P9-COO-722

How dare he?

How dare this besotted excuse for a tutor have the audacity to call her stupid during the sweetest moment of intimacy she had ever known?

"I believe you have an appointment at University in little over an hour, though I fail to see that you are in any condition to take an examination."

"Maybe not an examination, but I'll wager I could take you," the young man retorted, his voice ragged with frustration. "But I've never had to force any woman, and I'd rather you came to me freely."

"Mr. Phillips," Clarissa whispered fiercely, "for a scholar, you are incredibly dense. I'll never come to you at all."

"Could you be so haughty if you felt my lips on yours once more? Let's see, shall we?" Phillips queried, slurring his words as he swung around, only to be sidestepped by his suddenly reluctant student.

"Your time would be better spent readying yourself for an academic conquest, not a personal one. Since you consider intelligence such a masculine trait, perhaps you could demonstrate some . . . *now*!"

Dear Reader,

Kristin James is back, and Harlequin has her! Pick up *The Yankee* for a read you'll long remember. The town of Huxley, Texas, can't stop talking about the marriage of Andrew Stone—a Yankee, for heaven's sake!—to local girl Margaret Carlisle. It's the scandal of the year, but how much more scandalized will the good people of Huxley be when they discover that this unlikely pair, whose marriage began as a matter of business, have actually fallen in love?

Erin Yorke has long been another favorite with readers, and this month she offers *An American Beauty*. When a well-born British law student is asked to tutor an American girl living in London, the results are unpredictable. Theirs is a clash of cultures that leads to a passionate trial by fire and a life sentence—in each other's arms.

Next month, look for Lynda Trent and Louisa Rawlings, and in coming months expect books from Caryn Cameron and all your other favorites. History with a romantic twist—you'll find it in each and every Harlequin Historical.

Yours,
Leslie J. Wainger
Senior Editor and Editorial Coordinator

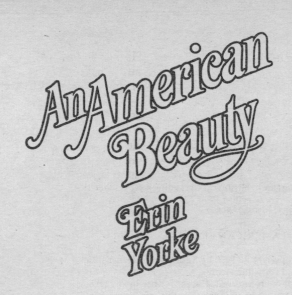

An American Beauty

Erin Yorke

Harlequin Books

TORONTO • NEW YORK • LONDON
AMSTERDAM • PARIS • SYDNEY • HAMBURG
STOCKHOLM • ATHENS • TOKYO • MILAN

Harlequin Historical first edition November 1990

ISBN 0-373-28658-9

AN AMERICAN BEAUTY

Copyright © 1990 by Susan McGovern Yansick
and Christine Healy.
All rights reserved. Except for use in any review,
the reproduction or utilization of this work in
whole or in part in any form by any electronic,
mechanical or other means, now known or
hereafter invented, including xerography,
photocopying and recording, or in any information
storage or retrieval system, is forbidden without
the permission of the publisher, Harlequin Historicals,
300 E. 42nd St., New York, N.Y. 10017

All the characters in this book have no existence
outside the imagination of the author and have no
relation whatsoever to anyone bearing the same name
or names. They are not even distantly inspired by any
individual known or unknown to the author, and all
incidents are pure invention.

®: Trademark registered in the United States Patent
and Trademark Office and in other countries.

Printed in the U.S.A.

ERIN YORKE

is the pseudonym used by the writing team of Christine Healy and Susan Yansick. One half of the team is single, fancy-free and countrified, and the other is married, the mother of two sons and suburban, but they find that their differing lives and styles enrich their writing with a broader perspective.

For Family Members who are very Special—
Frank McGovern,
the brother who has taught me so much
about life and courage;
and
Christopher and David Yansick,
two boys who make my world a better place.
And to Very Special Friends,
who've become Family—
Mildred O. Isaacs, my other mother;
and
Waltraut C. Amato, my second sister.

Chapter One

Lavinia Cooper nervously patted her fading red hair and watched her guests partake of the elaborate tea the servants had laid out. Though the middle-aged ladies present shared not only her table but an interest in gardening as well, Lavinia could not help but feel anxious. What if the scones appeared burned, or the jam a bit too tart? Responsibility of any sort, even that associated with entertaining, oftentimes caused her to become unduly flustered; however, much to her delight, Lavinia noted that all was going smoothly this afternoon. And now that the gathering was almost at an end, the hostess found herself finally able to relax.

As she leaned into the cushions of a plump, fashionable settee, she listened to the prattle around her and a small sigh of satisfaction escaped her lips. She was a maiden lady, and at forty-six her life was full and, what was more, serene, a quality sadly lacking in the lives of her married acquaintances, according to the snippets of conversation she was hearing at the moment. But then, her friends had only themselves to blame for that. Once one took a husband, one carried a double burden, until even that was multiplied by the arrival of children.

Lavinia was glad that she had escaped such a tumultuous existence. Why, in order to continue undisturbed in her placid sphere, the genteel spinster had even seen to it that her niece, who had come from Philadelphia to spend some time in London, had been safely ensconced in a finishing school situated in the country. Not that the girl couldn't do with a little finishing. Lavinia winced silently. Yet that hadn't been the main reason for the suggestion she had proffered to the girl's father. No, it had definitely been to protect her own quiet style of living. Without a doubt, the young ladies academy had been a brilliant alternative to opening the doors of her town house to her high-spirited niece, Clarissa.

Adjusting the lace at her wrists, Lavinia congratulated herself on the success of her ploy then silently raised her teacup to blessed solitude, sipping the hot, mellow brew with languid satisfaction. Once more, Lavinia counted herself fortunate indeed in that there was no one who could violate her tranquillity.

Dame Gwendolyn Briarley alighted from the carriage and stood before the fashionable London town house. Though she was glad to have finally arrived at her destination, her face wore a look of displeasure as if she found the reason for this journey highly distasteful.

The occupant of the imposing gray stone edifice before her might be a reticent gentlewoman, a paragon of social refinement and accepted within all the better circles, but Dame Gwendolyn had nevertheless determined to put an end to any close association with Lavinia Cooper *and* her family. Straightening her already stiff neck in a gesture of moral superiority, Gwendolyn turned and peered into the dim interior of the carriage, until her narrowed eyes rested on the impudent minx who had so recently been placed in her care, only to be quickly removed.

Eighteen-year-old Clarissa Manning, sitting so quietly, didn't appear to be a wayward, headstrong young woman. Her delicate features and quiet beauty endowed her with a rather angelic air, that is until one looked into Clarissa's deep brown eyes. There glinted the defiance and independence that Mistress Briarley had found upsetting. The gleam originating in those intelligent, dark eyes was a reminder of the rebellion that had so recently sullied the halls of the Briarley Academy for Young Women, and assured Dame Gwendolyn that her course of action was the only right one. Who would have thought that Lavinia Cooper could have such a niece? But then, Clarissa *was* an American, and in Dame Gwendolyn's mind, that explained it all.

With a curt nod of her properly bonneted head, the older woman once more indicated her displeasure with her young charge and motioned toward the town house. To the British matron's annoyance, the brazen girl complied immediately, remaining completely unruffled by the whole affair. One would think the shameless Miss Manning would have the decency to be humiliated, or at the very least frightened, by her present circumstances. She was, after all, the first young female ever to be dismissed from Briarley, and under such deplorable circumstances!

Dame Gwendolyn looked down at the massive length of thick red hair she held in her tightly clenched fist while Miss Manning, without a jot of contrition, stepped onto the pavement. Her recently cropped coppery curls matched the swatch held by her companion, and were now exhibited for all the world to see. Lacking the grace to cover her outrageous handiwork with a proper bonnet or to cast her eyes downward in some semblance of regret, Clarissa steadily met Dame Gwendolyn's stare. Indeed, a small, challenging smile played about the young woman's lips, a gesture that only further infuriated Mistress Briarley.

Squaring her shoulders in indignation, the founder of Briarley Academy quickly mounted the stairs that led to Lavinia Cooper's door. Gwendolyn was impatient to return Miss Cooper's wayward niece and retreat once more to the sanity of her school, a place where manners and proper behavior were held in the utmost regard, in a sedate atmosphere that had been carefully fostered through the years and that was certain to return after the removal of this American upstart. With a sense of relief, the older woman lifted the town house's heavy door knocker and employed it with emphatic determination.

"Oh, Clarissa!" Lavinia mourned after the gossiping ladies of the Horticulture Society had departed, "to be returned here by Mistress Briarley herself, in the middle of one of my garden society receptions..."

"Now, Aunt, it's not half as bad as you think," Clarissa consoled, though Lavinia's unsettled emotions were beginning to seem more enduring than her own patience. "I'm certain that the other ladies have no notion of Dame Gwendolyn's purpose in visiting here today.''

"No notion, you say?'' Lavinia wailed as she distractedly pulled and twisted a dainty linen handkerchief between her fingers. "What possible explanation could they have conjured up other than the truth when they saw the founder of Briarley Academy arrive here unannounced with you in tow? Whatever will I say when they begin to delicately inquire about your circumstances?''

"If you feel you must say anything, simply tell them the truth.''

"The truth?'' Lavinia trilled in disbelief.

"Well, then, say that I've been ill, and that Dame Gwendolyn has returned me to your care so that I could regain my health,'' Clarissa sighed, dismayed that her aunt should deem the opinions of others to be of such importance. "Such a story would even explain my hair, which I assume also upsets you.''

"It's not your hair that has me in a dither, Clarissa,'' Lavinia whispered anxiously, "it's your lack of it.''

Swirling around to avoid her overwrought aunt, Clarissa paced the floor of the morning room, letting her pent-up energy spend itself harmlessly. Her vibrant brown eyes flashed brightly, giving evidence of the quick temper suggested by her copper tresses, and belying the ladylike image presented by her delicate, high cheekbones and pale skin. Willowy though Clarissa might be in form, she had a determination that was unlimited when it came to getting her way.

Though the young American realized that Lavinia meant only the best for her, what could this woman remember of youthful yearnings? Still, in the bright sun streaming through the room's bay window, the matronly figure called forth Clarissa's earliest memories of her now-deceased mother, and these recollections curbed her natural fiery tendencies.

"Aunt Lavinia,'' she said, trying to reason gently. "I am no longer a child, despite Father's attitude, and I certainly have no need for the services of some exclusive finishing school that turns out proper ladies like well-stuffed sausages from the butcher, all identical in appearance and content. As independent as you've always been, living alone as you do, you must agree that a woman, even one of eighteen, should be capable of deciding her own future?''

"Perhaps I would agree, were we speaking of a woman of eighteen," Lavinia conceded, "but you are the topic at hand, my dear, and you have not shown yourself to fit that category! A well-bred woman does not have temper tantrums, Clarissa; above all else, women are always polite." As the ever proper Miss Lavinia Cooper stressed her last word, the delicate cloth in her hands shredded, reacting at last to its maltreatment of the past half hour.

"Aunt, you're not being fair to me—"

"Now, child, look what you've made me do! And to one of the handkerchiefs your grandmother gave me on my coming out. As for being fair, I don't have to be. I'm your guardian, at least temporarily. Now sit down there and listen to me before you bring on another of my spells. You know my heart is not what it used to be." Looking at her indignant niece, Lavinia removed her spectacles, pushed back her unruly auburn hair and motioned the girl to sit beside her.

The physical resemblance between the two was easily discernible in the stubborn tilt of their chins and the fiery highlights of their tresses, one's beginning to fade gracefully to tones of a warm summer evening's sun, while the other's, cut close to her head, shone with the sunlight captured in the glory of a spring dawn.

Grimacing in displeasure, Clarissa dropped into a chair across from her aunt, not willing to surrender an inch in what she suspected was to be a contest of wills. If only Father had allowed her to remain in Philadelphia, or for that matter had taken her with him on his lecture tour. Instead he had banished her to some foreign institution that was supposed to endow her with inhibitions, all because she had exposed an inch of ankle while sitting on the speakers' platform during one of his symposiums. Was it her fault that this simple act had garnered more attention from the young men in the audience than Dr. Manning's words? Though her father had been uncharacteristically upset, Clarissa vowed that she would not go on paying for that one incident! As Lavinia cleared her throat, Clarissa determinedly turned her face in the woman's direction.

"Now then, my dear, I do not wish to see you unhappy, but James Gregory did entrust you to my care, and no matter how difficult, I must see to that charge. Not that I resent the responsibility. I mean, you know you are very dear to me, Clarissa."

"And you to me, Aunt, which is why I can't understand your not accepting my need for independence. At home I am free to do as I choose without regard for petty rules and regulations."

"I fear that is all too obvious from your behavior, but this is not that free country of yours, even if it is 1893. And while I do feel that Mistress Briarley acted harshly in dismissing you for being individualistic, you must admit that rules are designed for obedience. Why else would the Lord have offered, that is, commanded us the commandments? And for thousands of years, they've worked out awfully well, don't you agree?" Not waiting for a reply, Lavinia continued her rhetorical conversation.

"At any rate, Clarissa, you must realize that Dr. Manning, I mean your father, of course, will be quite distressed if I do not manage to continue your education. Even if you cannot return to Briarley I'm certain I can manage to place you somewhere else. Perhaps if you were to wear a chignon. They are quite fashionable in society..."

Lavinia's words trailed on but all Clarissa heard were the phrases threatening her with a return to exile.

"No!" Again the slender form was in feverish motion. Clarissa jumped to her feet and moved to stand directly before her aunt. Grabbing the woman's restless hands, Clarissa squeezed them urgently to gain her attention. "If you do, I promise you that I'll be back here in less than a month. The kind of girls who attend such schools never do anything without consulting the etiquette manuals, which are the only books they ever read. No one is ever spontaneous about anything. Such a prescribed method of living is totally foreign to me!" Clarissa released her aunt's hands and strode toward the window, too perturbed to remain still. "As for my hair, it was my one way to be different from the traditional Briarley female who has no thoughts of her own. Besides, Aunt, this shorter style is really rather becoming, and I plan to continue wearing it this way." Turning to face Lavinia, Clarissa sank into her chosen seat with a smile born of bravado.

"Clarissa, a lady of proper upbringing, even an eighteen-year-old, does not seek to appear becoming. It is simply too plebian to discuss, even if you were raised as an American..."

"I am an American, Aunt!"

"True, but with a great deal of effort, that is something we might be able to overcome, or at least hide. If you would only realize the importance of decorum and morality, topics I fear were not emphasized strongly enough in your life since your dear mother passed on." Seeing the objections flashing in her niece's brown eyes, Lavinia decided a different tack might be more persuasive. "I do miss her so, especially at times like these," mourned the older woman.

"There are more important things in life than decorum and morality. Other people's rules are insignificant to me."

"That attitude is exactly what I am talking about, young lady. And after what you've done, how can you ever face my friends again ... that is, be seen in society?"

"I don't care what society thinks of my shorn tresses!" Clarissa's protest was overriden as her aunt continued.

"Your hair is just another example of your spontaneous foolishness, Clarissa, and it merely serves to exemplify your selfish disregard for others. I am certain your father will blame me for this new turbulence in his life, since I recommended Briarley to him. Not that he is not a good man, indeed, a wonderful man, and I am certain he tried, but he is still only a man, and when it comes to bringing up a young woman properly.... At least if you continue to receive instruction somewhere else, I would not feel quite the foolish old woman when I face his disappointment, and he will have every right to be disappointed in your outrageous behavior, I assure you."

"Father is well aware of my temper," defended the girl.

"Perhaps he is, child, but he did entrust your well-being to my care, and I have failed that charge." Lavinia's sigh was deep as she played with the torn piece of linen in her lap. "Your poor mother, not being able to rest in peace because I can't properly supervise her only daughter, oh ..."

Lavinia's deep sigh hung over the room as Clarissa considered her options. Seeing that she had been unable to sway her aunt from the need for further studies, Clarissa found her natural defiance tempered by her affection for her aunt, and she considered a compromise to Lavinia's proposal.

"If you insist upon continuing my education, perhaps I could attend lectures at University College. It is nearby, and I understand they've admitted women since 1872."

"But not women of our class, Clarissa. Besides, it's a nondenominational school that caters to common people. Certainly no young lady who has been gently reared in the church would think of going there . . . definitely not my sister's daughter."

As the girl heard the door to public-school entrance firmly closed, her mind searched for another alternative. While the idea of a hired tutor was extremely tiresome, the prospect of once more living within the confines of a school like Briarley Academy was emphatically more loathsome. Of course, having a tutor didn't necessarily mean she wouldn't be free to do as she pleased anyway, and who knew how long he'd last? If she chose, Clarissa was certain that she could be rid of such a monkish pedant with as little effort as it had taken to get herself dismissed from Briarley. Not that she objected to learning; in fact, she was better read than most men. It was just that Clarissa preferred to direct her own course of studies.

"Aunt," she proposed, "if I agree to be tutored here, will you abandon the idea of having me accepted at another one of your highly proper schools?"

"Here?" shrieked Lavinia, envisioning a sudden end to her well-ordered life.

Surprised at Lavinia's hesitation, the young woman decided to employ a bit of emotional blackmail of her own.

"Certainly, you would be a much better example of ladylike behavior than anyone else could ever be, and I would feel so much closer to Mother," said Clarissa.

"Well, I suppose I could help you with such matters as etiquette and stitchery, and, of course, my garden is renowned. Such an arrangement might be possible, though... Hmm, I do wonder if your father will appreciate this. He expects you to be receiving an education in British history and the classics. Why Dr. Manning believes a lady would ever need such knowledge is beyond my ken—she clearly could never discuss politics or such in polite society. Better to talk of gardens or receipts or the weather," opined Lavinia indignantly.

"Don't you think that women are equipped with the same intellects as men and that a woman should be able to learn whatever she wants?" Clarissa's outrage at her aunt's overly conventional comments energized her once more.

"Learn, yes, but that does not mean she need parade her knowledge openly in public. Really, Clarissa, think of Marie Antoinette or Helen of Troy; they are not remembered for their brains! Intelligence has never been a ladylike trait. If you should be unfortunate enough to possess it, you certainly do not advertise the fact."

"Honestly, Aunt, this absurd barrage of advice makes me feel like Custer!"

"Custard? But we've just finished luncheon."

"Not custard, Aunt Lavinia, Custer! General George Armstrong Custer, an American soldier who was massacred because of his rigid behavior. None of his troops survived the Indian attack on Little Big Horn; they were all scalped."

"There, now, do you see what I mean? How could such a gory piece of history be part of any proper drawing room conversation? Besides which, you are hardly one to talk of scalping after what you've done to your lovely hair. Perhaps it *is* better you do your learning here where I can supervise its content." Clarissa bit back a smile as she realized her victory. "To some degree, that is. You must understand I do not have very much free time; I am very involved with my own social calendar and obligations."

"Of course, Aunt," assured Clarissa smoothly.

"If this arrangement is to succeed, you must agree to cooperate with the tutor I engage to help with your lessons." Lavinia's tone was stronger and more authoritative than Clarissa had ever heard it, but before she could reply, the older woman began to muse aloud. "Perhaps if the tutor were a student of law, and I approach the matter with your father by emphasizing that your educational needs are being well met, he will be more easily reconciled to your leaving Briarley."

"Yes, Aunt, that's the way to handle Father. Anytime you can bring his beloved law into a situation, he's more easily managed," agreed Clarissa, wondering how long it would take her to escape the required lessons. "Your idea does seem best."

Dr. Michael Humphrey, lecturer in law, sat at the desk of his University College office. Deep in thought, he replaced the recently read letter in its envelope, removed his spectacles and began to clean them, a habit he had acquired in his own days as a student.

So, James Gregory Manning's daughter needed a tutor, did she? Why the young woman's aunt had set out to cull one from the ranks of his law students was beyond Humphrey's comprehension. They had enough to do managing their own studies; he saw to that. Surely someone reading theology, philosophy or even literature would be better suited to the position of assisting a young lady in her education.

Still, he had no wish to offend Manning or any member of his family. The American was a professional acquaintance and enjoyed an impressive reputation in international law. With this in mind, Humphrey sent forth a great outlet of breath as he decided to comply with Miss Cooper's request. He'd post the position, do the initial interviews and send around two or three candidates for the woman's inspection.

The lecturer wrote out the notice and placed it on his desk next to Miss Cooper's entreaty for help. Checking his pocket watch, Humphrey saw that it was time to meet with his lower classmen and expand their barely existing intellects. By next term, after careful molding at his hands, some of them might even be deemed intelligent. He'd enjoy the challenge, though he doubted his students would feel the same way.

Gathering his papers from the haphazard piles cluttering his desk, he uncovered the list of those noted legal figures he intended to invite to the reception for his third-year students. Michael Humphrey was of the opinion that his young men could benefit from his numerous connections, and he was determined to give his upper classmen that opportunity. With an inspired smile, the don added Manning's name to the list with heavy, bold strokes. After all, if he could help educate Manning's daughter, the American could be invited to attend the law school's social function. True, Manning would still be on the Continent, but upon his return, he would feel obligated to visit the school, and this would give the upper students the opportunity to meet one of international law's most impressive figures.

Adjusting his spectacles and straightening his academic attire, Humphrey assumed the crusty countenance that hid the pleasure he found in preparing England's future barristers. Those who survived their course of study with him would never be intimidated in a courtroom, he thought with satisfaction. Then he noticed he was smiling slightly, and quickly remedied the situation.

The professor sallied forth in a burst of scowling determination, leaving the door to his office slightly ajar, as he usually did when in a hurry to lecture. Watching from a nearby stairwell, Preston Waverly-Smythe saw Humphrey pass, and after observing that no one else was about, entered the vacant study. Since his second term, Preston had made it a habit to visit the offices of his professors when they were occupied elsewhere. Often these forays had proven quite productive. Scribbled notes concerning future lectures, topics for study and assignments had certainly helped Preston's class standing. His only competitor for First honors and a prestigious internship upon completion of his studies was Brandon Phillips, that unmoneyed nobody who had wooed most of the school into accepting him.

From their initial meeting, Preston had sensed there was something dangerously different in Phillips' character; though almost penniless, he seemed the sort capable of reaching any goal he set for himself, a man full of ability and purpose. Such an upstart, Preston knew, could be ruthless if pushed far enough, but Phillips' sense of honor gave Preston a distinct advantage. The man's personal integrity was as archaic as that of Michael Humphrey or Preston's father. It was, the intruder thought with a smirk, Phillips' only known source of vulnerability. Quickly ruffling through the papers on Humphrey's desk, Preston determined he'd find a way to bring Brandon Phillips down, and soon.

Today it seemed that Humphrey hadn't left all that much out in the open. There was a notice for a tutoring position. No doubt that would be an item of interest to Phillips, out of pocket as he was, some correspondence, and the list of those to be invited to the upcoming law reception. Scanning Humphrey's scrawl, Preston saw no surprises among the invitations to be issued until he reached the last name. James Gregory Manning! Now there was a prestigious guest. Old Humphrey was even better connected than Preston had supposed. The student decided he'd best research some of Manning's legal texts before the reception. Knowledge of a man's accomplishments never failed to charm one of these pompous old legal asses, and Preston knew that if he could extract a letter of recommendation from Manning, Phillips would no longer be any threat to him.

Preston replaced the list, and out of habit began to glance through Humphrey's correspondence. Nothing seemed of interest until he came across an envelope addressed in a decidedly feminine hand. So, Preston smiled scornfully, the old codger was part human after all! Thinking to amuse himself, he began perusing its contents and stopped in amazement. The tutoring position was for Manning's daughter!

Now here was an opportunity. He'd find some altruistic reason to offer old Humphrey that would explain his interest in tutoring without revealing that he knew the identity of the young woman's illustrious parent. If this aunt, Miss Cooper, were a lady of quality, he had no doubt that he would be chosen to fill the position. Then, he'd lavish both intellect and charm upon father and daughter. Earning some money in a reputable manner would also serve to impress his own father. Yes, things were going very well. Soon Dr. James Gregory Manning would be sponsoring a new protégé, and Brandon Phillips would be left to sharpen quills.

Carefully repositioning everything as he had found it, Preston Waverly-Smythe walked jauntily from Humphrey's office with every intention of celebrating his good fortune.

The interior of the Solitary Lion was dim but cheerfully so, bathed as it was intermittently with the soft glow of candles and gaslight. The dark half paneling was offset by whitewashed walls hung with tankards, and the benches wore an inviting patina that had come from nearly fifteen decades of use. Even the tables bade a welcome; carefully polished, their scratches revealed the innumerable tankards that had passed along their surfaces, and the dents told of those pints slammed down in celebration or friendly argument. It was a comfortable place, well stocked with wines, ales and liquors, the type of public house popular with males of all classes who easily recognized the hospitality that issued from every crevice of its sturdy structure.

The friendly proprietor, reasonable prices and lack of pretensions made the Solitary Lion a favorite retreat for the young men attending the nearby university. As usual, the rear of the taproom played host to clusters of students. Some had gathered to enjoy the fellowship of their peers, others to exercise their intellects by debating philosophies of all sorts. No matter what the purpose of their visits, all were prepared to add to the contagious good humor found within the Lion's walls.

Such a pair of young men were seated at a small trestle table in the furthest corner of the tavern. One was a tall, well-built man who evinced a certain air of authority and mystery. That he was a few years older than his companion was evident from his looks and demeanor. His strong, chiseled features, blond hair and molten gray eyes would have been enough to command a second glance, but these became almost subservient to his innate air of easy dominance.

The younger man was of medium height and slight frame, with a shock of unruly black curls that tumbled across his forehead. His frequent, enthusiastic smiles and twinkling brown eyes gave him a good-natured appearance, rather like an energetic and friendly young pup just set out on his first exploration of the wide world.

"Yes, Brandon," he was saying, "she was a delightful piece of fluff. I think I may be falling in love."

"Ned." His companion smiled indulgently. "You fall in love at least once a fortnight, and you'll be enamored of this girl only until the next comely skirt flutters her lashes your way. It's a good thing these females don't take you seriously, or you'd have broken half the feminine hearts in London by now, and been the defendant in a great many lawsuits charging breach of promise."

"But Brandon, there are so many enticing young things to choose from. How any man can settle for just one at this point in life is quite beyond me. Besides, mild flirtation is rather enjoyable. You should try a bit of it yourself. It would do you good."

"I don't have time for that sort of thing this term, and quite frankly, neither do you, my young friend," Brandon answered with mild exasperation.

"Just because you have a few years on the rest of us, you needn't act the old man. You sound just like Father."

Ned threw back his shoulders, extended his stomach and drew in his chin before launching into a blustering imitation of his parent, Lord Geoffrey Newcomb, Earl of Hammerford.

"Ned, my boy, this won't do at all. Here I am but newly knighted for my efforts on behalf of public schooling, a trustee of the so-called red brick school founded for the education of the common man, and I am saddled with a son who refuses to be educated at all! I sent you to University College as a statement of my firm belief that this institution is capable of providing as fine an education as the older, more venerable schools. And what do you do, you young scamp? You carouse and carry on so that not one of your instructors has yet to deem you fit to sit for an examination! I should disinherit you, my boy. Now try a bit harder, won't you?"

"You're incorrigible! I don't know why your father doesn't cut you off." Brandon chuckled in spite of himself at the manner in which Ned had so neatly captured his father's personality.

"You know exactly why. I am his only son, born after he'd already sired seven daughters. The old boy fairly dotes on me, and not," Ned added unabashedly, "without just cause. I am a rather charming fellow."

"So it would seem, at least as far as most of the young ladies in London are concerned. Still, I won't fault you for that, nor can I complain about your studies this term. You've made quite an improvement."

"That's your doing, Brandon," replied Ned, his voice serious for a moment. "As my tutor, you've been quite patient with me and my flaws. Without your help I'd have been sent down long ago."

Embarrassed by his young pupil's sudden declaration of gratitude, Brandon tried to brush Ned's exuberant compliment aside.

"Now, Ned, your father pays me quite well to help you with your studies. I merely feel he should receive value for his money."

"That might be true, but he doesn't pay you to be my friend," Ned continued, his natural buoyancy of spirit flaring once more. "Why, you've become the brother I've never had!"

"Thank you, Ned, but you'll find that older brothers are not always pleasant things to have about, such as now, for instance, when I tell you that it is time we head back to our apartments. You've had quite enough for one evening."

"It's still early!" Ned rejoined, his voice projecting a mournful tone. "Don't you think it's time you learned to enjoy yourself, Brandon?"

"Oh, I did plenty of that, my young friend. I was a bit like you before my situation changed."

"It's not fair, Brandon," the younger man answered, his normally uninhibited personality becoming more so due to his generous intake of ale. "If your uncle had been a better businessman, he wouldn't have lost the family wealth in his shipping ventures and you'd have been left a damned sight better off when he died."

"In spite of my lack of funds, things aren't as bleak as you paint them, Ned. My circumstances have taught me self-reliance, and in addition, I learned from my uncle's mistakes. He was an honest gentleman who put his faith in the wrong people. I've learned to be more discriminating."

"Well, you pegged Waverly-Smythe right enough!" blurted Ned. "He's a veritable villain, and would as soon let flow your life's blood as look at you."

"You exaggerate, Ned," Brandon replied with a half hidden smile.

"It's true, I swear."

"And all this time I thought he was studying law. I'd had no idea he was following the mortician's trade."

"You know very well what I mean, Brandon. I'm just looking out for your welfare."

"Thank you. I'm touched by your concern, but don't involve yourself, Ned. This competition is strictly a matter between Waverly-Smythe and myself."

"He's a cur!"

"You'll get no argument from me, but remember, he's a very determined individual. He wants to obtain first standing in class and with it the internship with Dobson and Whittaker as much as I do—"

"Like you, he may be set on being called to the Inns," Ned interrupted indignantly, "but certainly his motives can't be as honorable. You need a sponsor for the Inns of Court, but his family can pay his way. I've heard some talk, though, that unless he comes through at university, his family won't back him; he got into some sort of trouble in York before he came up."

"No matter what his reasons, Ned, Waverly-Smythe is as resolute as I am. You'd do well to remember that such individuals can be dangerous. Leave him alone. Now be a good boy and drain your cup so we can be off. There's an early lecture I want to attend."

"One more, Brandon, then I promise to leave...truly," Ned offered. "Besides, the proprietor relies upon my trade in order to feed and clothe his numerous offspring. You wouldn't want the young ones to go hungry, would you?"

Brandon looked at his young friend with amused affection. The boy had certainly applied himself to his studies this term. A bit of recreation would do him good, do them both good, actually. Having made up his mind, Brandon nodded, settled himself more comfortably and prepared to enjoy another half hour or so in the company of his fellows.

As he sipped his ale, Brandon experienced a rare sense of well-being. His pupil might benefit from Brandon's knowledge, but Ned had reminded him that life could be more than a struggle; it could be pleasant, as well. This was something Brandon had all but forgotten these past few years.

After the condition of his uncle's estate had become known, Brandon had been forced to put aside his plans and work for three years to keep the family shipping firm from being taken over by lien holders. Through his own sweat and perseverance, the company had become solvent—though barely. The sale of the business, however, had given him enough to satisfy his uncle's debts, and with that obligation gone, Brandon was free at last to follow his ambition to become a barrister, or at least as free as his limited financial state allowed. Too proud to borrow from family friends, he had provided an income of sorts by tutoring others as he attended university. This was how he had become acquainted with Ned, by far his favorite pupil.

At the moment, influenced by his companion's lighthearted company, Brandon felt he had had enough of hardship. Why not spend a few extra pence tonight and enjoy himself? The coming months would afford few such opportunities.

In the middle of sharing a laugh Brandon and Ned were joined by one of their fellow students.

"Here's something that may be of interest to you, Phillips," said the newcomer. "The Humph has posted a notice advertising for a tutor. I don't know the details, but I thought I'd mention it to you."

"Oh, Brandon, why bother?" exclaimed Ned. "I'll simply tell Father to raise your salary."

"Thank you, Ned, but your father is already quite generous as concerns my stipend. Besides," Brandon replied with a laugh, "keep on living as well as you do, and your father will be lucky enough to afford my usual fee, never mind a raise. I'm only surprised that you haven't already depleted the family coffers. Your father won't have to disinherit you, you'll have spent it all long before!"

Ned laughed and the men soon lapsed into easy camaraderie as they discussed the rigors of the present term. They became so deeply involved in their conversation that they paid no heed to the goings and comings of the Solitary Lion's other patrons.

When Preston Waverly-Smythe entered the popular establishment, he was anxious to celebrate his gleanings from Humphrey's office, though he would have to keep the cause of his good humor to himself. Stepping to the bar, he ordered half a pint of ale and nodded with an aristocratic smile to a handful of acquaintances. As his eyes became acclimated to the dim interior, he spied Ned Newcomb, a chap whose family connections could prove extremely useful. Preston was set to approach the young man until his eyes traveled across Ned's table to the seat on its opposite side. There in the recess of shadow sat Brandon Phillips, and the bitter taste of ale in Preston's mouth became more bitter still.

Chapter Two

In contrast, the next morning, Lavinia Cooper found life very sweet indeed.

"Oh, miss, these flowers are absolutely the most lovely ever. I know they are always unusual, but where anyone could find peach blossoms this time of year, I can't imagine." Ellen's voice held undisguised admiration for the woman who received such floral tributes.

"Now, Ellen, you know the flowers are merely a gesture of friendship," chided a blushing Lavinia as she examined the arrangement the maid placed on the breakfast table. "Thank you, that will be all, but when Clarissa comes down, you may bring her breakfast."

"Yes, miss."

Ellen left the room, and Lavinia smiled more comfortably as she explored the flowers. How very clever of that Greenaway woman to categorize the meanings attributed to flowers so that bouquets were more than merely pretty decorations. They were messages to those who knew the language.

"Aunt, what an extraordinary display of blossoms! Are they from your greenhouse and did you arrange them? Or have they been sent by someone special? What is the occasion? I know it's not your birthday." Clarissa always started her days at the same full-fevered pitch of enthusiasm that others would not reach till noon, but she never appeared to notice anyone else's early morning reticence.

"Clarissa, sit down and stop that noisy chattering. For mercy's sake, even the birds have more sense than to sing nonstop. The flowers, ah, are from a friend in the Horticultural Society whom I assisted with some social obligations, that's all. But enough about them," dismissed Lavinia as she took a sip of tea. "I must prepare to meet several applicants for the tutoring position today."

"Applicants? You mean there are actually law students willing to tutor me?" Clarissa could not contain her surprise; lack of response to her aunt's query had been a hoped-for possibility. Now, vague images of tiresome scholars dressed in dusty versions of the caps and gowns worn to university classes put a damper on the girl's morning.

"Well, I'm not certain Professor Humphrey mentioned the fact that you are female, but that will be obvious when the young men meet you." The attractive matron smiled as she looked at the girl. Unconventional as Clarissa might be in behavior, her beauty could not be ignored by even the most studious of men, though whether that would prove a blessing or a curse, Lavinia was uncertain. "At any rate, I have two gentlemen, or I would hope they are gentlemen, to interview, but I would think if the professor recommends them, they will be satisfactory."

"Yes, I imagine so," admitted Clarissa reluctantly. Michael Humphrey was a man whose opinion her father valued. But perhaps she could prove the chore of tutoring her too difficult for the young man chosen. After all, except for her father, Clarissa Manning had yet to meet a man she couldn't manipulate, and if she chose to be willful ... A thoughtful gleam appeared in her eyes as she buttered the toast Ellen had placed before her.

"You did agree to cooperate, Clarissa," reminded Lavinia chidingly as Ellen entered the room with a package.

"For Miss Clarissa, from Dr. Manning, all the way from Spain, miss," explained the maid.

"Oh, how thoughtful," breathed the young lady as she accepted the parcel eagerly.

"I wonder why he sent it here. He can't know you've been sent down already...at least I hope not," worried Lavinia.

"Aunt, I told you Briarley is like a prison; Dame Gwendolyn's young ladies are not permitted to receive gifts unless they are delivered by a member of the family. Undoubtedly, Father remembered that." Tearing the paper from the box, Clarissa found a folded letter and two wrapped parcels within.

"This one is for you, Aunt," cried the girl as she busily ripped the covering from her own package, only to drop the contents abruptly in her lap.

"Well, what did your father send you?" queried Lavinia as she daintily unfolded the wrappings from her own gift.

"I'd rather see your gift first, Aunt—oh, it's a fan, how beautiful."

Lavinia held up a delicate lady's fan of exquisitely carved ivory held together with black lace so fine it seemed gossamer spun by a magical spider. Fluttering her hand gently, Lavinia peered over the fan as though flirting from a balcony while suitors serenaded her from below.

"How exquisitely right! Father is so correct when he chooses gifts, it's uncanny."

"Well, then, what did he select for you?"

The young woman had the grace to blush as she lifted her hands from her lap to display her father's choice: two ebony haircombs, carved to perfection with small rosebuds that seemed ready to open and fill the room with their sweet aroma.

"Clarissa, they are perfect for your hair . . . or should I say they were!"

"Enough, Aunt. The combs will keep, and so could my education!"

"You leave that decision to me, my dear," replied Lavinia. "You'll see, we'll satisfy your father and our own needs."

"I hope so."

So do I, thought Lavinia as her eyes fell upon the bouquet, *so do I.*

"Miss Lavinia, a Mr. Waverly-Smythe to see you about the tutoring position." The maid's soft voice interrupted Lavinia's reverie, with a start, bringing her abruptly back from an imagined world shimmering with soft glances and whispered endearments.

"Oh, yes. Very well, show him in, Ellen."

Placing her spectacles on the tip of her nose and imagining herself to appear scholarly, Lavinia stood to her full height of five feet two inches and greeted her caller.

"Good afternoon, young man. Very glad you could come on such a cold day. You know, there was only one other applicant for the position, though possibly seeking a tutor from the law college was not the best of ideas. I did feel, however, that you young men would be of good moral character and, from what Dr. Manning has told me about a law student's training, you should be able to help my niece with almost any topic. Any topic within reason . . . not that I mean you would introduce anything untoward . . . Oh, I've forgotten my manners, please do sit down, won't you?"

As Lavinia paused for breath, Preston seized the opportunity to speak. A tall, dark young man of broodish good looks and handsome carriage, he was not accustomed to listening to others for any length of time.

"Please don't be concerned, Miss Cooper. I'm certain you have many more urgent things on your mind than manners. The responsibility for your niece, for example." A bone tossed to a starving mongrel would not have been grasped at more quickly.

"Oh, Mr. Waverly-Smythe, you really do not know the effort I have devoted to that girl and her welfare, and now, I am so concerned that she do well here while Dr. Manning is abroad. A qualified tutor would so relieve my poor worried mind." Waving a scented handkerchief before her face, Lavinia evinced the troubled sigh Preston had been expecting her to give.

"Well, I can promise you that any one of us from university, though naturally I must strongly recommend myself first, would be well equipped to aid in your niece's education, and would welcome the opportunity of doing so, especially if she is half so charming as yourself."

Lavinia smiled coquettishly at this and fluttered the lacy cloth in her hand. "Why, thank you. You are really quite the gentleman, though of course, I had expected no less from what my brother-in-law tells me of today's aspiring barristers. He's a lawyer himself, you know, and has written some important works on international legalities, though I do suppose you poor fellows are probably sorry that he did, what with having to read them and all. I tried once, but I fell asleep."

"Actually, I've found Dr. Manning's works quite valuable, but to change the subject if I may, who else did you say had applied for this position?"

"Dear me, sir, I do not think I did say, did I? I fear it wouldn't be appropriate for me to reveal your competition's identity. Why don't we discuss your qualifications instead? Since Dr. Manning is Clarissa's father, I must choose a tutor amenable to his peculiar views that a woman needs an education beyond the normal feminine arts, though personally, I feel a woman's role is meant to be buttered." Lavinia tittered as she demurely lowered her lashes.

"Oh, yes, Miss Cooper, quite amusing, yes." Temporarily uncertain as to which path to take, advocating women's education or his interviewer's sympathies, Preston avoided the issue altogether. "My qualifications, I believe you asked, ma'am? I'm a third generation student of British jurisprudence. My grandfather was a member of the Cabinet in the forties, and my father is a magistrate in York, having been a barrister in his youth. I wanted to earn my own reputation, however, and chose to study here in London. As a matter of fact, though, I wouldn't be at all surprised if Father knows Dr. Manning through their various fraternal organizations and the conferences he's chaired. Father is rather well known in the field."

"Why, dear me, that would be an amazing coincidence, wouldn't it?" bubbled Lavinia, pleased with the young man's suave tone, self-assurance and familial ties. "And is Brandon Phillips as well connected as you? Oh, heavens me, I really had not intended, that is . . ."

"Brandon Phillips? Really, Miss Cooper, he is far from well connected." Preston could not restrain his annoyance at hearing that his rival once again was that damned fellow. "He is barely able to afford his texts, and he certainly has no family to speak of, at least not of our class. Phillips has to tutor to earn the money for his meals and lodging, but why he bothers, I surely don't know. He should be content clerking somewhere in a solicitor's office in the country."

Suddenly realizing the ill-mannered nature of his comments, the young man caught himself and continued in a conspiratory tone. "But, of course, that is what I've heard others say of him. Naturally, I am not one to gossip about the less fortunate. I would hate, however, to see a woman of your candor and charm, Miss Cooper, be misled by the appearance of superficial intelligence he presents. Though I am quite certain that with your worldliness, you would not be."

"I would think not. At least I hope," trilled Lavinia, "that I can perceive sincerity. Tell me why are you interested in this position, Mr. Waverly-Smythe. I cannot imagine the stipend . . ."

"No, ma'am, but knowledge is such a marvelous thing. Reading Dr. Manning's works has so enriched my studies I feel that this is an opportunity to repay him in some small way for all that he has given me."

"Aunt, is tea ready yet?" Clarissa's voice preceded her into the drawing room. She stopped in the doorway, giving the handsome young stranger an interested glance. "Oh, I'm sorry if I've interrupted."

Preston was on his feet at once, bowing ceremoniously to the enticing vision before him, even as Lavinia commenced the introductions.

"Clarissa, this is Mr. Waverly-Smythe, who has come about the tutoring position. Mr. Waverly-Smythe, may I present my niece, Miss Clarissa Manning?" As the young people exchanged pleasantries, Lavinia watched quietly, noting the quick flush of Clarissa's cheeks as Preston took the hand she offered him, holding it just a shade too long.

"Aunt, might I show Mr. Waverly-Smythe the conservatory while you ring for tea? It is almost four," reminded Clarissa, smiling happily at this attractive male, most unlike the sniveling bookworm of her fears. This tutoring business might not be so bothersome after all, she mused.

"I don't think today is a good time, my dear," replied Lavinia, "though of course my plants and flowers have received numerous commendations from London's horticultural societies, but our discussion was just ending, Clarissa, and I'm certain Mr. Waverly-Smythe has his own work. We mustn't keep him from his books any longer."

"Well then, what about tomorrow, Aunt?" questioned the insistent female.

Especially vigilant when observing her unpredictable niece's behavior with young men, Lavinia saw at once the speculative glance that Clarissa cast in Preston's direction and the surprised yet pleased smile that passed fleetingly across his well-formed face. Why did the girl constantly place her in such uncomfortable situations? Flustered, Lavinia searched desperately for some civilized excuse to forestall issuing an invitation and fortunately found the perfect one.

"I'm afraid it won't be possible tomorrow, either, dear," she replied with apparent regret. "I've a lecture to attend at the Horticultural Society, and you have an appointment with Miss Simmons, my dressmaker, to be fitted for some new gowns now that you'll be staying in London."

"Well, I'll certainly be back for tea," protested the young woman.

"I doubt it, Clarissa. Miss Simmons is a very thorough seamstress, and when you've finished with her, there are some errands I'd like you and Ellen to perform since you'll be in the neighborhood."

"Then, may we say another day?" persisted the stubborn American miss.

"Certainly, dear," postponed Lavinia, perturbed by Clarissa's forwardness. "I do beg your indulgence, Mr. Waverly-Smythe, but I am still adjusting to this living arrangement. Perhaps we can set a date sometime in the future?" Lavinia concluded with the polite, dismissing smile that people of society employed when they wished to put off such an invitation for an indeterminate period.

"I'll escort him to the door, Aunt," offered the girl.

"Very well. My niece will see you out, and you will hear from me within a day or two regarding my decision. Good day." Rising from the settee and extending her hand, Lavinia added graciously, "I did so enjoy our chat."

Lavinia watched carefully as the two young people bid each other a restrained goodbye. Their words were proper and measured but their expressions spoke volumes. Clarissa's eyes were mildly flirtatious, and Preston seemed definitely interested.

Perhaps hiring a young law student was not a practical idea at all, mused Lavinia. She would interview the other applicant, and if he proved no more suitable than the first, she would have to advertise elsewhere, possibly among the retired professors, if any of them actually lived long enough to survive a career based upon intellectual encounters with their students. Offhand Lavinia could not number any such academicians among her acquaintances; they all seemed to stay in harness, lecturing and writing until they dropped in their scholarly tracts.

It was not that Lavinia disliked Waverly-Smythe. On the contrary, she found him quite charming. However, it was best not to allow these things to start before she had fulfilled her duties as guardian and thoroughly checked his background. Actually, she mused, it was time for Clarissa to be settled and placed under a doting husband's care.... It would certainly make her own life much easier. But better to let such matters rest until her brother-in-law returned to claim his daughter. How much more trouble could the girl cause?

"Mr. Phillips, I have heard so much about you from Mr. Waverly-Smythe, I feel as though I've already met you. Oh, dear, perhaps I shouldn't have said that. No, probably not," twittered Lavinia nervously an hour later, waving her ever-present handkerchief in the general direction of the settee. "Won't you sit down? We've just finished tea, but I could ring for some if you like."

"No, Miss Cooper, thank you. But tell me, why would you be speaking with Waverly-Smythe?" Brandon Phillips was momentarily nonplussed at the mention of his classmate.

"Oh, well, you see, he was... That is, you and Mr. Waverly-Smythe are the only two who replied to my advertisement, which really does not allow me much choice. Not that I mean you are not, ah, choice, that is, if Professor Humphrey...well, I meant..." This was most definitely a man who would be at home in the company of kings or peasants, and Lavinia had not meant to imply otherwise. As usually occurred when she had committed a conversational faux pas, Lavinia found herself so tongue-tied that she was unable to extricate herself from the resulting embarrassment.

"Don't worry, Miss Cooper," Brandon replied gently. Heaven help me, he thought, I understand her. "But, tell me, why would Waverly-Smythe be interested in such a position? Money is not a concern of his.''

''Well, he said it was to help others find the pleasure in learning he did, but,'' confided Lavinia in a whisper, ''I am afraid it might have something to do with my niece's allure. He seemed quite taken with her, and she with him, I might add. You know, as her guardian, I can't be too careful. Clarissa's such a pretty young thing; they say she takes after me,'' Lavinia revealed, turning her head toward the light to accentuate her silhouette.

Dear Lord, no! Brandon prayed silently for strength. Please let the similarity end with their shared looks, he asked, unable to imagine tutoring anyone as empty-headed as Lavinia appeared to be.

''What about you, Mr. Phillips? Why are you interested in the position as Clarissa's tutor? I must caution you, she can be a handful at times. Have you had any experience educating young women? Mr. Waverly-Smythe didn't mention it, but I had the impression he'd never done it.''

''Not that he would admit publicly,'' replied Brandon in amusement.

''And you?''

''I have tutored a number of students in university and can certainly provide you with references; however, if I obtain this position, I would limit my services to one other assignment, a young chap who is actually a friend, Edward Lowell Newcomb.''

Lavinia blanched but abruptly recovered to comment, ''Lord Geoffrey Newcomb's son? Then I can research your references quite easily. Lord Geoffrey and I are old... I mean, I see him occasionally at Horticultural Society meetings. Yes, that is what I meant to say.'' She breathed more easily. ''Do you enjoy flowers, Mr. Phillips?''

''I'd never really thought about it, Miss Cooper,'' replied Brandon with a bemused look at the flustered woman.

''Oh, dear me, Mr. Phillips, you must never ignore the beauties of life,'' chided Lavinia. ''Remember the lilies of the field. The Lord created them to show he cares for those he loves.''

"Perhaps, Miss Cooper, but he doesn't always show it. Remember his relationship with Job."

Lavinia studied the pleasing masculine form before her, gratified that he was familiar with the Scriptures, and noting the sense of purpose that seemed to emanate from his person. He did not appear to be someone whom life's difficulties could defeat. Clarissa did need someone who would be immune to her feminine wiles and manipulative tricks, but would this man's commanding air help or hinder him in dealing with her? Perhaps two such strong personalities would not mix well.

"Miss Cooper?" Brandon's voice recalled Lavinia's attention to the interview at hand. Caught so openly appraising the candidate before her, Lavinia blushed and hoped he didn't misconstrue her intent. Her discomfort was such that, for once, she couldn't think of a thing to say.

"Is there anything else you wished to ask me, Miss Cooper?" Brandon ended the woman's misery with the gentle query. She seemed nice enough, if a bit feathery.

"Well, actually, ah, yes," Lavinia gushed, thoroughly impressed by the rugged good looks and almost dangerous masculine grace of her visitor. "If I do employ you as Clarissa's tutor, do you think you will be able to refrain from being distracted by her charms? They are quite numerous, but I would prefer that you attend strictly to the business of education."

"Yes, ma'am, I understand she takes after you, but I believe I could manage." Brandon smiled into the vacuous eyes trained on him. "I cannot afford either the time or the money for romance. At the end of this year, I hope to attain a legal fellowship, and that is my priority now."

"Fellowship? But I would imagine you know many fellows at university..."

"To be a barrister, Miss Cooper, one must serve a set number of terms at one of the Inns—"

"Inns? Now I am confused. I understood you wished to be a lawyer, not an innkeeper."

"Not that type of inn, ma'am, the Inns of Court. Gray's Inn, Lincoln's, Barnard's, Inner Temple and Middle Temple." When the woman showed no sign of recognition, Brandon explained more fully. "They are schools of law, which date from the thirteenth and fourteenth centuries when the practice of law was limited to the clergy. Today young men wishing to become barristers join an Inn to gain practical experience. It is permissible to attend university while at the Inns, but it wasn't financially possible in my case. Each year, however, Dobson and Whittaker, two of England's most prestigious barristers, sponsor a graduate from University College for the Inns, and I hope to be this year's choice.''

"Oh, I see. How nice to have your future in hand; I wish you luck, but I do have other matters that require my attention now. I am quite a busy person and should inform you that, if you are my choice, I would hope my presence would not be required at these tutoring sessions. Running a household efficiently as well as seeing to my gardening interests takes so much of my time and energy; you see, it is imperative that I choose my niece's tutor wisely. I have many responsibilities, Mr. Phillips.''

"That is obvious, ma'am, but I think I could manage without any difficulty,'' Brandon answered as he rose to leave, giving Lavinia pause once again as his manly authority asserted itself. "Thank you for considering me.''

"Good day, Mr. Phillips. You will hear from me once I've made my decision.'' Brandon bowed politely and left the room, leaving Lavinia momentarily staring after him.

As Brandon descended the front steps, Clarissa watched from an upstairs window. She detected a horrid trace of masculine dominance and self-confidence in his step, an observation based primarily upon her determination to detest anyone who applied for the position of her tutor other than the charming Mr. Waverly-Smythe. Deciding to make her preference known and explore her aunt's intentions, Clarissa set off in search of Lavinia.

"Ah, yes, there you are, my dear.'' The woman's voice trilled before her as she reached the top of the stairs.

"Aunt, I was just coming to talk with you,'' began Clarissa as Lavinia swept past her up the hall.

"Very well, but you must talk as I move, dear, for I'm afraid I must hurry out. There is a society dinner that I hadn't planned to attend because of your situation, but I just now received the most dreadful news about the invasion, and that, of course, changes everything.''

"What invasion? Is England at war?"

"No, though it's almost as catastrophic. It's the peonies! They've got ants, and they were to be the starring members of tonight's centerpieces. Heaven only knows what we'll do now! Well, anyway, Clarissa, you'll simply have to understand that I must put my own wishes aside to step into the fray. After all, I've owed allegiance to the Horticultural Society much longer than I've been responsible for you... Not that I don't love you, my dear, but you do see my position?" Not waiting for a reply, Lavinia entered her room and headed straight for the wardrobe. Within moments a muffled voice continued.

"Cook has prepared a lovely dinner since she expected me to be here as well... Not that she wouldn't feed you, of course, but..."

"That's all right, Aunt. You needn't worry on my account; I'll find something to keep me busy." Clarissa's words halted Lavinia's breathless patter as the matron's head emerged momentarily from the wardrobe to peer at her niece. Pursing her lips in thought, she ducked once more into the recesses of clothing as the garments began to take on lives of their own, erupting randomly from their hangers.

"Yes, now, let me see, the colors for tonight's decor were to have been white and mauve, but of course that may change, depending on what's available in the hothouses. I wonder whether I should dress to harmonize with the surroundings or to stand out. After all," mused Lavinia thoughtfully, "as an organizer of this affair, I should be recognizable, however, since the flowers are our reason for being, perhaps I should try to complement the floral arrangements, but now I don't know their colors. You see my dilemma. Clarissa, what shall I wear?" asked the flustered woman. Changes in plans always disturbed her.

"Why not wear that ivory silk with the delicate lace insert? It's lovely, though it would be more fetching if I removed the lace," offered the girl. Lavinia's eyes widened at the suggestion, but Clarissa continued before her aunt could respond. "I know you've said a lady should always appear proper, but there's nothing improper about looking your best. As a matter of fact, I think I'll update my wardrobe when I see the seamstress tomorrow. What I've brought from home seems awfully dowdy." Although it was far from true, all her dresses appeared that way to Clarissa since she'd met Preston.

"Clarissa—" Lavinia chuckled "—if you wore a sack, it would not look dowdy, but I'm certain you'll be pleased with Miss Simmons' work. Now, what shall it be? The heather with your grandmother's amethysts or the ivory with her cameo?" Moving bewitchingly before her cheval glass with both gowns held before her, Lavinia debated.

"Definitely the ivory; it lends a glow to your complexion that's almost ethereal. You'll be the envy of every woman and the interest of every man at the dinner," stated Clarissa confidently. "Though either choice would be a good one, unlike the decision between the applicants for my tutor. Whom did you select anyway? Don't you think Mr. Waverly-Smythe is best suited to instruct me?"

"The question is, in what?" murmured Lavinia under her breath as she continued to peer at her reflection.

"I didn't hear you, Aunt."

"I believe you're right about the ivory, dear, but certainly not because I wish to be the object of anyone's interest or jealousy. But come help me with my hair as we talk." Seating herself before the vanity, Lavinia smiled gently at Clarissa as she removed the pins from her coiffure. "I am so pleased that you agreed to be tutored, my dear. Such a willingness to adapt to differing situations is a grand sign of maturity. You will indeed be a fine young woman," assured the matron as she patted her niece's hand and gave her the combs needed to dress her hair.

"Thank you, Aunt, but you haven't yet told me who will help me to be such a fine young woman," reminded Clarissa impatiently.

Watching the girl's face in the mirror, Lavinia couldn't resist the temptation to pretend to misunderstand her query.

"Why, Clarissa, I thought we'd agreed that I would coach you on the feminine arts of sewing and manners. Surely you haven't decided that you don't need my instructions now that you've seen the candidates from the law school? Ouch, be more careful, young lady!"

"I'm sorry, Aunt. Actually I'm anticipating my first lesson with great interest, but I do wonder who's to give it," replied the girl. "You haven't told me your choice."

"You've done a magnificent job with my hair, child, but as to which young man I've chosen, I really can't answer that. Instead, let's talk about your visit to Miss Simmons tomorrow. Ellen will accompany you, but there'll be no gowns with overly low décolletage, my dear young niece. You're much too inexperienced to advertise your charms in such a fashion."

"Advertise, Aunt?" Clarissa couldn't believe Lavinia's turn of phrase.

"Well, call attention to yourself, then. Men are only human, Clarissa, and a woman should not tempt them beyond reason. Help me, please, with these buttons; they create a marvelous draping effect, but they are difficult to unfasten, I mean fasten, when they're at the back... At any rate, your face is fetching enough without revealing your other attractions. Mr. Waverly-Smythe noticed you quite sufficiently this afternoon," chided Lavinia.

"Aunt, we simply exchanged pleasantries, but tell me, isn't Preston your first choice?"

"Preston, is it, then? Clarissa, you didn't even meet the other candidate, and you've made your decision, have you?" Smiling at her niece's lack of subtlety, Lavinia gave the girl a thoughtful glance.

"I can't tell you, my love, because I don't know yet myself. I'll have the opportunity to investigate the gentlemen's references at dinner tonight, then I'll make my decision and inform them, and you. You can't imagine that I'd trust my only niece to an untried... I mean, not fully researched... that is, I will tell you tomorrow," assured Lavinia. "Now, can I assume that while I'm out, you will remain quietly at home looking at my pattern books and deciding what fashions your father's money should buy?"

"Yes, Aunt, but do you suppose the seamstress could have the garments ready for my first lesson?"

"I don't think that is possible, and the object of your educational exercises is not to capture your tutor's heart, Clarissa, but to learn some history and classics, my dear. Well, have a pleasant evening." Squeezing her niece's hand tightly,

Lavinia laughed and exited gracefully while an amused chuckle escaped the girl's lips.

"There are many kinds of learning, Aunt Lavinia," murmured Clarissa, "and if this instruction is to occur, I will see the curriculum progresses to my specifications, believe me."

The next morning had come and gone without any sight of Aunt Lavinia, who had left the house on Hertford Court early. Since there was still no clue as to whom her guardian had selected as tutor, Clarissa put the matter from her mind and became absorbed instead in the selection of additions to her wardrobe. Though if truth be told, thoughts of the impression she would make upon Preston in this dress or that did occasionally cross her mind.

Standing swathed in material in the middle of Miss Simmons' fitting room, Clarissa decided that it was not a bad place to be. The shop's proprietress proved a witty gossip, intent upon dressing Clarissa in clothing designed to emphasize her alluring figure. Prompted by Ellen's encouraging smile and Miss Simmons' urgings, Clarissa chose materials and patterns for three new dresses. It was apparent that the dressmaker was more interested in the individual personalities and figures of her clients than in the current dictates of fashions, and Clarissa, with her predilection for the unusual, felt very much at home. She even considered ordering some gymnastic bloomers for cycling, but decided against it. They were not worth the distress they would cause Lavinia.

When she had dressed once more in her own clothing, Clarissa made an appointment for her next fitting, and stood chatting with Miss Simmons for a moment in the open doorway of the shop.

Although the interval was brief, it was long enough to signal her departure to the masculine figure that had been lounging in the bookseller's across the street and waiting for Clarissa to emerge to the pavement of the fashionable neighborhood. Gathering up his purchases, he left the shop and crossed the cobblestones separating the two establishments. With two books tucked under his arm and the third open for study, he appeared to be engrossed in his reading, but his eyes saw not one word printed upon the pages in front of him as he maneuvered his advancing steps to coincide exactly with Clarissa's descent to the street.

"I do beg your pardon." The low-timbered voice dripped with sincerity as he bumped ever so gently into the young American.

"It's quite all right," Clarissa began as she turned to face this walking disturbance. "Why, Mr. Waverly-Smythe," she exclaimed with genuine delight, "I hadn't thought to see you again so soon."

"Nor I you," he answered untruthfully, "and to think I might not have done so if my intellectual curiosity hadn't lured me to the bookseller's across the way."

"So it seems," Clarissa responded with mischievous amusement. She gleamed knowingly at Preston as the corners of her mouth turned upward and the couple shared a conspiratorial smile. "Ellen and I were on our way home for tea. Since fate has brought us together once more, why don't you join us?"

"I'd be most happy to do so, Miss Manning, that is if you don't think that your aunt would object."

Ellen studied the duo before her and cleared her throat ever so softly.

"Pardon me for saying so, miss, but I'm not certain that your aunt will have returned by the time we reached Hertford Court."

"That's of no consequence, Ellen." Clarissa laughed lightly. "You and Cook will be in the house, so I don't really think Aunt Lavinia would have any objection. The situation wouldn't warrant a second thought in America."

Ellen made no response. She'd done her duty as chaperone by stating the obvious. Were she in Clarissa's place, she'd have made the same decision. The gentleman appeared a decent sort, and he did have the nicest smile. Besides, they might be able to get him in and out before the old miss came home.

A moment passed before Preston made the obligatory reminder in a voice just slightly tinged with wistfulness.

"Unfortunately, this *is* England, Miss Manning."

"So it is, Mr. Waverly-Smythe, but *I* am an American. Come." She laughed as she reached out to take his hand and direct him to her aunt's carriage. "Let's live recklessly and share a cup of tea and some pleasant conversation this afternoon.''

Even if he had been so inclined, Preston would have been hard put to reject so engaging an invitation, and soon the young trio moved off toward the carriage in high spirits and an adventurous mood. As he smiled winningly and handed her into the coach, Clarissa began to anticipate the hours they would spend together when Preston began to tutor her. There was no doubt in the young American's mind that this was the man her aunt would choose for the position. After all, how could Lavinia do anything else?

Chapter Three

Two days later, Clarissa Manning's new tutor made his way toward Lavinia Cooper's Bloomsbury address. His precise and determined movement along the fashionable thoroughfare was direct and resolute, mirroring his personality. Though his gait was graceful and supple, his apparent sense of purpose made Brandon Phillips more emblematic of a prowling lion than a London gentleman about to call on a young woman of quality. Yet no matter what his destination, his stride always spoke of strength and independence, capturing an untamed essence of character that even the gentility of his upbringing could not eradicate.

His dress, while clean and obviously the result of meticulous tailoring, was nonetheless a few seasons old. The once expensive brown cloth of his jacket and trousers had lost some of its stiff body, and exhibited a softness that caused the material to lie closely against his lean but muscular frame. Still, his self-assured manner belied his dress, and he did not appear out of place in this neighborhood, one of London's most elite. In point of fact, until six years ago, he had lived in just such a place, and so was neither impressed nor awed by the imposing portals fronting the wealthy residences surrounding him.

But though Brandon appeared comfortable in his surroundings, his passage through the area was not unnoticed. And many of the glances sent in his direction originated beneath the long lashes of flirtatious females, whose interest was sparked not only by his build and bearing, but by his handsome, arresting features.

His face was pleasantly angular. A broad forehead and a slender, aristocratic nose combined with high cheekbones and a square jawline to create a regal air. Yet his countenance was spared from haughtiness by his sparkling gray eyes, in the depths of which there seemed to lurk an elusive twinkle, like the sun breaking through an early morning mist. His mouth, when not set in determination, added softness to his looks, his lips reverting from a thin line to their natural fullness when he allowed himself relaxation.

At this moment, his mouth was slightly turned down as he thought with no small degree of self-annoyance at the irony of his new position. Imagine! Hiring himself out to tutor some simpering young female because her rich, indulgent father thought her capable of grasping the rudiments of higher learning. He'd been tempted not to apply for this employment, lucrative as it might be, yet Humphrey had seemed rather anxious for him to do so, and the younger man had complied.

It was odd that Waverly-Smythe had also been interested in educating Miss Cooper's niece, Brandon mused as he neared his destination. After all, what did his competitor have to gain? But it didn't matter. Though Preston could exude charm and sophistication, the girl's aunt had chosen to hire the older of the two applicants.

Good Lord, that woman! God help him if his new pupil were anything like her Aunt Lavinia, Brandon thought, drawing his brows together, and he certainly had his suspicions about that. Why had the girl been unable to complete her term at Lady Briarley's academy, an institution dedicated to developing the marriageability of its students rather than their intellects? If the girl hadn't managed to do well in such a mundane environment, how could anyone expect her to understand topics of a more intellectual nature? Certainly her doting, doddering aunt could have undertaken to teach the young woman embroidery, music and the proper hiring and firing of a household staff. That was all the education a girl of her class usually wanted . . . or needed. He couldn't help but wonder if the time he spent with his new pupil would be more a source of intellectual frustration on his part than improvement on hers.

Still, Brandon was not one to dwell on the unpleasant aspects of life, and he considered that it was possible the whole business might not be too intolerable. Perhaps the girl would prove more parrot than magpie and at least possess the ability to mindlessly repeat the knowledge he attempted to impart. If that were beyond her capabilities and she were truly simple, Brandon hoped that she was, at the very least, pleasant to look at. That would certainly make the hours he spent in her company more bearable. He might not have taken a woman to his bed in a while, but he was certainly not immune to a well-turned ankle or blossoming bosom.

However, it really mattered not in his grand scheme of things if the girl were dull, homely or both. Her family had offered a more than generous stipend to satisfy their needs.

Ascending the three broad steps that led to the thick mahogany door set into the gray stone of Miss Cooper's home, Brandon lifted the heavy brass door knocker and allowed it to fall, announcing his arrival. He smiled as he noted that the ornament was cast in the likeness of a roaring lioness crowned with a wreath of daisies, and he supposed it to be the result of some fathomless flight of fancy on the part of Miss Cooper. Amused by the fierce glare of the metal beast, Brandon chuckled as he compared the image of female resolve to the dithering middle-aged woman and the niece who was supposed to be so like her. When the door opened, he certainly didn't feel as though he were entering the den of a beast of prey, and he had no doubt that he would manage to survive the time spent in this household and escape unscathed. Roaring lioness, indeed!

Brandon was shown to the morning room by a pretty, young maid. It was a place that readily reflected the eccentricity of the house's mistress, a jumble of intricately carved sideboards, tables and overstuffed furniture. The carpets strewn on the floor had no discernible relationship to either the color or patterns of the furniture or the elaborate draperies. Several ottomans made a walk through the room an adventure demanding one's complete attention, and paintings hung in profusion upon the walls while knickknacks filled every available surface. The decor, while highly fashionable, made Brandon uncomfortable with its disorder. The only ornament missing from the room was Miss Cooper's niece. He decided that the girl must be too well-bred to wait alone for his arrival and would make her appearance shortly in the company of her aunt, who would perform the proper introductions.

Brandon chose to seat himself in the chair nearest the window. It appeared least uncomfortable, and from this vantage point, he could look at something other than the clutter of the room while he waited for Miss Manning.

Soon he was studying the comings and goings in the small park across the way, and losing himself in his thoughts. He was disturbed a short while later by the sound of light footsteps rapidly approaching the morning room.

Deciding that the sound heralded the arrival of the tardy Miss Manning, Brandon hurriedly opened his Latin grammar and assumed a slightly stern and serious countenance in order to impress the highly desired quality of punctuality upon his new pupil. He decided he'd listen to her contrite excuses, then soften a bit so as not to disturb her delicate womanly constitution. If the girl became highly flustered she might well bolt from the room in tears. He had to remember that while Clarissa Manning was a student, she was a female, and thus a frailer creature than those he usually taught.

Hearing the door creak open, Brandon appeared cool and detached as he looked up from his text. However, instead of the apologetic Miss Manning, there was the same young servant who had admitted him, and who seemed not at all intimidated by his austere expression. Instead, she informed him in a saucy way that she had been sent to inquire if he would like some coffee and to inform him that the mistress of the house would be along directly.

Taken aback, a bewildered Brandon could only decline the coffee with a polite shake of his head. The maid turned with a flirtatious bounce of her skirts and moved from the room, leaving an increasingly irritated Brandon to snap the Latin grammar closed with annoyance at the impertinence of the females residing in this household. Saucy maid, dithering matron and *missing student*! He had yet to meet Clarissa Manning and already she was the irritant he had feared she would be. Dressing her hair was probably more important to Miss Manning than greeting her tutor. With her continued absence, his previously low opinion of her sank rapidly while his impatience rose.

Another fifteen minutes went by before Brandon removed his watch from his vest pocket and noted the time with mounting anger. Damn these people! Did they think him some fawning tradesman to be kept waiting or some ardent suitor better left to cool his heels? If he hadn't already severed his professional relationship with those students he had tutored last term, he would have left the house on Hertford Court at that moment. But in truth, he had placed his financial stability in the hands of Miss Cooper and her wayward niece, and circumstances forced him to remain where he was.

Suddenly Brandon's thoughts were interrupted as an emotional whirlwind swept into the room in the person of Lavinia Cooper, still placing the last pins in her upswept hair. Her eyes mirrored a soul that was simultaneously confused and apologetic as she noted Brandon alone in the room. A pitiful little sigh escaped her lips, and she seemed so vulnerable that the tutor hadn't the heart to berate the beleaguered woman as he stood to acknowledge her presence.

"Oh, dear," she whispered almost to herself then turned to Brandon to ask in a high-pitched, breathless voice, "what has Clarissa done that you've dismissed her already? I know the child can be vexing, Mr. Phillips, but do you think it wise to have allowed her to escape so early this first day? Not that I would presume to tell you how to conduct your tutoring sessions, but I know from experience that one must take a firm hand with her."

"In order to do that, one must first have her firmly in hand, Miss Cooper."

"Oh, Mr. Phillips," Lavinia blushed.

"It's but a figure of speech," Brandon replied with a hint of exasperation tinging his well-modulated, low-pitched voice. "What I'm trying to say is that I have not as yet had the *pleasure* of becoming acquainted with your niece. She should have begun her lessons almost an hour ago..."

"Well, where is she?" Lavinia asked, her voice rising higher and her large eyes growing bigger with a panic she didn't bother to disguise.

"I can assure you that I have no idea as to her whereabouts. *You* are her guardian, Miss Cooper. I should think that you would know where to find her."

"Oh . . . yes," Lavinia answered; her confusion grew more apparent, but she measured her words carefully as though she would not for the world give anyone the impression she was derelict in her duties toward her young ward. "Well, I'm sure, Mr. Phillips, that it is all really some little misunderstanding. Clarissa knows it's imperative that she attend to her studies, so she must have a perfectly good reason for not being here. We'll simply have to wait to find out what it is," she finished, trying to appear blasé about the situation, while her eyes traveled heavenward, imploring Providence to sort out a matter she found difficult to handle. "But please be seated. *I* can spare a few moments to keep you company."

Twenty minutes later, Brandon still sat, extremely bored and paying little attention to whatever Lavinia was saying. He merely nodded his head in agreement each time the older woman's conversation was punctuated by her simple, fluttering laugh. Looking out the window, he was soon ignoring her completely as he spied a young couple emerging from the park. His attention had initially been arrested when he had recognized the masculine form as that of Waverly-Smythe. Curious, his gaze had traveled on to the young female, and there it had remained. Tall and willowy, she moved with a sensuous grace that was accented by the close cut of her garments as they caressed her small waist and crested over her well-formed breasts. Her face was framed, beneath a fashionable hat, by the most beautiful, pale copper hair Brandon had ever seen. There was a wildness about it that made him want to touch that luxurious mane as curls escaped their restraints and rested against her high cheekbones. Brandon continued to inspect the young woman lazily until the unexpected stirring in his loins produced by the sight of her reminded him that it had been awhile since he'd had a woman.

Though his discomfort rose, Brandon continued to watch as she flirted with her companion, her smile suggesting promises a well-bred young woman would never utter. As she extended her hand coquettishly to Waverly-Smythe, who brushed his lips across the tips of her long, tapering fingers, it was against all logic that Brandon's temper began to flare. His reaction had to be a result of the intolerable morning he'd spent in the Cooper household, he decided. After all, he had never before been envious of Waverly-Smythe for *any* reason.

"I knew she had a good excuse." Lavinia's rather shrill voice intruded upon his thoughts. "Why, here she is now."

Brandon tore his gaze from the couple leaving the park and looked about the room for Miss Cooper's niece.

"Where?" he asked, annoyed, noting that no one had entered the morning room.

"Why there, coming toward the house. That is my niece with your friend, Mr. Waverly-Smythe."

This was Clarissa Manning? If the behavior he had witnessed during the past few moments was any indication, she was probably sent down for seducing one of her tutors, Brandon fumed. Well, comely she might be, but it was no excuse for her ill manners that morning, and for wasting her time and his own with the likes of Waverly-Smythe. Her aunt was right. The girl needed an education.

As they heard the front door open and close, Lavinia bustled from the room to scold Clarissa and to inform the girl of her tutor's presence. It was more than obvious to Miss Cooper that Preston's appearance this morning explained Clarissa's forgotten errands of a few days before, as well as the extra teacup Lavinia had found when she'd returned home. Really, her niece just had to be made to understand that behavior of this sort was totally unacceptable, and in loud, urgent whispers she tried to make her feelings known.

Brandon tried to ignore what was transpiring between aunt and niece in the vestibule. Seeking to salvage some tranquillity from this disagreeable morning, he continued to stare out the window, but the tutor's ire only increased tenfold as he noted Waverly-Smythe retreating from the house with a particularly jaunty stride, as though he were quite pleased with himself.

A few moments later, Brandon was still alone, and he stood tapping his foot in vexation. Forgotten was the carefully chosen look of mild sternness with which he had thought to first impress his new pupil. At the sound of the door opening behind him, he turned to glare at Miss Clarissa Manning and demanded in frosty tones, "Don't you know it's rude to keep people waiting?"

Though inwardly she was seething, Clarissa reacted to his attack with a cool, unperturbed stare. She hadn't wanted him as her tutor to begin with, and now he was compounding her disgruntlement by speaking to her in such an arrogant way!

She studied her new tutor with the interest of one preparing to engage in battle. In spite of his good looks, there was an air about him, provocative, yet dangerous. Though Clarissa found it attractive, she nonetheless decided Brandon Phillips would have to be brought under control, and had sufficient self-confidence to think she would soon enjoy the upper hand. It had been her experience with males of any age that a fragile smile, a flutter of lashes or, if the occasion warranted, an inch or two of exposed ankle, soon gave her the advantage in any situation.

Without relaxing his glare, Brandon waited for a torrent of apologies and excuses to pour forth, but none appeared. How dare this little vixen stand looking at him so innocently, offering a shy, tentative smile? Though the portrait she presented was bewitchingly lovely, Brandon knew it was but a pose. She certainly hadn't appeared innocent or shy with Waverly-Smythe. He resented the game she was playing with him and vowed she'd soon learn he was no addle-brained swain to be manipulated at will. Though it was obvious that she was used to getting her way, that was about to change, Brandon determined as he sat down and prepared to begin the lesson.

Strategy for control uppermost in her mind, Clarissa made her way with a graceful sway of her slim hips to a chair very near Brandon's. As she took her seat, he couldn't help but notice the trim, well-turned ankle exposed when she arranged her skirts. Then she leaned closer to him and extended her hand, saying in a throaty voice, "Mr. Phillips, how do you do? I am, as you have guessed, Clarissa Manning."

"How do you do?" Brandon roared, jumping to his feet in an effort to dispel the unsettling effect her voice had upon him. "What is wrong with, 'I'm sorry, Mr. Phillips, to have kept you waiting'? Young woman, do you have any idea how ill-mannered you appeared when you failed to meet with me this morning as scheduled?"

"Yes, I do seem to be a bit tardy," she replied in that same voice as she studied him from under her thick golden lashes.

She was beginning to grow impatient with his unbearable temper and immunity to her charms, but she restrained herself from showing it. He was going to be more of a challenge than she had supposed, Clarissa thought as she withdrew the hand she had offered in greeting from the empty air before her.

"You certainly are late, Miss Manning," he replied, steeling himself against the impulse to return the dazzling smile she was bestowing upon him. "For reasons quite beyond my comprehension, your father and aunt feel you are deserving of an education. I was engaged to tutor you in Latin and the classics; now it seems I must teach you manners as well."

Clarissa's teeth clenched imperceptibly as she made one last attempt to turn this madman into a civilized human being, staring at him with a flirtatious glance through lowered lids and pursing her lips in a manner that she had constantly been assured was adorable. Still, the man had the audacity to continue his reprimand.

"You are to be on time for our next session, as tardiness will not be tolerated. I hope I have made myself clear. You colonials still speak a semblance of the King's English, do you not?"

"Yes, Mr. Phillips," Clarissa responded meekly with a smile so winning that Brandon began to regret his harsh tone. Perhaps she was not as devious as he had imagined. His regret was short-lived, however, as his pupil stood and began unbuttoning her coat, her words in opposition to the sweet cadence of her voice.

"As long as we are making things clear, Mr. Phillips, let me tell you how I feel about these lessons. I have no need of tutoring from a hired man who is probably less intelligent and well-read than myself, especially when I find that person to be an odious bore!"

Clarissa smiled inwardly as she noticed Brandon clench his fists while thunderclouds gathered in his gray eyes and he fought to control his emotions. Removing her jacket to expose a trim white blouse that emphasized her pleasing bustline and a slim skirt that hugged her tiny waist, Clarissa enjoyed the conflict she read in his eyes as Brandon's irritation warred with the natural interest her actions aroused.

"I have no need of your services, Mr. Phillips. You see, my father is a scholar of the highest order, and I have aided him in his research for some years."

Aware of her tactics to divert his anger, Brandon's temper soared once again and he drawled an unimpressed response. "That indicates that you can read and write, so my task will not be as difficult as I had first assumed."

"Do you know why I was sent home from school?" Clarissa smiled, refusing to become visibly disturbed by his caustic comments as she reached up to remove her hat pin.

"It would seem it was because you're incorrigible," Brandon stated with finality.

"Not at all, Mr. Phillips," she replied, removing not only her hat, but along with it most of the lovely hair that had framed her face. She smiled smugly at his ill-hidden shock as she stood before him, hat and switches of hair in her hands, her own locks a cap of short, burnished copper curls.

"No need to look so concerned, Mr. Phillips," Clarissa responded, relishing the fact that she had been able to crack his icy facade. "I wasn't sent home as a result of illness, I was sent *down* because I refused to allow Briarley Academy to mold me into the sort of simple, empty-headed female your countrymen appear to esteem. As for my hair, I cut it off as an act of rebellion. I felt that if I were being forced to live like a nun, I might as well look like one. While Lady Briarley thought my action disgraceful, I view it as indicative of a desire for freedom . . . a trait common to my countrymen and probably unknown to you and the rest of the British, with your blind adherence to tradition and convention."

Brandon's eyes stormed with fury, and it was with great difficulty that he managed to keep his voice even. "A bit of convention might become you, Miss Manning. As for reminiscing about your girlish transgressions, you are wasting valuable tutoring time. As it is, I will be late to my own lecture."

"Please don't allow me to detain you any longer, Mr. Phillips," Clarissa replied with insincere concern evident in her response. "And you're not to worry. I'll arrange for you to be paid for the day."

"I'll be paid only because I will have earned every copper of it. I'm not leaving until we conclude your lesson. Since you claim to be so learned, try your hand at Caesar,'' Brandon demanded, tossing aside the Latin grammar and thrusting his copy of the *Gallic Wars* into her hands.

Clarissa opened the book and began reading. "All Gaul is divided into three parts..." When she had concluded an impeccable translation she looked at Brandon triumphantly. "Have I made my point, Mr. Phillips?"

"It *is* a famous passage. You may have memorized it. Before our next meeting, read the first three chapters on the origins of western society in this text," he commanded, handing her another thick volume. "I realize it's unfair of me to expect you to behave in a civilized manner if you have no concept of what civilization actually is."

"I'll read it if I have the time," Clarissa responded smoothly. "I've already made plans to spend this afternoon and evening in the company of Preston Waverly-Smythe. I'm afraid that appointment takes precedence."

Clarissa enjoyed the anger implied by the tension of Brandon's mouth and the muscles along his lean jawline. Preston had been truthful when he'd told her what a bore Phillips was and how much the two men disliked each other. Annoyed that her charms hadn't been able to overcome Brandon Phillips' air of superiority and control, she vowed to use his negative feeling toward Preston to her advantage. If he weren't going to quit, he *was* going to be managed. Except for her father, Clarissa had never met a man she could not manipulate. She had no doubts that, eventually, she would bring Brandon Phillips to heel.

Chapter Four

"That does it, Brandon!" exploded an exasperated Ned, slamming closed the cover of his text.

Brandon's molten gray eyes narrowed as he studied his fellow student from across the table situated in Ned's outer room. "What is the cause of this outburst?" the tutor asked, his voice distant and devoid of emotion.

"The cause?" Ned sputtered in disbelief. "What is the *cause*? Why, you've done nothing but scowl and growl ever since you arrived, even though I feel that my mastery of academics has never been so great. Something is afoot, Brandon, and as your browbeaten pupil *and* your close friend, I demand to know what it is."

"There is no reason for you to be concerned," the tall blond man mumbled, embarrassed by the reason for his vile mood and by his inability to keep his turbulent emotions hidden. "Let's return to your books, and I promise that I will be my usual, charming self."

"Now, now, Brandon, you can't fool me," Ned replied in a lighthearted manner that was persistent all the same. "Tell Uncle Ned what it is that's got you in such a state."

"It's nothing more than the remnants of temper provoked by my *other* pupil every time I see her," Brandon said hastily, attempting to brush the subject aside as unimportant. "I apologize. Now can we return to work?"

"Not so fast," Ned protested. "This student of yours sounds much more interesting than anything else we've been discussing this afternoon. Tell me all about her," the younger man demanded, eager curiosity shining in his eyes. "Is she beautiful?"

"Comely enough," Brandon answered grudgingly, at a loss as to how the Manning girl constantly succeeded in disturbing him, and wondering why he was answering Ned's inquiry at all.

"Then, my dear fellow," said Ned in all earnestness, "I fail to see that there could be any problem."

"Well, there is, I assure you, Ned," Brandon said. "You have never met a female as aggravating as Clarissa Manning."

"But then I'm the sort who has *never* found a good-looking female to be vexing," Ned shot back, his face breaking into an infectious grin.

"That's true," Brandon replied, as the muscles of his jawline softened in amusement at the veracity of his young friend's statements. "You're besotted by them all. There was even that audacious creature who rode bareback in P.T. Barnum's extravaganza."

"Ah, Eliza," sighed Ned, caught in reverie. "It was her boldness that I found most appealing, both in the show and out."

"But really, Ned. A circus performer?"

"I see nothing wrong with that. Why, even Queen Victoria herself has always enjoyed Barnum."

"Yes," Brandon replied dryly, "but not in quite the same manner in which you enjoyed your little performer."

Ned's only reply was a sheepish smile.

"You're hopeless," Brandon concluded with a laugh as his sharp eyes spied a hairpin near the chair in which he was sitting. Bending to retrieve it, he held it up for his companion's inspection. "I don't suppose this is yours?"

"It is now—" the young man grinned "—since the young lady to whom it belonged seems to have left it behind."

"You'd best watch your step, Ned," Brandon cautioned. "Should anyone learn you've been entertaining young women in your rooms, you'll be sent down. How would you explain that to your father?"

Ned shrugged his shoulders meekly. "Can I help it if the gentler sex finds me irresistible?"

"And just as eligible. Keep it up, my boy, and you'll find yourself on an unplanned trip to the altar."

"Enough about me," Ned said as he quickly changed the topic to one with which he felt more comfortable. "Tell me about your Miss Manning."

"She's not *my* Miss Manning!" Brandon stated emphatically. "And at any rate, there is not much to tell. All I can report is that she is, without a doubt, the most difficult, headstrong female I've ever had the misfortune to encounter. I've only tutored her three times since her aunt engaged me two weeks ago, and the girl has yet to be the least bit cooperative. She hasn't finished any of the readings I've assigned, and in discussion, she demonstrates the American penchant for rudeness."

"Ah, so that's the problem," Ned crooned softly. "Miss Manning is the independent type, and not at all impressed by your imposing masculine presence. Perhaps if you tried cajoling her instead of putting her off with your infernal commands things would be different. I'm certain you'd have no more problem with the young lady once she became aware of your true, congenial nature," Ned concluded in a wry manner.

"I'll do nothing of the sort!" Brandon exploded, annoyed that even now images of Clarissa's deep brown eyes and willowy figure flooded his mind. "I'm paid to tutor, not to coddle some rich family's spoiled daughter."

"If you tried to please her, you might reap more benefits than you expect," Ned continued logically.

"See here, I'm not her suitor. I don't have to win her over, and I certainly don't intend to attempt it."

"Fine, then learn to ignore her attitude toward you."

"It's her attitude that makes that impossible."

"Then, old boy," Ned stated without consolation, "I'm afraid you've met your match."

Lavinia scurried down the stairs only to find Clarissa before the hall mirror, pinching her cheeks and preening in her new afternoon frock, a simple yet delicate affair of pale yellow. Its straight skirt accentuated the slimness of her hips, draping behind to emphasize the roundness of her firm, young posterior. By contrast, Lavinia, in an attempt to enhance her femininity, had festooned her dress with yards of lace at throat, wrist and hem. Yet, different as they might be in temperament, age and tailoring, the two women complemented one another. A fact Clarissa noted with pleasure as she glanced in the mirror. It could only aid the plan she had laid for this afternoon.

"Clarissa, my dear, I really don't think this is appropriate behavior. After all, it isn't as though you and I were actually asked to this reception. The invitation was issued in your father's name."

"The envelope was addressed to Dr. Manning and family. Dr. Manning cannot be there, but his family can," Clarissa retorted, artistically attaching the switch of red hair Lavinia had insisted upon. "You worry too much about convention, Aunt Lavinia, like my stroll in the park with Preston. In Philadelphia, that would be perfectly acceptable."

"In Philadelphia, I fear, anything is acceptable, and what do you mean by *Preston*? You've known Mr. Waverly-Smythe little more than a fortnight and already you're on such familiar terms. I barely recovered from the shock of your being dismissed from Briarley Academy when you gave me palpitations upon seeing you and Mr. Waverly-Smythe emerge from the park unchaperoned. Scarcely two weeks have passed, and now I find we are attending an affair this afternoon to which we have not truly been invited. Have you no regard for either your reputation or my heart?"

"We've discussed that at length, Aunt Lavinia."

"I've discussed it, you have ignored it."

"Oh, dear Aunt, it seems to me that you are proper enough for both of us. As for our outing this afternoon, I'm sure the reception committee won't mind if we attend. Who could object to the presence of a beautiful, popular woman of society and her niece?"

"Do you really think so?" Lavinia asked, edging Clarissa away from the mirror so that she could study her reflection and thus verify the truth of her niece's statement.

"Yes, I'm certain. You know how the Horticultural Society depends upon you for all their affairs. Don't you think your presence would only add feminine elegance to this reception, as well?"

"I suppose we *would* provide some sparkle to an otherwise dull afternoon. Why don't you go out to the carriage and I'll be right along," Lavinia directed, standing before the mirror, humming as she made final adjustments to the lace ruffles at her throat.

Waiting for her aunt, Clarissa sat in the carriage and thought with relish of the excitement the afternoon would bring. When the invitation to the reception for University College's law department had arrived, she had tossed it aside, not wishing to spend the afternoon chatting politely in her father's stead with the dons, good but dull men, some of whom she already knew.

Though her acquaintance with Preston would not have swayed her decision to remain at home, her turbulent encounters with that barbarian, Phillips, had brought about her change of mind. Clarissa knew that duty would necessitate the upper classmen being present, and she wanted that horrible Brandon Phillips to see her in a social situation, and observe just how much she was admired and pursued. *He* may have been immune to her charms since their first meeting, treating her like a child, but now she would have the satisfaction of demonstrating to him that other men found her attractive and highly desirable.

Yes, Clarissa thought with a self-satisfied smile, settling back against the seat of the carriage, this afternoon would allow her to salvage a victory of sorts over her detestable tutor.

Clarissa moved around the reception room, chatting amiably. A great number of young law students, including Preston, had attached themselves to her, and as she walked about, they followed her en masse.

Listening for perhaps the tenth time to the peculiar anecdote explaining how the skeleton of Jeremy Bentham came to repose in the college's main entry, Clarissa wondered at Brandon's absence, chafing at the tedious trend of the conversation she was forced to endure. Lavinia, though, standing at her elbow in the role of chaperone, fairly preened at the attention given her as Clarissa's aunt. Suddenly the younger woman felt her relative tugging at her sleeve.

"Look, Clarissa, isn't that your tutor? My, but he does cut a handsome figure!" Lavinia bubbled, before adding in some embarrassment, "Not that you aren't as . . . um . . . attractive, Mr. Waverly-Smythe."

Clarissa glanced up at Preston with a twinkle in her eye, attempting to hide a smile at her aunt's faux pas. She had to admit there was some truth to Lavinia's statement, the latter half, at any rate. Preston *was* very attractive with his blue eyes and his black hair. Besides, he pampered her terribly. He was ostensibly everything she had dreamed of in a suitor. Still, Clarissa found her attention drawn to Brandon as he made his way into the room.

Some might think him handsome, she conceded petulantly, if it were not for the perpetual scowl he seemed to wear whenever she saw him. Today, however, he was actually smiling, and Clarissa's interest was piqued by the easy manner with which he greeted his fellows. But when his gaze met hers, the dazzling grin he had worn when he entered the reception room was replaced by an all too familiar look of displeasure. At that moment, an embarrassed Clarissa retaliated by entwining her arm in Preston's and asking to be escorted to the punch bowl, a walk that would place them directly in Brandon's path.

As she crossed the reception hall with her escort, Clarissa was at her most vivacious: her conversation animated, her eyes sparkling, her laugh gay and her smile enticing. Preston, pleased with this attention from Dr. James Gregory Manning's daughter, could not resist a smug glance at his rival, who was still unaware of the girl's illustrious parent. His pleasure increased as he noted Brandon's flaring irritation, like a tinderbox upon which Clarissa's obvious snub was striking sparks of anger. Yet, when the young woman turned with a sidelong glance to see what effect her presence at Preston's side had on her tutor, she received nothing more than a cool, mocking smile in return.

He's impossible, Clarissa thought. Vexed, she turned and said coldly, "Why, Mr. Phillips, I didn't expect to see you here at a social occasion. I had imagined you spent all your free time in some dreary little spot, poring over one boring text or another."

"On the contrary, Miss Manning, I like to socialize when I'm with people whose company I enjoy. Speaking of texts, I assume you've finished your readings for tomorrow."

"Oh, dear," Clarissa responded with false concern, "I'd forgotten them completely! I haven't had time for such trivial things, as Preston has kept me quite busy since last I saw you."

Assuming from her remarks that she had come to the reception for the purpose of joining Preston, Brandon found himself annoyed at the court his academic rival was paying to his student. But mostly he was irritated with himself for being at all perturbed about how the chit spent her leisure. It was no concern of his!

Managing to conceal his ire, Brandon replied smoothly as Preston turned to fetch some punch, "Miss Manning, I'm certain that if you apply yourself, you'll be able to read and retain your assignment with no problem. From what I observe, your sweet little brain should be more than capable of absorbing new knowledge, seeing as how uncluttered it is at the present time."

With that he took his leave before a furious Clarissa had an opportunity to say anything further. Throughout the rest of the afternoon, the red-haired beauty observed Brandon enjoying himself immensely, without so much as a glance in her direction, leaving her to seethe at his opinion of her as emptyheaded.

It took all Clarissa's self-control to continue smiling demurely at Preston as she silently vowed to demonstrate to Mr. Brandon Phillips exactly how intelligent she truly was. Indeed, she could converse with the brightest of men, a trait of hers that sent Aunt Lavinia into despair. Feeling that her pride was at stake, Clarissa determined to impress Brandon Phillips during their tutoring sessions, but it would be *she* who set the course of study. She would prove to him that she was capable of learning more than most, not because she desired his good opinion, she told herself, but because it presented such a challenge.

The door to the morning room opened, and Brandon was surprised to see Clarissa already there, perched on an oversize ottoman, reading a text, and to all appearances waiting to begin the day's lessons. He could not help but think she made a fetching sight when she was quiet. He crossed the threshold and his eyes took in the loveliness of her appearance. She was dressed in green, the blouse a delicate pastel, fitting closely under her well-proportioned bosom, with sleeves puffed above the elbow and tapered to the wrist. The neckline was properly high, but the yoke was made of a transparent material that hinted at the loveliness of her form beneath its confinement. The skirt, a much darker green, was like a forest glen in mid-summer, when one can smell as well as see the lushness of nature. All together, the effect was quite enchanting, and Brandon realized that even his highly disciplined self-control didn't exempt him from appreciating his pupil's stunning good looks.

She sat with her head bent, studying the book held by two delicate hands on her slim lap. Her short, curly hair formed a vibrant red halo around her head, which enhanced her graceful neck and the pale, delicate tones of her face.

Clarissa looked up to greet him with such softness and gentleness mirrored in her gaze that Brandon wondered if this epitome of femininity was indeed the same vixen he had encountered at the law school's reception just yesterday. Without his knowledge, Brandon's face softened when their eyes met, and his appreciation of her womanly qualities was evident, just as Clarissa had hoped when she had dressed with such care that morning.

"Good day, Mr. Phillips," came the low, throaty voice Brandon had tried unsuccessfully to erase from his mind these past few weeks.

"Good morning, Miss Manning," he replied as he took the seat she indicated directly behind her ottoman, paper, inkwell and pen placed for his convenience on the side table next to his chair. She swung around to face him, their knees nearly touching, and she looked at him with such a warm, winning expression that Brandon felt he could submerge himself in her large brown eyes.

Her friendliness, though a welcome relief, was bewildering to a suspicious Brandon, and Clarissa watched his confusion with well-hidden amusement, knowing he was afraid to accept her overtures of friendship, although it was obvious he was tempted to do so.

"Well, Miss Manning," he began, looking into her attentive, upturned face, fully cognizant of its graceful contours, "I think we are ready to start. Have you read the assigned chapters?'' he asked warily, waiting for another outburst of the temper with which he was already too well acquainted.

"I have," Clarissa replied in honeyed tones as she drew her feet up in front of her and hugged her knees. "But," she continued, her voice becoming sweeter still, "I really am quite knowledgeable in the history of western civilization. I've had access to those sorts of books since I could read, and every instructor with whom I've ever come into contact has belabored the topic until, I assure you, I cannot bear to discuss it any further."

"I see," Brandon stated, glad he had not allowed himself to be lulled into a false truce by her suddenly sweetened disposition, and wondering what game the minx was playing at now. "Are you attempting to tell me once again that these sessions should come to an end because there is nothing I can teach you?"

"Not at all, Mr. Phillips. I'm certain there are many things in which you can instruct me, that you're knowledgeable in many areas where I have had no experience. In fact," Clarissa continued in a whisper meant to conceal the mischief she feared would creep into her voice, "I've decided to take advantage of your expertise and ask you to teach me about things that have, to this point, been forbidden to me."

Noticing a glow in her magnificent brown eyes, and quite taken by the seductive quality of her breathy tones, Brandon momentarily ignored what it was the girl was saying, so lost was he in how she was saying it. But when he realized the content of her words, he was quite taken aback. Did she know what she was intimating, or was she speaking of some other matter entirely? Clearing his throat in an effort to maintain his composure, Brandon inquired, "May I ask exactly what it is you wish to study, Miss Manning?"

"This." Clarissa laughed merrily as she lifted the book she had been reading and placed it on Brandon's lap.

Giving Clarissa a quizzical look, Brandon opened the volume to the title page, and one well formed eyebrow arched in amazement as he read, *On the Origin of Species* by Charles Darwin.

"Miss Manning, where did you get hold of this? I hardly think any bookshop would sell such a controversial volume to a well-bred young woman. This work has done nothing but cause all sorts of theological and philosophical uproar. Many consider it nothing short of indecent.''

"How I came to possess Mr. Darwin's work is really not important," Clarissa replied, waging her own struggle for the survival of the fittest. "As for propriety," she added with a toss of her close-cropped curls, "I'm afraid my notions of that fall outside your society's conventions. Come now, Mr. Phillips, since we must endure one another's company, let us at least make our time together productive. Allow me to learn the things I want to know."

So her gesture of amiability today did have a purpose, Brandon thought with a trace of regret. Still, Clarissa's interest in Darwin impressed him, and he realized that he had underestimated her intellect. It might be amusing to see just how much she could learn, Brandon decided, although the slight pout of her lips brought to mind other things he would like to teach her.

"Of course, Mr. Phillips," Clarissa continued with a sly, sidelong glance at her instructor as she pretended to study the pattern of the carpet, "if you're not familiar with Darwin's theories, you could read it for our next session and we'll discuss it then."

So now *she* was attempting to give *him* assignments, Brandon noted, amazed at her audacity. Why did she have to become so devilish just when he had found her so angelic?

"I am quite familiar with the book, Miss Manning," he answered crisply, "but I find it rather shocking for you to be interested in it. I doubt your aunt would consider it a suitable topic for your study."

"My aunt would never object to anything you would teach me. Come now, Brandon," Clarissa whispered, placing her hand atop his, "be my friend as well as my instructor."

Even if he had been inclined to resist her plea, Brandon found that at the moment, he would have done anything she asked. The realization worried him, and he hastened to attempt more of a balance in the relationship.

"Very well, Miss Manning, but only if you promise to complete any other assignments I give you in the future. I cannot have the student conducting the class or dictating the course of study."

"Oh, thank you!" Clarissa replied, giving him a smile that was genuine rather than calculated. "I promise to be more cooperative, and please, if we are truly to be friends, you must call me Clarissa."

"As you wish. Now let us see what you have gleaned from Mr. Darwin."

Settling herself comfortably for her lesson, Clarissa was surprised to experience twinges of regret over this morning's plot to manipulate Brandon Phillips. Although she was pleased with the outcome, Clarissa began to hope Brandon had seen through her ploy and had acceded to her request only because he agreed with her in principle. But, she reminded herself in an attempt to soothe her unruly conscience, it *was* true that she had not won her desire without making some concessions, and this seemed to assuage her guilt somewhat. What she found most confusing, however, was that she should feel at all ashamed of her scheming when similar behavior had never bothered her as concerned Preston or any of the other men she knew. Was it possible that she really did wish Brandon Phillips for a friend?

A few weeks later, Clarissa stood before her wardrobe, perplexed as to what to wear. It should be something that enhanced her coloring, yet a garment that Brandon had never seen before. Not that she was overly anxious to impress him, she assured herself; it was merely that a woman should always look her best. If only she had ordered more, she thought, a frown creasing the natural pout of her lips as she searched through her clothing. Finally she settled on a rich brown skirt with a fawn blouse that emphasized her dark eyes and highlighted her rich red hair.

Critically studying her reflection in the looking glass, the girl was satisfied with the overall effect of her ensemble. But it probably wouldn't matter, she thought. Nothing she wore appeared to make any difference to her very proper tutor. Today they were supposed to discuss poetry, but even here, Clarissa was certain that her law student would select something suitably circumspect. Most probably by Tennyson, the poet laureate whose work was enjoying such popularity since his death less than six months before. Not that Clarissa would have minded reading the romantic *Idylls of the King* in the presence of her young and handsome instructor, but she feared he would wish to discuss some somber ode written to commemorate one tedious state occasion or another. Didn't the man ever think of anything that wasn't serious?

Once again, Clarissa wished that it had been Preston who had been chosen as her instructor. Then perhaps Brandon Phillips would look up from his books long enough to see that she was a woman, and not merely a student.

It wasn't as though she could complain about his treatment of her. After they had made peace with each other, Brandon had proven himself to be an interesting and extremely considerate companion. The problem was that her studious teacher was much *too* polite. Had he ever paused in their discussions to notice her eyes or hair or mouth the way she had noticed his? The answer appeared to be a resounding no, and it was all Clarissa could do to shake off the sting of her disappointment.

Slipping an arm through the sleeve of her blouse, Clarissa consoled herself with the thought that it didn't really matter. After all, it wasn't as if she actually felt anything of a delicate nature toward him. It was simply that in addition to his intelligence, Brandon *was* awfully attractive. And he was the first male of her acquaintance to ignore her subtle flirtations and be completely unmindful of her charms.

Catching herself thinking of her good-looking teacher yet again, Clarissa decided that her preoccupation with him had to arise from the challenge such a man presented. If only she could get him out of Lavinia's parlor and away from their books, maybe then he'd appreciate the fact that she was young and female.

Brandon grimaced when he realized how quickly he was approaching the Cooper residence on Hertford Court and could only admit that his accelerated gait indicated his anticipation of spending yet more time with Clarissa Manning.

Now that he and his pupil were on good terms, Brandon had discovered to his delight that the girl's beauty was matched by her lively conversation and keen mind. He was fast becoming quite taken by this unconventional young woman, and it was increasingly difficult to keep his thoughts on the girl's education rather than on her velvety brown eyes or gently swelling bosom.

Damn it all, thoughts of Clarissa Manning were intruding much too frequently, even cropping up when Brandon was deeply engrossed in his own studies. Today's images of his fiery redheaded pupil caused an unmistakable stirring in his loins, and he wondered in exasperation how he would manage to get through the morning with her without being conspicuously affected by the attraction he felt for her.

No, this morning was definitely not one to be spent with Clarissa behind closed doors while Lavinia Cooper was off tending someone else's garden. Brandon knew he was feeling decidedly too randy to place himself in such a situation. An outing! That would be ideal, he thought with satisfaction. Some public place where Clarissa might find enjoyment and he might find distraction. Perhaps one of the museums, such as the National Gallery. Certain there would be no objection, Brandon decided he'd broach the idea with Miss Cooper before she went off to do whatever it was she did with flowers.

"Out? You want to take her out of the house for a lesson?" Lavinia asked, wide-eyed. "But why? I agree that art is a valuable subject, but my library contains some excellent plates, and you needn't—" Lavinia hesitated briefly "—needn't travel in this cold weather."

"Miss Cooper, begging your pardon, but a sound education cannot evolve solely from books." Brandon's voice was firm, allowing Lavinia no options. "Besides, there is really no comparison between the original canvas and reproduced lithographs. As a woman of sensibility, I know you understand that."

"Well, Mr. Phillips, I didn't mean to suggest otherwise; I merely felt that . . . a museum? You know, all my friends have paintings in their homes, and I am certain many of them are good ones. Perhaps I could arrange for you to accompany Clarissa to view those?"

"Miss Cooper, please understand that though museums are a fairly new concept, and admit all classes of society, they are not amusement areas for the vulgar, but formal institutions founded by our government to preserve and foster great art.

They are quite respectable, and it's becoming very fashionable to be seen there, especially with the royals lending them support and visiting occasionally. Why, half of London has already been to see the National Gallery's newest acquisition, da Vinci's *Virgin of the Rocks*."

"*Virgin of the Rocks*?" Lavinia gasped.

"Why, yes," Brandon responded, exasperated by the emphasis of her last remark. He felt like informing this woman that if she insisted on shutting him up with Clarissa this morning then scampering off, *virgin* might be a word no longer in her niece's vocabulary. "Haven't you heard," he continued instead, mustering all his patience, "that the painting cost the museum a record nine thousand pounds? Surely you agree that the curators would not have purchased the work if it were not great art."

"But Mr. Phillips, I have an appointment and am unable to accompany you this morning. It's Ellen's half day, and I am not at all certain that it would be proper for you to take my niece to the National Gallery unescorted."

"The National Gallery!" echoed Clarissa's delighted voice as she appeared in the doorway of the morning room. "Why, Aunt Lavinia, you simply must allow me to go!"

"Now, now, Clarissa. You know I have only your best interests and your reputation at heart," chided Lavinia. "This is not your American society, where young men and women are permitted to mingle so haphazardly."

"Miss Cooper, please remember, I am your niece's tutor, not a suitor for her hand. There is nothing improper in taking Miss Manning to the museum as part of her education."

"No, I suppose not," Lavinia conceded slowly, afraid she might be called upon to alter her plans. "And my carriage could convey you there before it returns to take me to my...meeting. But you will have to hire public transport to bring you back here."

"Done, Miss Cooper. I shall have Miss Manning back in time for tea."

"How clever you are, Brandon!" praised Clarissa as he handed her into the family coach a few moments later. "You can't imagine how desperately I needed such an outing."

"I think I can," replied the virile male, remembering his reason for proposing the idea.

Clarissa turned her head and looked at the handsome man sitting at the opposite end of the carriage bench. Something in his voice . . . or was it her imagination? Clarissa pushed it from her mind; their time away from Lavinia's house was not to be wasted in speculation. Moving to peer out the window on Brandon's side of the carriage, Clarissa managed to move much closer to her tutor.

"I thought I saw someone I knew," she explained with a dazzling smile as she established herself next to Brandon.

"Shall I ask the coachman to stop?"

"No. I was mistaken. I think it's best to proceed as planned," Clarissa said innocently, her provocative smile unsettling her companion.

Good Lord! He'd been worried about resisting her in Miss Cooper's morning room. Now he found himself sitting quite close to Clarissa in much narrower confines. It was only extreme self-control that kept him from taking her into his arms and teaching her what happened when a man found a woman enticing. He'd like to broaden her education, all right!

For Brandon, the hours spent at the museum passed all too quickly. He found himself studying Clarissa as often as he did the paintings being displayed. Without questioning the reason for his opinion, he only knew that her animated beauty overshadowed the still forms created by brush and canvas, no matter how carefully they had been crafted.

During the course of their visit, it was obvious that his alluring red-haired charge found the museum a spectacle of excitement. To her, each new room was a surprise package to be examined gleefully in all its multiple detail. No artistic work could escape her scrutiny, though Brandon attempted to steer her to the most noteworthy pieces. While her firsthand knowledge of art history was not to be faulted, her exposure to the works opened new vistas of experience and painted a perpetual look of delight on Clarissa's features, which even da Vinci would have been hard pressed to capture, mused Brandon.

"Oh, Brandon, you must come see this small painting. I think the girl could be me—had I been alive two hundred years ago."

Viewing Rembrandt's *A Woman Bathing in a Stream*, Brandon couldn't help but agree that the woman did look like his young companion. "Yes, she's a unique little sprite, caught perhaps in the only quiet moment of her day, though I doubt that you are ever that tranquil."

"It's just so natural and wonderfully real, isn't it? She's lost in contemplation and her face is so expressive, as if Rembrandt knew exactly what she must have been thinking."

"Not difficult," replied Brandon wryly, "when the model is your mistress."

"Mistress?" echoed Clarissa, her deep brown eyes brimming with mischief. "So then there are men who, though thoroughly devoted to their work, could find such a woman attractive!"

"I can't think of anyone offhand who wouldn't call her beautiful," Brandon responded, staring at the young woman beside him rather than at the Rembrandt that claimed Clarissa's attention. "And yes," he added in a low voice, "she does look like you."

"Why, Mr. Phillips," teased his pupil, "that sounded remarkably like a compliment."

"It's merely an observation, and beauty deserves recognition, Clarissa, even from your tutor. On that note, however, I think it time for us to leave."

"Please, Brandon," said Clarissa, bestowing her most charming smile, "can't we stay just a bit longer? There's so much more I want to explore."

Brandon discovered that he liked the way his name fell so naturally from her lips; in fact, he liked it too much. "I don't think it would be wise to worry your aunt by returning late."

"You're right," Clarissa agreed reluctantly, "but before we go, just allow me to see what's in that alcove across the way."

"I don't believe there's anything there, but go ahead if you must." Brandon chuckled indulgently.

A curious Clarissa scampered off, her tutor following at a slower pace.

"Oh, Brandon," he heard the young woman's voice call as he came to the portal of the small, empty room. "You must come in; there's something here that simply begs your attention."

A few more steps brought a perplexed Brandon to join Clarissa. Looking about, he saw that the area was being prepared as an exhibition room, but at the moment, nothing hung on its walls.

"Whatever could claim my attention in here?" he asked.

"Just this," whispered Clarissa, as she stood on tiptoe and laid her hand along one side of his face, while she placed a small, quick kiss on the other. "I wanted to thank you for bringing me here. It has been one of the nicest days I've enjoyed since I've been in England."

Recognizing Clarissa's genuine expression of gratitude, Brandon was startled yet pleased by his pupil's impulsive action. Though the kiss had been an innocent one, quite chaste in every aspect, it aroused far different feelings in the tall, blond law student.

"If I had known that this was to be my reward," he replied without stopping to measure his words, "I should have taken you out to a museum long before."

"But now that you do know," Clarissa said, a saucy smile highlighting her fine features, "perhaps there will be other jaunts such as today's."

His skin still ablaze with the memory of Clarissa's touch, Brandon caught himself imagining a repetition of her kiss. Though it was a pleasant thought, the very fact that he was preoccupied with it alarmed his sense of honor as well as his practical nature. After all, he was accepting money from the girl's family to see to her education, and that did not include teaching her how a man and a woman responded to a mutual attraction. Besides, he had nothing to offer a woman at present, other than future dreams. Surely it was best to keep a good deal of distance between them. Clarissa Manning was altogether too much of a temptation.

Seeing from her expectant look that Clarissa was awaiting a reply to her proposal for future outings, he murmured hastily, "That remains to be seen. For now, let's retrieve our coats from the cloakroom. I must get you back to your aunt's or there will be no question of further trips. Besides, I must tend to my books. The day after tomorrow I sit for one of Humphrey's torture sessions, otherwise known as an examination."

As she donned her coat, Clarissa didn't know whether to be disappointed or heartened by Brandon's response. True, he hadn't jumped at her suggestion, but he hadn't said no, either. Though she wished for more of a reaction to her impetuous demonstration of appreciation, Clarissa tried to buoy her spirits with the thought that perhaps her handsome tutor was merely absorbed with preparing for his end-of-term evaluation.

Deciding it best for Clarissa to remain inside the museum's entrance while he went in search of a public carriage, Brandon welcomed the icy gusts of wind and pelting rain from the unexpected storm raging outside. The cold wetness brought him back to a sense of reality and helped to extinguish the spark of passion that Clarissa's impulsive kiss had ignited. Good Lord, Brandon rebuked himself as he walked to the next block in search of transportation, he was getting to be as bad as Ned. Imagine becoming almost undone as the result of a mere peck on the cheek by some chit, even one as bewitching as Clarissa Manning.

"Ah, here you are, right by the door. How fortunate," came the familiar masculine voice, startling Clarissa as she revelled in the day's memories.

"Why, Preston, whatever are you doing here?"

"I called at your aunt's to invite myself for tea. Miss Cooper had just returned home, and she was worried about your being caught in the storm. When she told me where you were, I volunteered to come in search of you. Besides rescuing you from the wind and rain, I thought to help you escape from a dreary afternoon in Phillips' company."

"Actually, I've had quite a lovely day," replied Clarissa, tired of Preston's constant condescension toward Brandon.

"Yes, well, I'm glad," Preston said. Angry as he was that Clarissa should find any pleasure in the presence of his rival, Preston's tones were congenial enough. "Now, however, I'm certain that you'll be happy to get home and enjoy some tea. Your aunt's carriage is right outside the door."

"But what about Brandon?" said Clarissa as Preston took her arm to escort her from the building.

"What about him?"

"He went to find a public carriage. We must wait for him. I know Aunt Lavinia won't mind setting out an extra teacup."

"That won't be necessary. Phillips is on his way to his rooms."

"What?" Clarissa questioned, disappointment etched around her pretty mouth.

"I saw him outside. When I told him I'd been sent to fetch you both, he remanded you to my care and said something about needing time to prepare for Humphrey's examination," Preston lied smoothly, at the same time quite satisfied that *he* wouldn't have to worry about prepping for his law professor's academic inquisition. Having a copy of the examination beforehand always made his life so much easier. "You know what a pedantic fellow Phillips can be," he added to persuade his indecisive companion.

"Oh," Clarissa said, not daring to utter another syllable for fear of giving way to the hurt she felt. After she had just kissed him, Brandon Phillips had gone off and left her to the care of another man! Could Aunt Lavinia have been right when she lectured that men disliked unconventional, forward women? Or perhaps, Clarissa wondered miserably, it was only she whom Brandon Phillips didn't like.

As they hurried to the carriage, Preston smiled, thinking of Phillips' reaction when he came back to find Clarissa gone. However, it would be prudent to leave a message with the guard at the entrance stating that the young woman had left for her aunt's house in the company of the gentleman who had been sent to fetch her. After all, Preston didn't want his afternoon interrupted by Phillips pounding on Lavinia Cooper's door to report that Clarissa was missing. Once his rival had found out that the young woman had returned home, he'd have no recourse but to be on his way. After all, that penniless upstart was merely Clarissa's tutor, and he had no right to question his employer's actions.

As for his companion, Preston thought it wouldn't hurt her, either, to think that Phillips preferred his books to his pretty pupil. In truth, she'd been mentioning that bastard's name too often of late.

Quickly settling Clarissa in the carriage before his rival appeared, Preston informed her that he wanted to inquire about a forthcoming exhibition. He was back within moments, his message to the guard delivered. Hastily he seated himself close to the unusually quiet girl. He tapped on the roof and the carriage moved forward, just as a chilled and wet Brandon alighted from a rig but a few feet behind them.

Recognizing the Cooper carriage, Brandon was surprised to see it there, and more surprised still when it moved away and rounded a corner, making the identity of its passengers easily discernible. After her affectionate display a short while before, Clarissa had left him and gone off with Waverly-Smythe!

And that Lavinia had condoned the whole thing was evident by their mode of transportation, Brandon fumed. While he could understand that Clarissa's aunt was the sort who could be easily manipulated by Waverly-Smythe, he was astounded that Clarissa would abandon him so easily.

He thought of how she had thanked him for the trip to the National Gallery, and even standing in the cold as he was, his face burned as he wondered how many kisses Preston would receive on the return to Hertford Court.

His first assessment of Clarissa Manning as a spoiled, willful female had been the correct one, Brandon angrily concluded. Besides, hadn't he told Ned often enough that as far as serious students were concerned, women were distractions? It was only too bad that he hadn't heeded his own advice.

Brandon's heart felt as empty as the carriage he turned to dismiss. There was no sense in wasting money on comfort for him alone when he could just as easily walk to his rooms. The trek would be unpleasant, but perhaps the rain would wash away his temper, activated so easily by that fickle American female. At any rate, by the time he reached his quarters, the storm would have seen to it that he'd be happy enough to be there. And though he'd be alone, his beloved books would be waiting. He determined not to waste any more time thinking about Lavinia Cooper's niece. His studies, he was sure, would be enough to eradicate all thoughts of the cruelly bewitching Miss Manning and the myriad emotions she had conjured up.

Chapter Five

"Damnation! Try to broaden someone's experience, do more than what's expected and what happens? Achoo! You stay up all night with a bloody cold and don't get a lick of studying done," stormed Brandon as he brewed yet another pot of tea. Not normally a man to fall victim to physical malady, he deeply resented the discomfort and inconvenience he was suffering. "The Marquess of Queensbury be damned; in life there aren't any rules, at least none that society plays by. If that fool Waverly-Smythe hadn't come along yesterday, we'd have returned home in the carriage and I wouldn't have gotten drenched."

Conveniently overlooking the fact that he'd been soaked from the instant he left the museum in search of a carriage, and still would have had to travel from Hertford Court to his quarters, Brandon felt justified in his annoyance. Pouring a liberal tot of rum into the steaming pot, he inhaled the fumes and sneezed again.

"How the devil can I concentrate on Humphrey's torts for the senior preliminaries with this bloody cold? That girl may have the face of an angel, but I wish I'd never been blessed with her as a student. She's nothing but trouble, from her odd preferences in her studies to her even odder partiality for a cur like Waverly-Smythe. What can she see in that bastard? Achoo!"

"Good God! Where did you pick up that lovely bit of congestion?" asked Ned as he stepped over Brandon's carelessly scattered legal briefs and settled himself in a comfortable chair without needing an invitation. "I saw your lamp lit late last night when I passed. Anxious about your examination and working hard?''

"Trying hard to study is more like it," Brandon snarled, grateful for a scapegoat to bear his wrath. "Not like some classmates I could name who choose to flirt with the socially elite. The hell with him. I got nowhere last night, thanks to a doe-eyed vixen who wouldn't leave me in peace.''

"You? Two days before exams wasting precious time on a skirt? You've got to be joking; that's more like the old Edward Lowell Newcomb before you reformed me. A woman's not something Brandon Phillips could enjoy with a test on the horizon." Ned's teasing only worsened Brandon's humor.

"Damn it all, why does everyone always think they know everything about me? It's that irritating Manning chit I've been tutoring.''

"She's gotten to you, has she? Well, you wouldn't be the first man to think himself immune to a pretty young face only to discover otherwise," Ned stated with a philosophical shrug.

"It's nothing of the sort," Brandon protested in exasperation. "It's simply that I find instructing a female a tiresome chore.''

"Actually I've always found teaching a pretty woman a rather exhilarating experience.''

"I'm talking about formal education," lied Brandon, not only to Ned, but to himself, as well.

"Naturally, what else would you think of but books, even with regard to the fairer sex?" needled the raven-haired youth. "But you needn't be so concerned about her education. I'm certain good old Waverly-Smythe is seeing to that in her leisure time.''

"Him again? He broke up a tutoring session we were having yesterday at the museum, but where could you have seen them together? You wouldn't be caught dead in a gallery.''

"If I were after a comely lass, I might give it a go, but Father mentioned that he had encountered Miss Cooper, her niece and Waverly-Smythe at the theater benefit last night where they'd gone to see the divine Sarah Bernhardt. Apparently he knows Miss Cooper from the Horticultural Society, and they happened to meet at the intermission for refreshments. I've no doubt old W.S. was busily trying to curry favor, as usual.''

"Isn't that cursedly typical? Old Maid Cooper in her prim and proper manner hesitates to allow me to escort her precious little darling to the museum, but she welcomes that bastard to her bosom. After she professed to be concerned about his motives regarding Clarissa, she allows him to accompany them to the theater. Ned, never believe a woman; they're all fickle, not an honest one among them." He punctuated his outrage with a sneeze, adding, "And this is her fault, too!"

"Well, as decadent as I might be, I'm afraid the alternative to women holds no attraction for me, old friend," replied Ned softly. "And from the protestations you're making, I'd say you feel the same."

"What are you babbling about now? Even with me as your tutor, you're becoming more obtuse by the day," growled Brandon, taking his annoyance at the world out on his friend.

"Nothing important. Look at it this way. If Waverly-Smythe was out on the town last night, that's one more advantage you've got over him, since you were hitting the books."

"Hitting them, yes, throwing them, yes, but learning? I'm afraid not likely. After what happened yesterday afternoon, I couldn't concentrate."

"All right then, forget about last night and enjoy this rum straight. Having finished my examinations this morning, and done rather well, I suspect, I brought us a few bottles to celebrate. If alcohol really has the antiseptic powers Lister goes on about, maybe it will restore your health as well as your spirits."

"Humphrey's inquisition is tomorrow," protested Brandon halfheartedly as Ned filled his cup.

"Don't be ridiculous. You're so proficient in international law that Humph himself invited you to lead the course summation last week. The written examination is merely a formality for you; besides, you need to relax. Let's drink to fickle women!"

"May they drown in their own tears," toasted Brandon, "when they learn the true nature of the Waverly-Smythes of this world." Swallowing rapidly, he refilled his cup and lifted his arm once more, sipping heedlessly while he mused aloud. "There probably isn't a man alive who hasn't been stung by the words of a capricious woman. The trouble is, we're too bloody polite to give them a dressing down about it."

"I doubt Miss Manning even realizes just how much she has offended you," mumbled Ned, his tongue becoming a bit thicker as the effects of the rum began to weave through his body.

"You haven't been listening, Ned. The girl means very little to me," said Brandon quickly, unwilling to admit, even to himself, how deeply Clarissa's rejection had stung him. "The actions of her aunt are what concern me."

Though Ned was aware of the unnatural color rising in Brandon's face, the younger man took his friend's words at face value, attributing his vehemence to the effects of the alcohol coupled with anger, not his tutor's ambivalent feelings.

"Well, I don't see why you allow the old girl to put you in such a dither," he replied as he filled their cups once more.

"Because she's my employer," said Brandon, finding that the rum was beginning to quell his unsettled emotions as well as extend his patience with a suddenly dense Ned. The feeling was a comfortable one, and in his present state, Brandon could see no reason not to prolong such a satisfying sensation by partaking of more drink. Though he remembered his impending examination, he also recalled the nights he had spent drinking with his uncle's sailors. He had suffered no ill effects then, and expected that his indulgence tonight would be no different. Besides, he rationalized, he had to do something to dispel the distracting visions of Clarissa that had been befuddling his mind of late.

"It's highly disturbing, Ned, to have the person who pays your salary say one thing and then do another," Brandon continued, attempting to forget the copper-haired American and concentrate on Lavinia instead. "I never know what she expects of me. The woman is quite beyond all logic."

"Why don't you simply tell that middle-aged pudding-headed frump just what you think of her?" enthused his slurring pupil.

"I should," Brandon declared. Inhibitions gone, he raised his voice and began his address. "To all the victims of fickle females," he proposed, "may they gain the courage to tell the gentler sex what they really think of them and the torment they employ. You hear me, Lavinia? You're a silly old fool, primping before your mirror for imaginary suitors and ignoring the temptress beneath your own roof. Waverly-Smythe will be her ruination, Cooper, believe me. You should watch out for that fellow. Right, Ned?"

"Certainly, Bran, old fellow. Pour me another before you finish that third bottle, though. Good man."

"That's something else I must remember to tell Cooper. I *am* a damned good man, a hell of a sight better than—achoo—what's-his-name, anyway. Don't you agree?"

But Ned had dozed off before the fire and gave no response. Frowning at his unsociable companion, Brandon stretched out a hand and pulled one of his notebooks from the untidy pile on the floor. Perhaps he should just look things over one more time.

Yet he'd barely turned a half dozen pages when he, too, was overcome by the heat of the room, the smoothness of his drink, and his black mood. Slouching down in his chair he drifted off, his books forgotten beside him.

The first gray streaks of dawn stole into Brandon's rooms causing shadows deeper than the ones that gloom had cast upon his soul. In a groggy stupor, Brandon sat up, cup in hand, staring morosely at the remains of last night's fire. Collapsed on the floor near the hearth, Ned had not stirred from where he'd fallen victim to the demon rum, but Brandon, haunted by the image of Clarissa, had been unable to rest for long. Her laughing vivacity and innocent lust for life had invaded the place in his heart once held by his first mistress, the law. Drinking so heavily was out of character for him, though this morning he was not quite sober enough to recognize this or the other changes Clarissa had so easily wrought in him.

The absence of the fire in the hearth caused the room to be cold and damp as well as dim, but rather than stoking the waning embers, Brandon arose shakily, remembering something about the hair of the dog, and staggered about, searching among the remains of the bottles Ned had brought. While the warmth the rum imparted couldn't warm his soul the way thoughts of Clarissa could, it was a far better companion than the woman in question; at least he knew what to expect from the rum.

The girl, on the other hand, was maddening in her unpredictability; he had thought she was enjoying their afternoon together and had come to appreciate his company, yet the moment he turned his back on her, she disappeared with Waverly-Smythe. It was all Lavinia's fault—not only Waverly-Smythe's interference in Brandon's plans, but also Clarissa's appearance at the theater with him. How could that so-called guardian condone such irresponsible behavior?

Emptying his cup and then another before draining the last dregs from the bottle, Brandon reached a decision. He would confront Miss Cooper as Ned had suggested the night before. She was no fit guardian for the girl. Where was Clarissa's family, anyway? Didn't her father, whoever he was, know better than to trust Lavinia? Anyone who would encourage the attentions of Waverly-Smythe couldn't be in full possession of her faculties. Someone who professed to care so much about respectability and reputation should be able to recognize that Waverly-Smythe's gentility was merely superficial, and Brandon would tell her so, right now, before he sat for the senior preliminaries. If he could just banish Clarissa and her ineffective duenna from his concerns, he'd be able to concentrate on the academic task before him and be one step closer to being the student recommended to Dobson and Whittaker.

Moving as quickly as his head would allow, Brandon splashed water on his burning eyes, performed a rapid toilet and threw a blanket over the now snoring Ned. Pulling on his greatcoat, he grabbed his gown and mortarboard from the hook beside the door and set off determinedly for Hertford Court.

"Miss Clarissa, Miss Clarissa, you've got to come downstairs." Ellen's voice conveyed her distress. "I wouldn't disturb you this early, miss, but your aunt's not around and Mr. Phillips is being most insistent. I can't get him to leave."

"Mr. Phillips is here? At half past six in the morning?"

"Yes, miss; he doesn't appear to be feeling too well, but he demands to see Miss Cooper. The gentleman claims he must meet with her before some examination today and he won't believe she's not at home."

"She's not here at this hour? Why ever not?"

"Well, er, you see, she often rises early and...she goes to the park, miss. She says it's one of her few opportunities to enjoy nature in its solitary state. But what shall I tell your tutor?"

"I'll be down shortly to deal with Mr. Phillips, Ellen. Just invite him to be seated and see that there's a fire started in the morning room to take off the chill."

"Yes, miss." Before the maid had closed the door, Clarissa was out of bed and at her wardrobe, pondering its contents.

"If the matter is really that urgent, I wonder if I should take the time to be properly gowned? It's not seemly to appear in dishabille, heaven knows, but this is not an ordinary social call. Yes, the apricot satin should do nicely."

Shedding the simple blue gown she'd worn to bed, Clarissa donned the chosen nightdress with its matching robe, adorned with lace at the neck and bodice. The Paris-designed outfit had been a gift from her father last season, and while its opaque fabric covered her young body adequately for even the most prudish aunt, it floated around her in such a sensuous manner its aura of sexuality was an open invitation more than a suggestion. Quickly washing her face, brushing her hair and pinching her cheeks, Clarissa went down to meet her fate.

Waiting below in the morning room, Brandon was suffering the effects of his night's debauchery. His walk to the Cooper home, rather than clearing his head, seemed to have made it heavier, and now the aroma of Lavinia's plants and the warmth of the fire were enough to set him half-nodding in his chair.

Suddenly before him there was an angel, but one robed in pale apricot instead of white. Her gown was long and loose and flowed softly from slender shoulders, accentuating her graceful neck. As he gazed on the soft coppery curls framing his heavenly visitor's delicate features, Brandon knew he'd found paradise.

"Well, Mr. Phillips? Are you going to sit and stare at me all morning? I understand it was urgent that you see my aunt, but in her absence, will I do?" Crossing to stand before the unmoving figure, Clarissa was surprised at the tutor's disheveled appearance, but more so at his apparent lapse of manners. What could be wrong?

"I should say so," Brandon muttered as he looked again at the beauty before him: was this really his pupil Clarissa? His brain could not accept it, no matter how often he blinked his eyes or shook his throbbing head. This elegant creature was no one to whom he could teach anything, save perhaps the thrill of loving. Attempting to stand to greet her properly, he sank back hurriedly as the room began to spin.

"Mr. Phillips, I do believe you are intoxicated!"

"Only from drinking in the sight of you, though I venture to say a taste would be ever more powerful." His usual control having been ravaged by alcohol, Brandon gave in to his natural instincts and the sight of his pupil so charmingly attired. Grabbing at Clarissa's hand, he drew it to his lips in what he imagined was a romantic gesture of gallantry. But before he could savor her, she wrested her arm from his grasp.

"Brandon Phillips! How dare you appear here in this condition? Especially after you deserted me the day before yesterday!"

"I deserted you?" Brandon tried to bellow before he realized such an action caused his head too much pain. Dropping his voice to a husky whisper, he added, "It was you who left me!"

"Now I know you're in your cups," Clarissa retorted. "What would my aunt say if she were to see you acting the besotted fool?" Clarissa's condescending tone pierced Brandon's alcohol-induced haze and reminded him of his purpose.

"Ah, yes, right you are, Miss Manning. Your aunt, the ever righteous Miss Lavinia Cooper, who is so damnably prim that she protests an educational excursion to the museum, but welcomes Waverly-Smythe's attentions, allowing him to escort you all over—the park, the legal reception and the theater. Heaven knows where else he's gotten with you!"

Initially outraged by Brandon's obvious drunkenness, Clarissa began to find the scene amusing as she recognized the jealousy in Brandon's proprietary tone. Perhaps this man had noticed her in more than a scholarly way, after all.

"About the museum, Brandon. Preston told me Aunt Lavinia had sent him to—"

"See? There's another example of your aunt's misjudgment!"

"But why? What does Preston have to do with this?"

"He's a . . . rogue, Clarissa. He's sly about using young and beautiful women, enjoying them then casting them aside. I don't know why he should be so damnably interested in you, but—" In casting unintended doubt upon Clarissa's desirability, Brandon's confused tongue had committed a blunder he didn't even recognize, so when she sharply interrupted him, he couldn't fathom the reason.

"Well, I thank you very much for your assessment of my feminine allure, sir. However, if you could just remember why you wanted to see my aunt so urgently?"

"Why, yes, of course," began Brandon, attempting to clear his head by shaking it, but quickly regretting the effort. "That is, I have already. I mean, she must be on guard against Mr. Waverly-Smythe. He is not the gentleman he appears, and I couldn't study for worrying about what was happening. I knew if I didn't warn your aunt, I'd never sleep or study again."

"It would seem that you found another way to occupy yourself last night," retorted Clarissa. Though still leery of the man's purpose, she didn't question his concern. "A bottle or two, apparently?"

"Yes, but they didn't help. I couldn't keep my mind on the law with you in my heart."

"Perhaps you'd better rest a little while, Brandon, while I fetch us some coffee," said a surprised Clarissa. "If you are to succeed in your examination this morning, you'll need to be sharp, and not as muddleheaded as you appear now."

Clarissa went to the kitchen, preferring not to alert the servants to Brandon's condition. How remarkable that this man, previously so somber and businesslike, could have become so uncertain and tongue-tied because of her. This perspective of Brandon had awakened a protective instinct in her she hadn't known she possessed. Imagine him worrying about her! She wasn't aware he'd noticed her in that way; she'd tried her best in the museum the other day, but when he'd gone off without a word, abandoning her to Preston's attentions, she'd given up hope.

Yet here he was going on about some kind of warning; he must really care or he wouldn't have come, especially right before that damned test. And in return, she'd spend the rest of the day worrying about him and his blasted examination. But wanting to caution her about a gentleman such as Preston, really! How foolish could men be?

When she returned to the morning room with the coffee, Brandon was stretched out on the settee, his academic gown and his boots on the floor at his feet, the deep, elongated breaths that indicated sleep echoing his exhaustion. Placing the laden tray within easy reach of the couch on one of her aunt's numerous tables, the young woman stood silently looking at him. This was definitely a man to achieve his goals. The power of his determination could be read even in the manner of his pose, arms folded across his chest, strong hands at the ready to dominate any task. But it was Brandon's face that drew her closest attention. For the first time she saw signs of his vulnerability.

He had been as worried about her as he said, she decided, noting the darkened circles beneath his eyes, the furrows in his brow and his unhealthy pallor, though Clarissa wasn't entirely sure if overindulgence wouldn't account for the latter. She longed to reach down and soothe the weary lines creasing his forehead, but hesitated to be so forward. From this vantage point the hard chin she'd imagined so stubborn and angry appeared masculine and strong, despite the hint of a smile on his lips. Perhaps Mr. Phillips might come to be much more than her tutor, but there was no time to explore that possibility today. She'd best get him off to his examination.

Seating herself on the edge of the settee, Clarissa softly touched his shoulder, intending to wake him gently. Brandon opened his eyes in a state of semiconsciousness to find his dream come true. Tenderly he pulled Clarissa to him and began to caress her silken neck and downy curls. It would seem there were many aspects of Brandon's personality that he had kept hidden. Clarissa discovered that the raw masculinity he was presently displaying thrilled her beyond all expectation. Acting under the influence of spirits not entirely his own, the dominant Brandon surprised his angel into submission.

"Clarissa Manning, you're too much a temptress for any man to ignore. You're driving me to the brink of insanity so that I want to sear your lips with passionate kisses, the way you have seared your image into my very soul."

Brandon eased his body back on the settee to allow Clarissa to fit more comfortably beside him. Lowering his lips to hers, he tenderly savored the softly yielding mouth beneath his own. Slowly Brandon gave way to his burning need and built the pressure of his mouth until Clarissa welcomed his tongue and drank as deeply from his being as he did from hers. They were alone in a world of discovery and enticing sensation.

As Clarissa's body began to tremble with his warmth, her heart sighed its contentment. The racing of her pulse and the delicious shivers along her spine were unfamiliar sensations to the eighteen-year-old, signaling her readiness to love had she been able to interpret her body's message. In her inexperience, however, she was uncertain how far she could allow her desires to lead her. This sensation intoxicated her in much the same way that Brandon's excesses had affected him, so that all rational thought was quite impossible.

Only when Brandon's adventuring right hand began to caress her lower back, the increasing pressure demanding uninhibited responses, did Clarissa become alarmed and attempt to pull out of his possessive embrace.

"Careful, little angel, since you're not equipped with wings, you might hurt yourself if you try to fly away." He whispered softly in her ear, his lips inflamed with the slightest of touches. At this moment, all Brandon knew was that he didn't want this bewitching female to separate herself from him. Her sudden show of reluctance urged him onward with gentle insistence, and in his desire to engulf her in his fervent ardor, he sought words of tender reassurance. But passion combined with alcohol to cloud his usually astute mind. When he spoke, the words intended to soothe the skittish Clarissa were chosen unwisely.

"Stay close to me, Clarissa. I won't hurt you; that's a promise. I only want you near. I may be your tutor, but that's no reason to be frightened. I am also a man, and while I never expected to be attracted to an intelligent woman, I suppose your mind doesn't make any difference, since your beauty surpasses your intellect by far.''

"Oh, does it?'' snapped Clarissa angrily, her unsettled emotions causing her to take this awkwardly tendered compliment as an insult. She tore herself from him, only to fall unceremoniously on the floor.

"What's wrong?'' wondered a startled Brandon, looking at the angel who'd flown from his side. Hadn't he just told her that as smart as she was, she was even more beautiful?

Gathering her gown about her and rising unsteadily to her feet, Clarissa refused to recognize the true cause of her reaction to Brandon's words, that she had been frightened by his overwhelming masculinity enough to grasp at any excuse offering an escape from his arms. Unwilling to admit her fears, she dwelt instead upon his unintentional affront and fumed inwardly.

How dare he! And he was the man she had been allowing such liberties! This besotted excuse for a tutor who, in the sweetest moments of intimacy she had ever known, had the audacity to insult her and call her stupid. How dare he! Her lips might have been bruised and tender, but her words were icily pointed.

"Mr. Phillips, I believe you have an appointment at university in a little over an hour, though I fail to see that you are in the proper condition to take an examination of any kind.''

"Maybe not an examination, but I wager I could take you,'' said Brandon, his voice ragged with frustration and his ego suffering. "But I've never had to force any woman, and I'd rather you came to me freely.''

"For a scholar, you are incredibly dense,'' Clarissa whispered fiercely. "I'll never come to you at all.''

"Could you be so haughty if you felt my lips on yours once more? Let's see, shall we?'' Brandon said in a slurring voice as he swung around, only to be eluded by his suddenly reluctant student.

"You'd better ready yourself for your academic conquest, and not this personal one, Mr. Phillips. Since you consider intelligence such a masculine trait, perhaps you could demonstrate some now,'' chided Clarissa as she pressed a cup into Brandon's shaky hands and turned to fetch the hot coffee. She only wanted him sober enough to leave the house on Hertford Court. After that, Clarissa thought as she pushed him into a seat, she didn't care what happened to Brandon Phillips. "This is the only thing you'll get from me. As you can see, I'm not interested in your games playing."

"Maybe not now, but what of five minutes ago? Remember what you felt then?" Reaching across to stroke Clarissa's conveniently positioned thigh, a persistent Brandon deflected the coffee she was pouring and instead of its streaming into his cup, the liquid cascaded off his hand to form a puddle on Lavinia's marble table.

"Damn it, woman, why couldn't you watch what you were doing? Cor, that's hot!" bellowed the law student, jumping up in an effort to shake the hot fluid from his fingers. As he rose to unsteady feet, however, he missed his footing and went down on the morning-room floor.

Feeling helpless, but realizing she couldn't involve the servants, Clarissa struggled to get her tutor back on the settee with no help from him whatsoever. It was apparent that the usually impeccably behaved Brandon Phillips was out cold.

Uncertain as to whether Brandon had hit his head or if his unconsciousness was simply due to the accumulated effects of his overindulgences, Clarissa debated her options. The only thing of which she was certain was that she couldn't wake him.

Hurrying from the room, the girl was thankful that Cook was already out to fetch the day's marketing and wouldn't ask time-consuming questions. Quickly locating the objects she sought, she returned shortly to the morning room with a basin of cool water, towels, dressing and the herbal salve Lavinia recommended for any and all ills. When Brandon's hand was thoroughly cleansed, she was relieved to see that the burns, though red and already blistered, wouldn't require a doctor's care.

"Oh, but the examination! With that hand, he won't be able to write for at least a week. Yet if he misses the test, he'll face dismissal... Brandon, wake up. Come on now..."

Shaking him roughly by the shoulder, Clarissa was rewarded with only a muttered groan.

"Damn, if only there were some way he could sit for that senior exam. Preston said all the students, medical, law and scientific, are in the same large hall, over four hundred scholars monitored by impartial proctors. No one would ever realize he was hung over. By Custer's cohorts,'' Clarissa said, her eyes glinting with a half-formed thought. ''No one would ever recognize him, I'd wager... or anyone else who arrives in his stead.''

The gleam that appeared in Clarissa's eyes deepened and her mouth began to twitch with the devilry of her idea.

''His boots would be a bit large, but his academic attire should disguise my figure sufficiently, and with my short hair... After all those lectures of Father's I've copied and researched, I surely have enough background to write an intelligent essay on international law... If only I dared, it would be better than his not showing up for the examination at all.''

A loud snore and hiccup interrupted her litany, confirming her assessment of her tutor's condition. He was in no state to prove his academic worth, let alone earn his precious placement at the Inns of Court. That left her no choice but to replace him! The only problem she could foresee was if he regained consciousness soon enough to appear at the examination hall before the preliminaries had ended. Well, she could fix that!

Clarissa crossed to the ornately carved sideboard and unlocked the cabinet where Lavinia kept her best brandy. Pouring a healthy glassful, she reminded herself that this really was for Brandon's own good, though why she should bother to help him after his behavior today, she had no idea.

''Brandon, sit up a little, that's it. Drink this. Now, come on, that's a fine fellow, a little more, finish it up.'' With slow coaxing Clarissa was able to induce Brandon to swallow almost all the brandy, and to her satisfaction, he promptly slipped into a deep sleep, replete with resounding snores.

Locking the morning room behind her, with a silent prayer, Clarissa called for Ellen and gave instructions for the carriage to be brought round to take Mr. Phillips to the college for his examination.

''Since I've delayed his departure, I feel it only right that we afford him the opportunity of arriving on time for his appointment. I'm certain Aunt Lavinia would agree.''

''Very well, miss, I'll see to it.''

"Just tell Andrew to wait in the court. Mr. Phillips will be out as soon as he has finished his coffee. I am going to dress then catch up on my correspondence and reading in the morning room, Ellen. I will ring when I want luncheon, but otherwise please do not disturb me."

"Yes, Miss Clarissa. What shall I tell Miss Lavinia if she returns before you ring?"

"That I am tired from this early conference and will see her at luncheon."

Once the maid had left the hall, Clarissa gathered Brandon's boots, greatcoat and scholarly robe, then scurried to the back entryway where, as she vaguely remembered, the gardener kept extra clothing. Fortunately Mr. Norris was a slight man. His garments felt strange, but didn't look all that ridiculous, she decided as she gave a final glance at the hall mirror. Attired in dark pants and a jacket that had seen far better days, but that would be adequately covered by Brandon's greatcoat, Clarissa was satisfied. With fingers crossed, she turned the collar high around her face, pulled Mr. Norris' woolen cap on her head and left the house with Brandon's gown and mortarboard beneath her arm.

"We shall see about my intelligence, Mr. Phillips," she mused smugly, still stinging from his earlier remark. "Though the handwriting will be awkward enough to support the injury to your right hand, this will be the finest exam you have ever written."

Clarissa strode rapidly across the courtyard in front of University College, attempting to lengthen her stride and move as one of the many young men streaming toward the examination hall.

"Heavens, give me the strength to go through with this! In Hertford Court I thought it would be simple, but now I'm beginning to wonder," Clarissa found herself mumbling. "If anyone looks at me closely, it would be Brandon who would suffer for my deception. Though what choice do I really have? Besides," she continued, bolstering her flagging courage, "there is absolutely no need to question my ability to answer the topic. I'll merely take a few deep breaths and find my, er, Brandon's seat."

Clarissa knew she was intelligent, despite her tutor's opinion; she would prove so with her paper this morning. Since the independent proctors wouldn't know Brandon or any of the other students, she was safe in her disguise. She had only the actual writing to survive. Noticing Preston seated six rows ahead of her, Clarissa ducked her head as he glanced her way, then remembered that in Brandon's nondescript academic gown and Lavinia's old spectacles, she was just another anonymous student among many.

Suddenly the proctors entered through their private door and began to position themselves around the hall. Before she could entertain any last thoughts or prayers for success, the chilling command was given, the die cast.

"Scholars, you have three hours. Open the examination booklets and begin!"

Chapter Six

Clarissa tugged the cap down on her brow as she hurried back to Hertford Court. Her head was bent forward in the face of the raw March storm, but the wind's force couldn't lessen her high spirits. Thanks to the upturned collar of the greatcoat, she appeared to any but the most discerning eye to be a slight, working-class youth braving the weather to reach his place of employment. The handy garment hid not only her delicate features, but the smug expression that played about her lips as the girl fought the urge to splash joyfully in the puddles.

Fate couldn't have provided a more opportune way in which to prove myself to Brandon Phillips, Clarissa thought as the corners of her mouth moved upward once more in a sweep of satisfaction. Imagine his surprise when he finds that I have managed to accomplish something that he, for all his so-called intellect, was in no condition to handle.

She had actually done it, sat for an examination at university alongside the *superior* sex, and no one had been the wiser, she exalted silently. Of course, much had been made of the fact that the college had opened its doors to women two decades before, graciously allowing the gentler sex to take part in the learning process. But though females were granted degrees, they rarely attended lectures or sat for examinations with their male counterparts because to do so would be unladylike and much too stressful, besides. It was this obstinate position on the part of higher education that kept Clarissa away from such institutions. She wanted no select morsel handed to her as one would feed a pampered pet. She wanted the whole meal.

Even many of those who advocated the education of females did so to provide the gentler portion of society with some sort of diversion, declaring that women should be exposed to harmless ideas as a sort of hobby, but not to anything that would cause them to think, mind you, or question their obedience to their husbands or their place in society. While such an attitude might satisfy the Lavinia Coopers of this world, Clarissa was a different woman entirely. And so she relished the day's success all the more.

Well, Brandon, she thought, what will you say when you find that it is I who am responsible for passing your examination in international law? It would have been virtually impossible for you to have signed your name, never mind to have composed any type of coherent essay.

Clarissa's eyes were shining with accomplishment as she thought of what she had written, assured that her arguments were forcibly made and her position the only acceptable one. The slant she had given the essay on the legalities of imperialism was original, refuting outmoded attitudes of the past, a brilliant piece that would be touted, she was sure, as outstanding work on Brandon's part. And then, after he accepted all the praise and accolades, she would tell him, privately of course, that it was she who had produced such marvelous results. That would diminish some of his insufferable self-confidence. Clarissa anticipated the triumph of that moment, even as she realized with surprise that in a little corner of her heart, she was truly glad she had been able to help her tutor.

Though Preston was a decent sort, Brandon was the one who needed the sponsorship for the Inns. Besides, until he had so unceremoniously abandoned her at the museum only to show up on Lavinia's doorstep this morning, Clarissa had come to prefer his company to that of Preston Waverly-Smythe. After she and her tutor had begun delving into Darwin, Brandon had introduced other interests, as well, including the ideas of Oscar Wilde and the cynical philosophies of George Bernard Shaw, so that her time with him had become learning as she enjoyed it.

He had tried to initiate a new subject this morning, she suddenly thought as a crimson flush stole over the contours of her lovely face. But then, he couldn't have been sincere; it was only the effects of the alcohol that had shattered his cool reserve. In fact, without his confident intellectual mask in place, Brandon had seemed as vulnerable as a small boy and endearingly human. But he certainly hadn't acted like a child, she reminded herself.

Recalling his whispered words and demanding kisses, her blush grew more furious. Vague feelings she couldn't name rose within Clarissa, causing her breathing to become shallow and fast. This was absurd, she decided, attempting to push away thoughts of Brandon and their effects upon her. After all, he had been inebriated and had not meant a word he said...or had he?

Clarissa was so caught up in her quandary that she completely ignored the uncomfortable elements of the storm, and almost walked by Lavinia's residence. An icy gust brought her back to her purpose and she turned to enter her aunt's home, catching herself at the last moment and bypassing the main doorway in the hopes of slipping in through the servants' entrance. If she could gain admittance to her room unnoticed, it would be one less problem with which she'd have to contend.

Stealthily she opened the door and stood still, hearing Cook and Ellen conversing in the adjoining kitchen. She had but to reach the back stairwell in order to ascend the two floors to her room, yet she remained rooted, astonished and embarrassed to find that she and Brandon were the topic of conversation.

"I tell you," said Cook, folding her plump, flour-dusted arms across her ample bosom, "our young miss is leading the Phillips gent a merry dance."

"Perhaps," conceded Ellen, "but it 'pears to me that he calls the tune."

"It don't make no never mind, my girl. Mark my words, they'll wind up partners in the dance of life. Why, any fool can see he's besotted with her. A few days ago, when I went up to the morning room to discuss the week's menus with Miss Cooper, the young ones were just finishing up their lesson and the way he gazed at her as she bent over her books, well, it told more than words ever could."

"But," interrupted Ellen, "it doesn't appear that the young lady returns the admiration. They were fussing only a few hours ago when you were at market."

"I'm always at market," grumbled Cook. "The number of plants in this house and its garden, and not an edible root or leaf in the bunch. But never mind, tell me what happened."

"You should have heard them feuding, and the old miss nowhere in sight to lend a hand."

"It would appear that Miss Lavinia Cooper is back to her old ways, and more power to her, I say. Do go on, though, about Miss Clarissa."

"There's not really all that much to tell. There were loud voices, and then things grew still. The next thing I know, Miss Manning is off to find some bandages; I'd give a month's salary to know exactly what went on, but that oak door is so thick that I couldn't make out what it was they were saying. I suppose that's why the old miss used to do her entertaining in there. At any rate, next thing I know, Miss Clarissa yells out that she doesn't want to be disturbed all day, and Mr. Phillips, he goes off to university. Since then, the door to the morning room has been closed. I fear Miss Clarissa has shut herself up there in a fit of pout. To my mind, that ain't exactly the mark of a couple in love."

"Oh, they scrap because our girl is an independent lass, and he's strong-minded as well. He's probably the most tempting man she's ever met, but I'm certain it's his strength of character that's at the root of her attraction to him."

"Well, for my money, the gent's got other attractions," Ellen gushed. "He's a damned good looker, and his frame makes me think he'd be agile enough between the sheets . . . I say he'd be more than a match for our fiery young miss."

Clarissa's cheeks burned scarlet and she quietly scampered past the open doorway as she heard Cook and Ellen retreating into the pantry. She didn't wish to overhear any more idiotic speculation on the part of the servants, but when she was not quite out of earshot Cook added, "Mind you, I'm quite certain I'll shortly be preparing a wedding feast."

"And from the looks of the groom to be," said Ellen, giggling, "there'll be a christening dinner soon to follow . . ."

"How dare they!" Clarissa said to herself as she entered her bedroom, the memory of the servants' laughter still sounding in her ears. "Why, it's none of their concern even if there *were* anything between Brandon and me," she continued aloud as she sat at her dressing table and spoke to the reflection in her mirror, "though of course what they think is ludicrous! Brandon has no real interest in me nor I in him, at least nothing beyond flirtation, and that's all his actions today indicated...and mine as well," she declared vehemently until she remembered this morning's ardent kisses and saw the expression on the face that stared at her from the glass.

The young female in the mirror blushed at thoughts of Brandon Phillips' advances, yet longed for more. Could this be *her* reflection? Had the game she had played with Brandon been so dangerous that she had lost much more than she had ever thought to wager? In the eyes that looked at her, she saw the answer. Brandon Phillips had won a place in her heart.

This revelation frightened Clarissa. What she felt for her tutor was a hundredfold more powerful than what she had imagined for Preston, charming as he was. This changed everything! The elation she had known as a result of the morning's scholarly accomplishments diminished, and worry took its place. She wondered if Brandon would understand why she had sat for his examination, or if he would think that it had just been a lark she had undertaken to embarrass and ridicule him. What's more, she had to decide if he really did love her as Cook said, or if it was merely romantic gossip on the old woman's part. If only she could speak to someone experienced in these matters. Of course, Lavinia would be no help. Lavinia!

Her aunt must surely be back by now. Clarissa jumped up and began to dress hurriedly, to return to the morning room before Lavinia discovered her deception. The young woman was in no mood for her aunt's palpitations, nor did she wish to take the proper Miss Cooper into her confidence. If her aunt became aware of the episode, she could inadvertently inform Brandon of a situation Clarissa was beginning to think might better be kept from him. After all, Brandon was so honorable that he would confess to someone taking his examination in his stead. Why hadn't she thought of that this morning, she wondered as she hastened her preparations to go downstairs.

Quickly divesting herself of the gardener's clothing, Clarissa rolled it into a ball and thrust the garments under her bed. She donned her light blue frock and ran her fingers through her curls, then placed Brandon's academic attire and boots in her oversize needlework bag and made her way to the main staircase. Seeing that no one was about, she silently opened the front door, sounded the knocker and loudly closed the heavy mahogany behind her before stepping into the morning room. Let them think Brandon had only now returned.

Standing just inside the doorway, Clarissa saw Brandon as she had left him. He remained sprawled on the settee, head to one side and a lock of his unruly blond hair falling carelessly across his forehead. His features were so relaxed and boyish that Clarissa's heart swelled with tenderness before she took hold of herself and set about doing what had to be done.

She removed Brandon's academic gown from the needlework bag and tossed it carelessly across the back of the furniture on which he slept. Then, walking to the desk, Clarissa dabbed the corner of a blotter in the inkwell and retraced her steps to the dozing man's side.

Dear Lord, give me courage, she prayed silently as she gingerly lifted his unbandaged left hand. She thought her heart would cease its function when he stirred slightly; but ascertaining that he remained asleep, Clarissa gently separated his index finger from the rest, smeared the blotter's inky residue along the finger's side near the top knuckle, and replaced the hand to its original dangling position.

Putting his boots in front of the fire, Clarissa smoothed her dress and returned the blotter to the desk before stepping to the bell pull and tugging on its heavily embroidered length. Then she crossed once more to look down upon Brandon Phillips and stood lost in thought, absently brushing the wayward lock of hair from his forehead.

A few moments passed before Ellen stood before her, the maid's widened eyes taking in the unusual scene with great interest.

"Oh, Ellen, I feared Mr. Phillips might be a bit feverish," Clarissa floundered as she sought some alibi to excuse the gesture of affection the maid had witnessed. "However, I think he is merely exhausted from his work at university this morning and his trek back through the storm. I've set his boots to drying, but I'd like you to see to his greatcoat. And ask Cook if she would send us up some warm broth, buttered bread and coffee... plenty of coffee. I've no doubt Mr. Phillips will be hungry when he wakes."

Clarissa managed to hide her nervousness as she looked at Ellen to see how much of her story would go unquestioned. When no probing looks or queries were forthcoming, Clarissa ventured a bit more. "By the way, Ellen, where is my aunt?"

Now it was Ellen's turn to fidget. "I'm sure I don't know, miss. To my knowledge, she hasn't returned as yet."

"Not home? It seems rather odd that she would be out communing with nature in weather such as this."

"Perhaps," the maid faltered, "when the storm broke, she stopped off to pay a call on one of her friends."

"Well, I hope that is the case. But, Ellen, you look so uncomfortable that I suspect something is afoot."

"I'm sure I don't know what you mean, miss," the maid replied elusively as she retreated hastily to the kitchen.

Curious, Clarissa sat in the chair by the window, trying to piece together what she had learned of her aunt's odd behavior. Well, it didn't much matter, the girl decided, dismissing the situation before she pondered it at any great length. Clarissa was content with the fact that her inquiry had diverted attention from her own actions.

Waiting for Ellen to return, doubts about her predicament began to materialize. What was she going to do? Before she had realized that she cared for Brandon in a special way, she wouldn't have worried what his reaction to this morning's escapade might be. In fact, she might have found his anger a source of extreme satisfaction. Now, however, it was another matter entirely, and she debated whether or not she should confess what she had done. Good Lord, she'd have to make a decision and rouse him soon.

But Brandon's response to what she might tell him was not the only thing that troubled Clarissa. Until today, she had come to rather enjoy their verbal sparring. But all that had been changed by a few stolen kisses and searing caresses.

The trouble was, though, did Brandon feel the same way or was it the alcohol that had made him so attentive this morning? She couldn't respond to her newfound emotions before she received some sign from him. To do so would give Brandon an advantage in the relationship that Clarissa did not wish him to have. Balancing an attraction to this man with her independence was going to demand great skill, and Clarissa was not certain she was equal to the task.

Ellen had brought in the tray and departed quickly, leaving the door ajar and giggling over Brandon's muttered endearments, which issued forth in his sleep.

"No doubt off to have a nice long chat with Cook," Clarissa muttered with exasperation as she closed the door. "And the longer he stays, the more they'll have to gossip about. I'd best awaken him."

Drawing closer to her slumbering tutor, Clarissa bent and touched his arm softly, shaking it while calling his name in as sweet a voice as she could manage. Her labor, however, evoked no response on his part other than a few incoherent utterings and movement that only served to make him more comfortable upon the small sofa.

Thinking that he might respond more favorably in a little while, Clarissa walked to the window to see how the storm was progressing. "Heavens, no!" she gasped as she looked out and saw a public carriage pulled to the curb in front of the house, with her aunt descending from its interior. Mustering her strength, she flew to the settee, determined Lavinia should not find Brandon here and in such a state.

Gone was her intent to awaken him gently. Desperation overtook her, causing Clarissa to push and poke her tutor while hissing angrily, "Brandon, get up! My aunt has returned! Damn you, man, wake up this instant!"

Brandon's dreams were interrupted by a bothersome buzzing in his ear. Try to block it out as he may, the irritating noise continued until he opened his eyes in some annoyance to see what was the cause of it. Focusing was no easy accomplishment; everything in the room was swaying and moving so that at first he thought he was back on one of his uncle's ships. But damn, these furnishings had no place on an oceangoing vessel, nor did the slight feminine form before him.

Sitting up quickly, Brandon learned that any sudden movement caused his head tremendous pain. Had he been set upon from behind and shanghaied? Where in damnation was he, he wondered as he struggled to gain full consciousness and shrug off the fog that numbed his mind.

Attempting to clear his vision, he blinked his eyes vigorously and found the consequences of the action more detrimental than beneficial. This caused his lids to drop again as he sat back, hoping to stop the thundering in his head. Instantly, however, the high-pitched buzzing began once more, adding to his discomfort. Slowly the noise began to take substance, and he grinned as he realized with satisfaction that he could distinguish it as the female's voice, though none too gentle, or genteel, for that matter.

"Wake up, you smirking sot. This is an entirely serious matter, and there you sit smiling like a fool. No more time for games. Wake up this instant!"

The mysterious woman by his side appeared to have the unfortunate quality of being a shrew, Brandon decided with rising anger, determined to subject himself to her sharp tongue no longer. With valiant effort, he managed to open his eyes and keep them open until the room stopped shifting and he could distinguish individual objects.

No, he decided, he wasn't on a ship, but in some sitting room. Again the feminine voice broke through to his consciousness, as shrill and insistent in its demands as before. Good God, was he in the position of having cuckolded one of the local gentry, and in imminent danger of being caught?

Desperately his eyes traveled the length of the woman's figure until they rested upon her face, and her features, after an instant, became recognizable. It was Clarissa Manning! Nothing to worry about there. Brandon almost sighed his relief. She was hardly the seducible type, although vague recollections of a honeyed mouth assailed his memory, causing him emotional as well as physical discomfort. Damn that girl! She never gave him any peace!

Quite suddenly, Brandon found a cup of coffee placed in his hands, one of which was bandaged, before Clarissa retired to the chair opposite him, saying sweetly as though there were nothing out of the ordinary, "How nice of you to come by, Brandon."

As he regarded her skeptically, desire stirred amid recollections of ardent kisses, whether real or imagined, he could not tell. Yet her face remained so demure and innocent that he was certain it was all part of some dream. In the midst of trying to separate fact from fantasy, he heard the front door open and shut and dainty footsteps ascend the main staircase as somewhere in the background a clock chimed. Two o'clock! His test had been at nine!

Hurriedly he searched his memory as best he could and found he was capable of recalling nothing other than coming here early this morning for a reason he couldn't remember. Had he been in the house since then and missed his examination, caught in some alcoholic stupor thanks to Ned's generosity and his own attraction to Clarissa Manning? The queasiness that rose in his stomach stemmed as much from the horror that he might have thrown his career away for a chit who cared nothing for him as it did from the effects of the alcohol he had consumed.

Brandon gingerly sipped the coffee, studying his decorous pupil over the rim of Lavinia's delicate china cup. He couldn't dismiss Clarissa's alarming appeal as she sat there smiling at him, and visions of her draped in an apricot dressing gown invaded his thoughts, to be shoved hastily aside. Of course he had never seen her in such a state of undress. Such images appearing so suddenly and vividly validated his suspicion that the girl held more than a passing attraction for him, and the realization only served to make him more bewildered.

Had he sacrificed all his past work for a young bit of fluff who had no idea of what it meant to strive for something? He had to find out if he had been here all day, but there was no way he would admit his loss of memory to Clarissa, not after all the lectures he had delivered on the topic of dedication to learning. He couldn't ask her exactly what had transpired since he had knocked on Miss Cooper's door that morning. And why the hell was his hand bandaged, he wondered as its throbbing called it to his attention. Perhaps in the course of casual conversation, Clarissa would reveal a clue that would spark his memory concerning the day's events. It seemed to be the only course of action that allowed him to escape appearing the complete fool.

"Excellent coffee, Clarissa. Miss Cooper is to be recommended on her choice of blends," he began tentatively.

"Thank you, but then anything hot would be welcome on a day such as this," Clarissa replied gesturing toward the window to indicate the storm raging outside.

Storm! It hadn't been raining when Brandon had arrived, of that he was certain. Glancing surreptitiously at his feet, the rugged, light-haired student noted with surprise that he wasn't wearing any shoes. What *had* happened here this morning?

"Where are my boots?" Brandon snapped as consternation began to overcome his attempt at manners in a stressful situation.

"Why, Brandon," Clarissa cooed soothingly, deciding to brazen it out, "they're in front of the fire, where I put them to dry. They were quite wet from being out in all that rain, and are still damp. Surely you don't mean to leave now and go out in this nasty weather; you'd only catch more of a chill. Have some pity on me and sit down like a dear fellow. I'd like nothing better than to pass this dreary afternoon in your company."

That's too demure a response to my bellowing, Brandon thought with some suspicion. This was definitely not the Manning girl he knew. What would suddenly quiet a lively lass like Clarissa and make her so loving? The only conjecture Brandon could make filled him with dread, yet if the shoes were wet, he hadn't been here all day, hadn't had the chance to... Not that he wouldn't want to, he admitted as his gaze came to rest on the provocatively graceful figure. Bloody hell! Here he was thinking of her again when he should be worried about his future.

Bending to retrieve his boots and place them on his feet, Brandon noticed the fingers of his left hand quite stained with ink, and allowed himself to hope that he had written his examination after all, though awkwardly, it would seem, if he had injured his right hand before then.

Clarissa remained silent, her great brown eyes bright and her lips pursed enticingly in obvious concern. Why was she looking at him so intently, as though waiting for some sign? Good God, he had to get out of here and find Ned. Once his panic had abated, perhaps his friend could help him fit the pieces together.

Brandon had just risen and asked for his coat when Lavinia entered the morning room, flustered as usual.

"Hello, Clarissa, dear. Good day, Mr. Phillips. I'm certain you young people have been working so diligently that you've been lost to the outside world," she said with an almost indiscernible note of hope in her voice. "Now I expect you learned a good deal today, dear."

"Actually, Aunt, I'm afraid that I've been rather a poor student this afternoon, but it was no fault of Brandon's," Clarissa responded with docility under her tutor's intense stare. "He was most determined to teach me, I must say."

Brandon's face colored slightly. He was not at all certain if he understood her allusions correctly, or if indeed she were referring to anything outside the realm of textbooks.

"Well, you just do as Mr. Phillips tells you, and I know you'll be thoroughly educated in no time," Lavinia absently directed her niece.

"Why, Aunt, I must admit that under Brandon's tutelage I've learned about . . . oh, all sorts of things," the girl replied, a faint flush stealing across her face while her mouth drew up into a disarming curve.

Brandon noticed her expression and heard her words with mounting anxiety. He had to immediately escape this room, which had taken on a suffocating air, though it appeared not to bother either of the women. Taking his greatcoat from Ellen with perfunctory thanks, he noted with some sense of relief that it, too, was damp. It stood to reason that if his shoes and coat had been out in the storm, he must have been, as well, but why in God's name couldn't he remember?

And why did Clarissa look more alluring than usual as she glanced at him, as though they shared some special secret? Like a hunted animal facing its predator, Brandon knew he must get away. He bade both women goodbye, his apprehension increasing as Clarissa boldly laid a restraining hand on his arm when he turned to leave.

"Brandon, I know that you must be terribly tired after completing your examinations, but don't you feel that we should celebrate a job well done? Aunt Lavinia and I are attending a concert this evening, and there is room in our box if you care to join us."

How could he celebrate anything until he discovered the truth about how he had spent his day, Brandon thought with frustration. The only thing of which he was certain at this point was that the young woman smiling so winningly in his direction was the cause of his emotional tumult, and this prompted Brandon to answer her invitation curtly.

"As you have said, I am quite fatigued, Miss Manning. And I pray that you can understand the stipend I receive for your tutoring, while quite generous, does not allow me to squander money on concerts. I will see you next at our regularly appointed time."

"How silly of me to expect you to celebrate your end of term with Aunt Lavinia and me. Of course you'll want to be off and carouse the way you students usually do. A little tippling, perhaps? However, Aunt Lavinia and I aren't dependent upon your company, I assure you," Clarissa answered with an impassive face and a saccharine voice, determined she would not allow this man to know just how deeply she was hurt by his rebuff. "Good day, Mr. Phillips."

Clarissa waited until the door had slammed behind an irritated Brandon before she gave way to emotion and flew up the stairs. Once inside her room, she threw herself on her bed, a flurry of tears flowing down her cheeks, the outward sign of her anger and embarrassment.

"Oh, that insufferable man! How could I have ever believed that Brandon Phillips was human enough to fall in love with anyone?" she thought angrily, throwing her history text on the floor near her bed. Sitting up, she reached for the small notebook containing questions she had jotted down to discuss with Brandon at their next session and ripped it into small pieces; but rather than making her feel better, the falling papers seemed only to fan her temper. She didn't care how handsome or masculine he was. What did it matter if his infrequent smiles stole her breath way? It made no difference that he was the most attractive man she'd ever met—he was also the most conceited, obstinate and domineering. How she would relish being able to entice him, simply for the pleasure of rejecting him. But he obviously *hadn't* been bewitched by her beauty or charms, no matter what Cook thought. The only way he would notice her was if she were blindfolded, wore a Grecian gown and carried the scales of justice in her hand. That beast!

A few moments later, a soft knock came at the door, and Lavinia entered.

"Oh, Aunt Lavinia, can't you dismiss Brandon Phillips as my tutor? I absolutely detest him!"

"That's nice, dear," Lavinia answered mindlessly, patting the girl's hand. "If you truly detest him, you have no reason to be upset by Mr. Phillips' reaction to your invitation. How can you fault him for acting with propriety? He's correct to keep your relationship on an impersonal basis. Why, if I thought he would be moved by your good looks, I would never have engaged him to begin with. Now, be a dear girl and help me clear away this mess you've made before we have to listen to Ellen's grumbling."

As Clarissa began retrieving the pieces of notebook and throwing them into the fire burning upon the grate, Lavinia bent to pick up the history text. In the act of doing so, her eyes caught sight of some clothing protruding from under the bed, and she clucked her tongue disapprovingly. Surely Clarissa knew that orderliness was a highly desirable quality. Pulling the clothing from its hiding place, Lavinia gave a little gasp, her hand flying to her heart as she discovered the garment to be a pair of men's trousers.

"Clarissa," she panted, sinking into a nearby chair, "have you no concern for your aunt's health? What is the meaning of this? How will I explain it to your dear father?"

"Oh, Aunt Lavinia," responded the girl with exasperation, "don't carry on so. The clothing belongs to the gardener."

"Our gardener? Mr. Norris? Why, he's older than I am! But then I know all too well that one can never be overly careful with those who dedicate their lives to nurturing plants. I . . . I suppose it comes of their poking about in all that fertile soil and sowing all those seeds. But Clarissa, I must tell you that I am shocked and gravely disappointed!"

"Aunt Lavinia, don't be so hysterical. How could you think such a thing of me?"

"Clarissa, nothing about you would surprise me any more. If you are not carrying on with the gardener, then why is his clothing in your room?"

"I simply borrowed it, Aunt. I thought it would be great fun to go around the city disguised as a boy. With my cropped hair,

I was certain I could carry the whole thing off, and I assure you, I did quite nicely, thank you!'' Clarissa replied, feeling that this half truth was better than either the actual facts or an outright lie.

''You think it a lark to gad about London dressed as a man, exposing the silhouette of your . . . your limbs to the population at large? My dear girl, you have gone too far! I've been too lenient with you, but I intend to remedy that very shortly.''

Clarissa had had enough upset with Brandon, and her emotions were tautly stretched. She was in no mood for Lavinia's emotional jabbering, nor did she appreciate the impropriety of which her aunt had accused her, and with old Mr. Norris!

''My dear Aunt Lavinia, it was a harmless prank, that was all.''

''I see nothing harmless about it! I am disheartened by your constantly indecent behavior. Lord knows I've tried to set you on the right path, but all to no avail. I am sick over this, Clarissa, truly quite ill. I would never have attempted such a thing in my youth! Your actions only serve to tell me that your father has not done at all well in raising you, but then what can one expect from a man, and an American at that!''

''Though I love you very much, I shall not stand by and hear you say anything against my father, Aunt Lavinia. As to all the effort you put into transforming me into a lady, why, you spend more time with your flowers than with me. You're always dashing off to meetings of the Horticultural Society, and if you had been home this morning, you could have stopped me from doing anything you consider highly improper. Where were you this morning, anyway?''

''Well, I was . . . I was . . .'' Lavinia sputtered, her face a vivid scarlet. ''I was off on business for my garden society.''

''In the storm?''

''Don't question your elders, Clarissa. It's most unbecoming. Besides, it is you who must answer to me, not I to you.''

''Dear Aunt, don't be angry with me. It's just that Papa has gone off to the Continent, and you are out almost every day. I am constantly left to my own devices and then taken to task for doing things I find entertaining.''

''Perhaps you are right,'' relented Lavinia, her palpitations ceasing and her sympathies aroused. ''You are left on your own quite a bit, but it is not as if I am engaged in frivolous activities—the work of the Horticultural Society is quite important. Why, when the Prince of Wales' son, dear Eddy, died so suddenly leaving his fiancée, Princess May, a widow before she was ever a bride, it was the Horticultural Society that supplied the bridal wreath of orange blossoms she placed on his coffin. Without our help, where else would she have found such blooms in the dead of winter? So you see, my dear, my work is important . . .''

"I've never questioned that, Aunt Lavinia, but it doesn't cure my loneliness," Clarissa said, though her thoughts were centered more on Brandon than on any sense of abandonment by her mother's sister.

"It's not that I don't enjoy your company, my dear," the older woman replied in a softer voice, "but if I were to abandon my life as it was before your arrival, what should I do when your dear father comes to take you home?"

"I don't want you to give up your hobbies for me," Clarissa stated truthfully as she played with the edge of her sleeve, "but there are times I am so bored that I wouldn't mind attending some of your meetings with you."

"But I'm afraid that's impossible," Lavinia answered rapidly, her cheeks burning once more. "It is a closed society. However, I think I have the solution to our dilemma. Mr. Phillips is between terms right now. Perhaps I can persuade him to spend a bit more time with you. Lord knows I don't agree with education for women, but at this point, I don't see that a bit more would do any great harm."

"I don't want to spend more time in Mr. Phillips' company. He's an impossible tyrant!" Clarissa shouted, thinking of the man who had been so rude this afternoon rather than the passionate male to whom she had been introduced that morning.

"Now, now, it won't be that bad, I'm sure. He's rather nice, actually, and perhaps I could permit some more trips to the museum."

"It could be that Mr. Phillips won't agree to your proposal, Aunt," Clarissa stated smugly.

"Oh, I think he'll be amenable to the idea. I'll just pen him a short note this instant and have it sent around to his quarters."

"Well, if you expect an affirmative response, you'd best promise him a bigger fee," Clarissa retorted with no small degree of sympathy for herself. "He appears to think of me strictly in terms of pence and pounds."

"Don't worry, dear," Lavinia answered, moving toward the door. "Leave it all to me. And please, Clarissa, return the gardener's clothing as unobtrusively as possible. It wouldn't do to have the servants speculating about our personal lives."

Chapter Seven

Buoyancy in his step, a euphoric smile on his face, Ned bounded into Brandon's quarters later that afternoon.

"I say, what's with all this gloom?" cried Ned gleefully as he pulled back the curtains and opened the windows wide. "I know this place was a morgue when I left this morning, but it's a whole new world out there now!"

"What are you trying to do, invite the weather inside?" objected Brandon as he closed the offending panes. Troubled by hazy memories of temptation satisfied and the sudden hurt in Clarissa's eyes when he had rebuffed her invitation, he was in no mood for jocularity. "I'm still suffering from that grippe, you know."

"Fiddlesticks! You drank enough last night to kill anything and this room needs a good airing. Enough small talk, though; what's important, Brandon, is that you did it!"

"My God, did what?" asked the blond man in alarm.

"You're a genius, a true champion, England's, nay the world's best," pronounced Ned authoritatively, slapping his friend on the back. "Congratulations!"

"Obviously you haven't recovered full use of your senses after our session with the bottle. Whatever are you rambling on about?"

"The grades are posted for first years students, *mon* tutor superior, and you, Brandon Phillips, succeeded in getting me, Edward Lowell Newcomb, heir to Lord Geoffrey Lowell Newcomb, Earl of Hammerford, K something or another, through royally! As a matter of fact, friend, scholar and confidant, you earned me a First, not with honors, granted, but a bloomingly glorious First, nonetheless.''

"Good job, Ned, but it was your doing, not mine. Congratulate yourself, old boy.''

Even in his elated state, Ned recognized his friend's peculiar lack of unrestrained enthusiasm.

"That's it? 'Good job, congratulate yourself'? Damn it, Brandon, we vowed we'd celebrate the way it's never been done before if I passed the bloody term, let alone earned distinction. I can understand your anxiety yesterday before your exam, but word is that Humphrey's question dealt with sovereignty and the expansion of the empire. Since you researched four papers this term on British imperialistic policies and international politics, you undoubtedly wrote the best exam in your class. Can't you relax enough to share my triumph?'' A note of exasperation crept into Ned's voice as he moved impatiently about the room in which Brandon sulked, but the younger student was determined to await his tutor's response. After a few moments of silence, Brandon raised his head from his hands and spoke in a despondent voice.

"That's the damnable uncertainty of it, Ned. I don't remember the test question and I can't be absolutely positive I even sat for the bloody examination this morning... That is, I had ink on my fingers, but all I can recall is that at some point I was kissing an angel.''

"Is that why your hand is bandaged? I mean, certainly you appreciated the Humph's choice of topic, but I don't think it was too politic to have kissed the man. No wonder the old codger attacked you; in fact you're bloody fortunate he didn't injure a more delicate part of your anatomy.''

"For Lord's sake, Ned, stop being such an ass or get the hell out! Can't you see I'm in no mood for your nonsense? I have no recollection of what really transpired this morning and what's a dream... I mean, I know you spouted some idiocy last night about my truly wanting Clarissa, but at the moment I'm not entirely certain I didn't take her.''

"You? Don't be absurd, Brandon. But you know I'll do anything I can to help,'' promised the young Newcomb more soberly, as he settled into a seat opposite his friend. "The last thing I remember last night was opening the third bottle of rum, and when I came to this morning you had already left, I presumed for the university."

Hunched over in a posture far removed from his usual stance, Brandon recounted the morning's activities as best he could. From arriving at Hertford Court and not finding Lavinia to the sensuous dreams of an apricot flavored angel to sudden pain and awakening with a bandaged hand; Brandon withheld nothing from his friend, not Clarissa's suggestive glances, or her atypical suggestion that he escort her out for the evening, or her surprise at his refusal.

"So now," he concluded, "nothing is really vivid in my mind until she woke me up, supposedly after I'd returned from the senior preliminaries, though heaven only knows why I would have returned to Hertford Court."

"Unless it was because you still had to speak to Miss Cooper. Remember, you hadn't seen her earlier."

"I don't believe so, but who knows for certain? I don't. I'm haunted by the vision of Clarissa—her perfume, the velvety texture of her skin, even the taste of her, and I can't rid myself of her, real or imaginary."

"Well, she can't have been all that good if you don't recall all the exciting details," said Ned facetiously. But before Brandon could give voice to the angry retort Ned saw forming in his eyes, he continued quickly. "Sorry for being flippant, old man, but do you really believe that Miss Clarissa Manning of Philadelphia would allow you such liberties as you imagined and then say nothing of your outrageous behavior later on?"

Brandon said nothing but seemed to mull over the question.

"Far more likely that last night's rum together with the intellectual efforts expended in your examination today combined to reward you with a desirable fantasy while the young lady was off ordering your lunch. You said yourself her kiss in the museum had almost changed your mind about her until Preston showed up. As for her scent, it was probably lingering because the settee was where she had last been seated."

"Perhaps..."

"No perhaps about it, I'm afraid, much as you might like to believe Clarissa desires you." Ned hesitated as Brandon snorted, but continued bravely. "And dotty as you claim her chaperone is, I very much doubt any young woman, even one as unorthodox as this American, could wrestle lovingly with you on the couch in the morning, then treat you so nonchalantly in the afternoon as to make you question your sanity.''

''I suppose you're right, Ned, but all my senses responded to her so completely I could have sworn it happened.''

''I'm sorry, but I still say wishful thinking. However, enough of this second guessing the past, we're off to dinner. Father insists that I bring my celebrated mentor round so you can partake of the praises showered in my direction this evening, not to mention the fatted calf he's certain to have commanded for his prodigal son.''

When Brandon hesitated and shook his head as if to refuse, Ned pressed on.

''Obviously you've been working too hard and need a rest, or your overtaxed cranium wouldn't invent such outlandish fantasies. Come along, relax with a good meal and a better friend.''

''All right,'' agreed Brandon with a sheepish chuckle. ''I haven't taken much time for myself of late, but with the trimester break officially beginning tomorrow, I plan to alter that. A little mindless feminine companionship would be welcome.''

''Now that's more like it. Tomorrow night I'll take you to the Holborn; they have some girls there who . . .''

As the pair approached Brandon's stairwell, however, one of London's street urchins, always prepared to run an errand for a copper, arrived with a letter for Brandon. When the lad indicated he needed a reply, Brandon opened the missive at once, wondering as to its urgency. After briefly perusing its contents, he groaned and passed it to Ned.

My dear Mr. Phillips,
I do hope you will excuse my addressing you as ''dear,'' but it seems only right. Though I am afraid this may be inconvenient for you, it is utterly imperative, in my opinion, that you meet with me tomorrow at nine o'clock promptly. I daresay you are aware of what has been happening with Clarissa and after what went on today, it is essential that you and I discuss your past and future relationship with her. I cannot stress the urgency of this mat-

ter strongly enough, but I believe you understand that
there are things that cannot be committed to paper. Until
tomorrow, I trust,

L. Cooper

"Yes, very well," murmured Brandon to the waiting child as
he gave him a few coins. "Tell the lady I shall be there."

As the lad scurried off, reward in hand, Brandon looked
questioningly at his friend.

"Still of the opinion I was fantasizing, Ned? Or doesn't it
sound like a summons to discuss not only Clarissa's behavior
but mine as well?" His resentment built as he pondered his
possible fate. "Where in tarnation was that old biddy this
morning when she should have been home, keeping an eye on
her niece—and perhaps me as well? Damn her! I wish I'd never
heard of Lavinia Cooper and her precious tutoring job. She's
nothing but trouble."

"Now you don't know that for certain," offered Ned. "Her
note may just have arrived coincidentally with your own guilt
feelings, for which I still say you have no cause. Besides, from
what you've told me of Cooper, *what's been happening with
Clarissa* might be merely that the girl can't curtsy properly."

"I can't help feeling there's something else in store for me
tonight to make the day even worse," muttered Brandon,
looking for all the world as though he would enjoy a scuffle to
release his pent-up anger.

"Nonsense, it's always darkest before the dawn. We'll visit
Father's wine cellar and that will brighten the evening. Since my
stepmother, Elsbeth, left town with the gardener, Father has
kept some very notable vintages available for those dark,
brooding moods when they strike. Though I must say, of late
he's not been in a bad way too often. Still, that means we've a
vast selection to choose from. Come on now, move along. Relief is ahead."

"I daresay I haven't anything else to do until tomorrow."

Shrugging his shoulders as though they bore the weight of the
world's ills, Brandon followed Ned, not particularly caring for
their destination, concerned only with what Lavinia intended
to do about what he had done, whatever that might be.

* * *

The Right Honorable Geoffrey Lowell Newcomb, ninth Earl of Hammerford and member of the board of trustees at University College, smiled vaguely at the portrait of his ancestor over the library fireplace as he polished his monocle and returned his handkerchief to the pocket of his smoking jacket. A man small in stature, he carried himself aristocratically, allowing his years in the military to be reflected in his regal bearing and posture. Only the graying at his temples and his silver-streaked eyebrows gave the lie to his belief that he looked just as he had twenty-five years earlier.

"Well," he reflected solemnly, speaking his thoughts aloud as he awaited his guests, "not all of time's changes are for the worse. Twenty-five years ago there was no Edward Lowell Newcomb, and this house was filled with the constant chatter of Annabelle's seven daughters; I thought I'd never know peace. Now, though, they've all gone off and married. Even Elsbeth left me, though I suppose running off with the gardener is not quite in the same category as Annabelle's departure," he mused, tamping the tobacco in his pipe. "The girls were right, though. I married too soon after Annabelle's death to know what I wanted. But a man's bed is meant to be warmed and Elsbeth knew how to do that well, though it seems there were other beds she preferred to hoe..."

"Who knew how to do what well, Father? Haven't you had enough problems with gardeners?"

At Ned's query, Lord Geoffrey gave a loud harrumph and moved quickly to embrace his son.

"An old man's ramblings, Ned, nothing of importance, I assure you. Lord, but you've made me proud today, boy. When I saw the postings of grades, I wanted the whole world to acknowledge your success. If I hadn't thought it unseemly, I would have stood all the university to a drink, but I fear that might have suggested a lack of faith in you, Edward, which is far from true. You've merely taken longer to mature than most."

Clapping his son on the back, the earl swung around to greet Brandon, pressing a glass into his hand.

"Brandon, how can I ever thank you for leading my wayward heir to a life of rewarding scholarship? A toast to you both, prime examples of today's youth striving their damnedest to do their best."

My Lord, thought Brandon irreverently, he meets Lavinia at the theater and in two days he's become as voluble as she.

"Thank you, sir, for your kind words, but I did no more than any other tutor would have done for Ned. The credit really belongs to him, you know. He earned the First, not I."

"Nonsense, Brandon, I'm sure you've earned one of your own," defended Ned quickly. "Yours will be posted tomorrow, undoubtedly with honors."

"Well, then, son, that should be your goal for next term—a first with honors. But how can I expect that of you when spring is soon upon us and a young man's fancy is apt to turn to romance. Though I fear yours is never very far from thoughts of young women to begin with. Who will it be this time, Ned...an actress, a governess or perhaps an Indian from Cody's Wild West Show?" The earl sighed. "Phillips here is a superior display of what a fellow can accomplish without such distractions."

"As you avoid them, Father?" quipped Ned, annoyed at his parent's continuing laudatory remarks directed toward Brandon. "I seem to recall that you've been known to fancy the ladies on numerous occasions—the Horticultural Society, for example."

"Perhaps—harrumph—on occasion I have dallied among the dahlias, but only on occasion. However, tell me, Brandon, what happened to your hand? I can see you have it bandaged."

"Yes, your Lordship. I have a bit of a burn, but to tell the truth, I can't honestly say how I..."

"Why, that's preposterous, lad!" expostulated Lord Geoffrey. "How could you not be aware of an injury? It would be understandable if it had been sustained in battle, perhaps as happened to me in Crimea in '54."

"It seems, Father, that a log fell from the fireplace while Brandon was studying last night, and he was so intent on his work," interjected Ned, flashing his friend a warning glance, "that he'd picked it up and tossed it back into the fire before he'd realized it was smoldering."

"Good heavens, Brandon, I recommend dedication to scholarship, but not to such an extreme. Be more careful in the future, lad. Another drink, gentlemen? You've no classes for nearly a month, I believe."

"Yes, sir, thank you."

"Thank you, Father, but isn't dinner overdue? It's after eight, and I know you favor punctuality in all things."

"Now, I've never said in all things, son. A little tardiness in a woman can be most charming and quite alluring, actually. However, I have had dinner delayed this evening. One of your classmates at university promised to bring me a photograph he'd taken of a new specimen of Pinwheel Jasmine, native to northern Borneo of all places. It seems he's quite the photographer. At any rate, I invited the young man to join us. His name is Waverly-Smythe."

The tense silence that greeted the earl's announcement surprised him momentarily, but he rebounded quickly, presuming the lads disgruntled by the delay of their repast.

"Now, don't worry. When we sit down, you will be able to satisfy your appetites fully and I've a few splendid wines to accompany our courses."

"Yes, Father. I've told Brandon of your wine cellar. But why didn't you tell me you'd invited Waverly-Smythe?"

"I didn't think, Edward, that I needed your permission to invite someone into my home; there are other facets to my life than those that concern you. Actually Miss Cooper introduced us the other evening at the Covent Garden benefit, and besides photography, I understand Waverly-Smythe is quite knowledgeable about the cultivation of *Gracillimum Jasminum* itself."

"Yes," agreed Brandon noncommittally, "Waverly-Smythe is interested in cultivation of all sorts." Especially, the young man thought, when his target is someone who can help advance his career. Damn, but he should have heeded the presentiment of a foul day ending in a fouler evening. Then he could have remained in his rooms without being forced to endure the company of his rival, the man who, after today's odd happenings, might easily win Dobson and Whittaker's sponsorship for the Inns of Court. Bloody hell, he should have begged off when he had the chance. But perhaps he still could; he'd claim a

sudden indisposition and exit before that ingratiating repro-
bate arrived. Brandon was about to put his plan into action
when one of the house staff entered the room.

"Your Lordship, Mr. Waverly-Smythe," announced the
servant.

"Very good, Martin. Tell Cook we'll adjourn to the dining
room immediately. Gentlemen, this way." Clapping Preston's
shoulder as he met him on the threshold of the room, the earl
led him toward the celebration dinner. "Good to see you again,
lad. You won't mind if we dine at once; I assure you there will
be ample spirits with our meal."

As Brandon and Ned stood to follow the pair, they exchanged irritated glances.

"I hope those wines you mentioned are extraordinary, Ned,"
communicated Brandon through gritted teeth. "To get through
this evening civilly, I fear we'll have need of them. If that bastard makes any mention of today's examination or the position at the Inns of Court, I can't vow that I won't smash his
arrogant, aristocratic face."

"Sorry, if I had known Father had broadened the guest list,
we could have found our own fatted calf, but leave it to Preston, always looking for a leg up on the rest of us. It would figure he'd see Father as an easy mark for a glowing recommendation to show the internship committee."

"Yes, I'm certain he knows your father can only recommend one of us, and with your success in the examination, he
must have feared Lord Geoffrey's choice is already made,"
agreed Brandon slowly. "Let's give him some competition,
shall we?"

The ninth Earl of Hammerford leaned back in his seat at the
head of the table, listening in amusement to the discourse surrounding him. Not one to enjoy a silent meal, he had been
prepared to introduce multiple topics to keep the minds of his
young guests enthralled, but his assistance had not been required, except to ease the forceful vigor with which they con-
versed.

"Gentlemen, gentlemen, this is not the taproom at one of
your student pubs. Kindly refrain from using such loud tones.
I have always understood from your professors that in the

courtroom often the more reliable witness is the most soft-spoken.''

"My apologies, your Lordship, but I must strongly disagree with Phillips here. The Liberal government under Gladstone will bring the Empire to ruin. The Prime Minister is, after all, called 'the old man.'''

"I believe, sir," retorted Brandon, "that the term is the 'grand old man.'''

"Grandiose is more like it, with his schemes for changing the plight of the common folk, though I suppose ideas of that sort would naturally appeal to you, Phillips.''

"Would you care to expand on that last remark?" Brandon asked, his face a mask of perfect civility, though his voice held a deadliness all its own. "Perhaps you feel the working classes don't deserve a larger share in the riches of the empire?''

"I don't think Preston means that at all," Lord Geoffrey interjected, trying to forestall a serious clash between his two guests. "If that were the case, why would he be attending a school like University College, an institution dedicated to the education of the common man? Surely you agree that with his family's resources, he could have enrolled in one of our older universities, elite as they are. I am certain that Preston, along with the rest of us, supports the reforms championed by Gladstone's party.''

"But of course, your Lordship," Preston lied smoothly, deftly changing his opinion to match that of his influential host. "My concern is based upon Gladstone's ability at eighty-three or eighty-four to engineer the changes England needs. And his commitment to Home Rule for Ireland could be the downfall of his government before he has had the opportunity to implement any reforms that might benefit the working class.''

"There, you see, lads," interjected Lord Geoffrey, "we all think alike. But now, I fear we've lingered too long at table. Shall we have our coffee and port in the library?''

How easy it is to satisfy such fools, Preston thought, proud of his ability to placate a man like Ned's father. These insipid idealists always responded to some sympathetic phrase or other, never suspecting that a man of intelligence such as he might not mean what he said. And, Preston gloated, he was certainly more intelligent than Phillips, for all his studious habits. The dolt didn't even realize that Clarissa Manning was the offspring of James Gregory Manning, world-renowned expert in international law. Though Phillips might tutor the chit, he, Preston, was courting her. Certainly if any help toward establishing a career was to be gotten from Manning, it would be the girl's sweetheart, not her tutor, who received it.

Accepting a cigar from the earl, Preston prepared to enjoy the rest of the evening, more than content with his lot in life. He had his photography, his studies, and soon he'd have the appointment in the chambers shared by Dobson and Whittaker, as well.

Managing to move his fractious guests to another locale, the earl felt he should also maneuver a change in conversation to a more familiar, less controversial topic.

"Now, tell an old man, Preston, Brandon, how went your examination today? We know of my son's success, but what issues did you throw at Humphrey in your discourses?" As he concentrated on filling and lighting his pipe, Lord Geoffrey failed to notice the consternation on Brandon's face. Preston, however, lost no time in replying.

"Sir, as I assured you the other evening at the theater, I am confident of my abilities; I know I responded to the issue in the only legitimate manner." Smiling at his pun, Preston paused momentarily to allow the others to appreciate his wit. "A few references to Disraeli's position of 1872, Clive's intervention in India. Why, I daresay the examination practically wrote itself. Wouldn't you agree, Brandon? Or have you been too entranced by your pupil's eyes to pay attention to your own studies?" queried Preston snidely, suspecting that his scholastic competitor was too honorable to permit romance to enter the picture.

"His pupil's eyes? What on earth would Ned's vision have to do with it?" questioned the ninth Earl of Hammerford in mystification. "I don't believe he needs spectacles, do you, Ned?"

"No, Father, not *my* eyes."

"What Mr. Waverly-Smythe refers to, sir, is my second tutoring position, instructing Miss Clarissa Manning. He applied for the same opportunity of broadening Miss Manning's education, and has apparently not yet recovered from losing out, once again, to the better man.''

"That's hardly the case, Phillips. You may be certain that when I visit the young lady, I do it for pleasure, not pay. But I suppose, in your financial circumstances, you have no choice."

Before Preston had finished speaking, Brandon was on his feet and across the room to confront him. The earl, however, stepped between the pair before blows could be thrown.

"Now, now, Brandon, I'm certain Preston didn't intend to give insult—''

"There we disagree, your Lordship; I am certain he did. Nonetheless, out of respect for you, I will merely reply that if the girl's guardian had any sense, she'd chaperone Miss Manning properly rather than sigh helplessly into her scented handkerchief and allow her charge to associate with someone like Waverly-Smythe."

"I beg your pardon, young man. What is it you're saying about Miss Cooper?''

"Nothing, sir. I apologize for speaking out of turn. Excuse me if I take my leave; I fear my sense of decorum has been overtaxed this evening.''

Turning abruptly on his heel, Brandon exited the room in much the same infuriated state he'd been in when he'd walked home from the gallery two days earlier. A man who believed vehemently in right and wrong, he was not one to see shades of gray, and too often reacted emotionally in personal situations.

Ned caught him as he was leaving the front hall.

"Brandon—''

"Leave it alone, Ned. I realize I antagonized your father with my rudeness, but Waverly-Smythe's pomposity, Cooper's urgent summons, Clarissa's temptation, if it existed, and my own uncertainties about today have emptied my resources of tact. I'll give Waverly-Smythe this round, but he'll have to be a lot more impressive to win the internship away from me. That I swear."

Allowing the door to slam behind him, Brandon stepped onto the darkened street and began transmitting his frustration and fury to the pavement over which he strode, an unleashed energy seeking refuge from his heavy heart.

Chapter Eight

How much has changed since I first walked down this street, Brandon thought. Making his way to Hertford Court early the next morning in response to Lavinia's note he was all too aware that only a month ago he had gone to see a new pupil, and now he was probably on his way to encounter all sorts of accusations. In fact, he quite possibly faced the end of his career before it had even begun, were his vague sensations of passion at all accurate.

If he could just remember what had happened, he might be able to prepare a defense, but having no recollection of yesterday's events, he would have to believe any charges Lavinia made and plead guilty. After all, ignorance of the law was not an excuse, as he knew only too well. If he had gone beyond the bounds of society's strictures, he would not be exempt from the penalty. Damn Clarissa Manning, but she had turned his very existence upside down and inside out and seemed to enjoy herself thoroughly while doing it! Before he had met her, his life was in order and his future carefully planned. Today, he worried, that future might be forced to include Clarissa as well as the law.

Of course, Brandon admitted, if he had initiated a seduction and actually compromised the girl, he would feel obligated to offer her his name. Though his instinct for self-preservation balked at the thought, he found himself considering the prospect for a fleeting instant. In reality, he'd often thought Clarissa enchanting as she sat with him during her tutoring sessions. Though her eyes flashed and her temper often flared as she debated some point, with the right kind of loving she might be quieted, and Brandon knew that he would enjoy the attempt to tame her, regardless of his success.

Yes, life with Clarissa might not be unpleasant at that, Brandon reflected, until he recalled her predilection for obstinacy and her ability to irritate him when he followed his own dictates rather than hers. She was the only female he had ever encountered who could provoke him beyond reason.

Arriving at his destination and lifting the heavy door knocker, Brandon no longer found the brass lioness crowned with daisies to be amusing. Instead it was indicative of the predatory females residing within who waited hungrily for him to step into their lair where they could pounce on him and devour his liberty with a few short roars. While they might eventually bring this prey down, he vowed as the door opened that he'd do a little roaring of his own beforehand.

After a sly glance and smothered giggle from Ellen, Brandon found himself shown into Miss Cooper's dining room. Here he discovered Lavinia seated alone at the end of a highly polished cherry-wood table. Where was the lovely Clarissa, he wondered mockingly, taken to her rooms until she could recover from the assault her enticing body seemed to demand?

"Mr. Phillips, I'm so glad you could come around," Lavinia enthused as she looked up from her toast and marmalade, indicating that Brandon should take the seat at her right hand. "Please join me in something to eat. Cook has quite outdone herself this morning," she went on, gesturing toward the heaped platters of eggs, ham, broiled tomatoes, grilled fish, toast and sweet rolls.

Brandon found Lavinia's composure and gracious hospitality confounding under the circumstances, but he sat as he was bidden. How apropos, he thought wryly as he studied the heavily laden table. The condemned man's last meal. The idea squelched any appetite he might have had, and he declined the offer of breakfast and tea, listening with mounting confusion as Lavinia went on to make small talk, quite pointedly ignoring any reference to the reason for which he had been summoned.

Brandon found this interminable tactic of skirting the issue much worse than the sudden outburst he had expected Lavinia to make. And while he experienced some sympathy for this genteel woman's predicament, he wished she would get on with it. He'd be damned if he would come to her aid by accusing himself of a crime he wasn't certain he'd committed. He saw himself in an imaginary dock at Lavinia's table. The situation gave him insight into the feelings of accused criminals as they waited to be questioned, and he vowed to remember the emotion if he were ever fortunate enough to practice law.

After her flurry of aimless conversation, Lavinia entreated Brandon once again to have something to eat. "It's all too much for me, I'm sure." She shrugged helplessly, indicating the full platters. "And Clarissa has no appetite after what happened yesterday, but I'll come to that later, when I've composed myself so that I can discuss it without giving way to the overabundance of emotion with which we women are afflicted." Lavinia finished breathlessly as she consoled herself with one last sweet roll.

Here we go, then, thought Brandon, relieved that Lavinia was at last getting to the point.

"You see, being Clarissa's guardian has been no easy task, Brandon...I may call you Brandon, mayn't I? After all, your relationship with my niece has practically made you a member of the family."

Brandon tightened his lips at this comment, the muscles of his lean jaw tensing as he waited for the accusations to be leveled.

"Brandon, I find it difficult that I must speak to *you* about Clarissa's latest escapade. But with your involvement with her, and all that she has learned from you, I felt, quite rightly I think, that I should turn to you for assistance in directing her once more to the right path. You do agree with me, don't you?" Lavinia sighed in lamentation. "Because I don't know how I could face her father and inform him of the situation if the matter were still unresolved."

At this point, Brandon would have liked to ask for details. Just what did happen yesterday? If he were going to pay for the crime, he might as well at least be able to savor the memories of what he had done. However, a man couldn't blatantly ask a woman of quality just how he had compromised her niece. And to question a maiden lady, to question Lavinia... No, she'd never be able to compose herself enough to tell him what had occurred, and he wasn't sure he was equal to one of her feathery outbursts. He'd already decided that if he had bedded the girl he would do the right thing. Acquiescing to Miss Cooper without argument would make it easier for everyone.

"My dear Miss Cooper, I am quite sincere when I tell you that I have no knowledge of the situation to which you are referring, but if I have transgressed, I am quite ready to set things to rights," Brandon replied, thinking unwillingly of Clarissa's delectable lips and the often stormy expression of her brown eyes. How challenging it would be to change that look to one of passion.

"Oh, Brandon, I knew I could count on you. You're such a sensitive, principled man, and I am only too well aware that this wretched business is all Clarissa's fault," Lavinia said, oblivious to Brandon's raised eyebrows. "While I know that Clarissa appreciates what you have taught her, I personally feel she has learned much more than a young woman of her age has any right to know. And most men, I am certain you will concur, would not choose so enlightened a girl for a wife. But since you are agreeable, and I can't see that it would do her any more harm than has already been done at this point, I would like you to inundate her with knowledge, keep her busy night and day, so to speak. It is my only hope that such a course will make her more manageable."

Brandon narrowed his silver-gray eyes as he looked at the woman before him. Was she aware of what she was suggesting?

"Now, of course, my niece may prove a bit reluctant to having you about so constantly, but I'll leave it to you to persuade her."

"I'm certain she will protest. The girl has never made anything easy for me. But I'll do my best to make her understand our new relationship is unavoidable," Brandon replied as he envisioned the inevitable confrontation looming before him. Now that he had agreed to protect Clarissa's reputation, the vixen would most likely want no part of marriage or of him.

"Now, Brandon, in light of what transpired yesterday, I think you should assume your new obligations as quickly as possible."

"And if Clarissa objects?"

"She lost any right to object yesterday," Lavinia retorted, her brows drawing together in disapproval. "This is a matter to be settled strictly between you and me. I've made up my mind."

"If that's how you feel, when may I see Clarissa to inform her of the understanding between us?"

"Shortly. I believe she is entertaining Mr. Waverly-Smythe just now."

"Waverly-Smythe?" repeated Brandon incredulously. Had the girl *no* sense of propriety?

"Yes, yes, but as I said, you may see her in a bit. They're in the morning room. Oh, Brandon, I can't thank you enough for agreeing to help me take the girl in hand," Lavinia babbled. "I'm certain you cannot imagine what it was like yesterday, finding the gardener's clothing under her bed."

"The gardener's clothing!" boomed Brandon, a steely look coming into his lightning-gray eyes. What in hell was going on here, and who had compromised Clarissa, he or the gardener? Though unexpected waves of jealousy washed over him, turning his skin a pale white as he thought of other hands caressing Clarissa, he wasn't fool enough to pay for another man's mistakes, gardener or anyone else. Through clenched teeth, he addressed Lavinia. "Perhaps we'd best forget our agreement, Miss Cooper. I had no idea. If Clarissa has been carrying on with the gardener..."

"Brandon! It's not what you think, but it's *almost* as bad," Lavinia sputtered, blanching at the impression she had created. Though she found it difficult to speak of such things, Lavinia knew she had no choice but to correct Brandon's misconception. "Clarissa is still quite innocent, her virtue unquestionable, I am certain. Yet it seems that she thought it high adventure to go about the streets dressed as a boy. That's why she stole old Mr. Norris' clothing. Mr. Norris, my gardener, has been with the family over thirty years, and the poor man is so arthritic that he has trouble lifting a hoe. He couldn't...she wouldn't..." Lavinia faltered with a blush. "It's her silly masquerade that upsets me. I never know what the girl is up to. You can see, can't you, why I need your assistance? If you could come every day to tutor her, keep her head in her books, so to speak, I'll at least know where she is and what she's doing. Should her father ever find out that she was prancing about London in trousers, I'm sure I don't know what I would do.''

''So you want me to give her additional tutoring? That's what your message was about?'' Brandon whispered.

Upon Lavinia's affirmation, Brandon breathed a sigh of relief. Yet he could not help but feel a twinge of disappointment as visions of Clarissa in an apricot dressing gown and half-remembered sensations of shared passion were relegated to the realm of dream. He knew he should be elated that he was not being called upon to forfeit his freedom by marrying Clarissa because he had compromised her honor, but damn, why did he have a feeling that it would have been a sweet compromise indeed?

''How many additional days do you think you could give my niece?'' asked Lavinia, intruding upon his thoughts.

''I won't be able to make any commitment until my examination results have come in, Miss Cooper, but they should be posted late this afternoon.''

''Send me word this evening, won't you, Brandon?'' Lavinia asked as she leaned over to pat his hand, oblivious to its bandage and causing more than a little pain. ''I know I can depend upon you.''

Leaving the dining room, Brandon could not help but chuckle at his apprehension about coming here this morning. How foolish he had been! Ned had been right all along. That realization helped to alleviate the heavy mood he'd been experiencing since yesterday. The only thing he had to contend with now was the result of his examination; he hoped that, too, would be a simple matter.

As he crossed the hallway to take his coat from Ellen, the door to the morning room flew open to the sound of soft feminine laughter, and Clarissa came into view with Preston. A giggle died on her lips as she saw Brandon standing there. All Clarissa could think of was the stinging rejection he had delivered when she had invited him to accompany her last evening, and the memory of her embarrassment and disappointment became a whetstone, sharpening her tongue and giving an edge to her words.

"Well, you appear to be in a jolly mood this morning, Mr. Phillips. I must assume the cause of your good humor is that you've just been paid for the time you have spent with me."

"My dear Miss Manning," Brandon responded coolly, careful to conceal the anger caused by Waverly-Smythe's presence, "surely you must be aware that there is not enough money in all of England to pay me adequately for the time I have spent with you. So you see, compensation isn't the reason for my joy. Rather, it is the fact that I am departing. Good day."

He turned on his heel and strode through the door, leaving a flustered, highly annoyed Clarissa in his wake.

That impertinent chit, Brandon fumed, descending the wide marble steps, fire mirrored in his deep silver eyes, how dare she accost me in that manner in front of Waverly-Smythe? And what was the little hellion doing with him again, anyway? I must have been totally mad to ever consider shackling myself to the likes of her, no matter what I might have done. I'm certain any sane jury would have acquitted me if I had murdered her, never mind attacked her. She is the most provoking little demon I've ever had the displeasure to meet!

Yet in spite of his anger, Brandon couldn't help but speculate as to how her slim hips and long legs must have looked in a pair of men's trousers. And much to his annoyance and discomfort, he found the image exceedingly arousing.

Clarissa, however, found it was her temper and nothing else that was aroused by Brandon's departure.

"Preston, that man drives me insane!" Clarissa railed as she stared at the door. It's only too bad there isn't a law against arrogant rudeness, Clarissa thought, seething. If there were, Brandon Phillips would have been imprisoned long ago. And she would be happy to see him there! Oh, she couldn't wait to take the wind out of his sails when he began to brag about how well *he* had done on his examinations! The conceited bully! How was he going to feel when she told him it was she who had been so brilliant?

"Don't mind him, dearest Clarissa," Preston consoled her, mindful of her distraction. "Breeding will tell, they say. He must have been annoyed to see us together, happy as young people should be. It's common knowledge that Phillips has no notion of how to enjoy himself, though why he's in such a bother now, I can't imagine. After all, examinations are over and the new term is still weeks away."

"Oh, yes, I'd almost forgotten. How *were* your examinations?" Clarissa asked, trying to regain her composure. After all, Brandon Phillips was not worth the upset.

"They presented no problem at all. In fact, International Law was the easiest essay I have ever been called upon to write while in university."

"The easiest?" Clarissa sounded a bit disappointed. "Then it would have been no difficult task to do well on it?"

"Not difficult at all. They merely wanted legal justification of Britain's imperialistic activities."

"Justification?" Clarissa repeated as her anxiety grew like a weed. "I'm afraid I don't understand. Wouldn't your instructor leave the question open to individual interpretation and judge you according to your ability to substantiate the position you chose to defend?"

"Hardly likely, Clarissa. Do you think our law professors are apt to encourage us to take a stand against the official policy of monarchy and government? They are breeding barristers who can sort out legal sanctions for Her Majesty's expansionist tendencies. In fact I'm certain that Humphrey expects all of us to take the silk when we are able," Preston declared, referring to those talented practitioners of law who, after ten years, applied to the Crown to become elite Queen's Counsels, and from that day forward represented only the interests of the monarch. "It wouldn't do for us to take the part of those nations who are less than anxious to be included in the Empire. But, since your own country is so self-contained and rather isolationist, you probably have difficulty grasping the reality of the situation. At any rate, it is nothing for you to worry your pretty little head about. You needn't understand things of this depth. Being beautiful is all you have to do, and that you manage quite nicely."

"How kind you are, Preston," murmured Clarissa, ignoring his intended compliment and dwelling instead on the horrifying realization that she had been laboring under the wrong assumption when she had given her answer to the examination question. Because of her impulsiveness and naïveté, she had written an entirely inappropriate essay. As angry as she had been at Brandon just a few moments before, her heart inexplicably began to swell with sympathy for him . . . and for herself, as well!

Good Lord, Brandon would throttle her if he were aware of the situation, she thought, as visions of his flashing gray eyes and thundering temper came all too readily to mind. Beside the vision of Brandon's anger, Preston's presence was all but forgotten until his voice broke in upon her thoughts.

"Clarissa, dear, have you been listening to what I've said? You appear to be off in a world of your own. Dreaming about some new frock to wear on our next outing?"

"Something of the sort," Clarissa replied as she was called back to reality, finding that she had to force herself to pay attention to her companion in order to stave off the remorse that was tightening in her chest like the mainspring of an overwound clock.

Brandon might be exasperating at times, she readily admitted, but he didn't deserve to have his future taken away from him so abruptly. Her reasoning that her tutor would most certainly have been sent down had he missed sitting for his examination provided no consolation. Clarissa couldn't help but feel that causing him to appear ignorant before his mentors was somehow worse. Her little excursion into academia seemed to have consequences she had never imagined. If only her pride hadn't prodded her into thinking she could do well writing on some topic about which she knew so little. Still... she *had* given an excellent defense, she argued with herself, and it wasn't *definite* that her attempt had been unsuccessful. Perhaps there was still some hope.

These thoughts were giving her a headache, and she wanted more than anything to be alone. She was about to send Preston gently on his way when she felt his arm reaching around her waist to draw her closer to him. It was a bolder move than any he had made previously, and Clarissa was quite taken aback. As he pressed his lips upon hers, she experienced none of the liquid fire she had known yesterday morning with Brandon, and she sighed loudly at being so attracted to a man whom she may have helped to destroy.

Preston, misunderstanding the source of her reaction, was encouraged that Clarissa could be moved so easily by his advances. But when he reached up to cup a firm breast with his hand, Clarissa gasped and pulled away in alarm.

"Dearest Clarissa," he begged with outward sincerity, "forgive my transgression, but you have no idea how your proximity bewitches me, until I am past all logic and propriety."

"You're forgiven, Preston," Clarissa responded, anxious to be rid of him and willing to play the weak female in order to attain her end, "but please go; I fear I am quite overcome."

"Certainly, sweeting, I know your innocence allows you no knowledge of desire, be it mine or yours, but someday, Clarissa, someday..." Preston whispered as he took his leave. Other conquests had taught him that there were times when things left unsaid could be more enthralling than any spoken word. He smiled with satisfaction as he buttoned his coat and stepped out into the brisk March wind.

While Preston thought Clarissa captivatingly beautiful, he found her too intelligent and headstrong for his tastes. Normally he would never consider any involvement with a female of her type, yet as Dr. Manning's offspring, Clarissa was an object worthy of pursuit, and Preston was determined to woo her. With the girl his adoring little paramour, it would be but a small matter to obtain a recommendation from her father. Such a reference was certain to outweigh those written by Lord Geoffrey Newcomb and his like, or even the Humph himself. Yes, one word from Manning would see to it that he was chosen for the fellowship over Brandon Phillips. Garnering such an honor could very well recapture his place in his father's will.

Thinking of his own parent caused Preston to consider for an instant if Phillips had discovered just who Clarissa's father was. He doubted it. After all, no matter how vexing Clarissa could be, no one, not even his ill-bred rival, would be as rude as Phillips had just been to J.G. Manning's daughter. Still, Preston thought with a shrug, it didn't really matter. Phillips was too blindly honorable to take advantage of this sort of opportunity. Hadn't this morning's tiff proved just that?

Later that afternoon, the senior law students stood outside Dr. Humphrey's office, congregating around the recently posted results of the exam in International Law. Brandon strode purposefully to the door, determined to learn the truth about his presence at the test once and for all. Quickly he scanned the list and breathed a relieved sigh to see his name. But before he could turn his gaze to the corresponding standing, he felt a hand on his arm and heard Waverly-Smythe's condescending tones.

"Here you are; I want to have a word with you about your impertinence to Miss Manning earlier today. Really, Phillips, my already low opinion of you has sunk to new depths. Your cheek merely accentuated your place outside of society. No matter how you and your class are educated, you are still unfit for genteel company and will never be accepted by it other than in the capacity of employee."

"I realize this may come as a bit of a shock to you, Waverly-Smythe," Brandon replied in even, icy tones that belied the ire burning beneath his calm exterior, "but I have no great desire to be embraced by any society that also accepts you. As to my breeding, Mr. Darwin suggests that we all share common origins, and it would appear that my branch of the family has evolved, while yours has not."

Brandon's comments drew some good-natured guffaws from the other students, who had been following the exchange between the two competitors. Annoyed by the laughter, Preston turned to leave, calling nonchalantly over his shoulder, "I hope, Phillips, that you find your standing in International Law as amusing as your inane remarks to me."

Preston's words caused Brandon to turn sharply and scrutinize the posted notice. There was his name, but next to it only a blank space. He slowly exhaled in bitter disappointment and was about to walk away to mourn the death of his future in private when the door to Dr. Humphrey's office opened abruptly and the professor's shaggy white head appeared.

"Phillips, I thought I heard your voice," he growled. "Step inside, we have something to discuss."

As Brandon presented himself in the office, the don commanded, "Be seated, Phillips. I suppose you have guessed that I wish to question you about your examination."

The instructor watched the young man before him quite closely for his reactions.

"I had assumed as much," Brandon answered unflinchingly.

"I found your paper quite astonishing, Phillips," Dr. Humphrey declared, surprising Brandon with the fact that his paper existed at all. The professor sifted through the examination booklets and removed one signed with the young man's name, thrusting it across his desk for Brandon to examine. "It was extremely articulate and presented impressively logical arguments," he continued coolly. "Unfortunately, the position you chose to take is entirely unacceptable. I want an explanation as to how you could compose such a piece as this."

Brandon opened to the first page and noticed that the handwriting was unsteady and awkward, but then, he had been drunk, and his right hand hurt, its still bandaged state now capturing the attention of the sharp-eyed professor. Under the circumstances, both men concluded that the scrawled script could have indeed belonged to Brandon.

Reading the question, in all of its unremembered intricacy, Brandon went on to peruse the answer, his color mounting and his eyebrows drawing one to the other in ill-concealed consternation. Good God, he didn't remember any of this! Some of the points raised within the essay had never crossed his mind, while sober, anyway, and others he should have been astute enough to exclude from an examination in International Law. While the expanding Empire was something he viewed with mixed reactions, he knew better than to openly condemn it in this situation. Dr. Humphrey, staunch monarchist that he was, would never stand for it.

How in bloody hell could I have produced such tripe? I've never discussed ideas of this sort with any of the other students, in fact I've never discussed them with anyone at all . . . except Clarissa Manning! Christ, that damned girl and her odd views have influenced me more than I thought, he fumed. Once more in the space of a few hours, his temper flared at that impossible chit who had turned his quiet, orderly life into one of chaos.

Though he took full responsibility for his actions, including this wretched excuse for an essay, he couldn't help but feel that this was her fault, too. *Damn her!* he thought, *and damn me, too, for being swayed by anything she does and says! Give me* a pair of dark brown eyes and a well-turned ankle, and I'm parroting what *she* thinks! Just who has been the tutor and who the pupil these past few weeks anyway, he chided himself in disgust.

"Phillips!" the don intruded, seeking his pupil's attention after a few moments of intently studying the young man before him, noting every detail of his reaction.

"Sir?"

"What bloody well happened to you, Phillips?" the don raged impatiently. This, after all, had been one of his star pupils.

"I can't remember, sir," Brandon answered stoically, seeing his future crumble before him, but too proud to try to make excuses.

"Can't remember! That's hardly what I expected to hear from someone of your caliber. You've a good head on your shoulders, Phillips, or at least I used to think so, and you're a bit older than the rest. I cannot accept your explanation."

"If you want something less than the truth, I'll tell you anything you want to hear, but as it is, I can't recall either your question or my answer."

"Were you ill?"

"I certainly wasn't myself, judging by my paper."

"If you were indisposed, the intelligent thing to have done would have been to send a note around informing me of the fact. That way, I might have persuaded the trustees to permit you to sit for another essay at a later date. As it stands now, you have taken the test and failed. My hands are tied."

"I'm aware of that, sir."

"Well, I didn't call you in to berate you, Phillips. Contrary to reputation, I do not enjoy browbeating my students, the better ones, anyway. The point is, I cannot write you a letter of recommendation as promised when I don't find your examination acceptable."

"I understand that, sir," Brandon replied, wishing the man would be done with it.

"The question is, what in God's name are we going to do about it?" Humphrey asked, his brow wrinkling in concern.

"I don't know there is much to be done, Dr. Humphrey," Brandon said slowly, something in the professor's voice causing the handsome blond student to wonder if indeed all hope had been lost.

"The point is that we must do something, Phillips. I am aware of your financial situation, I understand that without the fellowship at the Inns you would have to give up your plans to become a barrister. I can tell you that I would consider that to be a loss to the legal profession."

"Thank you, sir." Brandon smiled at the unexpected compliment.

"No need to go about grinning like a fool, you young pup. You still have much to learn about being an acceptable practitioner of law, and the first thing is to keep your opinion to yourself, especially in the courtroom. I really don't care how you feel about British Imperialism. I only expect you to justify it in legal terms. As for my reasons in wishing to recommend you, it is simply a matter of elimination. You seem a bit more worthy than your cohort, Waverly-Smythe, though my judgment may be in error. After all, I had, at one time, considered you a shade more intelligent."

"Thank you, Dr. Humphrey," Brandon said with enthusiastic sincerity. Contrary to reports from the School of Anatomy, the old boy had a heart after all.

"No need to thank me, Phillips, I haven't done anything for you yet, other than to point out your recent stupidity," Humphrey growled. "Now here is what I will do for you. During the break between terms, you will be assigned extra work, beginning with a legal defense of Rhodes' position in Africa. If I find that you have done an outstanding job, I will put off any letter of recommendation until the end of next term. At that time if I determine that you are first in my class, and you seem to have learned something about International Law, then, and only then, will I write to Dobson and Whittaker on your behalf. Have I made myself clear?"

"Perfectly, sir. Thank you," Brandon responded, shaking his mentor's hand vigorously.

"Yes, well . . ." Humphrey sputtered then coughed in embarrassment. "Get out of here, Phillips, and see that the Rhodes case is completed by next week. Then I'll give you the next topic. And do a good job on that paper!"

Brandon left Humphrey's study caught between dejection and elation. He was devastated by his failure on the examination. Still, the old gaffer had been almost human about it, and there was one more opportunity to become a barrister. It was almost impossible, he knew, to attain first standing in the don's class with this failure upon his records, but if he pushed his efforts to the limit of his endurance, it just might be done.

Still, logistical problems remained. Lavinia Cooper was expecting him to take charge of her niece during the upcoming weeks. That girl! Again Brandon heard the stinging remark Clarissa had delivered that morning, and he liked it no better now than he had then.

It was true, Brandon admitted with what he perceived to be true magnanimity of spirit, that he had been somewhat brusque when he had rebuffed Clarissa's invitation the previous evening, but surely she must have seen that he'd been upset. He hadn't behaved at all like himself in the hours following his examination . . . or in the hours beforehand. He winced. In fact, he thought, trying to push the idea and its implications from his mind, he hadn't been himself since he'd met Clarissa Manning.

Still, no matter how he had acted yesterday afternoon, Clarissa should have understood, Brandon decided, his pride wounded and his self-pity very much aroused. And certainly *nothing* he had said or done was cause enough for her to address him in such a waspish manner this morning...and in front of Waverly-Smythe!

The memory of a laughing Clarissa, on the arm of his rival, exiting the morning room where he himself had spent so many hours with her, set Brandon's teeth on edge until he reined in his emotions and attempted to exert self-control. This burst of anger was completely out of character, he muttered under his breath, and it, along with everything else that was troubling him, could be traced back to Clarissa Manning. When he wasn't thinking about her, he was in her company. In short, she took up altogether too much of his time. His performance on Humphrey's preliminary proved that, Brandon concluded with a grim set of his lips.

And what was she, he asked himself as his temper rose. Why, she was nothing more than a child masquerading as a woman while *he*, by God, was a law student, and not some nanny looking for hire. Miss Cooper could get someone else to take charge of her wayward niece, Brandon decided as he neared his rooms. He had other things to do, this assignment of Humphrey's chief among them.

He'd begin planning his defense of Rhodes this afternoon, and when he finished outlining the legal strategy, he'd pop around to Miss Cooper's and inform her of the decision to give his notice. That settled, he mounted the stairs to his quarters, a determined gleam in his eyes.

"So you see, my dear," Lavinia bubbled as she raised the glass of champagne to her lips, "I believe I have finally solved our problem concerning Clarissa. I'm certain Brandon Phillips will send round an affirmative response this evening, and as of tomorrow, I will be an unencumbered woman. That's not to say that Clarissa is not a sweet girl, really; still, it takes so much time and effort to watch over her properly. It has been most disconcerting, but you have been as patient as a lamb about the whole thing, and I appreciate your behavior."

"Perhaps you'll appreciate it even more as the night wears on," responded her companion.

"Whatever do you mean?" Lavinia replied coquettishly, leaning her head into the crook of the large masculine arm that traveled along her body and wrapped itself around her waist.

"Shall I show you?" asked her escort in a husky voice, ripe with passion, as the moonlight streamed through the window, casting a romantic glow over the pair.

"It *has* been a while; I'm sure I have forgotten completely what you mean."

"You're a greedy little kitten, aren't you? It hasn't been forty-eight hours since last we were together."

"It seems like centuries," Lavinia simpered. "Still, I think engaging Brandon Phillips to come around more often will do the trick. He brooks no nonsense from my little niece."

"Yes, Phillips appears to be a fine fellow and a good influence, though a bit hot-tempered at times."

"Perhaps merely hot-blooded, like most of you men." Lavinia giggled, running her cool palm along the broad, masculine chest of her companion. "Still, he manages to control himself admirably around Clarissa, and I trust him implicitly. He's wrought some welcome changes in the girl.''

"I can't say he hasn't done the same with Ned. But let's stop speaking of the children and concentrate on more adult pursuits,'' the man demanded as he began to tease Lavinia's fingertips with his lips.

"Oh, Geoffrey, if your Ned grows up to be anything like you, he'll be quite a man, indeed,'' Lavinia murmured as Lord Geoffrey's kisses pushed thoughts of Clarissa from her mind and she floated on a sea of sensation.

Chapter Nine

Damn it all! It was half past eight, Brandon noted as he looked at his pocket watch, and he was barely a quarter of the way through his case outline. Ordinarily work of this sort was second nature to him, yet today it had been a struggle. Was it the complexity of the case, or was it his own provocative yearnings spurred on by a pair of delectable lips and fleeting images of dark, laughing eyes? He pondered the issue wearily, running a hand through his thick, pale hair.

"Bloody hell!" Brandon yelled suddenly to the empty room as he brought his fist down on his table so that it shuddered, as though in fear of this irrational man. Even when he wasn't with her, the girl gave him no peace. But that was about to change, and soon, he vowed impulsively, getting to his feet and grabbing his coat from its peg on his way out the door.

He was going to put an end to this bewitchment tonight—right now! Once he severed his relationship with that enticing hellcat, he'd feel better. At least he'd be able to concentrate without wondering how she would receive him when next they met. Christ, but the woman had driven him to the brink of madness, kissing him so sweetly one day and spurning him another.

Stepping into the cool night air, Brandon considered waiting until tomorrow to make the journey to the Cooper residence, but decided against it. He had told Lavinia that he would inform her this evening about the amount of time he could afford to spend with her niece during his term break, and by God, tell her this evening he would, no matter what time it was when he arrived at Hertford Court.

He started across the cobblestone street, the sound of his firm, rapid steps loudly echoing his scowling determination to rid himself of his troublesome student. Each block he traveled saw his anger with Clarissa Manning and her aunt grow, so that by the time he reached his destination, he was in a rare mood indeed.

"Why, no, sir, I—I'm sorry," said an uncharacteristically flustered Ellen, remembering Mr. Phillips' insistent behavior the last time he learned Lavinia was not at home. "Miss Cooper is dining with friends this evening and won't return till quite late. You were not expected... but I'll be certain to tell her of your visit, sir. Good evening." Intending her words to be a clear dismissal, Ellen tried to ease the heavy door shut, only to find her motion halted by the visitor's pressuring hand.

"I assure you, miss, there is no need to push me out the door. Since I am made welcome in the daylight hours, I see no cause for this ill-treatment just because the sun has set. Miss Cooper requested me to return with an answer for her as soon as possible."

"An answer?"

"To nothing that concerns you, Ellen." Brandon's tone was no longer even remotely civil. The day had been difficult enough without this inhospitable behavior to boot. He was going to see Clarissa!

"No, sir, but you must understand that this is a female establishment. I mean, that is, we do not usually have male—ah, gentlemen callers at night. May I give Miss Cooper a message when she returns?" Apprehensive of the cold sparks in Brandon's eyes, Ellen only wished him gone. He was a man no woman could safely ignore, and her pulse reacted so to his nearness, she could hardly decide what was appropriate.

"Damn it all, you're still trying to make me leave, aren't you? I don't suppose you'd keep Waverly-Smythe on the front step all night, or should I feel honored not to be directed to the servants' entry?" Surprising Ellen by his sudden movement, Brandon stepped forward, lifted her from his path and, moving across the threshold, placed her to one side of the door. "Tell me he's not welcome company during eventide."

Not knowing what reply might soothe the raging man before her, Ellen nodded, then shook her head in confusion as the rugged male groaned.

"I suppose Miss Clarissa is in the morning room? You needn't announce me; I'll do that myself." Familiar with the layout of this part of the house and determined that he should be properly acknowledged as a caller, Brandon moved purposefully down the hall. He might be engaged as a tutor, but he'd be damned if he'd allow them to treat him as a tradesman.

"No, sir. She's upstairs in Miss Lavinia's small conservatory. Miss Clarissa enjoys the flowers almost as much as her aunt and often goes there in the evening to read." Realizing she could not prevent this willful figure from doing whatever he chose, Ellen sighed ruefully as he mounted the stairs. If only a man like that would seek her . . .

"Not to worry, Ellen." Brandon's voice gentled as he looked over his shoulder to where the maid stood beside the open door. "I give you my word of honor as a gentleman that I shall neither steal the silver nor tarnish anyone's reputation." Brandon's dimple showed faintly as he flashed her a brief smile to make amends for their confrontation, thoroughly undermining Ellen's resolve to alert Cook to his presence. Instead she firmly closed the door, said a prayer for Lavinia's heart should she ever learn of this visit, and returned to her own quarters. If the young miss were anything like the old, she'd handle that devilish fellow quite nicely without anyone's assistance.

Stopping as he reached the head of the stairs, Brandon hesitated. He'd foolishly taken it into his head to speak to her immediately, but he'd been too proud to ask exactly where the conservatory was. He glanced about but saw no indication as to which door might open onto a private parlor, a bedroom or whatever else might be up here.

Surely the conservatory must be on the south side of the house to get the most sun, probably over the kitchen. Mentally envisioning the lower floor, Brandon surveyed the doors before him and moved to the entryway at the far left of the hall. Throwing it open, he stepped inside to warmer air. As he moved into the room, he saw Clarissa's coppery tresses glowing in the gaslight as she bent over the volume in her hands. The sight of her dispelled the anger he'd been feeling. She was wearing the pale blouse and gray skirt of their first encounter, and angelic visions danced across his mind as he studied her. She presented so peaceful an image, compared to the heat pulsing within him. How could she set his spirit afire yet appear so untarnished?

"Clarissa?" His lips caressed her name in a gentle whisper as he shed his heavy coat.

"Brandon? What—what in the world are you doing here? Aunt Lavinia's not home." Startled by his sudden appearance when he'd been so much a part of her thoughts, Clarissa was less than welcoming in her tone. What had he come for? Did he know about her part in his examination? Preston had said the results would be posted today.

"One generally greets one's callers politely before cross-examining their intent, Miss Manning." Wanting her so much he could taste it, yet not recognizing the source of his discomfort, the young Englishman fell into the familiar trap of responding to her barbs by baiting her further.

"Good evening, Mr. Phillips. While you might believe I have nothing better to do than wait for uninvited guests at this time of night, that is not the case. I'll have to ask you to leave." Still smarting from his rejection the day before and fearing the reason for his call, Clarissa stood up from the lounge chair on which she'd been seated and took refuge in an offensive strategy. "I trust you haven't been drinking again. I would have thought you had learned your lesson yesterday."

"Yesterday, ah, yes, that was a day for the record books, I fear." Moving toward the gas fireplace, Brandon rested his forehead against the cool marble of the mantle and stared into the small flames licking greedily at the air above them, almost in the same way as she destroyed the very essence of his self-control.

"Fear? I didn't imagine the word to be in your vocabulary," challenged Clarissa as she came to stand beside the unmoving figure of her tutor. What had happened to bring him here after he'd left so abruptly that morning? Too nervous to be polite, she spoke her mind openly. "Perhaps you have financial worries, but that's where your shortcomings end. For the sake of the mere mortals among us, I only wish you didn't always succeed."

"When it comes to you, I don't," he growled, revealing more than he'd intended and annoyed once again at how easily this vixen could pinpoint his weakness and strike. Would he ever learn to remain calm around her? He should have known better than to come; this conversation would serve no good.

"Now you're talking in riddles and it's much too late for conundrums, Mr. Phillips. If you're trying to demonstrate the art of a barrister, I'm not impressed." She knew she should simply ask him what had happened on the examination instead of picking at him, but the words wouldn't come.

"You never are, unless Waverly-Smythe is in the vicinity. Well, then, I should tell you that your fawning suitor did remarkably well on his most recent examinations."

Thank God he was finally getting to the topic that concerned her most.

"Oh, really?" Unable to see Brandon's eyes as he admitted his competitor's success, Clarissa couldn't fathom the pain searing his soul. "And I suppose next you'll explain how very much better you did?"

"Unfortunately, no," he replied curtly. "Perhaps your aunt hired the wrong man."

"That's what I've always contended," the young beauty retorted with a forced laugh, trying to calm her jumping nerves. So, Preston's essay had been better than Brandon's; that didn't necessarily mean disaster. She knew that he could never settle for second best; at least he'd been recorded as having taken the test, more than he would have done without her help. "Come sit down and tell me about your essay," she suggested, taking his arm and leading him to the sofa. Once he was seated, however, she was too nervous to join him and paced before the fire.

"Actually, I don't remember sitting for the examination, and based on my results, it would probably have been better if I hadn't," he began, not knowing why he should respond so wholeheartedly to her newly displayed empathy. Perhaps exhaustion had finally extinguished his temper.

Hearing the anguish in his voice and seeing it echoed in the steel depths of his eyes, Clarissa feared the worst.

"You don't mean you've been sent down? They couldn't, not you, since you didn't... I mean, I can't believe that they would dismiss you on the basis of one inconsequential little paper."

"I'd hardly call the senior preliminaries inconsequential, but no, I haven't been sent down, though considering the work I submitted, perhaps I deserve to be," Brandon mumbled, his head in his hands. Somehow he hadn't expected to feel so distraught; he'd come here to set up his future, not to seek sympathy.

Concern for Brandon uppermost in her mind, Clarissa had to do something to ease his suffering and quell the guilt assaulting her in tumultuous waves. Reaching out to the crushed spirit of this man who'd captured her concern, she moved behind the couch and placed her hands gently on his shoulders in a show of support. Slowly the slender fingers with a mind of their own played against his tight muscles and began to ease the tension evidenced in the knots in his neck. When he sighed but offered no resistance, she urged, "Slip out of your jacket and let me try to soothe your distress while you tell me what happened."

It had been so long since a caring woman ministered to his needs, the exhausted scholar complied without question. Already he could feel her magical touch easing the pockets of his pain as her fingers danced across the rocklike chains weighing him down.

"Move over and let me sit beside you," Clarissa said, needing to eliminate even the furniture that formed a barrier between them. "Now turn the other way." Again he did as she asked, permitting her to manipulate his body as she had his soul.

"I don't know what to say. I must have still been drunk or delirious to commit that kind of claptrap to paper."

"You saw your examination?" Her hands hesitated in midair, but she was seated behind him, so Brandon didn't notice her reaction.

"Just briefly, but believe me the ideas therein were totally foreign to me.... I think even you would have had second thoughts about committing such liberal fantasies to paper, knowing who'd read it. Had I been in my right mind, I would have written..."

As he detailed the traditional arguments of a royalist position, Clarissa debated whether to interrupt. He'd have to learn of her part in his academic failure sometime, but her instincts cautioned against using this moment for revelations. She was just getting him to relax; there was no purpose in upsetting him further.

While it was guilt that had initially driven Clarissa to soothe him, it was something else entirely that urged her on, so that she stretched forward, reaching over his shoulders, and fumbled to undo the top buttons of his shirt till he began to help. Her gentle hands slid the shirt off his muscular shoulders, giving her greater access to his neck and upper back, so cramped with tension that Clarissa ached at the pain she'd caused him. Trying to alleviate his discomfort, the young woman found herself growing languid as the fiery touch of his skin erased all thoughts from her mind. As her slender fingers persisted in their healing motion, she leaned close and, without thinking of the possible consequences, tenderly kissed the nape of his neck.

A shudder shook his body, and his unbandaged hand unexpectedly captured hers, drawing it to his lips.

"Clarissa," he whispered softly, his lips teasing the delicate softness of her milky palm, sending quivers down her spine as his tongue flicked across the sensitive tissue between her fingers. "Once I dreamt you were my angel; tonight you've shown me how real dreams can become."

"Brandon, I feel so terrible about your test. Maybe if you hadn't spent so much time with me..."

A masculine finger pressed her lips together gently, stilling her words. Without hesitation Brandon shifted his body till he faced her. Still reverencing her silken hand with tender attentions, he drew Clarissa's slender form into his arms, content for the moment to hold her close, enjoying the scent of her as she rested her head on his bare chest. Urgency might come later; now was the time for tenderness.

"Hush, this isn't the time for regrets," he admonished, tracing the sensuous outline of her mouth, setting it aflame with desire, making her the recipient of tenderness rather than the instigator.

Brandon supported her slight weight effortlessly. She marveled at how naturally she fit against him, making all the world seem right. Banishing the lingering trepidation over his exam, Clarissa snuggled closer, allowing her cheek to rest on his firmly muscled torso. Yesterday was gone and tomorrow was far away. Tonight Brandon was hers and she wasn't going to allow anything to intrude on their intimacy.

As if by mutual agreement, the couple sensed each other's readiness to move forward into a universe where words ceased to exist. Brandon's gentle touch elicited quickened breaths and sighs of rapture from Clarissa. His lips caressed her slowly, kissing her eyelids, the tip of her pert little nose, the tender pulsing in her neck, till his mouth at last returned to hers. Parted and waiting, her lips claimed his with an insistence demanding more and giving all as their easy patience evaporated in the heat of growing passion.

Not wanting their tentative explorations to end yet not wishing their first glorious moments of discovery to be marred by too hurried a fulfillment, Brandon eased the pace, stroking Clarissa's fiery tresses and bringing her head to rest once more on his rapidly heaving chest.

"Clarissa, are you sure you . . ." He hesitated, but he cared too much not to offer her an escape from this commitment. "I mean we needn't . . ."

"I've never been more certain of anything, Brandon," she replied artlessly. He'd laid claim to her heart with his vulnerability the morning of his examination, and it was time he possessed the rest of her. Standing, she hurried to unbutton her blouse, wanting to free her body from the feminine trappings of its confinement.

"No, let me do that," instructed her tutor in a voice husky with anticipation.

The fingers of his bandaged hand began to stroke her breasts through the soft fabric as he eased the garment's fastenings slowly open until Clarissa wanted to cry aloud in impatience. After what seemed an eternity, she stood before him as Eve had once transfixed Adam, the lushness of her youthful body revealed in all its glory.

Knowing with innate certainty that this would be Clarissa's first time, Brandon embraced his beauty, drawing her to him with a reverent eagerness born of devotion and the determination to make this night special for her. The trust in her eyes said all he needed to know, as he discarded his trousers.

"Come over here," he suggested softly, leading her to the fire. Throwing down the afghan from the settee, he knelt on the blanket and urged her down beside him. Igniting her smoldering passion once again with his kisses, he invited her soul to heaven while his fingers massaged the soft pink rosebuds of her breasts. The swollen nipples called, and he lowered his head to answer, savoring their promises as he set his obedient fingers tracing a slow path downward over her sweetly aching body, moving in slow circles lower and lower, till they threatened to set her ablaze.

"Oh, Brandon." Her words were a groan as she panted in an attempt to slow her staccato heart. She'd never felt this way before. It was as if every fiber of her being were really and truly awake for the first time in her life. Arching her back she strained her body closer to him, shivering as she felt his fingers stroke her feminine core.

"Brandon?"

It was a prayer more than a question, and he answered it swiftly, moving astride her and covering her mouth with his as he pierced nature's protection. Anxiously absorbing her involuntary shudder with a molten kiss, Brandon withdrew slightly and began the rhythmic motion that would carry them to ecstasy. An instinct older than time came to her assistance as Clarissa locked her hands behind him, matching his thrusts with her own, echoing his movements, introducing her to a pleasure apart from anything she'd ever imagined.

"Oh...oh...Brandon." With a euphoric gasp, they were at the pinnacle of creation, joined as one for eternity. If she had to die now, life would have been worthwhile.

"Yes, my love?" For Brandon it was ironic that he should find such exquisite release with a woman from such a different world, yet undeniably they were made for each other.

"Nothing." She sighed, knowing that speech could never convey her absolute joy. Instead she nestled closer to him, willing the night to last forever.

It was a sleepy-eyed Clarissa who dreamily greeted her aunt very late the next morning.

"I understand Mr. Phillips called last evening." Lavinia addressed her niece with mild reproof. "He could have merely left his message for me. It wasn't seemly for you to receive a gentleman at such an hour."

"You're right," Clarissa agreed, reveling in a contentment that made argument impossible. "But it was an emergency of sorts."

"That's what Ellen seemed to indicate, but I do hope he left early."

"Yes, Aunt," Clarissa said, adding silently, *early in the morning*.

"And just what was the nature of this emergency?" Lavinia continued in a halfhearted attempt at her role as guardian as she busied herself pruning a plant in her dining room window.

"One of Brandon's professors has assigned some sort of legal studies between terms."

"That's nice, dear," Lavinia said, grimacing at the sight of a brown-edged leaf, "but I fail to understand what that has to do with you."

"Only that he wants me to help him with his work the way I help Father," replied Clarissa lightly as she walked to the sideboard and selected a small orange from the ever-present fruit bowl.

"I don't know if that would be proper," said Lavinia as she stopped her delicate snipping and cocked her head to one side. "After all, we pay Mr. Phillips to tend to your education and not you to his... Don't misunderstand me, he's a dear boy, but how your father would feel about the matter, I'm not quite certain."

"It's not as if he'd expect any fee for all the time we'd be spending together," Clarissa explained patiently, surprised by her aunt's reluctance, and formulating a plot to circumvent it. Had Ellen noticed the hour at which Brandon had left? No—or Lavinia wouldn't be so calm.

"Still..." The older woman hesitated.

"Well, it's up to you, Aunt Lavinia," remarked Clarissa all too casually as she began peeling her fruit and releasing its aromatic fragrance into the stuffy dining room. "Though of course," she continued with a shrug, "if I don't help him, he'll be too busy to tutor me at all before Trinity term begins."

"What?" asked Lavinia, her attention finally diverted from her fern to the young woman sitting at the table.

"It's just that without help he'll need all his time to complete the extra assignments. But it doesn't make any difference. I'll do whatever you think best," Clarissa stated in her most obedient voice, which Lavinia, if she had been less flustered and more astute, would have noted was at odds with the sly, stubborn gleam in the girl's eyes. "After all," the girl went on, "I could use the break, and it *would* give us an abundance of time to spend together, dear Aunt."

"Yes, wouldn't that be...lovely?" Lavinia replied with a wan smile as her brain worked feverishly to find a way out of this predicament. Her niece was a dear, sweet child, but four weeks in her constant unrelieved company, in this house—away from Geoffrey? Her finger played with a warm auburn curl as she fought her rising panic. What was she going to do now? In the midst of her anxiety, however, inspiration found its way through the haze.

"You know, Clarissa, as tempting as it would be to selfishly indulge in each other's companionship, we mustn't allow that to sway us from our obligations."

"What obligations?" Clarissa asked, a cavalier note in her voice. "Brandon Phillips is my tutor, not a member of the family," she added for good measure, biting into her orange to hide her satisfied smile.

"Why, my dear, he's given you so much of himself that he's certainly *like* a member of the family," Lavinia twittered, unaware of the truth of her words. "And it is our duty to aid the less fortunate," she continued, thinking she would be added to their number if she couldn't persuade her niece to spend more time with that nice tutor of hers. "If Mr. Phillips needs our assistance, we must do all we can to comply."

"Aunt Lavinia," began Clarissa.

"I'm sorry, dear, but I've made up my mind. As your guardian I simply can't allow you to be selfish. I'll send Mr. Phillips a note this very moment saying that you can begin assisting him this afternoon. And please, Clarissa," Lavinia concluded as she placed her pruning shears in their case and began to clear the debris, "be gracious about this, won't you?"

"I'll try," said Clarissa, hiding her elated mood with a mournful sigh, "but only because you insist."

Chapter Ten

Hours later, Clarissa waited impatiently in the morning room for Brandon's arrival. A devilish smile tugged at the corners of her mouth as she congratulated herself on the success of her ploy with Lavinia. By the time she had finished, it was obvious that aunt had been just as anxious as niece to have Brandon call at the house every day. Musing about Lavinia's often flustered state and the high color that flitted across her cheeks, Clarissa suspected it was not the business of the Horticultural Society that called the older woman from Hertford Court so consistently. The young woman doubted that plants and flowers could exert such allure. Still, she was not about to question the reasons for her aunt's numerous absences. As long as Lavinia was satisfied that her sister's daughter was behaving decorously, Clarissa knew she could do whatever she wanted.

But what, exactly, *did* she want to do, the young American wondered with a frown as lines puckered her forehead. Now that she had given herself to Brandon, what would he expect from her in the future, or she from him? She had no experience with this sort of thing, and no idea of what was to happen next. Would Brandon want to make love to her at every opportunity or would he ever want her again... And how would she *know*?

Though it was true that he had spoken words of endearment, Clarissa had heard whisperings among older, wiser women that men often said things in the heat of passion that were later forgotten. She began to wonder, like so many unmarried women before her, whether a man saw the act of love as the culmination of a relationship or only the beginning.

After debating the possibilities, Clarissa decided that this business of loving was not an easy thing. It was much less unsettling to adhere to mere flirtation, keeping a man interested but at a comfortable distance. Still, she thought when a tingling sensation played along her spine as she recalled Brandon's powerful arms encircling her, those rewards were not as great.

As Clarissa peered through the window, her heart began to beat more rapidly as she recognized a familiar figure approaching her aunt's doorway with a firm tread, notebooks and texts tucked under one arm. The sight of Brandon's broad shoulders, hidden though they were under his greatcoat, recalled the delicious sensation she'd known while exploring the skin of his brawny chest, and Clarissa remembered with indolent satisfaction the way his torso tapered so sleekly to his narrow hips. Such intimate recollections raised another question, and Clarissa began to panic as she wondered how a woman greeted her lover when meeting him for the first time after their initial excursion into the realm of forbidden passion. What would Brandon anticipate! Lord, but she wished she knew!

The noise of the heavy door knocker violated the silence of the house, so quiet with Lavinia gone to yet another meeting of her garden society. But as Brandon's voice sounded in the hallway, confident virility invaded the premises, dispelling the sedate atmosphere, and replacing it with delicious anticipation. Then suddenly he was there beside her, his presence unmistakably filling the room.

Clarissa stood and took in his raw good looks, yet hesitated to move forward to meet him. She, who had always been brazen and opinionated, found herself shy and uncertain near this handsome man who had been first her tiresome tutor, then her good friend, and finally her very ardent lover.

When his red-haired beauty remained where she was, Brandon felt the tension, noting the unsettled look in Clarissa's eyes and her reticent silence. Her innocent bashfulness touched him, and no matter that there had been no licence, he couldn't help but tenderly compare her to any blushing bride. Placing his books on the table, he came quickly to her side, took her in his arms and kissed her gently on the mouth.

Even in the soft touch of his lips upon hers, Clarissa recognized an unmistakable possessiveness that reassured her and made her heart beat all the faster. The naturalness of his actions quelled any anxiety she had felt, and Clarissa only knew that she belonged in Brandon's embrace no matter what society might say.

"Mmm, that tasted wonderful," he murmured, after a few moments of holding her close. "But as delectable and tempting as you might be, I'm afraid that there are other things that claim our attention at the moment."

He glanced ruefully at the stack of texts and notebooks as though begging her indulgence with an expression so boyish that Clarissa couldn't help but laugh, her voice a melody of happiness and contentment.

"Come on, Braxton," she said merrily, alluding to the famous recorder of English law. "Let's see what sort of trouble you've gotten yourself into."

No, said a little voice inside her head. *It's what sort of trouble you've gotten him into. You have to tell him.*

I know, I know, she answered herself, *but not yet. I have to wait for the right moment. His temper can be as fiery as his lovemaking. This man doesn't do anything halfheartedly. Besides, how angry could he be with me after I've worked hard to help him out of this mess? I'll tell him. I promise I will, but right now it's more important that I assist him with this research.*

Attempting to assuage her conscience, Clarissa threw herself into the task at hand with all the energy she could muster, and Brandon was surprised and delighted by the assiduous effort she was providing. That Miss Cooper's niece had a quick mind he knew, but her diligence could only mirror her concern for him. For his part, even this tiresome chore seemed agreeable in her company. They worked so well together that for an instant, a fleeting image of doing this in years to come passed through his mind. Shocked, he shook his head to rid himself of such imaginings. He was in no position to plan his future with or without Clarissa until Humphrey had been satisfied. Though he was tempted, there was no permanent place for a woman in his life right now.

Yet every once in a while, as disciplined as he was, he couldn't help but glance hungrily at her profile, the graceful arch of her neck, the gentle swelling of her bosom beneath her delicate peach blouse. He remembered the silky warmth of her skin and its honeyed taste. It would seem that intimate knowledge of her luscious body had not conquered his yearning or curiosity but only increased his ardor, her sweet mystery summoning him again as he felt a familiar stirring. Damn, he was as healthy as any male, but no other woman affected him in this manner, and it was only with extreme effort that he managed to begin reading the case before him once again, though this time with much more difficulty than before.

"Well, well, so this *is* where you've closeted yourself, as though I harbored any doubts when you told me this morning that you might be here," came an exuberant voice from the threshold of the room, distracting Brandon from his physical discomfort.

"A Mr. Newcomb calling, miss," Ellen announced belatedly, obviously unnerved that this energetic young man had outdistanced her on the short walk between the main entrance and the doorway to the room that contained her employer's niece. "I'm sorry, miss, I tried to . . ."

"No need to apologize, Ellen," interrupted Brandon. "As much as I am reluctant to do so, I'll take responsibility for this gentleman. I can vouch for Edward Lowell Newcomb's impetuous nature," he went on with an infectious grin, "if not his good name. And should Miss Manning decide she can endure his company for more than five minutes, I'm certain she'll be able to bear me out. Come in, Ned, and meet Miss Clarissa Manning."

"Ah, so this is Miss Manning," the ebullient whirlwind enthused as he moved to the center of the room and deposited a bundle of notes. "Why, you're more delightful than I had *ever* imagined," Ned raved with an approving glance in Brandon's direction.

"Might that be because you've listened to far too many of Brandon's complaints about me?" asked Clarissa, her dark brown eyes twinkling in amusement at the unrestrained good humor of the highly personable young man.

"Why, not at all! Brandon has never said anything about you that wasn't complimentary," Ned protested with a laugh, the glint in his laughing eyes belying his words.

"So I imagine," Clarissa retorted wryly. "However, if you swear that you have never believed a word of this man's slander, then I am pleased to make your acquaintance, Mr. Newcomb. Correct me if I'm wrong, but doesn't my aunt know your father?"

"So it seems, but let's not allow that to stop us from having fun. I promise not to divulge anything about *you* to Father, if you keep *my* behavior a secret from your aunt. There, now that bargain has been struck, we can all be ourselves. What sort of devilment do you suppose we can get into?" Ned asked, nodding his head toward the bundles of paper he had brought with him.

"Well, I have a feeling that whatever it is, it will be strictly legal," Clarissa said, laughing.

"More's the pity," Ned responded, sighing heavily as he fixed Clarissa with an absurdly mournful gaze, "especially with temptation so near."

"But we wouldn't want to break any rules, would we, Ned?" inserted Brandon with mock severity, moving to stand next to Clarissa. "Especially the bonds of friendship. And you, Miss Manning, should beware of this scamp. He's broken half the female hearts in London, and never means a word he says when talking to a woman."

"I always mean what I say," protested Ned, "at least I do at the time."

"Mmm?" inquired Brandon, fixing his friend with a skeptical stare. "Well, never mind, tell me what's that you've carted in with you? A stack of breach-of-promise suits?"

"I was down at the Royal Courts of Justice early this morning, I'll have you know—me, who hates to rise before noon—searching the court records for something you might find useful. And then I went to your rooms, only to have to follow you here." An elaborate sigh of exhaustion emphasized Ned's complaint. "Well, at any rate, I've brought a copy of a decision that may interest you. Here I am, in between terms, working when I should be ruining my health by enjoying life's pleasures to excess, and what thanks do I get? However do you put up with this fellow, Miss Manning?''

"Please call me Clarissa, and I shall call you Ned. It makes it easier, don't you think?'' Clarissa asked, falling into an easy alliance with Lord Geoffrey's son. "As to how I endure Mr. Phillips here, Lord knows it isn't easy. But then I don't have to tell you that, do I? After all, Brandon is your tutor, also, so I know only too well what you've had to endure."

"All right, you two,'' Brandon said with a laugh. "You've repaid me tenfold for all my bullying." Taking Clarissa's hand in his, he turned to Ned and asked, "Isn't she everything I said she was?''

"Yes,'' agreed Ned, an expression of exaggerated perplexity creeping slowly across his face, "but what I can't understand is why you thought anyone so refreshing to be so aggravating."

Though Clarissa laughed delightedly at Ned's buffoonery, she also took pleasure in Brandon's rising color as she thought of her behavior at their first few meetings. It seemed the highly controlled Brandon Phillips hadn't been as unbothered by her capricious tactics as he had pretended to be.

"That's enough, Ned. Stop before she believes you," Clarissa's lover ordered, only half in jest. Wait until he spoke to this young rascal in private, Brandon thought, but if truth be known, it was Clarissa he would rather have had alone.

"Though I'd love to listen to your patter," Clarissa said, intruding upon Brandon's thoughts just when they were becoming interesting, "I'm afraid your Professor Humphrey has dictated otherwise. Unfortunately, I think we should get busy."

Soon the trio was industriously at work scanning briefs and taking notes, the silence punctuated only by an occasional question. Though the going was slow, Clarissa knew she had never felt so content. Here she was, doing something useful yet challenging, sitting next to the man she loved and being accepted wholeheartedly by his best friend. Suddenly even Aunt Lavinia's morning room seemed a wonderful place, and Clarissa doubted that anything could mar the day.

Her feeling of serenity was short-lived, however, when the door knocker sounded once more, and Ellen appeared to inform her that Mr. Waverly-Smythe was calling. A groan from Ned and Brandon's conspicuous silence convinced Clarissa that the morning room was not the place in which to talk with Preston.

"Ask Mr. Waverly-Smythe to wait in the library, and tell him that I'll join him in a moment," she directed.

"Yes, miss," replied Ellen, scurrying from the room, her eyes raised heavenward as she anticipated relating this interesting bit of news to Cook. Imagine! The old miss was gone, and the young one was entertaining three men at one time! This house had never seen the likes of it!

Though both Brandon and Ned were extremely polite when she excused herself in order to deal with her latest visitor, Clarissa could detect Brandon's frosty displeasure as she left the room. What a proprietary male he was, she thought, surprised that this discovery was not in the least offensive. In fact, it didn't threaten her sense of independence at all. Rather, the realization was an exhilarating one, and it prodded Clarissa into sending Preston on his way all the more quickly.

"Ah, so there you are," Preston greeted her, rising to his feet, his face beaming as she entered the room. "I thought you might enjoy some riding this afternoon."

"I'm sorry, Preston, but riding is out of the question today."

"A stroll, then?"

"No, I'm rather occupied at the moment . . ."

"Cycling? I could borrow a pair of bicycles and be back within an hour."

"No cycling, either, I'm afraid," Clarissa replied, unable to keep from smiling at his tenacity.

"It's a glorious afternoon, Clarissa, but it would be even better if I spent the remainder of the day in your company. Come now, what can I use to tempt you?" He took her hands in his and gave her his most charming smile as he wondered why she was being so evasive. How the hell was he going to get a recommendation from James G. Manning with Clarissa being so standoffish? However, he was not one to give up readily.

"I know! I could get one of my cameras and we could take some photographs in the park. That would be fun!"

"Preston, you're very sweet, but I'm entertaining guests right now."

"Oh well, then, we *could* spend the afternoon indoors. Why don't you take me along and introduce me?"

"You already know them," Clarissa said, seeing that there was no easy way out, yet wanting to avoid any unpleasantness between Brandon and his rival. Why had she ever welcomed this man's attention, she wondered as she studied her guest. It certainly complicated matters. Still, it wasn't his fault, she reminded herself. Preston had only responded to her encouragement, and he had always been amiable enough so that now she felt especially guilty for sending him packing. It was perhaps her own culpability in the matter that stifled her urge to lose her patience with him, though there was no doubt in her heart as to who deserved the opportunity to intern with Dobson and Whittaker.

"Someone I know?" intoned a puzzled Preston slowly until the answer became obvious. "Don't tell me it's Phillips again." At Clarissa's nod, he continued, "Well, that won't pose much of a problem. We can ditch him easily, and Miss Cooper will never be the wiser."

"But I don't want to ditch him," Clarissa said, taking her stand. "He hasn't come to give me a lesson; this is something else entirely."

Preston's blue eyes narrowed as he considered the meaning of her words. When in damnation had Phillips crept into Clarissa's affection? But it didn't make any difference, he thought determinedly, as he prepared to fight for what he wanted. He was not about to allow that penniless upstart to best him and obtain a connection with J.G. Manning that should be his!

"Clarissa," he scolded with spurious fondness, "I thought you considered Phillips a bore? When did that change?"

"As...as I've come to know him," Clarissa stammered, a blush spreading across her pretty cheeks. "We've spent a lot of time together, and he's always been kind and attentive."

"It would seem to me, Clarissa, you'd best remember that his kindness and attention are bought and paid for by your aunt," Preston retorted, giving way to some of the venom he felt for Phillips. But as Clarissa opened her mouth to protest, he recovered his poise and placed a finger on her lips, resting his other hand quite naturally along her shoulder. "I'm sorry if I've upset you. Ordinarily I wouldn't do that for the world, but I spoke out because I care for you, and I don't want to see you hurt." His gentle expression hid the rage in his heart, and Clarissa, unable to see through the mask, allowed him to continue as he removed the finger that had hindered her defense of Brandon. "I'm only afraid that Phillips' gallantry has some ulterior motive . . . perhaps your father's credentials . . ."

"I don't know if Brandon is even aware of just who my father is," Clarissa declared hotly. "Brandon Phillips has never mentioned anything *about* my father."

"No, and he never will," Preston responded softly, attempting to gentle her mood. "He's too intelligent for that. But when it comes to a place at the Inns of Court, he can be quite a ruthless fellow. Do what you want, my dear, but just promise me you'll be careful. You know how much your happiness means to me," he lied convincingly.

"Thank you for your concern," Clarissa said, summarily rejecting this man's strictures concerning Brandon. After all, Preston's sentiments had to rise out of rivalry. Still, he had chanced her anger by giving voice to his suspicions, and this softened Clarissa's attitude toward the attempt to interfere in her life. "However," she added gently, "you mustn't worry about me."

"But I do worry about you, Clarissa," Preston said, orchestrating a credible tone into his voice ever so carefully. "But," he resumed brightly, "just because you've decided to befriend Phillips doesn't mean that we can't continue our relationship. I'll pop around again soon, when you're less busy."

Clarissa had no time to react to this proposal before Preston was placing a light kiss on the tip of her nose then linking his arms through hers. "Now at least consent to see me out," he commanded good-naturedly, "or I shall be quite hurt."

"Well, well, look who has turned up." Ned's voice rang out as Clarissa and Preston entered the hall on their way to the front door. Lord Geoffrey's son had made himself very much at home, lounging next to the open doorway of the morning room. "If I didn't know better, I'd swear this was university, what with the number of students who turn up. Brandon Phillips is here as well, you know," he announced, unable to contain the gloating expression on his face. "But I believe he'll be staying the *entire* afternoon."

Clarissa could feel Preston's body stiffen beside hers. And though she couldn't help but be amused by the mischievous glimmer in Ned's bold brown eyes, and by his devilish mood, she nonetheless felt sorry for the man she was escorting to the door.

Angry as he was, Preston bit his tongue. It wasn't judicious to offend Lord Geoffrey's heir. All he could do at the moment was accept Ned's gibes, playing the part of someone who expected these quips in a spirit of easy camaraderie.

"Then since I'm leaving and you two are staying, you and Phillips can only be considered the luckiest of men," Preston replied. "As for me, I'll have to be content to wait my turn and come back again."

Underneath his ready smile, fury raced through Preston's veins. Ned's transparent taunts could only be the result of Phillips' influence, and Preston Waverly-Smythe vowed again that he would somehow or other destroy that penniless bastard, and he'd do it soon.

Clarissa bid Preston goodbye, then entered the morning room, her composure strained by the interruption so that she was flushed and her breath came in uneven little spurts. She certainly hadn't expected Preston to be so persistent, and all the while she was speaking with him, she was conscious of Brandon waiting for her in the other room, wondering what *his* reaction to this intrusion would be. She only hoped Preston's casual arrival at the house on Hertford Court wouldn't spoil the mood of an otherwise idyllic day.

"There you are." Brandon greeted her with a quietness he didn't feel, his dazzling smile and endearing dimple giving reassurance of her welcome. "We missed you."

That was all he dared to say as he shuffled some papers and made room for her again on the settee. Anything else would only have led to a roar of wounded resentment. He couldn't tell her that all during the time she was gone, which was probably much shorter than he estimated, he'd been unable to concentrate, English law taking second place to his jealousy over a pretty American girl. Nor could he mention that in all probability it was his irritable restlessness that had driven Ned from the room. Brandon had never felt more at sea than when she'd been off with Waverly-Smythe, not even when he'd been a-drift in one of his uncle's ships. Yet how could he relate the irrational outrage he'd experienced when he'd seen Clarissa and Preston passing by the doorway arm in arm? After all, what right did he have to be incensed by the attention Clarissa received from another man?

He'd made love to her, yes, but what else could he offer her at the moment? From deep within his soul, he knew the answer: nothing at all, until he'd earned his degree and a place in the practice of law. And the first step toward that end was finishing this bloody case. With this in mind, he attempted to settle down to work once more, handing Clarissa a sheaf of papers and requesting her assistance in perusing them.

Clarissa began her task, aware only of Brandon's serious demeanor and not the reason for it. She knew she should be pleased that Preston's arrival hadn't interjected discord into their afternoon of quiet work, yet nevertheless, she found herself nonplussed that her handsome tutor had so nonchalantly accepted another man's pursuit of her without protest. Didn't he care that Preston had come courting? But then, she thought impishly, perhaps Brandon only needed a little reminding of just how much she meant to him. With an idea of how to show him firmly in mind, she was able to attend to work once more.

The clock had just chimed ten as Clarissa held her breath, attempting to unlock the door used by tradesmen in her aunt's home. Her delicate hand slowly turned the key then tried the handle, which did nothing more than promise her an escape to the outside world. A few days ago, this door had given her easy access; now it refused to allow her to leave. The night air must have woven some mischievous spell. The girl swore as the tumbler emitted a series of clicks that she was certain never sounded when the door was used during daylight hours. All she would need now was for Ellen or Cook to hear this racket in their rooms, which were situated down the narrow hallway, and then what would she do?

Even though she had known that Lavinia intended on spending the evening in her company, the problem had seemed easy enough to overcome when Clarissa had formulated her plan in the afternoon. Complain of fatigue, pick at her food during dinner, retire early, then steal out. Lavinia had never been one to stay up until all hours, so freedom beckoned no later than ten o'clock. At least that had been her intent, until she had been confronted by this confounded door.

If only she could get outside, a brief twenty minutes would see her in Brandon's arms. Swaddled from head to foot in her hooded cloak, no one who saw her could possibly know who she was. And though her heart beat rapidly at the prospect of venturing along the streets of London on her own at night, the idea of being discovered standing here ready to go out so late in the evening was even more alarming. Perhaps, she deliberated, she should return to her room. As the thought crossed her mind, she gave one more flick of her wrist, and another loud click reverberated through the stillness of Lavinia's household. Suddenly the door opened.

Clarissa exhaled slowly as the night air found its way into the house through a widening slit between door and frame. The coolness caressed her face, refreshing her, and invited her to step outside and begin her adventure. Impulsively she did so, her decision made. Brandon had certainly surprised her in the conservatory last evening, she reflected, her lips forming a slight smile, and tonight she would do the same for him.

Finding his rooms would be simple enough. She'd traveled sufficiently around London in her aunt's company to know the city well. Once, they had passed Brandon's street, which Aunt Lavinia had been kind enough to point out. Besides, Clarissa proposed to walk but a block or two anyway. Then she could hire a carriage to convey her close enough to Brandon's residence to be convenient, yet far enough away to be safe. She didn't want any witnesses to her boldness as she entered the premises, yet for both their sakes, she knew she had to see him that night.

A bleary-eyed Brandon scowled as he gathered his notes into a neat pile. With the help of Clarissa and Ned, he'd accomplished more research today than he had thought possible. Yet for all the headway he'd made on Humphrey's paper, Brandon Phillips wasn't happy, and he knew it stemmed from Waverly-Smythe's casual arrival at the Cooper residence and the familiar way in which he'd looped his arm through Clarissa's.

Damn it, Brandon fumed, *he'd* been the one to make love to Clarissa, not Waverly-Smythe, and he thought it should count for something. But the question was, did she? Apparently not, if her behavior with his rival was any indication. Then, too, after Preston's departure, when he'd tried to speak with Clarissa concerning tonight, she'd mumbled something about having to stay at home with Lavinia. With Ned nearby, Brandon hadn't pressed the matter, but now he couldn't help but wonder if it was Lavinia she was really with.

Christ! Here he was thinking about Clarissa again after spending the entire day in her company. Why couldn't he seem to get enough of her? He'd never met a female like Clarissa Manning, and he pondered whether her mystique came about because she was so very American or so much a woman. It made no difference. No matter which it was, he was ensnared, and so totally captivated that he was no longer trying to escape.

Shrugging his shoulders as he set about making ready for bed, Brandon thought it odd that acknowledging the cause of his symptoms shouldn't grant him some immunity to them. No wonder Lavinia Cooper was always in such a dither. The poor woman had no defenses against the girl's unpredictability, and, it would seem, neither did he.

Brandon had just entered his bedroom and removed his shirt when he heard a knocking at his door. Since when had Ned learned manners, he thought with a grumble.

"Come in; it's unlatched," he roared, speculating just what his young friend wanted after ten at night. The sound of the door opening and shutting quietly pervaded the otherwise silent flat. He hoped it wasn't another of Ned's endless celebrations. Brandon felt damnably tired tonight, and he couldn't think of anything offhand that could keep him from some well-deserved sleep.

Poking his head and shoulders out of the bedroom in order to greet his friend and possibly send him on his way, Brandon's words caught in his throat. There in the center of the room stood Clarissa, her cape at her feet, swirling along the floor like some rich velvet cloth used by a gem merchant to display his most costly jewel. And jewel she was, bathed in the glow of the gaslight, her tender smile giving form to her evocative lips as she stood there, slowly and seductively unbuttoning the front of her pale green dress.

"Hello, Brandon," she murmured in a throaty voice that gently invaded the stillness of the room, as the gaslight cast her shadow on the walls, making her actions appear larger than life.

"Clarissa," Brandon uttered incredulously as he moved into the outer chamber. The effect of the sight she presented raged through his body, wiping away all vestiges of fatigue. "I thought you were spending the evening with your aunt."

"I was supposed to," Clarissa confessed, a twinkle igniting her dark eyes, "but I gave her the slip when I realized I just couldn't stay away from you, you handsome rogue."

Brandon grinned broadly at her laughing admission. None of the women he knew would be so forthright, even in their jesting; they always found coyness to be ever so much more fashionable. But not his Clarissa. She usually spoke her mind. Though there had been times when he had not appreciated this trait, he saw now that there were instances when it definitely had its advantages.

"I hope you don't mind some unexpected company," Clarissa said, giving him a sidelong glance as she stepped out of her dress.

"Not at all," Brandon replied, his voice husky and his gray eyes shining with desire. "In fact, there's nothing I'd like more."

"Perhaps I can think of something," Clarissa said. Uncorseted and clad only in fine, semisheer undergarments decorated wickedly with French lace, she walked to where he stood, stepped up on her tiptoes and folded her arms lovingly around Brandon's neck.

Her delicate laughter illuminated Brandon's spartan rooms as the sunlight never could, and filled the cold atmosphere with the heat of love waiting to be consummated.

"You little she-devil," he chided with a smile. "Don't you know you shouldn't be here?"

"No one saw me, Brandon," Clarissa said earnestly. "You know I wouldn't cause you any trouble."

"It's not me I'm worried about, dearest girl," Brandon interrupted. "It's you."

"Well, don't agonize over it," Clarissa retorted as her fingers smoothed his broad shoulders and began marking the path her hands had traveled with fervent kisses.

"Oh, woman, you drive me to distraction," Brandon groaned. "You are such a greedy little creature."

But it was his own greed that brought his lips down hard upon hers. Though his mouth demanded reciprocation for his torrid spirit, there was no need for it to do so. Clarissa gave herself wholeheartedly, responding not only to Brandon but to the need he wrought within her.

It was he alone who had set free a compelling force that her innocent flirtations with other men had only vaguely suggested. There was nothing that could diminish the capacity of her longing other than to have her desire fulfilled by this man, whose blood seemed to smolder with a passion to match her own.

They were like moths to the flame, drawn to love's blazing exaltation, an immolation they welcomed, knowing that like the phoenix, they would find renewal within the fires of their scorching union.

With an agonizing slowness, Brandon began to undo the ribbons that kept the mounds of her breasts hidden from view.

It was all Clarissa could do not to shred the fragile ties herself. God, if she didn't feel him suckling her soon, she was certain she would go mad.

Suddenly the chemise fell open and Brandon quickly removed her underdrawers and stockings so she stood before him in naked glory.

Still he resisted temptation. She wanted to cry with frustration, until his actions caught her notice, and she stood transfixed as Brandon removed the remainder of his own clothing. Hungrily, Clarissa's eyes devoured the clean, smooth lines of his tight belly and trim buttocks. But, it was the physical proof of his desire that intrigued her the most, so that she reached out to touch him, and found that the velvet texture of his masculinity aroused her even further, although a few moments before, she would have thought that impossible.

Hearing Brandon's sharp intake of breath as she played a slender finger along the length of his manhood she increased her toying until an iron grip caught her wrist and forbade her further exploration. Letting go of her Brandon picked her up and carried her into the other room, where he placed her upon his bed and lay beside her.

As he leaned over her, Clarissa cupped one breast and offered it to him. And when the hot, moist pressure of his mouth closed over the rigid tip, she couldn't restrain her wordless sounds of joy. But the gentle tugging at her nipple and the touch of his hands didn't rid her of her craving. Instead, his touch increased the sweetness of her agony until she thrashed around on the bed, moaning and calling Brandon's name, urging him, then begging him to give her release.

The taste of Clarissa and her wild abandon as she moved beneath his stroking destroyed Brandon's plans for a leisurely session of lovemaking. The flames of her urgency stoked his own fire, so that instinct took control of both their movements.

As he positioned himself to love her, she encircled his waist with her long, slender legs, embracing him and drawing him to her with a fervor that moved him to a passion that knew no restraints, no inhibitions.

In a mindless frenzy, driven by pure sensation, a possessive Brandon couldn't get enough of Clarissa. He thrust inside her deeply, as though attempting to leave his imprint, or a bit of his soul, marking her as his woman, and his alone.

Clarissa responded in kind, reveling as everything was concentrated in her secretmost center while their bodies pressed against one another again, and again, and again.

Finally, just when she thought she could withstand no more, a thousand stars collided within her, and Clarissa gave herself over to their impact, while Brandon groaned deeply and shuddered in an eruption of passion. At the moment of greatest intensity, each called out the name of the other, because for them, no one and nothing else existed in their universe.

There was no other man for her except Brandon, Clarissa mused contentedly as she lay beside him, surfeited with love. As serious and self-controlled as he could be at times, she understood that his soul was full of searing emotions, and that *she* could ignite him with just one touch. Snuggling beside him to rest her head in the crook of his arm, she was enthralled by every aspect of their relationship: the spiciness of indulging in the forbidden, the command she could wield over such a confident, dominant man, but most of all, she savored the love that he tendered with such intensity. Quiet and gentle yet savagely primitive, it gave her a security and joy unlike any she had ever known.

A satisfied smile passed over her face. After such glorious lovemaking, Brandon had to be aware of just how much she loved him. And Clarissa was quite certain that he would never again be so complacent about Preston's attentions to her.

Watching her from the corner of his eye, a sated Brandon lazily stretched the arm not entwined around his lovely Clarissa and reached over to play with her absurdly short curls. He smiled anew at Clarissa's disregard for society's conventions, and suddenly her cropped, red tresses endeared her to him all the more. She was his, he exalted. The hell with Waverly-Smythe, Brandon thought, running the back of his hand along Clarissa's finely drawn cheek. He had nothing to worry about from the likes of him!

Preston Waverly-Smythe stood in the doorway of the building across from Brandon's flat. A scowl marred his good looks as he stared at his pocket watch in the glow of the lamplight. Clarissa had been in there three hours, and that boded no good.

It wasn't the fact that Phillips was in all probability indulging in sex with the girl that choked Preston with jealous wrath. What infuriated him was that the chit's attachment to Phillips could very well sway her father to use his prestige for that bastard's benefit. But after all the time and attention he himself had lavished upon Clarissa Manning, Preston Waverly-Smythe was not about to allow that to happen.

And to think he would have been unaware of the seriousness of Clarissa's involvement with his penniless rival if it had not been for chance!

Over the past years he had learned that nothing relieved frustration so well as a few hours spent with his cameras. They always enabled him to rid himself of tension, then don the mask of his public life once more. Without question, being ushered out of the house on Hertford Court this afternoon while Phillips remained had been frustrating in the extreme.

As a result, Preston had been on his way that evening to a cheap set of rooms he used as a photography studio off of Holywell Street. To get to that unfashionable neighborhood, he had cut down Brandon's rather shoddy block. It was while doing so that he had seen a carriage stop at the opposite end of the pavement and a woman descend to make her way to Phillips' door. Always anxious to obtain information that might later prove useful, Preston had tarried in the shadows to see who was visiting that arrogant upstart so late at night. But he had not been prepared to recognize the tall, slender figure standing in the light from the street lamps. The sight of Clarissa Manning joining Phillips in his rooms had so enraged him that any pleasure his photography might have given him that night had been destroyed.

When it became obvious that the girl was not leaving soon after she arrived, Preston had been tempted to alert the university authorities to the fact that his rival had a woman in his rooms, but discarded the plan quickly. By the time he returned, Clarissa could be gone, and even if she were still there, being instrumental in involving James Gregory Manning's daughter in a scandal could be detrimental to his own career.

Besides, investigation of the morality of one applicant for the place in Dobson and Whittaker's chambers might result in a similar examination of all who had applied, and Preston couldn't chance anyone scrutinizing his own activities.

The only thing he could do was wait. And wait he had, fury consuming him with each passing minute until his rage silently exploded when the door across the street opened to reveal the detested couple, Phillips' hand possessively at Clarissa's waist. There was no mistaking the cause of his proprietary gesture, and Preston ground his teeth as he watched them hurry off in the direction of Lavinia's house.

But Preston was not ready to accept defeat, graciously or otherwise. Tonight, he would attempt to console himself with drinking and whoring, but in the near future, he promised himself, he'd find comfort in *revenge*.

Chapter Eleven

Brandon grinned as he caught himself whistling a jaunty tune. He hadn't been this lighthearted in years. He should feel exhausted, having been up till all hours last night and rising early in the morning for a conference with Humphrey. But unexpectedly, he found himself full of vigor now that his life had gone from treadmill to garden path.

Unfolding his razor and stepping up to the mirror that hung over his washstand, Brandon was surprised to see the youthful reflection in the glass.

"For the past few years I've felt the old man, but by God, I look scarcely older than Ned," Brandon stated in astonishment. Gone were the creases caused by the determined set of his lips, and the brow that was usually wrinkled in concentration or concern was now quite smooth.

That woman is truly a witch, he thought with an affectionate laugh as he studied himself in the mirror, appreciating the changes Clarissa had wrought. At the thought of her, his eyes gleamed wickedly then glowed as he recalled the particulars of the previous evening.

"Lord, you're one lucky man," Brandon told himself following the final swipes of the razor. Then he threw back his head and laughed aloud, delighted by the ironies of life. The same woman he now adored had been considered a monumental irritation only two days before. How could he have been so blind? No one in the world could be as loving as his Clarissa, and certainly no other woman was as enchanting, as beautiful, as alluring, as giving, as sweet, as ... Dear Lord, this litany could only mean one thing, Brandon realized, as emotions that had been dormant these past few years awakened like a spring flood breaking through an ill-constructed dam. He was truly in love—hopelessly, irrevocably in love—and the reflection in the mirror smiled in benevolent agreement.

With a bounce in his step, Brandon went to his wardrobe and removed his meticulously kept garments. Eyeing the bed and its jumble of linen while he donned his shirt, Brandon shrugged his broad shoulders sheepishly as a familiar stirring began in his loins. Good God, he was acting like some pubescent boy, but the idea didn't disturb him at all.

Only the thought of arriving late for his meeting with the Humph was enough to dampen the reaction that had been spurred on by the sight of his bed and by the faint vestiges of Clarissa's perfume lingering in the air.

As he eased his trousers over his slim hips, Brandon consoled himself with the fact that once his command performance before his mentor was concluded, he would be free to continue on to Hertford Court and spend the remainder of the day in Clarissa's company. True, their time together would be limited to sifting through research sources, but even that seemed a delightful chore when it brought him into contact with Clarissa. And though Brandon didn't dare entertain the possibility of possessing his red-haired beauty once more in her aunt's house, just how much his Clarissa would dare caused his eyes to dance in speculation.

In the midst of anticipating a few stolen kisses, Brandon impulsively turned to the wardrobe, his hand fumbling along the bottom until it found what it sought. Lifting a small leather box from its recessed hiding place, he brought it into the open. The antique patina of the leather covering gave evidence to the fact that the box was several generations old, as did the slight creak of the hinges when Brandon's sure, strong fingers pushed back its lid.

There, nestled on a bed of black velvet, rested the bulk of his inheritance, two pieces of jewelry, a brooch and a ring, that had been his great-grandmother's before being passed on to her daughter-in-law, and finally to his own mother.

When he had been forced to sell off the family possessions to settle his uncle's debts, Brandon had retained these two pieces, a hedge, his practical nature had told him, against emergency. But now that the warmth of Clarissa's love had begun to melt the shard of ice with which he had surrounded his heart, he admitted it had been sentimentality that had prompted him to keep the jewelry.

Gently he moved aside the brooch, a heavy gold affair studded with pearls and emeralds, so that he could look at the ring for the first time since he had snapped shut the lid of the box on the day he had turned the keys of the family home over to strangers.

Even in the dim light of early morning, its central square-cut ruby glowed intensely, capturing in its fiery depths a reflection of generations of love. Brandon's mouth curved upward when it struck him that it was not all that impossible for Clarissa to one day wear this ring. But it was still too early for thoughts such as these, he chided himself. He couldn't offer anything until he had earned his degree and captured the internship. He closed the box, delighted at the possibilities it presented.

Brandon returned the jewelry to its secret spot and was brushing off his jacket, humming a slightly off-key version of a popular dance-hall tune, when a voice at the threshold of the room disturbed him.

"Good God, hasn't anyone ever told you it's downright rude to be so bloody cheerful at such an early hour?"

"No worse than intruding into someone's bedroom uninvited *and* unannounced," Brandon commented wryly, thinking he really should learn to latch his door after fetching water for his morning washing.

Looking at his friend, Brandon couldn't help but snicker. There he stood, Edward Lowell Newcomb, bleary-eyed and hat askew, holding a basket of strawberries, and quite obviously on his way home after a night of carousing.

"I brought you some breakfast," Ned muttered, though the start of a smile was beginning to slip into place now that Brandon had ceased that godawful racket he would most likely call a musical rendition.

"Strawberries?" Brandon asked in surprise. "Wherever did you get them? I'd almost say they were a forbidden fruit at this time of the year."

"They're greenhouse bred. I filched them from Father's study early last night. He'd been judging a contest through that damn horticultural society of his, and these are the losers...at least I don't think they're the winners, though they taste fine to me," Ned said, popping one into his mouth and savoring its sweet, juicy flavor as if to demonstrate. "But speaking of forbidden fruit, old man," he continued, spying the feather mattress and pillows with their telltale indentations, "what's the cause of your exceptional good humor this morning?"

"I'm sure I don't know what you mean," Brandon bluffed as he busied himself adjusting his tie.

"Come now, Mr. Phillips," Ned badgered, assuming a stern tone of hyperbolic proportions, as though he represented the university board of directors, sheriff of London and head of the Spanish Inquisition all rolled into one. "When last we met, you assured me that you would be spending last evening working diligently on Humphrey's assignment. But surely you can't mean for me to believe that now, not when the looks of this place and your own exuberant demeanor offer such strong evidence to the contrary. Out with it, sir, what were you up to last night?"

"Not now, Ned," said Brandon in an attempt to brush him aside. "I've got to meet with the Humph in less than thirty minutes."

"Well, if it will take that long to tell me about it, your good humor explains itself," Ned replied, a twinkle in his eyes. Though he more than approved, Ned was not above playfully repaying Brandon for the numerous lectures he had been forced to endure.

"See here, Phillips, I can't have my tutor sent down for entertaining women in his rooms. Think how that would tarnish my own reputation. Keep up this sort of behavior, and you'll be meeting with the board trying to explain your wicked, loving ways."

"You're one to talk!" the bedroom's inhabitant retorted. Though he regarded his friend with the same affection one reserved for a younger brother, Brandon realized at the moment just how much of a nuisance a younger sibling could be, and for the first time he could recollect, he was glad he had been an only child.

"Those days are gone," Ned protested with a laugh. "You'll no longer find any women sneaking into my rooms."

"Oh, really?" asked Brandon, a tone of amused skepticism dominating his words. "Have they *all* given you keys?"

"Not at all, old boy. I've simply followed the example of some of you older, more decadent students, and taken a flat in another part of town. Though the area is not as fashionable, there's less chance that way of running into anyone you know," Ned confided in a dramatic whisper.

"How many times since I've met you have I called you incorrigible?" Brandon asked in humorous exasperation.

"At least a dozen times that I can think of offhand," responded Ned, not at all impressed by Brandon's jesting reproach.

"By the sound of you, it hasn't done any good. Perhaps it should have been two dozen."

"If you *had* been successful at reforming me, then I wouldn't be able to offer you this," Ned replied, fishing in his pocket then pressing a key into Brandon's hand.

"What's this, then?"

"What does it look like? Eleven Derham Court is the address that goes along with it. Right now I'm only using the place on Tuesday and Thursday evenings after eight. Other than that, it's at your disposal."

"Ned!" Brandon snapped indignantly as he tried to return his friend's gift.

"It's not as though you'd be going there by yourself, Brandon," Ned insisted, jamming both hands in his jacket in an effort to forestall the return of the key, "so perhaps it isn't a decision you should make on your own. Before you give it back, why don't you discuss it with the lady—" he paused, attempting to make his tutor and friend more comfortable with the situation before adding in an offhand manner "—whoever she may be?"

"Ned, I really mustn't keep Humphrey waiting," Brandon said, quietly pocketing the key though feeling awkward with his friend's keen perception of the situation. "And from the looks of you, you haven't seen a bed all night, at least not one that you've slept in. What were *you* up to last night?"

"Me? Why, I merely spent some time at the music halls, took in the show at The Palace, went to a private club and prowled around in the area of my new digs. I wish you had more time this morning so I could tell you about this brunette they have at The Palace. She's . . ."

"No wonder your father despairs of you." Brandon couldn't help but chuckle. "Really, Ned, you're a student, not a dilettante."

"I'm not the only one who frequents these places, you know," Ned interrupted, his fatigue beginning to get the better of his natural good humor as he foresaw another lecture in the making. "It does take others to keep them in business."

"Yes, but those others aren't fledgling scholars of law."

"No, they're upper classmen," Ned shot back smugly.

"What?"

"I saw at least eight of our fellows on my rounds last night, Waverly-Smythe among them."

"Preston? Where was he?"

"I saw him from the window of my new flat."

"Hmm. What could he have been doing there?"

"The same thing I was doing when I was prowling the neighborhood," Ned mumbled, starting to feel exceedingly drowsy. "He was having a good time. And from the looks of the tarts on his arm, he was quite successful at it, too. He went off somewhere with two of them and came back an hour later, only to link up with a third. That's what I call stamina."

"It's hard to imagine the aristocratic Waverly-Smythe in such a setting," Brandon muttered speculatively.

"Maybe it's merely the fact that Preston and people like him frequent the area that makes it less than fashionable. However, my rooms and their furnishings are quality, I assure you," Ned said with a yawn, "or near abouts, anyway. Take a look at the place if you have the chance."

With that he bit into one more strawberry and made ready to depart. But at the doorway, he turned and addressed his chum.

"Listen, Brandon," he said in as serious a tone as he was capable of employing, "I'm glad you've found someone. If this morning's mood is any indication, it's about time a little happiness found its way into your life."

"It's not really something I'm ready to discuss with you, Ned, good a friend as you might be," Brandon replied in a voice that was gentle yet firm.

At that, the visitor nodded, once more the typical Ned, his smile cheeky and his eyes mischievous. "At least I won't have to worry about you any longer," he said.

"Worry about *me*?" Brandon asked in confusion.

"Yes, now that you're on the right path, I can stop my agonizing. I'd been quite certain that you were going to end up a crusty old bibliophile, cranky and unapproachable, just like Humphrey." He was gone without waiting for a reply, so that the hurled book missed its mark and crashed against the doorjamb.

Completing his preparations before leaving for the university, Brandon had to chuckle at Ned's antics. Thinking he'd never had a better friend, he placed some coins in his pocket, his fingers coming into contact with the key. The possibilities it unlocked played through his mind, producing a temptation that ignited his imagination. Maybe Ned was right; he should tell Clarissa about the offer of the flat, and ask her to make the decision. After all, for her sake as well as his, he couldn't have her showing up on his doorstep at all hours of the night. Such risk-taking could destroy both their lives. With this thought in mind, Brandon went off to meet his mentor, the key burning a hole in his pocket in a way that money never could.

Clarissa hurried into Lavinia's little-used library. Brandon would be here in less than an hour, and she still had a lot to do. True, there would have been plenty of time, she admonished herself, if she hadn't lain abed so late this morning. But she'd been feeling *so* deliciously lazy and cozy wrapped in her blankets and warmed by the memory of last night's visit to Brandon's rooms that for once she had found it difficult to rise and begin her day.

When she had come downstairs, her aunt was already departing. Stopping only long enough to make perfunctory inquiries about her niece's headache of the evening before, Lavinia had left, to aid in judging some berry contest, she'd explained breathlessly, scurrying down the steps to the waiting cab.

Left on her own, Clarissa had uncharacteristically dawdled away most of her morning, though there had, of course, been the task of choosing her ensemble for today. This and dressing were punctuated by periods of languorous daydreaming, so that the morning had seemed to evaporate altogether.

Now, however, as Brandon's arrival drew near, she remembered that she had wanted to check one of the texts her father had written. Though it didn't deal directly with the topic Brandon was pursuing in his defense of Rhodes, her father's work was so scrupulously documented that Clarissa suspected it might provide a trove of valuable source material.

Clarissa assumed the book would be displayed on one of the shelves in Lavinia's library, not that it had ever been read by the sister-in-law to whom her father always dutifully sent a copy of each new publication. Scanning the rows along the walls, Clarissa smiled in bemused affection. Among the numerous books on flowers and plants was a copy of Thomas Bowdler's *The Family Shakespeare*, an edition that added nothing to the text of the Bard's plays, but prided itself on the fact that it had expurgated any words or expressions propriety might deem objectionable. How like Lavinia, to attempt to civilize even Shakespeare, Clarissa thought with a grin.

Seeing some books protruding from the corner of a lower shelf, Clarissa tried to push them into line until she felt resistance. Removal of the offending volumes solved the mystery and revealed other books behind them. Thinking to straighten the bookshelves, Clarissa lifted them out and couldn't contain a delicate peal of laughter when she saw what they were—several of Ouida's raciest novels!

Under her pseudonym, Marie Louise de la Ramée had written dozens of books dealing with passionate love. Though it was claimed that no decent woman would read her work, the novels had sold extremely well, and it looked as though Lavinia had bought more than her share. To think that Aunt Lavinia was one of Ouida's admirers! Why, her aunt was nothing more than a devilish romantic, Clarissa thought as she carefully replaced the forbidden books with the intention of retrieving them and reading them at a later date. It would appear that there was more to her very proper aunt than met the eye.

Running her finger along the rest of the shelves, Clarissa could find none of her father's works and had resolved to ask Lavinia about them when a familiar masculine voice intruded upon her thoughts.

"Hello, dear girl. Ellen told me you were in here, and I said she needn't bother announcing me. It's too splendid a day to be cooped up in a library, don't you think?"

Clarissa turned to greet the man standing inside the doorway and studying her so intently.

"Why, Preston, I hadn't expected you to call today."

"No, I suppose you didn't," Preston responded in a lighthearted fashion that admirably concealed the rage he still tasted more than twelve hours after seeing her scampering into Phillips' rooms.

For now, it served his purpose that she had no idea of what he'd seen or how it had made him feel. He had to be at his most charming if he wanted to woo her away from that scum who made pretenses at being a gentleman. Yet perhaps it wasn't Phillips who had lured her out last night. It could be that Clarissa only wanted a man to warm her sheets, and if that were the case, Preston decided he'd be willing to oblige.

However, should Clarissa Manning want no part of him, Preston knew he'd want her anyway, or at least what she could do for him. And to that end, he realized, he mustn't scare her off, but play the attending lovestruck swain who would be willing, quite pathetically, to settle for friendship if his lady chose to offer nothing else.

"I thought I would surprise you," he began in an appropriately tentative voice, "and come by to see if you'd like to accompany me to a lawn tennis match."

"Why, Preston, I appreciate the invitation, but I'm afraid I have other plans," Clarissa responded gently, hoping to end this conversation and see him gone by the time Brandon arrived.

"Perhaps tomorrow?" he inquired, projecting the image of a man trying damnably hard to hide his disappointment.

"Tomorrow's not possible," Clarissa fluttered, all too conscious of the awkwardness of the situation.

"Oh, I see," he responded, just the right degree of dejection creeping into his voice.

Damn, she didn't want to hurt him, and there it was, pain, reflected in his eyes. She *had*, after all, accepted Preston's attentions prior to her relationship with Brandon, and the obligation she felt to this man weighed heavily upon her. Yet as she glanced at the clock and saw that Brandon would be here in a mere twenty minutes, she wished this could be settled easily and quickly.

"I know it's not proper to mention it," Preston began, seeking to gain Clarissa's sympathy since she was unwilling to give her affection. Though he might not be able to remove Phillips from the scene immediately, if he could manipulate Clarissa into feeling enough guilt, the girl might still press her father to do something for him. In the end, that was all that counted.

"It's just that," he continued as if experiencing difficulty in talking about it, "well, I'm afraid that my boldness of a few days ago might have caused you to view me in a different light and..."

"Preston, you don't have to—"

"But I must, Clarissa," he said thinking it would be amusing at any rate to watch Phillips' slut play the innocent. "You see, I wouldn't have offended you for the world. I know in your inexperience you were shocked, but I was carried away and..."

"Preston, please," Clarissa implored.

"Clarissa, just say you forgive me," he blurted, "and I promise you'll never have to worry about behavior of that sort again."

"I forgive you, Preston, but..."

"Enough to still consider me as a friend? That's all I dare ask, to be your good friend."

"Oh, yes, Preston, we're still friends," Clarissa gushed, only too glad to learn that was all he expected. After all, what harm could it do if she treated their relationship circumspectly? Surely she owed Preston that much.

"And we always will be?" he asked tenderly.

"Certainly," Clarissa said with a soft smile.

"And may I come to call on occasion, just to see how you're getting on?" Preston asked.

The enticing redhead nodded in affirmation, touched by his generous and forgiving spirit. He truly was a marvelous man, and if she hadn't met Brandon, she might easily have fallen in love with Preston Waverly-Smythe.

Two weeks later Lavinia was alone in the library; it had long been her habit to attend to her personal correspondence before tea on Mondays and Thursdays. After all, the woman reasoned, if it weren't for the promise of a warm scone or plate of strawberries and clotted cream as a practical reward, who would ever write all those dainty notes of appreciation? The words flowed so much easier when the scent of fresh baking offered a timely respite. Thank you letters for visiting, for gifts, for attendance at charitable functions, best wishes on birthdays, anniversaries and the like, messages of condolence, a lady's obligatory correspondence would never end but for the delicate chime of four o'clock and the appearance of the tea tray.

"Cook made sherry trifle for you, miss," announced Ellen as she placed the tray on one side of Lavinia's desk.

"But isn't Clarissa joining me? There's only one cup," chided the mistress of Hertford Court as she closed the inkwell and put aside her pen.

"Miss Clarissa said you shouldn't wait for her. She was doing research with that young man of hers again, I believe."

"Yes, she certainly has become the studious one these past few weeks, Ellen. With mornings spent on her work and afternoons helping young Phillips, we barely see her. I do hope she doesn't do too much, though since Geoffrey's boy is with them, I'm certain there's no cause for us to be concerned," admonished Lavinia, more to herself than the maid.

"Yes, ma'am." Though I wager young Newcomb might wink at a friend's dalliance, Ellen thought, especially if the lad takes after his father. Phillips has probably closed his eyes to countless indelicate liaisons on the part of young Ned, and turnabout is fair play. "Would you like me to pour?"

"No, thank you. I'll see to it. But would you bring me the afternoon mail and see that these get to the post?" asked Lavinia as she gave Ellen the completed correspondence. "It does seem ironic that there's always more coming in when I've just got these written to go out. Thank heavens there's no delivery on Sunday or I'd never get caught up." As the comely spinster filled a dainty cup, Ellen returned to hand her the incoming letters.

"Oh, how nice, there's something from James Gregory. He'll be so very proud of Clarissa's growing maturity and dedication to her studies. I can't believe the change in her myself."

She's dedicated, all right, reflected the servant as she left the room, but if you can't see that it's not books that's got her attention, I'm not the one to tell you.

Behind the oak door, Lavinia scanned her brother-in-law's letter with interest. He always commented in the driest manner on his travels and experiences that, as she told Geoffrey, "The Continent seems so intriguing from his descriptions that sometimes I'm tempted to see it for myself." This time, however, there was little about himself. Instead he devoted most of the letter to his approval of Lavinia's arrangements for his daughter, apologizing that her letter detailing Clarissa's dismissal from Briarley Academy had taken so long to catch up with him.

"Clarissa...sometimes headstrong and needing direction...you handled a difficult situation most artfully... Humphrey clearly well qualified to assist you...outstanding initiative on your part...perhaps the tutoring was Clarissa's idea...do appreciate your devotion to my daughter...must not take advantage...can only hope I can do more than repay your financial inconvenience...perhaps a trip...southern France, Italy...when I return...could not continue my speaking tour without the assistance you provide...thank you for your sacrifices..."

Imagine me on the Italian Riviera, or better, Geoffrey and me...I wonder, what would I pack? Hmm...If James Gregory had been pleased before, wait until he gets my reply, she thought, deciding to postpone her tea until his letter was answered. She certainly couldn't have him thinking that Clarissa wanted to be tutored. It had, after all, been her aunt's suggestion.

Dear James Gregory—
In an effort to encourage Clarissa's study habits, I've taken it on myself to arrange extra sessions with the same young gentleman. Despite the inconvenience in my schedule,

rather than twice a week, Phillips is instructing Clarissa daily and the improvement in her demeanor is so dramatic, dear James, that it would appear your notions of female education might have some merit after all . . .

Writing steadily, Lavinia had soon filled three pages with her cursive script, regaling Clarissa's father with only the choicest of anecdotes and omitting all reference to the museum outing. That was better forgotten. There was only so much even an American parent could be expected to tolerate.

Clarissa fairly bloomed with each passing day as she reveled in Brandon's affection. Though society would have censored the girl had it known of her relationship, in her own heart, Clarissa recognized nothing sinful about her love for Brandon Phillips. These were halcyon days, the young woman mused one afternoon as she handed her tutor a stack of notes, but the peacefulness they enjoyed together was far from dull. Ever since Brandon had tenderly but hesitantly offered her a duplicate key to Ned's new rooms, their existence had been sprinkled with rapturous stolen moments. It was at times like this sunny day, when they'd been engaged in academic tasks for hours, that Clarissa found the memories of the other times they shared made the task at hand almost impossible.

"All right, children, enough work now. Put your books away and look at what Uncle Ned has brought for you today." Ned's laughing voice came to the rescue, preceding him into Lavinia's morning room, causing Clarissa's futile attempt at concentration to cease altogether.

The pattern of their days had become so quickly established, Clarissa reflected with an indulgent smile, that Ellen never questioned Ned's arrival anymore. She and Brandon would spend the morning on her lessons, lunch together, then spend the afternoon perusing whatever references were needed to satisfy Humphrey's ever-increasing assignments. They'd adopted Ned almost as a mascot and he fulfilled his role well, inevitably arriving near teatime with some outrageous bit of gossip, obscure point of law, suggestions for an outing or, on one rare occasion, a young lady for them to meet. Reflecting how she'd miss these days when Trinity term began, Clarissa welcomed the life and the glorious camaraderie of their trio.

Ned and Brandon had escorted her to Madame Tussaud's, where she'd been fascinated by supposedly accurate depictions of her country's presidents, to the Tower of London, and even for a forbidden ride on the Underground, though Lavinia would have been scandalized had she known her niece had ventured into those sulphuric depths. The Royal Botanical Gardens at Kew were considered a more permissible diversion.

"Ned, we've only another few minutes reading to finish," protested Brandon halfheartedly. "Can't you wait? This could be the final evidence I need—"

"Until tomorrow when you'll discover another essential source you simply must see," Clarissa said with a knowing smile. "Our jailer is releasing us early, sir, enjoy it," she instructed, removing the pen nib from his hand and closing the text before him, allowing her hand to linger on his. "It's play time."

"I'll tell you what I'd like to play," he whispered softly, rising to stand beside her, his hand resting gently on her hip.

"Never mind that, I've something better," promised the persistent younger brother he'd never had.

"I seriously doubt that, but all right, let's see this seventh day wonder of yours," invited the long-suffering scholar, winking at Clarissa. "That? It's just two sticks and a ragged piece of cloth; why should we be interested—"

"Oh, Brandon, it's a kite. I haven't played with one since I was a child," cried Clarissa as she claimed Ned's prize to examine it more closely. "Did you make it? Will it fly?"

"Dear girl, I'm afraid if I had made it, it certainly wouldn't fly, but since I can't claim that credit, this one will take to the air as soon as you get your cloak. I've filched a bottle of Father's wine, some cheese and fruit, and his carriage for us to have an impromptu tea party in Battersea Park. The weather is perfect."

"For kite flying?" asked Brandon dubiously.

"Don't tell me you've never done it, old man," said Ned in surprise. "Everyone has flown a kite at some point."

"Maybe not everyone," disagreed Clarissa gently, "but it's quite simple and a lot of fun, Brandon. Let me teach you; you'll love the way the wind takes the kite higher than you could ever imagine and suddenly brings it back to your feet, rather like that soaring sensation of two people..." Modesty stopped Clarissa from finishing the sentence, but she could see from her lover's sudden grin that he understood. "Do let's go."

"Go where, my dear?" interrupted Lavinia from the doorway.

"To Battersea Park to fly kites, ma'am," explained Ned. "Father always had kites to amuse my sisters, and I thought your niece might enjoy an outing."

"How very thoughtful of him, and you, of course," said Lavinia graciously, beaming. "The time was when I'd enjoy a quick romp after a dancing kite, but I'm afraid those days are beyond me at this point. Besides, I've too much to attend to, but of course, you children must go. Have a good time."

"Thank you, Miss Cooper, and don't worry about Clarissa. I'll keep an eye on her and Mr. Phillips here," assured Ned with a straight face, ignoring Brandon's scathing look. "Having seven sisters made me an experienced, if unwanted, chaperone."

"I would imagine so," agreed Lavinia with a titter. Geoffrey's boy was such a dear lad; she had no qualms for Clarissa's well-being when he was with them. "Just be back for dinner, Clarissa, half past six, no later."

"Kite flying?" said Brandon to Ned as he handed Clarissa into the carriage.

"It got you the afternoon together in the spring sunshine, didn't it?" defended Ned with a smirk.

"As I see it, three's still a crowd."

"It won't be after we pick up Miranda. I've a kite for you and Clarissa and one for us—and the park's a very large one," said the lovable scamp, winking. "Once we leave the carriage we might not see one another for hours."

"Ned, you're a scoundrel," chided Brandon with a wide grin, anticipating the sweetness of Clarissa's kisses.

"And we thank you for it," added the woman at his side, already enjoying the special warmth only Brandon could generate.

"Think nothing of it. Just manage to fly the kite a little bit, anyway, in case your aunt or my father asks how the afternoon went."

"Of course," said the young American with a shy smile. "I've a feeling Brandon may reach new heights today."

It was almost half past six in the evening during the first week of Trinity term and Brandon was still fussing with his borrowed finery, an evening jacket Ned had procured so they could accompany Clarissa and Lavinia to the theater. His gray eyes stared at him in irritation as he stood before the glass, trying once again to conquer the uncooperative tie. It had been years since he'd had the need to wear such clothes.

"Ned, how you talked me into this, I'll never know," he snarled, losing his battle with the small piece of fabric. "I feel like a monkey in this getup."

"Well, you do more for the suit than an ape does, or you would if you'd hold still long enough for me to fix your tie properly," soothed his impeccably dressed mate. "You want to look worthy of Clarissa, don't you? And besides, it's high time her aunt began to view you as her niece's admirer and not simply the girl's tutor."

"Then let her look at the man and not his attire. Damn it, what's wrong with my old gray jacket, anyway?"

"Nothing but that it's old and out of style. If you want to attend the theater opening—"

"But I don't. This scheme was your idea, and her aunt's," protested the aggravated young man, viewing a stranger in his mirror. Unused to primping to satisfy the expectations of others, he resented the need to impress anyone.

"With someone as lovely as Clarissa on your arm, you've got to look the part, especially with Preston always waiting in the wings to show you up. One more refused invitation and I believe Miss Cooper would have questioned your upbringing rather than your inadequate wardrobe. And you certainly don't want her encouraging Preston to court your lady."

"The hell with Lavinia Cooper," declared Brandon in irritation, having found a scapegoat for his discomfort. "What does she know?"

"Nothing, I trust, and I hope it will stay that way if you two continue your circumspect behavior in public, but..."

"But what?"

"But you'll have to compromise with society occasionally, Brandon, if you're to be accepted by Clarissa's family. You can't meet in my rooms at Derham Court forever, you know. What happens when her father returns? Could you let her go back to the States?"

Silence greeted Ned's query, but it was a question that haunted Brandon all evening, coming back to trouble him when he was alone in his rooms at the end of the night. His friend was right. The past month had been a delightful fantasy, but it was time to consider the future. What he had was fine, but he wanted more.

Clarissa had given her body sweetly, but now Brandon craved her soul, and nothing less would satisfy him. He wanted her wholly, completely and without reserve, now and tomorrow. He wanted from her what he was prepared to give in return.

Turning to the wardrobe, Brandon once more sought the small leather box containing the jewelry that had been worn by the women in his family as symbols of the love their men felt for them. Maybe it was time for the ring to once more adorn the finger of a beautiful woman, he mused, envisioning the sparkling heirloom on Clarissa's slender hand.

Ned was right; he couldn't remain silent forever. But he was penniless, and his pride insisted that it was too early to speak, though fear of losing Clarissa said otherwise. Yet Brandon had never been a man to act out of trepidation; he decided to compromise. Though he knew that he would offer the heirloom to Clarissa one day soon, he would wait a little longer. At the end of term, once the appointment to Dobson and Whittaker's chambers had been announced, he'd be in a position to offer Clarissa not only the ring, but also his heart and the promise of a bright future together.

Chapter Twelve

Friday afternoon, finally, thought Brandon gratefully as he headed to his rooms after yet another session with Humphrey. The end of the second grueling week of term, and what good did it do him? Humphrey'd just assigned two research papers to be completed by Wednesday! God, that man is an irascible ogre! Granted, he gave me the chance to prove myself, and I knew it would be hell satisfying his demands, but he delights in finding peculiarly esoteric points of law then grilling me on their significance. Unleashing his angry stride on the pavement, Brandon moved hurriedly toward his quarters, anxious for a bit of stolen relaxation—and Clarissa.

Someday you'll be thankful, admonished his argumentative lawyer's mind.

He's probably waiting to see if I come out with any more tripe like that examination paper, acknowledged Brandon with a grimace. Six weeks after the fact and I still can't believe I wrote that.

Maybe, argued his pedantic legal soul as he turned the last corner on his route homeward, if you're so overworked and exhausted, you should just finish out the term and be satisfied with a clerking position in some small country firm, like Preston suggested. At least then you'd have some time for yourself instead of running nonstop between classes, the library, Ned's tutoring sessions, Humphrey's tutorials and, of course, Clarissa.

Ah, that girl is worth every bit of it. He broke into a broad grin, suddenly anticipating their meeting this evening at Ned's rooms. By all rights, he should be paying Ned's rent, considering the amount of time he and Clarissa had spent in that locale of late. Shifting his books to the other arm, he opened the door and took the stairs at a run; he didn't have much time to wash up and get over there, but he didn't doubt she'd make it worth his while.

Not only was Clarissa Manning more spectacular to look at by the day, but she'd become so loving and gentle, he barely remembered the feisty child he'd first met. Her teasing eyes encouraged him when he was too exhausted to read another line, her hands massaged his spirit, and her heart beating so close to his when they made love reminded him of the wonder of life. She's right by my side whenever and wherever she can be, he marveled anew.

But doesn't that seem strange? wondered his legalistic side. What makes you so special?

"Not today," snapped the man within the scholar as he opened the door to his rooms. "I've enough critics without self-doubt. Oh, what's this?"

An envelope waited on the floor at his feet, an unusual occurrence; since he had no family left, it was rare he received any mail other than university notices. Maybe Clarissa couldn't get away tonight... but it wasn't her handwriting.

My dear Mr. Phillips—
It was with some concern that I learned of my sister-in-law's engaging a young law student to tutor my daughter. As you've surely discovered by now, my daughter has quite a penchant for mischief when left to her own devices.

Yes, thought Brandon with a chuckle, the man does indeed know his flesh and blood. Remembering how Clarissa had appeared for her lesson earlier in the week, attired in a split skirt and bloomers, insisting they could just as easily discuss Ptolemy on bicycles as in her aunt's morning room, he had to agree with her father. The girl had a decided knack for unexpectedly overturning one's best laid plans, though not necessarily with negative results. Even their relationship wasn't what he'd anticipated, but he certainly wouldn't complain! He turned back to the letter at hand.

I trust you will excuse the liberties I took in contacting Michael Humphrey, but we are old classmates and a father's protective instincts can't be ignored. At any rate, having received only glowing reports of your scholarship, dedication to learning and general decorum, I must commend you on a job well done. With such glowing commentaries on your success, young man, I can assure you that the internship with Dobson and Whittaker is yours, if you want it.

Mine? Who the hell does this American think he is? Just like that, because I'm tutoring his daughter, I've got the legal job of a lifetime? Brandon's incredulous eyes moved down the page to the signature. James Gregory Manning... James Gregory Manning... Manning?

"Lord, how could I have been so stupid? J.G. Manning's books are required reading for every first-year student, but I assumed the man was in his dotage," exclaimed a startled Brandon. "I mean, anyone who's written fourteen law books can't be young enough to be Clarissa's father! Oh, bloody damnation, what have I gotten myself into?" Feeling a complete jackass, he fell into a nearby chair and resumed reading the missive in his unsteady hands.

I know the two barristers quite well and am certain that a few words from me, along with your impeccable academic record would take care of your career. On the other hand, anyone capable of taming my troublesome offspring might be someone I'd like close at hand, so perhaps we could discuss a junior position at my law firm in Philadelphia. We'll confer about the matter when I return to London.

Until then I remain (not James the Great as I understand you young scalawags call me, but)

James Gregory Manning, Esquire.

The signature was firm and dramatic, written by a man who told the world what would happen next then watched it comply, mused Brandon with a frown, though he seems to have a sense of whimsy to refer so casually to his irreverent nick-name.

Damn it, who would believe I truly didn't know who Claris-sa's father was until today? That I never made the connection between a vivacious young redhead and the man I presumed to be an old codger.

But I'll wager Preston did. Realization suddenly dawned. This does explain why he suddenly took such an unusual inter-est in tutoring, and in Clarissa. Pacing the worn carpet, Bran-don tried futilely to absorb the impact of the letter.

Bloody hell, not only didn't I know I was teaching the daughter of one of the greatest legal minds in the world, but I challenged her ability to think, let alone learn. No wonder she thought me an utter boor. But why didn't she tell me who he was?

"Why should it matter who my father is?" That's what she'd say. And it's true; it wouldn't have affected my behavior, ra-tionalized the young man in midstride. I've done my best teaching her—

And bedding her, added that condemningly legalistic whis-per. *After all the times you ribbed Ned about breach-of-promise suits, you've compromised J.G. Manning's daugh-ter—and now he's offering you entry into the legal profession on a silver platter!*

Damnation, how can life get so complicated with the arrival of one little piece of paper? It doesn't really change anything. I've still got to earn a First at the end of term to get Hum-phrey's recommendation. His letter to Manning had to have been written before that cursed examination or the man would never have allowed me near his daughter.

But, whispered his persistent critic, *with the appointment to the Inns in your pocket if you keep Clarissa and her father happy, who gives a hoot about the Humph?*

No! I won't trade on her like that, he argued, waging a war of honor.

Then break it off—just till the end of term—and see if you can earn Dobson and Whittaker without the Mannings' help, challenged an overly noble conscience.

I can't hurt her like that, she'll think I was just using her to get to her father.

She knows you better than that.

The way I know her so well that I don't recognize her name? His mind a jumble of questions, his heart torn by the impulse to be honorable and his need for the woman he loved, Brandon tossed the letter on his desk and headed for Ned's hideaway. He was already late, but maybe something would come to him on the way... Damn! James Gregory Manning's daughter! It was like suddenly learning your barber was Delilah's son, an unquestioned expert, but could you be comfortable in his chair ever again?

Ten minutes of brisk walking in the cool evening air helped clear Brandon's mind, and he approached Derham Court in an optimistic mood. The young man had decided that since Clarissa's parentage hadn't posed a problem to date, there was no reason to expect trouble now. He'd simply finish out the term working his damnedest, loving his lady and earning his First with honors. No matter how difficult Humphrey tried to make it, with Clarissa's encouragement he could succeed, then they'd confront the future and the decisions that had to be made together.

Passing a flower cart, Brandon stopped impulsively and pulled a crumpled bill from his pocket. He'd never bought flowers for Clarissa, since Lavinia might have been suspicious, but in Ned's rooms, no prying eyes would question their presence.

"Here, whatever this will buy. I want something that smells as lovely as the lady."

"Ah, she's a lucky one, she is, with you caring so," said the old woman, grinning, quickly pocketing the money and thrusting two bouquets of violets at her unexpected customer.

"I'd like to think so," he answered with a chuckle, "but then I suppose I'm biased."

"Get on with you, lad. I wager with your looks you could have whoever you had a mind for, but don't keep her waiting," urged the flower seller. "The good ones get away too fast sometimes."

"Thank you, but I'm not about to let that happen." With a gallant bow, Brandon was off around the corner and up the front steps of number eleven, anxious to forget his day and enjoy his belated evening. He had just put his key in the lock when the door opened of its own accord and a green-clothed beauty was in his arms.

"When you weren't here when I arrived, I was afraid some-thing had happened to you," she chided softly, pulling his head down to hers and kissing him.

"Clarissa, the street—" Pleased as he was by her greeting, Brandon was still concerned with propriety. Trying to grace-fully accept her affection, extract his key from the lock and close the door before curious passersby witnessed Clarissa's enthusiastic welcome, he dropped the delicate bouquets he'd just purchased. Stepping back to retrieve them, his foot found the violets before he did, and suddenly their scent filled the hall as he inadvertently crushed their beauty underfoot, their ten-der message lost in the confusion.

"Now look what happened. Clarissa, I've told you before, it's dangerous enough to your reputation for you to be in this neighborhood, let alone flaunt yourself in the doorway for all the world to see."

"Flaunt myself?" Her voice echoed her surprise at his un-characteristic tone. "Brandon, I merely kissed you. It's not like I undressed in Piccadilly Circus, for Lord's sake."

"Even if you won't consider yourself, Clarissa, *I* worry about you. Granted, as you always tell me, you are an American, but if anyone were to see you here with me and start asking ques-tions..." His hand reached out and stroked her soft cheek, asking her understanding with this tactile gesture of affection. "I'd hate to cause you trouble when you're so good about helping me out of mine." He drew her into his arms, and his lips tenderly erased the lines of worry from her forehead as he murmured softly, regretting his sharpness.

So good, echoed Clarissa's conscience. You promised to tell him the truth about his troubles. When?

"You know I care less about my reputation than your ca-reer, Brandon, but we've been through all this before. Let's go upstairs," she urged, ending the conversation as she linked her arm through his and moved to the staircase. "I'm sorry about the flowers, but I brought us sandwiches, cheese, wine and some beautiful strawberries for dessert."

"Where did you—"

"Not to worry. I didn't raid Aunt Lavinia's pantry. I shopped for our dinner myself after I visited the dressmaker this afternoon. Then I kept it all hidden until it was time to leave tonight."

"And just where are you supposed to be?" he asked with a laugh as he opened the door to Ned's rooms.

"Right here in your arms," she answered with a giggle, closing out the rest of the world as she shut the door behind them and moved closer.

"You won't get any argument from me, but what about your aunt?"

"Oh, somehow she got the impression that Ned's taking us to the concert at St. Paul's this evening."

"You said Ned was going to church? Clarissa, white lies are one thing, but you're tempting a lightning bolt with that story. For as long as I've known him, Ned hasn't been inside a church except at Easter or Christmas, and that only on his father's threat of disinheritance."

"That's what's so very perfect about it; besides love, he's found religion this time. Priscilla is a lovely blonde whose father is the choirmaster—" Brandon's shout of laughter overrode her explanation as he sat and pulled Clarissa into his lap.

"I should know better than to doubt my two best pupils. When you have a willing accomplice like Ned, there's no stopping you."

"Now, don't be jealous. We can be alone this evening without a problem because of his romantic heart, and I, for one, am deeply appreciative of his talented help."

"Forget Ned. I'm more interested in your talents," responded Brandon gruffly, nuzzling her neck with his teasing lips, his hands already beginning to open her blouse.

Welcoming his attentions, Clarissa encouraged his advances as she nibbled gently on his left ear, her hands playing with the small hairs on the nape of his neck. In short order, passionate kisses had eased the earlier tension and their breathing was wonderfully constrained.

"Mmm, you're absolutely right," whispered the red-haired temptress, already enjoying the growing warmth in her feminine core. "Just don't start anything we won't have time to finish. Ned and Priscilla are joining us around nine for a late supper."

"Oh, Lord, and I didn't arrive until after eight. I'm sorry." Looking toward the small table by the fire, set with covered plates and wineglasses, he sighed. "I don't suppose we could just not answer the door when they knock?"

"No. Besides, Mr. Phillips, we've got grand things to celebrate." In a sudden burst of energy, Clarissa was out of Brandon's embrace and across the room, rummaging in her bag. "Father sent me the most wonderful letter today."

"Oh?" Brandon's tone was noncommittal as he saw his evening's pleasure evaporate before his eyes.

"He's thrilled with the job you're doing with me—my education, I mean. Aunt Lavinia wrote him, and anyway, he said you shouldn't worry about that internship you want. He's known old Mr. Dobson and Lord Whittaker forever, and he'll see that the position is yours if you want it. Or even better, you can come home to Philadelphia with us and he'll give you a job in his firm and..." Triumphantly extracting a rumpled envelope from the depths of her reticule, Clarissa waved the letter in the air and returned to sit on the arm of Brandon's chair. "There! You can read it yourself if you want. Anyway, now you don't have to worry about doing all those stupid assignments of Humphrey's that don't mean anything, and we—"

Ignoring the letter in her hands, Brandon turned to look Clarissa in the eyes.

"Why didn't you tell me you were James Gregory Manning's daughter?" His eyes were hard gray stones, his voice cool, the unwelcome subject no longer avoidable, but still a cause for heartfelt ambivalence.

"Well, I knew you weren't aware of it at first, but later on I thought..." Something was wrong; he was looking at her as if he'd never seen her before. He should be thrilled, not angry. "I just assumed since Preston said Father's books are mandated for study..."

"His law texts are, but his biography isn't." Ignoring the proffered envelope, Brandon shook his head. "As a matter of fact, no, I didn't have the slightest idea. Much to my chagrin, I never connected the woman I love with a giant of international law." Contrary to the habits of reticence long-instilled in his being, Brandon had revealed too much, but when hadn't she been able to manipulate him? Abruptly he got up from the chair to distance himself from the vixen who claimed his heart. Why hadn't he been still?

"What difference does it make who my father is? I don't understand." Hadn't he just said he loved her? Then why worry about anything else? She followed him to the window, and putting her small hand on his rough cheek, Clarissa turned his head from the world outside. "Darling, look at me and tell me why my father's identity should change anything."

"Clarissa, listen to what you're saying. Five minutes ago you told me your father could guarantee me the position with Dobson and Whittaker at the Inns if I wanted it, and now you don't see what difference it makes?" The troubled Englishman shook his head sadly as his lady remained silent. "I won't have anyone saying I got the appointment because of you—or your father. I've always stood on my own two feet and earned my way in the world, without help from anyone or anything, and I can't change that now. Don't ask me to."

Again she stroked his cheek with a gentling touch till he caught her hand in his and kissed it softly.

"Brandon, no one wants you to change, least of all me, but can't you be easier on yourself? If you weren't qualified to start with, Father wouldn't intervene on your behalf, but—with Humphrey withholding his recommendation until the end of term, J.G. Manning's word would go a long way. Can't you just say thank you and accept with grace? You know you're the best qualified for the position."

"I used to think so, and so did Humphrey until I wrote that damned fool senior preliminary. If it weren't for that examination, the internship would have been mine already...but there's no changing the past."

Instead you have six more weeks of hell, doing penance for something you didn't do in the first place. If it would make him accept her father's help, now was the time for the truth. Clarissa's eyes began to water as she realized she didn't really know how Brandon would react, but if he did love her... "Brandon—"

"Clarissa, I'm sorry if this hurts you, but I really can't let your father—"

"No, Brandon, listen to me, please." Placing a soft finger across his lips to hold back the flow of words, Clarissa took a deep breath and plunged ahead. "You didn't write that paper Humphrey is punishing you for . . . I did." There, she'd said it. Now, if only he would understand.

"What?" He couldn't have heard what he'd thought she'd said; it made no sense. Yet looking down at her suddenly white face and seeing her lips begin to tremble, Brandon felt vindicated for the first time in weeks. It hadn't been his work that had failed to please; it had been hers. Hers? He reached out and lifted her chin, forcing her to meet his questioning gaze. The words he spoke were a sharp command she dared not disobey. "Tell me."

"I . . . That morning you were drunk and you kissed me. I suddenly realized how much I cared about you and . . ."

"And so you decided to make me fail the examination so fair-haired Preston would earn the fellowship and you could take me home to Philadelphia as a souvenir of your stay in London?" His voice cut through her like a blade, scarring their delicate relationship.

"That wasn't it at all. I wanted you to pass with honors, but I couldn't wake you. I knew you'd be sent down if you didn't appear for the examination, so I wore your robes and no one noticed me. I thought I knew enough to answer the questions from researching for Father, but I never realized you'd be expected to defend the Crown's position. I suppose I just wrote from the American viewpoint, but not to hurt you. Never . . ." She faltered, unable to bear the look of anger in his face, the dark emptiness in his eyes, the stiffness of his stance. How could she make him understand? "Brandon, I love you. I would never—"

"Love? What do you even know about love? Years of working like a slave on my uncle's ships so I could finally settle his debts and finance my studies, and I was almost there. One more term and I would have done it, but because of your love, I'm out on my ass, or will be as soon as I—"

"No!" Her anguished cry stopped his movement toward the door. "Don't go to Humphrey. What difference would it make? He's already got you working ten times harder than any other student; you're paying for that paper a thousandfold, but at least this way, you'll earn your degree. I just thought since I endangered your career, Father's help—"

"Can't you understand?" In seconds, he was before her again, grabbing her shoulders and shaking her. "I don't want his help, and I certainly don't need any more of yours." Thrusting her limp form from him, a tormented Brandon turned to leave, betrayed by emotions he couldn't master.

"All right, hate me, but don't throw your life away because of my stupidity. I couldn't live with knowing I destroyed your chance at a career... That's what started all this."

"That's what started all this?" Brandon exploded in outrage. "Are you telling me that you slept with me out of sympathy?"

"Brandon, it's not—"

"Well, your virginity was a pretty high price to pay for your guilty conscience, don't you think, madam?" His scorn punctured her heart.

Tears coursed down her pale cheeks as she witnessed his painful fury. He was right to be outraged, but she hadn't meant any harm. Couldn't he see that she felt his suffering as deeply as he? "Brandon, please don't go. I'll—"

"You'll what? Help me research the new topics Humphrey dumped on me today? Forget it—and forget me, Clarissa. I won't have time for you, and you'd better tell your father the same thing. Brandon Phillips will get that fellowship all right, but it will be in spite of the Mannings, not because of them."

The door slammed hard behind him, and she could hear his angry tread on the stair. In the distance another door reverberated against its frame as she sank to the floor in tears. Tonight should have been so perfect... now she wasn't even certain she wanted to see tomorrow.

By the time Brandon made his way to his rooms the next morning, the sky behind Big Ben was no longer inky black. He'd wandered the city for hours, keeping pace with the Thames, arguing before the Houses of Parliament, detouring past the Cooper house on his way to the Inns of Court, but the stone buildings were frustratingly silent, unable or unwilling to see his anger.

He kept telling himself he should be happy. He hadn't failed. Yet if he explained the situation to Humphrey, he'd be sent down. Clarissa was right about the need to keep silent. Confession might be good for the soul, but it would castrate his career in one easy swoop as easily as she had destroyed his love. Much as he hated to live a lie, it was the only way to salvage his future; he had to continue his academic probation, satisfying every problem Humphrey threw his way and proving Brandon Phillips was up to any challenge. At least, his conscience acknowledged, he'd be more than earning his sheepskin, and he hoped the coveted position with Dobson and Whittaker would follow.

As he opened the door to his building, Brandon felt his pulse begin to race again at the thought of the temptation Clarissa offered. How dare those cheeky Americans presume to influence British traditions? Had they no scruples? Climbing the stairs softly, avoiding the squeaky tread on the fourth step, he admitted to himself that he already knew Clarissa didn't, and it would appear her father was of the same ilk. Damn them both; he'd rather see Waverly-Smythe get the fellowship than accept their help!

Moving into his rooms without bothering to turn up the lamp, Brandon tripped over the outstretched legs protruding from his armchair in the darkness and found himself face down in the worn carpet, spewing anger at his uninvited visitor.

"What the hell is wrong with you? Haven't you done enough to destroy my career without sneaking in here behind my back? I told you I wanted nothing more to do with you and I meant it!" Bone weary with fatigue and grief, Brandon had expended his remaining patience. As he got up from the floor, he stormed to the door and, holding it ajar, he continued to bellow. "Damn it, go home to your aunt, and leave me in peace!"

When the figure in his chair didn't move, an exasperated Brandon turned up the lamp, but instead of finding Clarissa, huddled and apologetic, as he'd expected, a heavy-eyed Ned blinked at the sudden glare of the gaslight.

"And just where have you been, Mr. Phillips? Or should I ask with whom? You abandon an angel like Clarissa then tramp around the streets looking for pleasure? I'd thought more of you," chided the young man, standing and stretching in an attempt to shake the kinks out of his body.

"For God's sake, is sex the only thing you ever think about, or are you standing guard over the fair Priscilla ensconced in my bed since Clarissa took yours? Damn it, I've had enough tonight. What in bloody blazes are you doing here, Ned? Nobody named you my guardian."

Had Ned come out of friendship or the need to censure? While he couldn't be certain, Brandon knew he was in no mood for either. "Why don't you just collect your newest lady friend from the bedroom and leave me to my work? It's going to be a long weekend and I'm not up to conversation."

Dismissal was evident in his tone, but with the long practice of friendship, Ned ignored the implicit warning, going to the door but only to close it before he spoke.

"I don't expect you to become engaged in a conversation, Brandon, but you damned well better listen for a change. In the first place, you needn't worry about your precious reputation as a gentleman—I wouldn't sully it by bringing a woman to your rooms, though given your behavior tonight, your civilized image is questionable indeed. Not that you seem particularly concerned, but I saw Priscilla and Clarissa safely home hours ago." Still getting no response, be it thanks or a curse, Ned shook his head in bewilderment; the unemotional statue before him was not his friend.

"Brandon, what the hell is wrong with you? For all you seem to care, Clarissa could have been attacked and killed on her way to her aunt's and you wouldn't shed a tear. Damn it, that girl has spent entire days of her life, not to mention nights, taking care of your needs, be they research, text transcription or physical companionship, and you just walked out and left her distraught, all because her father offered to help establish you as a barrister? I mean, I've heard of prime jackasses in my time, but—"

A heavy fist struck the wooden desk across the room, leaving Ned in no doubt as to what Brandon would have preferred to smash.

"Leave it alone, Ned. You don't know the half of it, and I'm not about to explain." He spoke quietly, but the words warned of violence should the topic be pursued.

"What I know is that you're both my friends and I can't understand your behavior," snapped the youngest Newcomb, playing on the privilege of friend. "I've listened to you condemn my romantic dalliances time and time again, but in every case, my ladies and I were mutually interested only in having a good time. I suspect that's not true of you and Clarissa. Brandon, she cares for you deeply. Can you just ignore that and walk out of her life?"

"If I'm lucky," retorted the anguished scholar, knowing full well all the hours he'd spent traipsing through London hadn't erased her haunting eyes from his memory. Perhaps nothing would, but he damn well couldn't go to her and thank her for failing the senior preliminaries for him. And he certainly couldn't compromise either of them by explaining the situation to Ned . . . unless she already had.

"And what bloody sob story did Miss Manning dish up, anyway?"

"Not much of anything," Ned answered grimly, at a loss to comprehend Brandon's peculiar behavior. "I was afraid you'd been detained and someone had broken in and attacked her, she was crying so. I was about to fetch a constable when Priscilla calmed her down enough to understand what the girl was saying."

"And that was?"

"I told you, nothing. Only that her father is *the* J.G. Manning and that you were furious at her father's offer to help your career. Why did you storm off? I mean, for heaven's sake, Brandon, if you permit my father to write you a letter of recommendation, what's wrong with J.G. Manning doing so?"

"It's not the same thing at all," snarled the cornered male, rage sparking in his eyes at the need to defend himself when it was Clarissa who had been wrong.

"Because you've bedded his daughter? Why should that enter into it? She's a student of yours just as I am, and her father, like mine, is grateful for the scholastic assistance you've given his offspring. What you and Clarissa do on your time has nothing to do with her old man. Period, end of discussion, no personal obligation engendered."

"You're damned right there's no personal obligation because I'm finished with that whole damned family, the crazy aunt, the seductive daughter and the absentee father. Let them find themselves another tutor—I quit!''

''Brandon, you can't.''

''Watch me. I'm supposed to show up Monday at ten; instead I'll be at the library working on Humphrey's papers.''

''Look, if you won't reconsider because of Clarissa, think of yourself,'' implored a quick-thinking Ned, believing the two would settle their differences once he got them together. ''After all, the Humph recommended you for that position. If you just leave without giving notice, don't you think he'd hear about it? Given that examination of yours, I doubt you need another strike against your character.''

''All right . . . I'll give a week's notice, but that's my limit. And, Ned, I swear, if you mention her name to me once more, you'll be seeking a new tutor, as well. Now get the hell out of here and let me get some rest.''

Knowing when he was ahead, Ned gave a mock salute and departed quietly, pleased that at least they'd be seeing one another on Monday. By then, he hoped the pair of them would have cooled down enough to make sense of the situation. He bloody well couldn't.

Chapter Thirteen

By two o'clock that afternoon, Lavinia was concerned. Her niece hadn't appeared for either breakfast or luncheon, and when Ellen took her a tray, Clarissa had said she felt too ill to eat. The night before, Lavinia hadn't thought much about it when her niece had just picked at dinner before departing for the concert at St. Paul's, but now... James Gregory would never forgive her if she neglected his daughter's health! The Horticultural Society and Geoffrey had been taking up a lot of her time, she reflected. Perhaps too much; maybe the girl needed a bit of extra attention.

Deciding to look in on Clarissa, Lavinia climbed the stairs with a purposeful tread. The bedroom door was shut tightly, but a brief tap on the frame and Lavinia swept across the threshold, stopping in surprise at the dimness of the normally bright boudoir.

"Clarissa, why on earth are the curtains drawn? The sun is lovely today, and its cheery warmth would do you a world of good. Let's admit a little light; I promise you, dear, you'll feel better for it." Moving quickly to the bay window, Lavinia pulled the drapes and opened the glass ever so slightly. "Just a touch of fresh air to clear your mind. You'd be amazed at how sunshine and nature can heal. But now, tell me what's wrong."

As she saw her niece in the afternoon sunlight, the older woman was amazed at how poorly the child looked. She was still in her nightclothes, her hair atumble, her cheeks drawn and ashen while deep circles had appeared below her usually happy eyes. Yet Lavinia felt the most worrisome symptom of the girl's malaise was her singular lack of spirit. Never before had Clarissa been so quiet and unresponsive.

"Clarissa, is your stomach upset? Did you eat something untoward? Perhaps if you had a healthy dish of Grape Nuts—"

"No, Aunt, really, it's nothing. I—I'm afraid I didn't sleep very well last night, and I'm quite fatigued. That's all," said the young American listlessly. She knew she should distract her guardian from prying further, but she didn't really have the energy or the desire to send her away. At least Lavinia cared what happened to her.

"Do you suppose you're feverish? Perhaps I should have Ellen fetch the doctor?" Lavinia's fluttering hand stroked the girl's forehead, but felt no unusual heat. "Did you overtax yourself working with Mr. Phillips yesterday?"

"No, I don't believe so. We did no more than usual." Actually, we did much less, Clarissa thought with regret. For the first time in six weeks, she hadn't spent at least part of the night in Brandon's embrace and the rest sleeping blissfully. Yet after their bitter exchange last evening, it had been all she could do to get to her aunt's house, let alone go to sleep. Of course, explaining that was out of the question.

"Then I think the doctor should see you. I'm certain he'll be able to give you a tonic that will perk you up in no time." Her niece's eyes did look red, perhaps from too much reading. However, Lavinia still felt most alarmed by their peculiar lack of sparkle. It was as though Clarissa's inner light had been extinguished, and she was at a loss as to how to rekindle the fire.

"No, Aunt Lavinia, please. It's nothing more serious than a tiresome nightmare that seemed to recur everytime I dared close my eyes." But Brandon's reaction to her deception was no dream that would evaporate with the dawn. She had thoughtlessly endangered his career, and for that, he'd never forgive her.

"Oh, bad dreams, well, why didn't you say so in the first place?" Seating herself on the bed beside Clarissa, Lavinia smiled and patted the girl's hand reassuringly. "I used to be troubled by those until I decided the best antidote was to dress up, look my best and go out of my way to make my life a great deal more interesting than some nightborne chimera.

What sort of nonsense kept you awake, dear? I remember your mother always dreamed wild dogs were chasing her, and she'd climb into my bed to hide. You could have done the same thing, you know.''

Lavinia was not her first choice for a comforting bedmate, reflected Clarissa, a small smile flickering across her face as she envisioned her aunt's reaction had she bounded in on her with the story of Brandon's rejection. While her life at the moment was truly a nightmare, it was one she'd have to deal with alone. If Brandon didn't want her, then she certainly wouldn't have him around, either—and Lavinia had just provided the best means to that desirable end.

''Maybe you're right. Perhaps I have been overdoing my studies, Aunt. Everytime I tried to close my eyes last night, Brandon Phillips was standing over me, screaming and shaking me...''

''Shaking you? Why, I never would have thought that such a nice young man...'' Lavinia hesitated. After all, what did they know of him aside from Geoffrey's recommendations? ''But that never really happened?''

''No, of course not,'' lied Clarissa anxiously, admitting to herself that she deserved far more than a shaking. ''But he was so frighteningly angry, calling me dreadful names and saying I didn't deserve to learn.''

''I never! And he seemed so well-mannered,'' blithered the startled Miss Cooper. ''You know, Clarissa, some of the ladies in the Horticultural Society believe our dreams are really trying to tell us a truth we won't recognize when we're awake. I wonder... But I'd thought you two were getting along so much better, sharing your work and his research as you are.''

''So did I. However that's not the case,'' said Clarissa, but as she realized her error, she continued, ''at least not in my dreams. Though frankly, after last night, I'd rather discontinue my lessons and face Father's disappointment than have another session with Mr. Phillips. Perhaps your friends are right and I've sensed a side of him we haven't seen before.'' There, she'd said it; if only her aunt was receptive. But as Clarissa held her breath waiting for the answer, a knock at the door interrupted them.

"Excuse me, ma'am," began Ellen, "but there's a gentleman downstairs to see Miss Clarissa."

"I do not want to see Mr. Phillips today; send him away, Ellen," interjected Clarissa hotly. "This is Saturday and I don't intend to spend it studying."

"Yes, miss, but it's not Mr. Phillips. Your caller is Mr. Waverly-Smythe."

Disappointment cut through her unexpectedly as Clarissa swallowed quickly, blinking back unbidden tears when she heard her hopes crushed. Not that she would have agreed to see Brandon, but the pleasure of turning him away was now forfeit.

"Oh, isn't that lovely, dear? Ellen, please tell the young man that my niece will be with him shortly," instructed Lavinia as she moved toward the wardrobe on the far wall, thankful that the issue of terminating Mr. Phillips' employment could be postponed until her niece was herself again. After all, James Gregory would be returning shortly. Let him handle it; she had enough on her mind.

"Come along now, Clarissa, get out of that bed. It's a lovely afternoon for a stroll in the park to empty your head of those nasty dreams. And when you return, Cook will have a tea prepared for us to enjoy," she coaxed.

"I—I don't think I feel up to a walk," Clarissa protested halfheartedly, still wishing the visitor had been an apologetic Brandon.

"All right then, I'll have the carriage brought around and Preston can accompany you for a ride in the sunshine. You'll feel much better, I venture to say."

"I just wish it were that simple," muttered the redhead, throwing the covers off and joining her aunt before the wardrobe.

"What did you say?"

"I just want to wear something simple, Aunt, no frills or lace. I haven't the patience for style today."

"Very well, dear, you know what suits you best, except of course for that hair, though it is growing a bit. I'll leave you to your toilet, and I'll entertain Mr. Waverly-Smythe. You needn't rush." Feeling quite pleased with what she saw as her manipulation of Clarissa, Lavinia headed for another target. She was certain a few quiet words with Preston would produce a relaxing afternoon for the young people, something that would restore Clarissa's spirits in no time.

The sun was so brilliant Clarissa was thankful for her hat as she descended the steps to the waiting carriage. With Preston's thoughtful hand to guide her, she was soon seated against the soft cushions, feeling more relaxed than she'd imagined possible. Perhaps Aunt Lavinia's method of banishing nightmares had some merit after all, she thought, bestowing a beatific smile on her escort.

"Drive us through Regent's Park, no hurry about it," said Preston to the coachman as he entered the cab, choosing to sit next to his lovely charge rather than opposite her. Sensing Clarissa's surprise at his choice of seat, he viewed her suddenly downcast eyes and reached for a gloved hand, bringing it ceremoniously to his lips.

"It does my heart good to escape the dreary world and spend the afternoon with you," he confided, releasing her hand and settling his body more firmly next to hers. Just because he'd agreed to friendship rather than romance was no reason not to remind her of the joy she could find in his physical closeness. "Believe me, you're much more desirable company than stodgy old Blackstone," he said, referring to one of the mainstays of British law.

If only Brandon thought so, Clarissa wished, but catching herself, she determined to put him out of her mind. If he wouldn't trust her and try to understand why she'd taken that examination in his stead, he certainly couldn't love her, no matter what he said. And Preston was a dear friend who asked nothing in return except the chance to be near her. Turning to face him, she rewarded him with a smile.

"I should certainly hope so, sir, especially since the man's been dead for at least a century."

"Ah, yes, I'd forgotten you were familiar with legal references."

"And a few illegal ones, I venture to say." It was refreshing to exchange pleasantries without the emotional upheaval that so often accompanied those with Brandon.

"Miss Manning! I can see you need some instruction on the avoidance of voluntary confessions," said Preston with a forced chuckle as he recalled her late arrival at Brandon's rooms weeks ago. Though he'd kept a watch, he'd never seen her there with Phillips after that. "Hasn't your tutor explained the dangers of self-incrimination?"

"All too well, I'm afraid." Suddenly the girl's smile evaporated, her lovely forehead furrowed with worry, and her upper lip began to twitch ever so slightly.

Apparently there was a guilty secret here all right, decided Preston; maybe they'd been meeting somewhere else? Was this the illegality on her mind, and if so, could he get her to confide in him?

"And what could such a beautiful young lady as yourself need to hide? Don't tell me you snitched an extra pastry at tea when your aunt wasn't looking?" His tone was humorous, yet his eyes coldly calculated her response as he reached over and solicitously soothed her brow. "Why do I sense your tutor plays a significant role in making you so unhappy?"

"That's all Brandon Phillips is, Preston, a tutor—a hired hand whose job is my education and a bit of chaperoning. I think if it weren't for my age, Aunt Lavinia would have been happier hiring a nanny, but he serves the same purpose and she pays him well for his services. We both know he's willing to do just about anything for a copper." Why didn't it make her feel any better to think of Brandon in monetary terms? Maybe, said her heart, because you don't believe it for a minute.

"I hesitate to speak against a classmate . . ."

"But?"

"But I did warn you that his interest in you was totally self-serving, you know. I'm certain your father's reputation drew him to the job more than the salary, just as Ned's father is undoubtedly the key motivation in Phillips' working with that lad. Not that he can help his upbringing, of course. After all, tutoring isn't necessarily selling one's soul, especially if one's charge is as lovely as you, and if the tutor isn't seeking professional favoritism as well as financial remuneration."

Silence greeted his words, and when Preston looked at Clarissa, she was swallowing hard and making a point of staring busily out of the carriage window, her hands restlessly toying with her gloves. Better for him to remain quiet and let her deal with her doubts, he decided.

Clarissa had no doubts, however. Preston had read the situation incorrectly, but she was not about to tell him. Instead she urged with a sudden passion, "Let's just enjoy the afternoon and forget our studies and those involved in them. I've always wanted to see the zoo in the park," she continued in a confidential tone, "but Aunt Lavinia isn't very fond of animals. Preston, do you suppose . . . ?"

"Of course, if that's what you wish." Somehow, he'd lost the moment, but there'd be others when she needed a friend, especially if he took care to stay amenable. "Driver, the zoo, please. At least there, unlike our world, the animals are all in cages, my dear, and none of them can harm you. I hope the antics of the monkeys will make you laugh a bit."

"Let's hope so; I've had enough of gloom," answered his companion truthfully. "I feel as though I've been under an awfully dark cloud lately."

"Then we'll just chase it away, I promise," replied Preston, congratulating himself on the fact that J.G. Manning's distrait daughter was allowing him to comfort her. And what would it cost him? He was prepared to spend the afternoon in childish pleasure since his evening promised more adult satisfaction.

"I told you to wash yer face, Beatrice," the small brunette scolded her friend as they walked along London's Wych Street in the fading evening light. "*He* only takes 'em clean, and you've a streak of grime on yer cheek the width of Regent Street."

"Well, la-di-da," grumbled the petite blonde who'd spent most of her life in back alleys and on unfashionable thoroughfares. "Most men of my acquaintance like a woman in her natural state, and believe me, I've known a good many of them," she added with a shriek of laughter.

"Oh, do subdue yourself and try to act grand, won't you?" the brunette pleaded. "I tell you this one is different. He likes 'em scrubbed and he likes 'em young. And for God's sake, if whelping that brat of yours has left any marks on yer belly, try and hide 'em. Otherwise, Mr. Walker will take his look and send us away without a farthing."

"But what about if he likes what he sees, Alice? What then?"

"That depends on his mood," Alice admitted, her eyes clouding with concern, "but it's never been so bad that I wouldn't come back when I need money. And listen here, it's important to remember we're not more than fifteen."

"Fifteen! Cor! I ain't seen fifteen in a good five years. Still, I suppose we're both tiny enough to get away with it. Though if this gent wants London street girls who've never been in the family way, he'd best start looking for 'em younger than that. Why, I was fourteen when I had my Evelyn."

"Just play the part, Beatrice," the exasperated brunette ordered, "or we'll find we have nothing for our troubles at the end of the night. He don't want girls with babies."

"Just what is our part, then?" demanded a petulant Beatrice. "This bloke don't think he's getting a virgin, does he?"

"No . . . he just likes those who look innocent but who know enough to act the whore. Besides, what he's interested in mostly is taking our photographs."

"Photographs? What sort of photographs?" the blonde asked skeptically. "He's not some sort of crazy, is he?"

"No." Alice sniffed. "They're *art* pictures . . . and classical art, too. That's why we have to take off our clothes, he says, so that we look like woodland spirits. Last time I was there—" she giggled "—I wore nothing but a wreath of flowers in my hair. I was an ancient Roman slave girl, holding a huge platter of fruit, with my bosoms resting among the grapes and oranges. This man's fancy is without limit, I tell you."

"What does he get out of this, then, if all he does is pose us? Can't he make use of what nature gave him?"

"Don't you worry none about him. He sells the pictures to some private dealer on Holywell Street, so he makes a pretty pence. And that ain't all. After the modeling session, that's when we pleasure and amuse him. And if you think his imagination is unusual when it comes to photograph taking, it's nothing compared to later on. Take my word for it."

"Yeah, well, that sort of thing I don't mind, long as a fellow keeps a bottle of gin handy. My old man, Freddie, may suspect how I help support us, but he don't know for sure. Lord! Posing for pictures to be sold on Holywell Street! That would give him plenty of evidence, and if my mister ever gets wind of that . . ."

"Oh, come on, Beatrice, how would he know? He certainly couldn't afford to squander money on such things."

"Not when he has the real thing warming his bed."

"Then there's no harm in it, and plenty of money to be made."

"Yeah, I suppose you're right," the blonde conceded as they arrived at their destination in a back alley and Alice knocked timidly on a door. "And you know, if there's really a few quid to be had, I'll mention it to Freddie's sister. She's nearly thirteen and a real looker. Course, I'll take half of what she makes for finding her work."

"Just be careful involving Annie," Alice cautioned. "She's young yet, and while you and I know how to handle a man of this sort . . ."

At that moment, the door swung open, inhibiting the brunette from finishing what she had to say.

"Well, hello, Alice. It's good to see you," said Preston Waverly-Smythe, his salacious tone making innocent words seem perverse. After quickly assessing the small blonde standing behind his regular and finding her satisfactory, he went on smoothly, "And look, you've brought along a little friend. But where are my manners, to keep two young things like you standing out on the pavement? Come on in, girls, you can *play* in here."

"Monday morning," Clarissa whispered, though she needn't have bothered to remind herself of the day. Over the weekend, she could pretend that by the time their usual tutoring session came around, Brandon would have gotten over his upset, appear as usual, and they could start again with no secrets between them. Today, however, was the day of reckoning, and her listless brown eyes and pouting lips gave evidence that she held little hope that the man who had brought her to womanhood would materialize.

The clock on the mantel ticked away. Each swing of the pendulum increased her certainty that she would spend the morning alone, so that seconds before Brandon's scheduled arrival, Clarissa found she had deserted the settee and was pacing back and forth and whispering fiercely to herself, "I don't *want* him here this morning, anyway! I *don't*! I *really* don't!''

She whirled with a start as the door opened softly. But it was only a reticent Ellen who stood beneath the lintel.

''Mr. Phillips is here, miss,'' she announced in a hushed voice, though to Clarissa it had all the ominous ring of a thunderclap. ''And I think I should say, miss,'' she added in a whisper, ''that the gentleman seems quite put out about something. I've never seen a man so arrogant.''

Arrogant and put out, was he? Not at all the lover coming to make amends? Obviously *he* hadn't suffered the way she had since Friday evening. True, her actions had caused this altercation originally, but Brandon was no less to blame. *He* was the one who was drunk on the day of the examination, and *he* was the one who should have forgiven her if he really loved her. Clarissa's already flaring temper increased. Though she had wished him near at least a hundred times in the last two days, wanting to kiss him one moment and slap him the next, Clarissa decided that she had no reason to put up with his foul humor and insufferable male superiority. Why had he come to her aunt's house this morning anyway, to count her teardrops and notch them on his belt?

''Tell Mr. Phillips I have no wish to see him this morning,'' Clarissa directed in a terse voice, fierce pride entreating her to push away the remembered sensations of Brandon's demanding lips upon hers, the recollections of the security she felt lying in his arms, and the physical anticipation she was experiencing even now, knowing that he was only a few feet outside the door. But her heart was still too tender and bruised to permit Mr. Brandon Phillips the liberty of trampling all over it again so soon. ''Tell him he'll have to come back at another time,'' she directed Ellen.

''I'll do that, miss,'' replied the maid as she edged over the threshold, dreading the thought of having to be the one to deny access to the commanding male waiting in the hallway.

''That won't be necessary, Ellen,'' said a stormy voice that entered the room before the man. ''Miss Manning *will* see me. She has no choice.'' With that, Brandon was in the morning room and shutting the door, leaving a flustered Ellen to run to

Cook with the news that the young ones had indeed engaged in some tiff.

Brandon had closed the door to signal a desire for privacy and not expected intimacy; to make his point clear, he maintained a distance between himself and the traitorous beauty who glared at him without speaking. In the heavy silence of the room, he couldn't help but appraise her coldly in return. There was that sunrise cast to her hair that had warmed his blood since he had first set eyes on her, and the porcelain smoothness of her skin, which glowed with the vigor of youth. The willowy bend of her body and the seductive curve of her full lips began to lure him into doubting his decision, but then his gaze fell upon the defiant gleam in her eye, breaking the enchantment.

No, he assured himself, as he concentrated on the stubborn set of her chin, he could not forgive this thoughtless girl for what she had done to him. Yet, as obsessed as Brandon had been with his situation these past few days, the fact that Clarissa had been afraid to tell him about the examination had never entered his mind, nor did the possibility that she had always intended to inform him later on. He saw her actions only in terms of manipulating betrayal, and the idea that she could do this to him, when he cared for her so deeply, wounded him as he had never been hurt before. His torment had been constant since Friday night, so that his heart, which had just begun to open after so many years, constricted once more.

Clarissa perceived Brandon's frosty attitude. Its icy gust left her breathless and shivering so that she almost gasped before she broke the stillness, her heated words intended to melt the frigid stance of this man who was not her Brandon, but the frightening Mr. Phillips to whom she had been introduced on Friday last.

"I'm afraid a tutoring session is impossible," she said curtly as she watched intently for his reaction.

"Suit yourself," he replied, no trace of disappointment evident in his tone. "It's of no consequence to me. I'm here because I had given my word to be here."

"Oh, Brandon!" Clarissa cried, frustration and anger growing at his continued reserve while she had never been more on edge. The memories of their argument came rushing back to overwhelm her. "How could you even think of walking in here as though we had never loved, as though we had never quarreled, and think you could pick up tutoring where we left off?"

"Actually, I didn't anticipate doing any such thing, nor do I want to," came the stony reply, accentuated by the cold expression on his handsome features. "I came by only because I had promised your aunt . . ."

"My aunt!" Clarissa yelled, her outrage overcoming any vestige of remorse she might have. "In that case, we've nothing more to say to one another today."

"Or perhaps ever again," he replied, his deep, sure voice hiding the struggle that was even now being waged between his pride and the passion that this girl, this woman, awoke in him so effortlessly. How tempting it would be to take her in his arms once more, to feel the taste of her lips upon his as his traitorous body was demanding. But with long-standing training, logic overcame desire, and he remained where he was.

"That would make it difficult for you to remain my tutor, wouldn't it?" Clarissa retorted. Straightening her back, she continued. "I think it best to terminate that relationship, as well."

Clarissa moved about the room, carefully keeping her eyes averted from this good-looking man, waiting for the word or gesture that would reject the finality of the statement she had just made.

But none came. Never had she experienced a more devastating silence. It could only be explained by his continued obstinate refusal to attempt an understanding of why she had sat for his damned examination. He didn't love her, could never have cared for her at all. Damn him and double damn him! Why didn't he say something?

Her words still ringing in his ears, Brandon's rage prohibited his speaking. So now she was dismissing him, was she? Leave it to Miss Clarissa Manning to assume the manner of a grand lady, sacking him as though he had never been anything other than an employee, and stealing the thunder from his intended resignation. She was nothing more than an impudent American who put on more aristocratic airs than any English countess he'd ever met. This time, however, he was not going to allow her to get away with it.

"I'm glad you feel that way, Miss Manning," Brandon said at last, his voice firm and sure, yet soft of tone. "It makes it easier to tender my week's notice."

"Your week's notice? Why bother?" Clarissa retorted as her anxiety gave way to pride. "We can end our relationship as of now."

"If your aunt is agreeable, that suits me," Brandon replied, his eyes as dark as storm clouds and his voice becoming strident as he moved to the doorway. "But as far as I'm concerned, the relationship, as you so endearingly term it, ended last Friday."

"Why is that," Clarissa yelled "because you had what you wanted by then, both me and my father's offer of assistance?"

"No," said Brandon from the doorway, bitterness shaping his words, "because I finally understood how much you were costing me."

In the next instant, he was gone, leaving a distraught Clarissa to sample the acrid taste of a love gone wrong.

Brandon was like a man possessed as he moved rapidly to put Hertford Court *and* Clarissa behind him. Stomping along the pavement, oblivious to all, the young law student cursed Clarissa, her father and his good friend Ned. But most of all, Brandon Phillips cursed himself and his lingering attraction to a pair of deep brown eyes.

Chapter Fourteen

It was after a fortnight of Clarissa's doldrums that Lavinia found herself sighing as she leaned her head against Lord Geoffrey's ample, heaving chest.

"Oh, dearest," she mourned, "who knows when we'll have the chance to be together again?"

"Now, now, kitten," he consoled with an indulgent smile, "there's no need to worry. Haven't we always made our own opportunities?"

"Yes," she said, smiling wanly, "but you must admit these past two weeks since Brandon Phillips resigned, I've been able to sneak away only sporadically."

Lifting her hand to his lips, Geoffrey kissed Lavinia's fingertips. "But we've appreciated each other all the more, haven't we?"

"You're so understanding; I couldn't ask for a better man. But how patient will you be once my brother-in-law arrives tomorrow? There will be even less time for me to call my own, and lovely afternoons such as this may become a thing of the past."

"But how long could he stay before he and his daughter go home?" the earl asked in nonchalant tones that belied the rising anxiety he was beginning to experience.

"Probably at least a fortnight. James Gregory has written that there are some acquaintances he wishes to renew here in London."

"Two weeks, that's not all that bad," Ned's father bluffed before an idea entered his head and he proceeded to voice it optimistically. "Besides, once he's in town, surely he'll take charge of Clarissa and we'll be free to go on as we did before the American invasion."

"I'm afraid not," Lavinia said quietly, feeling very much like one of Ouida's heroines as she and Geoffrey sat in his drawing room, their clothing in disarray while they discussed the obstacles that blocked the culmination of their passion. "James is a wonderful man, but he's a busy one, as well. Two weeks could turn to three, and then four. And while he loves his daughter without question, I fear he will become immersed in his work with very little thought for her, until he emerges later, full of guilt and remorse only to pamper the girl terribly. I am sorry to say that it has been his habit to alternately ignore and then indulge Clarissa. That's why the dear child, as loving as she is, was so spoiled and willful when I first took her under my wing."

"And an admirable job you've done with her. Why, even my Ned is quite taken with her," Geoffrey assured Lavinia before placing a moist kiss on her wrinkled brow.

"With a great deal of help from Brandon Phillips...at least initially," she responded with ladylike modesty. "But now that he's decided to return to his books, Clarissa has become a problem all over again, though of a different sort."

"How's that, sweeting?"

"You know how headstrong and independent she was before Brandon took her in hand. Well, since he gave notice, my niece has been quite a different girl. She's moody, picks at her food, and is altogether much too listless and compliant to the wishes of others."

"I'd think that would make her easier to handle," the earl commented in confusion.

"Not at all, dear," Lavinia replied, patting his hand. "But then, though you've seven daughters of your own, I can't expect a man such as yourself to understand what it takes to raise a young girl properly. This new Clarissa needs much more care and attention. I don't know what James will think of me and my efforts when he sees the change in her," she lamented.

"If the girl misses her studies, then get her another tutor to keep her occupied. That way we can see both father and daughter safely busy," Geoffrey suggested with a facetious leer.

Lavinia blushed and giggled like a schoolgirl at her lover's actions, but all his good intentions couldn't solve her dilemma. "Now, Geoffrey, what kind of doddering old woman do you take me for? Don't you think that I would grasp at any possible solution to see us together as often as possible? I had only one other applicant for the position of tutor, and it was yesterday, as a matter of fact, that I made arrangements to engage him."

"Then what is the problem?" Lord Geoffrey asked, trailing his fingers along the back of Lavinia's neck as she snuggled closer.

"I think I've told you that I suspect Waverly-Smythe is attracted to Clarissa, and I just can't go off and leave him alone with her. It wouldn't be prudent."

"You did with Phillips." The earl sulked, seeing no resolution to his impending abstinence.

"I didn't have to worry with Brandon. Clarissa detested him at first, and then Ned was always around to chaperone. But come, let's not allow the bleakness of the next few weeks to mar our last few hours together," Lavinia invited, moving her lips closer to the clean-shaven face beside her. "James might be arriving tomorrow, but if we can put him from our minds, there will be nothing left to interrupt us."

"All right," Geoffrey conceded, allowing himself to be cajoled out of his doldrums. He brought his mouth down upon Lavinia's with all the passion he could muster. He didn't want her to forget during the coming days that she had every reason to come running back to him as soon as she could.

As always, Lavinia's response was exquisite, and he was just beginning to remove her clothing when the door to the drawing room flew open, and his hellion of a son came charging into the room.

"Ned! What's the meaning of this?" the earl roared as he and Lavinia disentangled themselves.

"Father, I need your advice," Ned began hurriedly, his brow puckered in consternation until it dawned on him exactly what it was he had interrupted.

For the first time he could remember, Edward Lowell Newcomb stood completely abashed. His father and Clarissa's aunt?

"This had better be important, Ned, for you to come barging in here unannounced," the earl growled while Lavinia demurely turned her back and began fastening the tiny pearl buttons of her fawn blouse. "Miss Cooper and I were discussing the Horticultural Society's next project."

"Oh," the young man replied, the only response he could think of while he worked to collect himself. "Well, that...that sounds very important," he stammered as he began to back toward the door and escape. "Much more important than..."

"Do you think we could possibly deal with your problem at another time?" his father asked quietly, annoyance spread all over his face like jam on a scone.

"Yes, sir." Ned swallowed, inching toward retreat. "I'll see you at our regular weekly dinner."

The embarrassed student had just turned to escape when the earl's stentorian voice stopped him.

"Where are your manners, boy? Bid Miss Cooper goodbye."

So the old boy wanted to play the game as though nothing had happened, Ned realized with admiration. His father was more the bon vivant than he had thought. But if that was the way he wanted it, Ned was only too willing to oblige.

"It was nice to see you, Miss Cooper," the young man began obediently until Lavinia's sudden and furious blush caused him to realize just how his words could be interpreted. "That is to say," he continued in a deep and sober voice meant to remove all doubts concerning his previous comment, "good day, Miss Cooper. Please give my regards to Miss Manning."

"Yes, I'll do that, Ned," Lavinia replied in as nonchalant a voice as she could employ, yet fidgeting all the same. "But why don't you come by and see her yourself," she added, amazed at her own effrontery in brazening out this awkward situation. "I know it was Mr. Phillips who first brought you to my house, but you can always come around with Clarissa's new tutor, Mr. Waverly-Smythe. I believe he's an acquaintance of yours."

"Yes, yes, I'll be certain to do just that," Ned said, his flashing smile drawing attention from his widening eyes as he continued to back out of his father's drawing room turned love nest.

Once the retreat was accomplished, young Edward Lowell Newcomb turned on his heel and quickly exited the family home, his head in a spin. He had come to his father with one dilemma and left with two. It was true, he grudgingly admitted, that he shouldn't have gone running into his father's drawing room like the small boy he had once been, but he'd been at his wit's end and wanted advice.

Since Brandon and Clarissa had quarreled, *nothing* had been the same, and he had felt like a choice walnut caught in the grip of some grotesque nutcracker. On the one side was Brandon, stubborn and unreasonable, at least as far as Ned could see. Why his tutor should be so incensed that J.G. Manning had offered help, Ned still couldn't fathom.

And on the other side was Clarissa, who, it was true, exerted less pressure but whose predicament tugged at his heart nonetheless. And there he was in the middle, unable to give Brandon, his dearer friend by far, his unquestioning loyalty, and unwilling to ignore Clarissa's sad plight. He didn't know what to do. How could he go about censoring Brandon and prodding him into a reconciliation with the Manning girl while maintaining the older student's friendship?

It was desperation that had pushed Ned to his father's house that day, looking for fresh insight. But it was certainly embarrassment that had driven him out. His father and Lavinia Cooper! The impact of that jolt had still not abated, even though his swift departure had taken him at least a mile from the scene of his discovery. He didn't know whether to be indignant or amused by what he had learned. Imagine, people that age indulging in physical contact of *that* sort.

Obviously he was more like his father than he had thought, Ned concluded with a wide grin, made all the wider when he realized that his own enjoyment of the fairer sex could very likely extend years past any projections he had previously made. What a joyous thing to discover, he thought happily, until he remembered Lavinia's announcement concerning Waverly-Smythe, and the smile faded from his face as he wondered how he was going to break this news to Brandon, who despite his protestations to the contrary, Ned suspected, still cared for Clarissa.

* * *

After pricking her finger for the third time in five minutes, Clarissa threw down the embroidery hoop in disgust. Aunt Lavinia and her antiquated notions of a woman's duties! The piece would never be finished in time for Father's homecoming; it was a major accomplishment just to avoid staining the pristine linen with her blood.

"But, child, you said I was to be your model of feminine deportment and you know how I value my flowers and needlework," Lavinia had admonished when she'd presented her niece with the cloth and dainty threads. "Your father is returning shortly and I think it appropriate that you have something tangible to show of your accomplishments. After all, your mind isn't visible—the man can't see your education. Besides, now that you're not so busy with Mr. Phillips, you'll need other activities. A well-crafted needle piece may even distract your father's attention from your hair."

Her hair! Of late that seemed to be her aunt's major concern, fussed Clarissa as she moved to the mirror. In her opinion, it was quite attractively modern, despite Preston's silent disapproval and her aunt's vocal reaction. The two months since she'd cropped her tresses had allowed the hair to fill in naturally so that soft ringlets curled brightly around her face, just touching the collar of her gown at the back. As a matter of fact, the girl realized, it was over a month since she'd worn the hair switch Lavinia had insisted upon having made. Brandon, after his initial shock, had come to love the simplicity of her hair. He'd tease her by capturing a curl with his lips and tracing a path of worship to the sensitive nape of her neck, his kisses telegraphing passionate anticipation to her very soul.

Brandon... Her heart sighed as she watched a public carriage pull up before the park and a couple alight. Since the morning he'd left the house in such a fury, every time the mail arrived or the doorbell chimed, she hoped there'd be a message from him. Times like now when she was too restless to study or read, her body would ache for his touch and she'd find herself at the front window, as if by wishing, she could make her lover appear. Her ex-lover, she should admit, but it was so hard to accept the end when she'd dreamed of a future with him. She should hate him; there were moments when she did, but they didn't last. He was the only man who had ever made her feel precious. She knew she'd been a fool, yet so had he, and a sanctimonious ass, to boot.

Why couldn't he be more reasonable, less temperamental, like Preston? Preston, her heart chided, doesn't set you on fire the way Brandon did and can't engage your heart or mind in appealing pursuits.

But he does respect my wishes and the limits I've set on our relationship, she argued. He's safe and comfortable; I'm better off this way, with no complications.

Then why did the smell of crushed violets haunt her, even in Lavinia's morning room? Why did she still wake from dreams of depthless gray eyes filled with the pain she'd caused? It would have been so simple if Brandon were not so highly principled. Well, she acknowledged with a grateful sigh, at least he hadn't confessed to Humphrey and was still eligible for the fellowship. Maybe she could convince Father to intervene without Brandon's knowledge, if only she could invent an explanation as to why it was necessary.

Father! Clarissa came out of her reverie with a start as the man in her thoughts materialized out of a hansom cab before the house. But it's the wrong man, she told herself; he's not due to arrive till tomorrow; I'm not ready. But a sharp tattoo of the door knocker said he was. James Gregory Manning had returned.

Taking long, slow, deep breaths to calm her heart as she stopped before the mirror and ran her fingers through her short curls, Clarissa uttered a silent prayer that the sight of her wouldn't horrify her somber parent. Then he was in the room, capturing her to him in a crushing hug.

"Well, well, child, I see your aunt, for a change, didn't exaggerate."

"Exaggerate?"

"She wrote that despite your hair, you were looking quite well and behaving so, too. I can't attest to the latter, but I'd concur with the former. You do look quite the young lady, very becoming, Clarissa, very." From her father, this was high praise indeed, and Clarissa blushed, rendered speechless by his unexpected affection.

He studied her quietly for a moment and continued.

"Perhaps you're becoming too much of a handful, though? Where is your aunt this afternoon?"

"We didn't expect you until tomorrow, Father."

"Come now, Clarissa, you should be aware that one of my foremost courtroom strategies is to catch the opposition off guard. Tomorrow all would have been as Lavinia thinks I would expect it; today I see the truth. Now, where is the woman? The maid who admitted me didn't seem too certain."

"I believe she's at a committee meeting for some Horticultural Society function or another. She said she'd certainly be home in time for dinner, and perhaps tea," said Clarissa reluctantly.

"And she's left you alone till then?"

"Father, I am eighteen."

"Joan of Arc was fourteen and look at the trouble she caused when left to her own devices." Prowling the room with the air of a hunter, the man noticed everything: the discarded embroidery, the scattered history and philosophy texts, an open issue of *Punch*. Yet his attention was arrested by the law book that had slipped down the side of a small reading chair, and he reached for it, unerringly extracting the reference work from its hiding place with a look of surprise.

"A legal text, Clarissa? Don't tell me your aunt is encouraging you to read law? Or were you hiding it from her?"

"No, Brandon and I were using it to document some points for a paper. I didn't realize he'd left the book behind." Almost two weeks ago, added a small voice within; he must truly despise you if he hasn't come to claim it.

"You always did target the most valuable references in any case, my dear. I trust Mr. Phillips appreciates you, that is, your research skills, as much as I."

"I—ah, he's never really said," answered the flustered Clarissa, anxious to end the discussion of Brandon Phillips yet knowing she had to say something to explain his absence. "Actually, Father, he's no longer tutoring me."

"Your aunt didn't write me of this," rebuked the legal authority, annoyed at this unexpected turn of events. He'd thought the lad available. "Why not?"

"I suppose you were already en route from the Continent," she extemporized, seeking a story with which to appease her father. "He simply became overly demanding of my time, and I couldn't tolerate his smug superiority and outrageous assignments. It was as if he decided women have no capability for higher learning and could never hope to be half as creative as their male counterparts."

"Clarissa, I can hardly believe that the case if he permitted you to help him with his own work. Surely he noticed you're a female, and yet he must have felt you were of some value to him."

Only in bed, came the unbidden accusation of her heart.

"Only in terms of the price he earned for his time," she said aloud.

"But I understood from your letters and your aunt's that you were spending more time together than ever before," he said. He knew Clarissa's explanation didn't ring true, and he'd be damned if he'd let a bright young law student like Brandon Phillips disappear because his daughter was moody and resented a strong hand. "If he were truly concerned only with his recompense, wouldn't he want to continue his position, especially as you also served freely as his research aide?"

"Only Heaven knows what Phillips might do, sir, given the opportunity," replied a male voice from the threshold. "Clarissa, I'm sorry to intrude; I didn't realize you had a guest."

"I'm not a guest, young man, I'm her parent. The question is who are you to come walking into my sister-in-law's home unannounced?" demanded the protective father of a comely daughter. Damn it, it was a good thing he'd come a day early if males regularly took such liberties in this household. Lavinia could enjoy her life as she would, but his daughter would have a proper moral upbringing or he'd know the reason why!

"Oh, sir, I'm sorry. Clarissa said you'd be home tomorrow and I..." Caught unaware, Preston was momentarily befuddled in the face of the man he'd envisioned as his patron. How to make amends and fast? "Dr. Manning, please accept my apology for what must seem inexcusable rudeness. I am Preston Waverly-Smythe, and it's my pleasure to tutor your lovely daughter now that Phillips has given notice."

"Was dismissed," interjected Clarissa hurriedly. "I was just explaining to Father that his attitude had become unbearable—"

"Yes, very bourgeois, not at all suited to a young lady of your sensibilities," concurred Preston, "but what can one expect when a job is performed solely for monetary compensation?"

"Then I take it," said the American thoughtfully, "that you have taken over Phillips' responsibilities without the stipend attached?"

"Ah, no, sir. That is, Miss Cooper wouldn't hear of it," claimed Preston, only half in truth, since he'd never suggested it. "Your daughter has such a quick mind, though, that her education is pure pleasure."

"Clarissa could always hold her own when she chose to," commented Dr. Manning dryly. "But, tell me, would you know if young Phillips has taken on any other position since leaving Miss Cooper's employ?"

"I wouldn't think so, sir, not at this point in the term. He's too wrapped up in law books to do any but the most essential work. He certainly didn't have the intelligence to appreciate Clarissa's, ah, Miss Manning's abilities," curried the overly ambitious Preston.

"Well, then, since she is so bright, Mr. Waverly-Smythe, you'll excuse her from her lesson this afternoon. I have need of a research clerk, and until I can procure one, perhaps Mr. Phillips, I'll need Clarissa's assistance."

"Well, of course, sir," affirmed the startled tutor, seeing his chance to impress Manning rapidly disappearing. "But if I can be of any assistance, please let me know."

"Thank you, but I couldn't impose. Nice to have met you."

"And you, sir. I've long been an admirer of yours. Well, Clarissa, I'll see you then tomorrow."

"Better make that next week, lad. I know Lavinia has a party set for the weekend and I'm certain she could use Clarissa's assistance," advised Manning. He didn't quite trust this fellow. He was altogether too polite and, at the same time, too familiar to be proper. Better to look into the matter before he welcomed a stranger into Lavinia's household.

Having been curtly dismissed, Preston had no choice but to depart without speaking to Clarissa alone. He could only hope she'd remember the elements of his background he'd wanted her to stress to her father. Damn, but he needed something to discredit Brandon, especially if Manning were serious about employing him as a clerk. Since that preliminary examination six weeks ago, Humphrey had more time and use for Brandon than anyone else, yet he hadn't posted a grade for the paper. What was it that made Phillips so special? Maybe a look at the paper would give him an idea. He'd have to get into Humphrey's office and see. With a set purpose in mind, Preston left Hertford Court with a much more jaunty step than he'd expected.

"Father, you're not serious about hiring Brandon, are you?" asked Clarissa hesitantly after Preston had gone.

"Certainly I am. Given the superior credentials Michael Humphrey wrote me about, and your aunt's, not to mention your enthusiasm for his abilities, I can't allow what I must assume a trivial disagreement to deprive me of a first-rate assistant...unless of course there's something you haven't told me."

"No...but why can't I do your research? I've always helped you in the past."

"Yes, and periodically complained about how it hampered your social calendar, as I recall," chided the lawyer. Taking Clarissa's hand in his and squeezing it gently, he continued. "We're in London for another month and I want you to enjoy it, my dear, not be cooped up in stuffy law libraries. You've enough of that at home."

"Another month?" echoed Lavinia, startled, as she entered the morning room in a rush.

"A little over, actually. I've booked passage to the States for five weeks from tomorrow."

"But I thought you wrote you had urgent work to complete," protested his sister-in-law.

"Lavinia, you haven't changed a bit," said James Gregory, kissing her cheek. "It's so like you to be worried about my work. Well, I do have a book to finish, but research and writing for one particular chapter can be done better here than in Philadelphia, and Clarissa deserves some time in this wonderful city. I trust we won't be inconveniencing you unduly. We can always move to a hotel."

"No, no, I won't hear of it. I've plenty of room," said Lavinia, sinking down on the settee with a sigh. As if lodging were the only issue she'd have to contend with... "Clarissa, why don't you go ahead and ring for tea. I think I'll just go upstairs and lie down a bit before dinner. Today's meeting left me rather drained. James, will you excuse me?''

"Naturally, Lavinia, and thank you again for all you've done for Clarissa and myself.''

And for all I haven't done for Geoffrey and myself, she added softly, and won't be able to do... Family!

Sitting in Humphrey's office the next afternoon following another grueling tutorial, Brandon regarded the don's gruff exterior with mounting indignation.

"Sir, this term I have buried myself in torts, I've fetched and carried inordinate amounts of research materials until I've worn a rut between the library and my rooms. I've eaten, slept and breathed law without complaint. But *this*, if I may say so, is going too far.''

"No, you may *not* say so, you young ingrate. If Manning wants you, he'll have you. Hadn't I already placed you as tutor to his daughter? But somehow you managed to muck *that* up. I understand your rival has that position now.''

Brandon nodded curtly, noting that bile still rose in his throat at the thought, just as it had last night when a nervous Ned had given him the news.

"Well, then, now that the great man himself has requested your help while he's staying in London, though only God knows why he should do so, you will comply with that request.''

"But, sir...''

"No buts, boy," Humphrey growled, ignoring the fact that the man before him was older than his usual students. "You'll do it.''

"That's completely unreasonable," Brandon muttered. "How am I supposed to keep up with my own work and...''

"Your *what*? Why, your job is to complete any assignments I give you, and your next one is to clerk for Manning whether you consider it reasonable or not," the professor pronounced with pompous finality, refusing to entertain any curiosity about his protégé's reluctance to jump, if not leap, at such a marvelous opportunity. Evidently it was a personal matter, and Humphrey had, many years before, made it a practice to stay out of his students' private lives. His only concern was to turn out fine practitioners of law, and to that end, he utilized whatever resources were available to see that his better students were firmly established. Did these innocents think that they could become successful and serve Imperial Britain solely on the basis of talent? Why, that didn't even enter into it! Connections were what counted, and only after they had been made could talent be given the chance to grow and flourish.

"Now I'll hear no more about this, Phillips. What I would have done to have worked with a man like J.G. Manning when I was your age! But the way you're squawking, one would think I was asking you to enter the gates of hell rather than offering you a golden opportunity."

"But the point is, Dr. Humphrey, that you are *not* asking. You're commanding," replied a hotheaded Brandon, thinking how much like hell it would be to hear Clarissa's laughter, to see her in passing, to be tormented by her nearness, and yet to be constantly aware that she had never really cared for him.

"That's correct, Phillips, I *am* telling you what to do. And if you feel that you are unable or unwilling to accommodate me, you can walk out that door," Humphrey said with a jerk of his head, "because right now, you are completely out of line."

Brandon knew he had never worked so hard to control his temper as he did at that moment. Unaware that his face had turned red with anger, the young law student glared at Humphrey but managed to hold his tongue. The self-control he demonstrated impressed his mentor. Humphrey silently congratulated himself on his astute assessment of his student. The professor knew that given the right circumstances, this was one falcon who could soar far above the others, and the possibility made him all the more determined to push his fledgling out of the nest and force him to fly.

For his part, Brandon wondered whether the old tyrant had really done him a favor by keeping him in university this term; perhaps it had merely been a ploy to exact additional punishment for the abominable paper Clarissa had written. After all, if he had been sent down, he would have been beyond Humphrey's reach, and free from further chastisement.

And now the heartless codger wanted him to crawl back into the lion's den as though he had never escaped to begin with. Only this time, the young man wasn't fending off the females, but the leader of the pride. He should remind Humphrey that this student's given name was Brandon and not Daniel.

Attempting to protest once more, Brandon was given no chance as the professor turned to his desk, and with his inimitable scrawl, wrote an address on a slip of paper. "This is where you'll be working with Dr. Manning. We've managed to secure some offices near the Inns of Court for his convenience. See that you report there in the morning. He'll be expecting you."

"Yes, sir," Brandon answered, his demeanor leaving no doubt that his compliance did not mean complete submission. He couldn't help but chafe at the yoke Humphrey had placed around his neck, and the irritated student decided without ever having met the man that it was unlikely Manning was any different from his offensive offspring. This whole clerking situation promised to be nothing less than distasteful, but at least, he thought as he rose to leave the room, he wouldn't be expected to work with the American at Lavinia's residence. That was the one bright spot in this whole sorry business. It meant there would be little chance of running into Clarissa. Just let Manning mention his precious daughter, though, and Brandon determined he would tell this false messiah of the law exactly what he thought of the fair Clarissa. With a sigh, he turned the doorknob to leave the don's office, consoling himself with the fact there was very little else Humphrey could do to him. This had to be the worst of it.

"One moment, Phillips. Your time with Manning tomorrow means you'll miss my lecture," the professor called over his shoulder. "See to it that you do the required readings and obtain the notes before our next session."

The only response was a curt, "Certainly, sir," that was almost drowned out by the slamming of the office door. Preparing to vacate the office, Humphrey shook his head and smiled proudly. Phillips was going to be a fiery barrister indeed!

Damn, but the Manning bitch was making him lose his mind. Preston frowned as he stealthily picked the lock to Hum-

phrey's inner sanctum later that night. He should have realized weeks ago that there was something grievously wrong with
Phillips' examination, something that could possibly benefit his
own standing if it became public. But he'd been concerned with
cultivating Clarissa's affection instead; he'd be more careful in
the future, he promised himself as he located the paper in
question in Humphrey's labeled files. At least the old man
hadn't tried to hide it; of course, he hadn't expected a visitor,
reflected the intruder with a sneer, more the fool he is.

Turning up the lamp, the young law student quickly scanned
the almost illegible first page before tossing the paper down in
disgust. What inexcusable drivel. No wonder Humphrey hadn't
given it a grade. Phillips should have been sent down post haste
for the nonsensical arguments he'd committed to paper, but
then no one except Humphrey had seen the examination—or
would see it, according to ordinary procedure set by the board
of trustees.

Well, what about the extraordinary? wondered the brooding male, considering the options before him. If I anony-
mously reported Humphrey to the university board as showing
undue partiality, I could be dismissed as easily as Brandon were
anyone to discover how I happened to see his paper. Besides,
since student examinations are viewed as sacred documents and
a professor's grade is inviolable, it's doubtful Humphrey would
even be censured. It's too bad, though, that this indefensible
tripe can't be utilized to discredit Phillips sufficiently to eliminate him from competition for the position with Dobson and
Whittaker. Humphrey might be swayed by the fool's original-
ity, but a scholar like Manning . . .

Manning! What if he were to see the paper? Would a man of
his stature be willing to accept such a radical thinker as his law
clerk, even temporarily? Not bloody likely, decided Preston
with a wry smile, returning the other files to Humphrey's desk.
With a bit of luck he could have the paper delivered to Manning tomorrow, giving the American plenty of time to digest the
piece before Lavinia's party and look elsewhere for an assistant. And of course, as his daughter's tutor, I'll be readily
available, he thought smugly.

"Hello? Who's that in my office?" Humphrey's angry voice
took Preston by surprise. What in blazes was he doing here at

this hour? Before he could consider an answer, Preston's well-honed instincts made him knock the desk lamp to the floor and dash past the startled professor.

"You there! Stop, I say!" Shoved abruptly aside by a hurtling body, Michael Humphrey landed ignominiously on his rump, the sudden force dislodging his spectacles from his nose and his briefcase from his hand. A moment or two passed before he could pull himself together sufficiently to understand what had transpired.

"A hooligan in my rooms? Nothing is sacred anymore; what is this place coming to? These student pranks are getting out of hand; usually they wait for the last week of term."

Chapter Fifteen

When the day of Lavinia's social gathering arrived, everything was as it should be for the staid guests invited to honor Miss Cooper's prestigious brother-in-law. For that reason, there was more amusement below stairs than in the reserved atmosphere of the parlor.

"Oh, you're never going to believe this one," Ellen gasped between giggles as she hurried into the kitchen, her nose deep in Kate Greenaway's *Language of Flowers*.

"Come along, then—tell a body," chided Cook, impatiently working at the last-minute preparations for the afternoon's party. With the menu Lavinia had ordered, she had little patience left for riddles. "You were gone long enough to read the botanical history of the world, never mind a few bouquets."

"I had to wait till the miss was through with the book, didn't I?"

"All right, then, what do his red carnations and laurustinus leaves mean?"

"No, no, you have to appreciate the increasing desperation of the poor man," disputed the maid, chuckling at the ongoing floral communication between Geoffrey Newcomb and her mistress. "First he sent her corchorus, 'impatient of your absence,' and she responded with the myrtle and oxeye for love and patience.

"Yes, yes, then yesterday the jonquils arrived: 'I desire a return of your affection,' and she sent him the daisies, 'I share your sentiments.' Get to today's tokens of affection."

"'Alas! for my poor heart. I die if neglected,'" read Ellen in a voice of wonder.

"I die if neglected? Oh, I've got to get my Andrew a copy of this message book." The older woman sighed wistfully.

"A book won't help Andrew," contradicted Ellen without thinking. "I mean, he couldn't get the specific flowers like these two can when they want them. Isn't the earl the most romantic man you ever heard of? But he is a devil to tempt her with a house full of guests; she's just wild enough to go off and leave them."

"A devil he may be, but what a gallant one," said Cook admiringly. "And there's nobody to suspect that the flowers are anything but that."

"Well, her brother-in-law surely didn't notice anything, and the way Miss Clarissa's under the weather of late, keeping to her rooms, I doubt she's even seen the arrangements."

"She hasn't been eating proper since that nice Mr. Phillips of hers stopped coming round. She just picks at her plate, no matter what dainties I make special... Maybe she ought to send that young man a posy or two," Cook nodded as she finished garnishing the tray of cucumber and watercress sandwiches. "You know this new lad just don't compare to the other."

"Aye, but he'll be handy enough to make the other fellow jealous. With them both coming today, I bet that's her game. Our little American miss will chase him till he catches her," predicted Ellen with a knowing smile. "She's not one for sitting on the sidelines."

But at that moment, Clarissa was attempting to avoid the party altogether.

"Aunt, I'm not feeling up to entertaining," she said softly, still clothed in a chemise and wrapper. "I'd rather stay up here and avoid Father's guests."

"Nonsense. A well-bred woman of manners does her duty first and worries about her feelings after," snapped Lavinia in a surprisingly harsh tone. Here she was, sacrificing her pleasure for James Gregory, and his daughter wasn't willing to cooperate in the least. "I am ashamed of your attitude, Clarissa. Isn't it about time you did something for someone else?"

I did, and look what happened...he hates me. The girl frowned. Avoiding her aunt's eye, she moved to the window and parted the curtains to look down at the street and the park across the way. Anything to avoid seeing the disappointment on Lavinia's face, but her mother's sister wouldn't understand that she really was feeling unwell.

"Just look at the exquisite job Miss Simmons did on your frock, dear. The hand embroidery on the bodice and sleeves of this silk took hours and hours, and this creamy ecru will complement your coloring remarkably well." Lavinia was losing the little self-control she had left. "Clarissa, you did badger her to finish the dress in time for today, you can't leave it hanging there..."

Still there was no reply from the silent figure watching the early arrivals. Going to her, Lavinia put an arm around her niece's shoulders and gave her a hug, at a loss as to how to reach the child short of strangling her. Fortunately, recognition of one of the guests provided an opening.

"Oh, look, dear, isn't that Professor Humphrey with Brandon?"

"What is he doing here?" To Clarissa's embarrassment, her voice caught in her throat at the reference to her ex-lover. Over the past two days, her father had done little but praise him to the skies, and she was sick of hearing about Brandon Phillips. She certainly didn't need to see him, especially when she was already unwell. Her stomach was definitely not right.

"Why, we met him at the law reception, don't you remember? And since he is a colleague of your father's—"

"Not Humphrey, Phillips."

"Oh, Brandon?" asked Lavinia in amazement. Was that what this was all about then? "Clarissa, that was a bad dream you had, but it was more than two weeks ago, and you did say Brandon had never been anything but absolutely proper and polite to you. So I don't understand why his presence should disturb you, especially since he is working for your father."

"It doesn't," denied the pale young woman, torn by the intense desire to throw herself into his arms and the need to deny his existence. How could he make her feel worse by coming to the house? "I was merely surprised to see him."

"But I told you the best of the law students would be attending along with some of the law faculty. Preston will be here, and Ned, as well as a handful of others. You have nothing to fear from Phillips; you probably won't even have to speak to him."

"I'm not afraid of him," declared Clarissa hotly, *only of myself when I'm near him.*

"Good, then we will expect you downstairs in twenty minutes," said her aunt in a tone that would tolerate no contradiction. After all, if anyone were to spend the afternoon in bed, it should be her and Geoffrey, not her innocent little niece!

Smoothing her skirt and donning her social smile, Lavinia swept into the parlor like a peripatetic whirlwind, determined that the afternoon would be pleasant for James Gregory, if not herself.

"Professor Humphrey, how delightful to see you again. I'm so pleased you could leave your texts and scholars behind and join us for the afternoon."

"But, dear lady, I haven't," said Michael Humphrey with a startled glance. "You alleviated that dilemma by inviting the better students along as well as myself."

"Oh, but you're not on duty teaching them, though," fluttered the attractive matron, as she smiled across the room at Preston.

"No, ma'am. I must, however, gauge their social presence and etiquette, especially that of the advanced fellows looking to leave university next month for the Inns. One can't be lax in measuring their suitability for the bar when they will, after all, be representing me and my colleagues to the world at large."

"Of course." Lavinia nodded, already moving to her next target, a professor with silver-streaked eyebrows. "Excuse me, won't you? I must greet our other guests."

"Certainly," said Professor Humphrey. "But please don't encourage them to be too at ease."

"Come now, Michael," challenged Dr. Manning with a grin, "just between us, aren't you overdoing the scholarly ogre role? I know for a fact that there's a heart beneath that gruff exterior of yours, and I imagine you've let it slip to a few of your young men as well."

"Not for publication, but perhaps one suspects," admitted the Humph begrudgingly as he watched Brandon stiffly decline Ellen's offer of punch. Brandon seemed ill at ease, frequently glancing at the door although whether anxious to leave or awaiting another guest, Humphrey couldn't decide. "Occasionally a young man stands out as worth a bit of extra trouble."

"Yes, Ellen, thank you. Michael, have one of these sandwiches, they're a special concoction of Lavinia's cook." Handing his colleague a sandwich and a napkin, Dr. Manning returned to their conversation. "Well, if you're talking about Phillips, I concur wholeheartedly. I want to thank you for sending him to tutor Clarissa, and more personally, to clerk for me. He's invaluable when it comes to research and even more so when it comes to legal analysis, despite his standoffish manner. Believe me, you've done an excellent job with him. I doubt I've met another student as accomplished as he in all my lectures abroad this term."

"I don't know that I'd go that far in his praise," disputed Humphrey with a frown, noticing Waverly-Smythe lingering nearby. "Some of his ideas rather border on the outrageous."

"If you're speaking of that examination paper of his you sent me—"

"*I* sent you?" To the best of his knowledge, that paper was still locked in his file drawer with the rest of the senior preliminaries.

"Yes, two days ago. I must admit I was surprised you'd part with such a brilliant piece of work, but it certainly gave me a perspective of young Phillips that's quite different than the one he presents when working with me, and of course, I'll return the paper."

Brilliant? My lord, how could a scholar like Manning consider that tripe passable, let alone brilliant? Was he losing his mind? In his anxiety for an answer, Preston edged closer to the conversationalists, ostensibly studying the portrait of Lavinia over the fireplace.

"Different isn't always synonymous with good, James. Say what you mean," instructed the ever-vigilant educator, suddenly understanding the invasion of his rooms Wednesday night. He didn't doubt the paper had been taken, but who would have stolen it to send it to Manning? Brandon hadn't wanted to clerk for the man, or so he'd said; could he have thought his examination would shock the American into rejecting him? As the questions crossed his mind, Humphrey looked quizzically at his silent host. "Well, James, surely that isn't such a difficult query?"

"Not at all, Michael, and I'd love to lunch with you Monday to discuss it at length, in private," stressed the American, staring pointedly at the lone student within earshot. "After all, this is supposed to be a social occasion, not a business discussion. Let me tell you about the most fascinating thing that I ran across in Milan..."

Following his glance, Humphrey nodded agreeably. So Manning, too, felt less than charitable towards Waverly-Smythe, did he? Now he was a character more likely to commit a theft to better himself than Brandon Phillips. Besides, decided the senior law professor, Phillips was intelligent enough to realize Manning would applaud his innovative approach to historical imperialism. On the other hand, the politically conservative Waverly-Smythe would have been scandalized at the essay's nontraditional approach, considering it akin to heresy. Yes, he was the candidate for the crime, mused the barrister, but without evidence, he had no cause to press charges. Still, it was something to file away.

"Dr. Manning, Professor Humphrey, I just wanted to say how exhilarating it is to be in the company of such great legal minds," said the lad in question, hearing their conversation cease and believing now was the time to ingratiate himself. "I only hope someday to have a reputation even one third as formidable as yours."

"One must earn a reputation before one can possess it, sir," countered Preston's legal mentor dryly as he noticed Brandon watching the door again. "Tell me, James, where is your lovely daughter? I haven't seen her since the law reception in February, and then these young scamps kept her too busy to notice us old codgers."

"I'm surprised she's not holding court already, but then, knowing Clarissa, I imagine she wants to make an entrance, eh, Preston? Has she ever been on time for a tutoring session?"

"Ah, yes, sir, almost always," replied the uneasy student. Why couldn't the conversation deal with law and his knowledge of it rather than lessons? "Though of course, when one is as lovely as your daughter, her arrival at any time is a pleasure. There she is now, and she looks ravishing, doesn't she?"

Ordinarily Clarissa would have been pleased to see all the masculine eyes turned in her direction; now it only made it harder to ignore the stormy gray ones that were swiftly averted at her entrance. She knew she looked becoming in her new frock, but she wasn't prepared for the silence that greeted her, or the sudden movement of young men in her direction. Miss Simmons' creation molded her bosom to a luscious size, then emphasized her slender waist before falling gracefully in soft folds around her hips, ending six inches off the floor so her soft kid slippers and trim ankles were revealed to all. The soft pastel flowers embroidered on the sleeves and bodice of the gown were detailed enough to be photographs, but the men's eyes didn't stop there, drinking in the beauty of the entire young woman, each man save one wishing she belonged to him.

"Clarissa, you've met Professor Humphrey, I believe." Dr. Manning's words broke the spell, and once again conversations resumed their pace as the lovely American joined her father and his guest.

"Miss Cooper, how nice of you to include the lower classmen in this fete," said Ned with a roguish smile. "It's rare that anyone thinks of us underlings, unless it's to pile on the work."

"Ah, yes, Ned, it's my pleasure," lied Lavinia as she moved to join Ned and Brandon, wondering just how much the young scamp had told his friend of their recent meeting. Best to brazen it out, she decided. "We didn't really have much chance to talk the other night—"

"I'm sorry, ma'am, but I'm afraid I haven't seen you since our theater outing with Brandon and Clarissa a few weeks ago," corrected Ned, the twinkle in his eye reminding Lavinia of Geoffrey's own gleam.

"Oh...I must have been confused. I thought I saw you, but it was definitely someone else entirely," dithered Clarissa's aunt, pleased at the boy's tact.

"I fear I've been keeping him much too busy for the theater, Miss Cooper," explained Brandon. "Between completing his don's course work and satisfying the demanding tutor in me, young Ned hasn't had much time for play lately."

"Unlike a few weeks ago," commented Lavinia regretfully. "When the three of you worked here, it seemed more fun than drudgery, at least to me. It's unfortunate you couldn't continue."

"Time moves on, Miss Cooper, and life changes. Your niece seems to have adjusted to her new tutor quite nicely," said Brandon icily, nodding at Clarissa, who had allowed Preston to offer her his arm and escort her to the other side of the room. Feeling Brandon's eyes upon her, Clarissa turned to face him, but just as pointedly, looked quickly away and laughed with Waverly-Smythe. It was enough of a message for Brandon.

"Forgive me for leaving so early, ma'am, but clerking for Dr. Manning is quite demanding, and I find I must steal time to complete my own work from whence ever I can," said the blond law student. "Ned, I'll see you later."

The next time Clarissa looked around the room, he'd gone. Maybe he was in the kitchen fetching something for Lavinia, she thought, noticing her aunt was also absent from the crowded room. Slipping from the confines of Preston's grasp, she excused herself and went into the hallway that led below stairs.

"Cook, I'm looking for my aunt and Mr. Phillips," she explained as she entered the kitchen, empty but for the almost clean platters.

"Mr. Phillips?" emphasized the cook with a grin as she nodded to Ellen, who'd just arrived with more trays. "I'm sorry, miss, but I haven't seen him. Perhaps Ellen has."

"Not recently, miss. As a matter of fact, I believe I heard him saying his goodbyes to your aunt about half an hour ago."

"Well, then, where is she?"

Embarrassed glances passed between the women but nothing was said.

"Well, what happened to her? She can't have gone to a horticultural meeting today!"

"I'll see if I can't find her, miss and send her back to the party. She's probably taken a few of the guests to see the new seedlings in her garden," Ellen volunteered in a rush. "I'll check for you."

"Very well. I'll go upstairs," agreed Clarissa, already tired at the thought of still more small talk and lascivious glances from the law professors and their students. Maybe Ned could say what happened to Brandon.

"I warned that woman she'd oughtn't have him come here today," hissed Cook. "But would she listen? Heavens no, not when her blood's boiling. You'd better get out to the gazebo with some lemonade and cool that pair off so she can return to her guests. After all, when there's only two women present, it's damned obvious when one disappears."

"Clarissa, you look absolutely stunning," said Ned, boldly kissing her cheek with the easy familiarity of a friend when the restless young lady approached him a few moments later. "How are you keeping these days?"

"Fine, and why shouldn't I be?" countered the red-haired girl sharply. Did he expect her to fall apart because Brandon was a stiff-necked prig who wouldn't try to see her side? She had more stamina than that!

"I don't know, your aunt mentioned something about your not being up to par, but you certainly are the picture of loveliness today," replied the confused male. He was concerned about her, not trying to belittle her; why was Clarissa so touchy all of a sudden? But he knew the reason, just as he understood Brandon's increased irritability; they wanted each other yet were too bloody proud to admit it. "I'm afraid you've missed Brandon; he left on another of Humphrey's research marathons. We could certainly use your help."

"I'm afraid my schedule won't permit it, but do give him my regards, won't you?" she suggested as Lavinia joined them, her hair slightly mussed from the attentions of her unexpected visitor.

"There you are, Aunt. I was concerned when you weren't here. Some of the guests have started to leave."

Not enough of them, thought Lavinia, anxious to escape should the chance arise, but then I'll see to that right now.

"Well, then, let's stand by the door and bid the rest of them farewell. It's been a long afternoon, and the food is almost gone anyway. Goodbye, Ned, do call when you have the chance."

As he climbed the steps to Lavinia's front door four days later, Brandon was more than a little annoyed. "Be a good fellow and pop over to Hertford Court, will you?'' the young man muttered, mimicking J.G. Manning. ''I'm afraid I've left some notes in my sister-in-law's library, and I'll need them for my ten-thirty appointment.''

So here he was returning, for the second time in the space of a week, to the house that sheltered Clarissa, a house that he hadn't ever wanted to enter again after their last argument. But life seemed to send him where inclination never would. First there had been that damn party and now this!

If it weren't for the possibility that Miss Manning might be at home, he wouldn't have minded fetching something for her renowned father. It was highly irregular for the keen-witted James Gregory Manning to forget anything, and even more unusual for him to ask Brandon to run trivial errands. In all his dealings with his new clerk, Manning had treated the young student as an equal, listening to his opinions on the issues at hand and never requesting Brandon to perform any task he wouldn't undertake himself. The older man was nothing like the demigod Brandon had envisioned, but a brilliant, affable human being, who was fast earning Brandon's loyalty as well as his respect. Without a doubt, if Manning weren't Clarissa's father, clerking for him would have been nothing short of enjoyable.

As it was, Brandon thought while he employed the ominous lioness knocker that graced Lavinia's door, Manning had been more than civil to him, in spite of anything Clarissa might have said, although it was quite obvious that she hadn't told her father *everything*. At their first meeting, he had asked a few questions about the tutoring sessions, and seemingly satisfied, he'd rarely mentioned his offspring again, preferring to build his conversation around points of law and amusing legal anecdotes. Even during the awkward hours of Lavinia's soirée, Manning had treated Brandon as pleasantly as he had treated Clarissa.

Brandon's musings were interrupted when the front door opened and a flustered Ellen stood within, regarding him with wide, uncertain eyes.

''It's all right Ellen,'' Brandon said gently as he stepped over the threshold. ''I'm only here to retrieve some notes for Dr.

Manning. He told me they were in the library. Now if you'll let me pass, I'll get them and be on my way before anyone even knows I'm here.''

Imagine Mr. Phillips coming to this house and not even asking after Miss Clarissa, Ellen thought. She and Cook knew something was afoot, but they hadn't thought it was anything more serious than some lovers' quarrel! She stood aside for the tall, handsome man, and as soon as he entered the library, she turned and ran to the kitchen.

A moment later, Clarissa started down the stairway headed for the morning room when she felt a small, sour flutter in the pit of her stomach. She gripped the handrail and stopped, making certain that the discomfort had passed before she continued on her way. She didn't want anyone to see, to suspect, what she herself had only just accepted.

Growing up without a mother or any close female relatives, Clarissa had never had the benefit of observing a pregnancy firsthand, but the girl was no fool. She'd missed her monthly courses already, and knew that she would miss the next one, as well. At first, she'd put the disturbance in her cycle off to nerves, but these frequent midmorning bouts of nausea and the complete exhaustion she experienced every night when she sought her bed wouldn't allow her to deny it any longer. She was carrying Brandon's child.

Coming to the bottom of the stairs, she paused to take stock of her feelings toward this newest twist of fate. She was distraught over Brandon, afraid of informing her father and anxious about the stigma a fatherless tyke would endure. Yet surprisingly, Clarissa discovered in the midst of all these negative emotions, there existed an impractical spark of joy and contentment. It was not altogether some horrible tragedy; she wanted this baby. And her acceptance of the situation, she knew, would make whatever she had to do much easier.

But what *was* it she should be doing at the moment? Was there anything to ease the ill effects of pregnancy? Though she doubted it, the idea occurred to her that Aunt Lavinia might have some book in the library that dealt with female anatomy.

With a determined tread, Clarissa made her way down the hallway, as much to keep herself busy as to search for some insights into what she could expect during the forthcoming months. Breezing through the doorway she didn't immediately notice the well-built male sorting through the papers on the desk her father had commandeered. But a deep-timbred cough held her where she stood.

Slowly she turned, and her amazement turned to yearning as she beheld the father of her child. Somehow, he looked a bit older, more somber and serious than she could recall seeing him. The jaw was still as lean and strong, the nose as straight and aristocratic as ever, yet Brandon had changed. The mouth that she had taught to smile had reverted to a thin, determined line, and the smoky gray eyes that had once smoldered with desire now seemed as lifeless and cold as ashes abandoned in the grate.

That he should appear at this instant, the two of them alone and unhampered by the presence of others, could only be an omen, Clarissa decided. If she were ever going to tell him about this baby, she should do it now; it might be the only such chance she would ever have. Yet, try as she might, she couldn't. Any words that came to mind stuck in her throat in the face of his frosty indifference. And so she stood, looking at him, but unable to speak.

Brandon took in the sight of her, drank it in, breathed it in, like a man who had been kept in a dark dungeon finally set free into the sunlight. Her skin glowed with a radiance he'd never seen. But basking in the sun could burn, a lesson he had learned only too well when he had given his heart to this woman. He wouldn't allow his feelings to once again become an offering on the altar of this cruel goddess, no matter how brightly she might shine. Instead, he kept his powerful, churning emotions hidden behind a wooden mask as he wondered which one of them would be the first to speak, or if indeed one of them would.

Finally, it was he who broke the silence. He wanted to hear her voice, to revel in its melodic quality, to listen to her say his name, if only once more. And so he addressed her, using her name as though it were an incantation entreating this heartless deity to speak.

"Good morning, Clarissa," he began tentatively, his uncertainty concerning her response causing his own tones to sound clipped and brusque.

"Brandon," she replied with a nod of her head, not daring to say more, afraid that her secret would come pouring forth. If only he would show a little warmth, a little caring, or at least an indication that he missed what they had once shared, then perhaps she could find the courage to tell him about his child. Just give me a hint of a smile, Brandon, she implored silently, so I can invite you to sit down, so that we can talk, so that we can knock down the wall we have built between us.

"I'm here to retrieve some papers for your father," he said, maintaining the distance between them. "I should be done in a moment and then out of your way."

"But you're not in my way," Clarissa said, daring to take a step in his direction. "Why don't you stay awhile?"

"I can't, your father is waiting for these, I'm afraid," he said, running his hand through his thick blond hair, the gesture alerting Clarissa to his indecisiveness and giving her the feeling that all might not be lost.

"Perhaps you can come back another time, then," she offered with a shy smile, its sweet invitation tormenting his soul.

"Maybe," Brandon replied quietly, wanting to see her again but still wary of how little effort it would take this woman to twist his heart once more.

"Please try to come by again," she said winningly. "I really do think we should talk."

"We may have said too much already," he rejoined. "Why not just leave things as they are?"

"Because there's something I think you should know," Clarissa persisted.

"What's that?" he asked in speculation as he eyed her intently.

"Just that I...I'm..." Clarissa stammered, wishing that he would make this easier.

"Clarissa," rang a masculine voice from the direction of the morning room, "where are you, dearest?"

Dearest! Brandon raged, recognizing Waverly-Smythe's voice. It appeared that Clarissa hadn't undergone the same loneliness and torment he'd faced. *"Dearest!"* he snorted in derision, ashamed of himself for being such a damn fool that he'd almost fallen victim to her ploys a second time.

At the sound of Preston's voice, Clarissa's eyes grew large with confused apology. What a moment for him to appear. She *had* to tell Brandon now, before all opportunity was lost. She opened her mouth to speak once more, but the bedeviled man on the other side of the desk stopped her.

"What were you going to tell me, Clarissa," Brandon sneered, "that you've a new tutor? That you've taken up with Waverly-Smythe? I only hope you enjoy what he's *teaching* you. Are you as apt a pupil with him as you were with me?"

Oh, good God, Clarissa thought, he thinks that Preston has taken his place in every way possible.

"Brandon, I..."

"Tell it to Preston," Brandon interrupted fiercely. "Whisper it in his ear while you're lying in his arms the way you used to whisper in mine. As for me, *I'm* not interested in *anything* you have to say."

Ignoring Clarissa's attempt to explain, Brandon scooped up the required papers from the desk and was gone, along with any hope she had to settle things between them.

Clarissa remained where she was, paralyzed by his reaction. Did he hold her in so little regard that he thought she would jump from his bed to Preston's? And if that *was* what he assumed, he would *never* believe that the child she carried was his! The question was no longer how could she tell him about the baby, but why should she bother? It was obvious he wouldn't want to know. Tears welled in the corners of her deep brown eyes as she wondered what she was going to do.

"What's Phillips' problem?" Preston asked as he came into the library. Catching Clarissa wiping away a tear, he moved quickly to her side and took her hands in his. "But more importantly," he continued, his voice rife with concern, "what's bothering you? Did that upstart do or say anything to hurt you?"

"No, no, I'm fine, really I am," Clarissa protested with a weak smile.

"Come now, my dear, you can't hide anything from me. If you won't tell me what's wrong, at least tell me what I can do to make things better." Preston would do anything to endear himself to J.G. Manning's daughter.

"There's nothing."

"You underestimate me, Clarissa. You know that I'd manage anything that would bring a smile to your lovely face," he said, lifting her hand and barely grazing her fingertips with a soft kiss. "Just command me, and I'd move heaven and earth to set your world right."

The concern in Preston's voice and his gentle gesture of affection caught Clarissa off guard. He was good to her, so unlike Brandon, who, moments before, had destroyed their future and that of their child with a few terse sentences. How different things would be if it were Preston's baby she carried.

She was touched by his kindness, and another tear rolled down her cheek. Ever ready to appear sympathetic, Preston let go of her hands and used the side of his thumb to wipe the tear away.

"The world's a wonderful place. All you have to do is realize it," he said in a soothing voice that invited confidences. "On such a bright, sunny morning, how can such a lovely woman have a problem that would make her weep?"

Though she fought to keep her despair at bay, Clarissa found she couldn't manage it. She gave in to the temptation to press her head against this strong, male shoulder and sob out her pain. Lately Preston was the only person who made her feel special, who took the time to listen to her, who inquired about her happiness. It was impossible to think of sharing her troubles with her father or aunt, wrapped up as they were in their own worlds. Preston, it appeared, was the only one who truly cared about her, and more importantly, he was here now, when she needed someone more than she had ever needed anyone in her life. It was a simple feat, deciding to unburden herself to Preston Waverly-Smythe, as she felt his hand gently stroking her hair, and heard his consoling whispers of assurance.

"Everything will be fine, my dear, if only you'll permit me to help you," he was saying. "Remember, you promised you would always consider me your friend. Now tell me what I can do."

"There's nothing anyone can do," Clarissa said, dabbing at her eyes as she composed herself and moved from Preston's embrace. "You see, I've really gotten myself into a mess this time, and I'm quite convinced there's no way out."

"We'll see about that," Preston murmured, beginning to lose patience with this infuriating girl. "Just tell me what's wrong."

"You know that Brandon had been my suitor," she began.

Had been! The words echoed in Preston's mind. Was it possible that all chances of reconciliation were gone? How opportune for him if that should be the case. Women whose hearts had been broken were such easy prey. They were so willing to believe the first endearment that someone else whispered in their ears.

"Yes, I knew, much to my own disappointment," he said. "And I also know that ended a few weeks ago. Do you want me to help you reconcile, Clarissa?" Preston asked with appropriate sincerity, ruminating upon what he could do to widen the rift.

"Unfortunately, that's impossible," Clarissa said sadly, "especially when Brandon thinks I've...I've been sharing your bed."

"How dare he think of you in such a way?" Preston erupted. He patted her hand and added, "But surely I can talk to him about that." *Yes, I'll tell him exactly what a passionate little hellcat I've found you to be,* he thought.

"It won't do any good," Clarissa replied, unaware of Preston's malevolent intent. "He won't believe you any more than he would believe me, just as he wouldn't believe—" she paused then rushed on, needing to verbalize her plight to someone "—that I'm carrying his child and not yours."

"Child!" Preston repeated incredulously. Clarissa had filled her belly with Phillips' offspring? This bit of news undermined every possibility he himself had for obtaining Manning's assistance. "What did that bastard say when you informed him?" Preston asked coolly.

"I haven't told him anything," Clarissa said, fighting tears once more. "From the accusations he made today, he'd only charge there was a possibility that the child isn't his, and I couldn't drag you into this, Preston, not after your kindness."

"So he doesn't know," Preston said softly while his brain worked feverishly to study the advantages of the situation. "Clarissa, he doesn't have to know—ever," Preston said at last.

"But Father had indicated that he might invite Brandon to come to Philadelphia. If that happens, he'll become aware of my condition eventually, and he'll have to wonder if..."

"Not if you're married to someone else, he won't," Preston interjected, his mind made up. What could be more perfect than to marry Phillips' whore and steal his child? But revenge was not Preston's only motivation. As J.G. Manning's son-in-law, Preston would become heir to one of the most prestigious international law firms in existence, at least he would when he informed the American lawyer later on how he had saved the precious Clarissa from scandal by giving her his name. Such an accomplishment would put him back in his father's good graces as well and, more importantly, in his will. Never had Preston's future been so bright and he owed it all to Phillips' inability to keep his trousers buttoned.

"What *are* you talking about, Preston?" Clarissa asked.

"Marry me, Clarissa."

"But that's impossible!"

"Why, because you don't love me? I've enough love for the two of us, so you see, that's no problem."

"I'm afraid it is."

"You don't have to worry, I can offer you a marriage in name only," he persisted, willing to tell any lie that was needed in order to gain his objective.

"But why would you be willing to do that?" Clarissa asked in puzzlement.

"Just to be near you, my dearest girl," he fabricated, "seeing you across my breakfast table every morning, taking you riding in the park, sharing quiet conversation in the evening. That would be more than enough to make me content, if that's all you wished to offer. In time, I believe we would find love to share."

"Are you certain?" Clarissa asked, beginning to envision a solution to her dilemma.

"Quite. And don't worry about the baby, either. He might have a fool for a sire, but I'll be a father to him, and love him because he's yours," Preston rushed on, thinking of how easily a child could be banished to the nursery, and ticking off the number of years before it could be sent away to school.

"And once we've become man and wife," he continued, "people might count the months between the wedding service and the time that you give birth, but no one will say anything. There'll be no scandal for you, the infant or your family. In fact no one, not even your father or aunt, need ever know that the baby is not ours."

"Oh, Preston," Clarissa cried, tears shining once more in her dark brown eyes, "you're so good to me—I don't deserve it."

"Nonsense, you more than deserve the future I have planned for you," Preston answered, seeing no obstacles in pursuing his hobbies after his marriage. "I sit for my exams in just three weeks, and after my degree is conferred, I'll be free to take a bride. Just tell me that your answer is yes. Say that you'll marry me."

Clarissa gazed softly at the man before her. She'd have to be a fool to turn down such an offer. It would be so easy to agree to become Mrs. Preston Waverly-Smythe, and never have to read the hurt in her father's eyes, or scandalize her aunt. It would mean her child wouldn't be an outcast from society. Yet taking vows would also cut her off from Brandon forever. Though her heart had withered when he had walked out of her life with such finality just a short while before, part of her still yearned for him. But this was no time to be selfish. She had to think of others. "Yes, Preston," she said quietly, "I'll be your wife."

Chapter Sixteen

James G. Manning rose from the partner's desk he'd been using and strode purposefully to the window overlooking Lincoln's Inn fields. The argument he was preparing had left him somewhat unnerved and, as generations of lawyers before him had discovered in these rooms, just the sight of Mother Nature offered soothing inspiration. Personally he would have preferred to be located at Gray's Inn, since he'd always been partial to the gardens designed by Sir Francis Bacon; however, as an American seeking temporary office quarters, he didn't qualify for an office in any of the Inns of Court and had to rely on professional contacts for assistance. He had Dobson and Whittaker to thank for lending him the extra rooms they maintained for consultations, but then he'd given them an unofficial glimpse of a prospective intern at work. Dobson had already commented on Phillips' "unusually astute legal mind in one so young."

Noticing two bewigged barristers cross the square en route to the law courts, his mind lifted the haze off years of history and he reflected that the men might have looked exactly the same two hundred years earlier. In fact, little about the Inns had changed since the Middle Ages, when the law and clergy had parted ways. At that time, the Inns of Chancery and the Inns of Court were created to be the home, the training grounds and the courtrooms of the legal profession all on one turf. Over the intervening years, territorial clashes between solicitors and barristers and modern convenience had established a separate law courts building. Now many students attended university rather than the Inns of Chancery prior to their final training as barristers at the Inns of Court, but tradition held firmly to the establishment of one's law office at one of the Inns of Court still scattered about the city, each with its pleasant garden, chapel, dining halls and library, in addition to individual offices and living quarters.

Opening the casement, the lawyer breathed in the fresh spring air, pleased that at least his secondary purpose in locating his office here had been successful. Given Dobson's remark, there was no question that the barristers would be willing to sponsor Brandon for the Inns, and, just as Clarissa had requested, he'd achieved it without any actions that even his highly principled clerk could find objectionable. If only his other plans had been half as successful, the perturbed father mused. Why was it that when one's relatives were involved, right and wrong were no longer so clear cut?

He had to speak to Brandon today, no matter how distasteful the conversation might be; he'd postponed the inevitable long enough, and the fellow did deserve to know. Perhaps, just perhaps the sparks he'd seen in Brandon's eyes when Clarissa's name had come up on carefully chosen occasions meant he was interested in the girl. Manning had hoped so when he'd sent the lad round to Hertford Court for those unnecessary papers a fortnight ago, but judging from his clerk's black mood when he'd returned, things had gone awry. Since then Brandon had politely found innumerable excuses to avoid any errands at Lavinia's home, and Manning was too much the professional to force his daughter upon any colleague, especially one he respected.

But then, Preston Waverly-Smythe had asked for his daughter's hand in marriage . . . Preston! In his heart, he feared such a union would be a disaster, but when he'd tried to speak to Clarissa about her seeming lack of enthusiasm, she'd rejected his concern. She told him she had matured beyond the schoolgirlish mania of "being head over heels in love," and accused him of trying to deny her the right to choose her own husband.

Maybe Brandon could... Ah, there he was now, crossing the field at his usual fast pace, apparently anxious to be at work.

Maybe not today. J.G. Manning frowned, fully aware of how awkward the coming session would be.

"No! Sir, I am very sorry but I cannot, I will not speak to your daughter," said Brandon emphatically. "It is not my place."

"The hell with your place, son. The girl needs a friend."

"Then that also excludes me." Brandon's words were clipped, but a telltale flush was creeping up the back of his neck as his emotions seethed beneath the shell of propriety. How dare this man ask him to question Clarissa's love when he had done little else since he'd heard Preston call her "dearest." The two of them deserve one another, Brandon fumed to himself, deceitful liars both.

"Now listen, I'm certain I'm not the only man to question my daughter's choice of husband," Manning continued doggedly, attempting to eat away at Brandon's resolve. "With that realization in mind, I could learn to accept Waverly-Smythe as my son-in-law..." Dr. Manning hesitated, uncertain as to how much he should admit to his clerk. "Well, I wouldn't be ecstatic, but I would accept him if I knew he would make Clarissa happy."

Brandon moved away from the desk, holding a wooden letter opener, turning it this way and that, occupying his hands with something tangible while his mind grappled with the inconstancy of a woman's love. He'd believed he had closed his heart to her, but the news that Clarissa was set to marry someone else set him on fire again. Was it merely that she was no longer available—or did he still care? Yet how could he go to her and protest her engagement to Preston, of all people? She would think he was only trying to please her father, and, if she was so foolish as to really love Preston, then...

"Brandon, my daughter refuses to discuss the marriage with either Miss Cooper or me. You worked with Clarissa for almost ten weeks, and you know her intended. Do you really think they're well suited?" Brandon realized the desperate cry of an overwhelmed father in the man's voice, not the carefully crafted argument of a renowned lawyer. Yet even Dr. Manning's pain could not force him to confront Clarissa.

"As far as my relationship with Miss Manning, she was an apt pupil when she chose to be," he replied carefully, remembering the pleasure of teaching her to love. And now that bastard Waverly-Smythe would benefit from his lessons! "Concerning the suitability of the happy couple, I believe they are well matched," Brandon stated, still stinging from the unexpected news of Clarissa's impending nuptials.

"Oh, really?" asked the American lawyer all too casually. "I find it difficult to understand her preference when I see better men around me."

"Sir, I'm sorry for your daughter if she loves Waverly-Smythe and even sorrier if she doesn't, but it's no business of mine," stated Brandon firmly, ignoring the older man's overt pressure and trying to empty his mind of the unbidden image of Clarissa undressing in his rooms.

"Very well, I suppose I must accept your decision, but Phillips, this is one time I don't agree with your interpretation of the facts," said Manning sadly. Perhaps he had misread the situation and his daughter and the clerk had never cared for one another. Still, it was too bad, he thought as he picked up a paper from his desk and made ready to return to business. "Here, this is the list of cases I need you to check for me, then after that—"

"Actually, sir, after that I'll need the afternoon off. I've some business of my own that won't keep," lied Brandon, envisioning the cups of ale awaiting him. Maybe then, Clarissa wouldn't be in his dreams.

"Certainly, Brandon. You've never needed time before, but I understand." And maybe I do, hoped the American, praying that young Phillips had been more perturbed by Clarissa's plans than he'd let on. Perhaps he still might come through to save the girl from disaster.

Lavinia, caught up in the joy of planning a wedding, was not as pessimistic as her brother-in-law.

"Oh, there you are, dear," she bubbled as she poked her head into the library and saw her niece curled up in an easy chair leafing through the current copy of *The Illustrated Strand*. "I've finally been able to locate some lovely white rosebuds. Even now, they're being nurtured in Mrs. Halpern's hothouse on her prizewinning rosebush, and they'll be in full, glorious bloom by the time the wedding takes place," Lavinia announced triumphantly, coming to stand before her niece. "I thought along with the traditional orange blossoms, that roses and ferns with swathes of white tulle would add a festive yet feminine element to the celebration at the house. There might even be enough to place on the altar at St. Pancras. Now tell me, what do you think?"

"That's nice, Aunt Lavinia," Clarissa replied listlessly, not even looking up from her magazine.

"If you don't like roses, perhaps we can find something else," the older woman sniffed, put off by the girl's unenthusiastic response.

"No, really, roses are fine," Clarissa said, turning a page and keeping her eyes trained on the periodical so that Lavinia wouldn't see their red rims.

What was wrong with the girl now, Lavinia wondered with exasperation. Lord knew that nothing *she* did pleased her niece, and it was unlike her to be so quiet and sullen for such a long period of time.

True, when the girl had made the announcement concerning her intended nuptials, she'd done so quietly. Yet she had been extremely firm about her plans, so that Lavinia hadn't voiced any doubts she might have harbored on the subject. Instead, she had quite naturally accepted Clarissa's decision, and tried to share in her joy. But each day saw the pretty American grow more distant and appear more peaked. Both Lavinia and James thought it was prewedding jitters, but this morning's behavior made it clear that Clarissa wanted no part of planning either the ceremony or the wedding breakfast to follow. Something was wrong, and Lavinia determined to find out what it was.

Clearing her throat, she sought to engage the brooding Clarissa in conversation.

"You know, dear, it's no easy task putting this wedding together in so short a period of time so that you, your father and Preston can travel to America as planned."

"I know. Thank you for your efforts," came the proper response conveyed with indifference.

"Thanks are all well and good, Clarissa, but I could use your help with managing the details. Coordinating everything is becoming quite complicated."

"It needn't be such an elaborate occasion. A simpler affair would be better for all concerned, and certainly less taxing on you."

"But Clarissa, yours will be the only wedding our family will see until your own children marry. Of course your father wants it done up properly. The wedding *has* to be appropriate to your station in life."

"All right then, do as you wish," Clarissa said peevishly. "Whatever you plan is more than acceptable to me."

"Whatever *I* plan? My dear, it's *your* wedding. Most young girls would want a say in the matter. Yet *you*, who have always had plenty to say about everything, exhibit no interest at all whenever I broach the topic of the wedding."

"That's not true," Clarissa said, looking at Lavinia with a smile meant to hide the misery she felt. Her pregnancy was proving to be a troublesome one; tender breasts, bouts of nausea and utter exhaustion did nothing to alleviate the unhappiness that beset her as a result of losing Brandon. How could she pretend to be an ecstatic bride when everything she ate, everything she did, everything she *thought*, had such awful consequences?

"I'm afraid, Clarissa, that things are as I have described them," Lavinia continued, fooled not at all by her niece's denial. "You don't want to speak of the floral arrangements. What the wedding guests eat is of little or no importance to you. Why, it's even becoming a chore to get you to Miss Simmons' establishment for fittings on your wedding gown."

Why couldn't this woman leave her alone, Clarissa thought resentfully, snapping the magazine shut. She had enough to contend with without adding a prying aunt to her list of problems.

"Aunt Lavinia, I assure you," the girl said, her voice louder than usual, "you have completely misread the situation. It's simply that you have far more expertise than I in organizing social gatherings, and I thought to place everything in your capable hands. If you are finding it troublesome..."

"Not troublesome, merely bewildering. Something is plaguing you, and I intend on discovering what it is."

Good Lord, her aunt was not about to give up, Clarissa realized, and at present the young girl couldn't bear to be besieged by any additional unpleasantness. Undoubtedly, she would have to tell Lavinia something, and now was as good a time as any.

"All right, Aunt Lavinia, but if I confide in you, you must promise me two things."

"Why certainly, dear," the girl's aunt assured her, anxious to get to the bottom of these mysterious circumstances.

"First, you are not to tell another living soul," Clarissa commanded, "and secondly, you must try not to become unduly upset."

"Me, upset?" Lavinia bubbled. "Why, if I have done something wrong, made arrangements that you find intolerable, let me know and—"

"Promise me. Swear on the love you had for my mother," Clarissa interrupted, intending to disclose only half the truth in order to obtain some semblance of peace from this dear but meddlesome soul.

"Consider the vow sworn, Clarissa. Now is it the menu for the wedding breakfast, or the guest list, perhaps?"

"I'm pregnant," Clarissa said in a voice so small and quiet that Lavinia thought at first she hadn't heard correctly. However, the haunted yet defiant gleam in Clarissa's sad, brown eyes informed the older woman that there had been no mistake. Lavinia swallowed a gasp. The girl was in a family way, and all probably as a result of those unchaperoned walks in the park. But even in her frazzled state, Lavinia realized that this was not the time for lectures. What her niece needed now was compassion.

Reaching out, Lavinia Cooper took Clarissa's hand in hers. No wonder the dear child was so at odds with everyone and everything. But as her aunt, it was her duty to do what she could.

"Clarissa, things are not as horrible as you may be imagining them. After all, there *is* to be a wedding, and with any luck, the baby will be small. But if that's not the case, your friends in America needn't know the month in which you married.

Look on the bright side, my dear, the baby's father has agreed to marry you, and that's all that really matters!''

"But that's not so," Clarissa cried as tears slowly burned their way down her face. She had never expected Lavinia to be so understanding, and her aunt's behavior, along with her own need to unburden herself to someone she loved, prodded the girl into disclosing more than she had originally intended.

"What's not so?" asked a suspicious Lavinia, as she wondered what piece of news was about to beset her now. "Preston *is* going to marry you, isn't he? Tell me that these wedding preparations are not in vain," she pleaded.

"Oh, there'll be a wedding, all right, and Preston will be the groom, though I don't love him," sobbed Clarissa as she dabbed at her eyes with a dainty handkerchief.

Lavinia was tempted to tell Clarissa that she should have thought of that before she set off along the primrose path. Instead, relieved that there was to be a ceremony after all, she bit her tongue. Then, she bent and put her arms consolingly around her unpredictable niece. Though her sense of morality told her that the girl should consider herself lucky Preston had offered marriage, Lavinia still couldn't restrain the sympathy that tugged at her heart at the sight of her sister's unhappy daughter.

"Oh, Clarissa," Lavinia crooned as she would to a child, "he's good to you, and there's no reason that one day love won't bloom. Until then, just think of your child, *his* child. The baby will forge a bond between you."

"I doubt it," Clarissa whispered urgently, driven by the need to confide in another woman. "The baby isn't his."

"What!" Lavinia croaked, her arms dropping to her sides as shock took its toll.

"It's Brandon's child, Aunt Lavinia," Clarissa said, "but Preston's willing to marry me anyway."

"And what of Brandon? What does he have to say about all this?"

"He doesn't know."

"Clarissa, you must tell him!"

"Why?" asked the girl, a forlorn note creeping into her voice. "He detests me, Aunt Lavinia. He told me so. And, even if he were willing to do the right thing for the sake of the baby, how fortunate would I be, joined for a lifetime to a man who wishes he had never met me?''

"But still, Clarissa..." Lavinia fumbled as the confusing events of the past few weeks began to make some sense to her.

"No, I won't listen to another word. What I'm doing is best for all concerned. It's what I want to do."

"Are you really so certain?"

"Yes, I am," Clarissa replied with a stubborn tilt of her chin. "Now remember your promise, Aunt Lavinia. Nothing I've told you is to be repeated. You gave your word."

"Yes, so I did," Lavinia agreed sadly. She stooped to place a quick kiss on Clarissa's forehead and left the room before she added to her niece's troubles by fussing with her to reconsider informing Brandon. She couldn't force her will on the girl. After all, it was Clarissa who would have to live with the consequences.

Without thinking about it, Lavinia headed for the morning room and poured herself a large snifter of brandy, though it was barely eleven. This was all *her* fault. What kind of guardian had she been, after all, that Clarissa now found herself bedded by one man and scheduled to marry another? Why, if James Gregory knew... But he wouldn't, and neither would Brandon Phillips. She had promised Clarissa, sworn on her own sister's memory, to remain silent, and though she had failed her niece as guardian, she would not commit the same crime as confidante.

Even as she made her decision, Lavinia doubted its wisdom. In despair, she poured more brandy, brought it to her lips and tilted her head. But she found no consolation in the fiery trail it left. What was a mere stinging in the throat and chest when compared to the pain of a heart that was breaking?

Sitting alone at a table in the Solitary Lion, Brandon found that the whiskey he sipped produced no solace. Clarissa was getting married—and to Preston Waverly-Smythe. Damn! How could the girl do this to him? He'd thought he was beyond any harm she could deliver, but he'd surmised incorrectly. At the moment, his heart pounded dully, as though it suspected it had lost all possibility of future happiness. Never had he felt more miserable or at such a loss.

And tomorrow he sat for Humphrey's senior examination. He laughed softly, the bitter cadence carrying no farther than his own table. Clarissa always did have impeccable timing. How the hell was he supposed to study tonight when all he could think about was Clarissa climbing into Preston's bed quite legally?

In frustration, Brandon's hand unconsciously gripped his cup tightly, as though the inanimate object were the twist of fate that caused his unhappiness, and could be eradicated through sheer physical force.

With unseeing eyes that focused on a life as empty as the cup he now held, Brandon signaled the barmaid for another whiskey. It was his second drink and would be, he decided in spite of his earlier intentions, his last. He refused to allow himself to be carried away on a sea of self-pity, especially when he recalled the consequences of being drunk before his last examination.

Today was a day for self-control, a strategy applied to both his intake of alcohol and his desire to go storming into Lavinia's house in an attempt to talk some sense into Clarissa. In all actuality, he had wanted nothing more than to comply with Dr. Manning's earlier request, but pride forbade him from doing so. Not that speaking with the girl would make any difference. The independent Miss Manning had always touted her intelligence and acted out of obstinacy; no word from her ex-tutor concerning the wisdom of her proposed actions was likely to change her mind. It was best to let it be.

A shadow fell across his table, jarring Brandon from his reflections, and he looked up in surprise. His present demeanor certainly wouldn't have induced anyone to join him or attempt to socialize—anyone, that was, except Ned Newcomb.

"Brandon, I didn't expect to see you here until after the Humph's final go at creating hell on earth!" Ned exclaimed as he slipped easily into the seat across from his frowning mentor.

Brandon couldn't bring himself to reply, afraid that his voice might express more than any words he might carefully select. His unnatural silence, however, didn't deter his young companion. Though their relationship had remained strained since Brandon had walked out on Clarissa, it had not been because of Ned's reticence. Indeed, the word had no place in his vocabulary. Even now, he tried to revive the easy camaraderie they had once shared.

"Never mind. No matter what the cause of your celebration, I'm glad to see you here. We can share a cup or two as well as a few laughs," Ned said wryly.

"Sorry, I was just leaving."

"No, you don't, Brandon. I'll have no more of that. I'm tired of this polite formality that has existed between us these past few weeks. Look, whatever is happening between you and Clarissa—"

"Nothing is happening. That's the point, Ned," Brandon said sharply as his gray eyes narrowed dangerously.

"All right, let's change the topic, shall we?" Lord Geoffrey's son replied. "We'll converse about something less lethal and see if we can't enjoy being mates once more."

When Ned chose, his charm proved irresistible, a fact which even Brandon found impossible to dismiss as he sat regarding the friend he'd been treating so shabbily. He didn't want to hurt Ned any more than he already had, and besides, though lighthearted banter wouldn't ease his pain, it wouldn't add to it, either, Brandon concluded. It was time this feud with Ned was ended. He'd been too good a friend.

"All right, Ned," Brandon said slowly, exasperated brotherly affection creeping into his voice in lieu of apology, "tell me about your latest exploits. As much of a scoundrel as you are, that should provide us with a needed chuckle."

"Actually, my adventures have been rather mild of late, Priscilla's gentling influence, I suppose. Though that's about to change—she's becoming much too possessive. However, our friend Waverly-Smythe appears to have immersed himself in the good life."

"Yes, doesn't he, though?" Brandon replied in a deadly voice as his splayed fingers beat a loud rhythm on the ancient, scarred table beneath his hand. It seemed that news traveled quickly. He couldn't believe that Ned would so callously broach this topic. But then, what could he expect of a man who had never seriously loved any woman, he pondered as he found himself dwelling upon the one thing he wanted so desperately to forget.

"Ned, what Preston does is of no concern to me," the handsome older student began in an attempt to put an end to the forbidden subject.

"Not even when I tell you that I think he spent last night in the company of a soiled dove?"

"That's enough, Ned," a red-faced Brandon bellowed, bringing his fist down on the table so that the cups skittered along its surface.

"But—but—I thought you'd want to know," Ned stuttered, taken aback by Brandon's outburst.

"Don't you think I already know?"

"That Preston has rooms near mine?" asked Ned in bewilderment.

"What are you babbling about?" Brandon growled, in no mood for nonsense.

"Just that when I was crossing over to my rooms late last night, my *other* rooms, that is, I saw Waverly-Smythe being accosted on the street by some bawds. Apparently he refused what they were selling, and as I drew nearer, they turned their attention upon me."

"So what's the point of all this?"

"Allow me to finish, will you? I laughingly told them that I had another engagement, but that I couldn't understand how the other gentleman managed to resist them. And they told me that Mr. Walker only likes very young girls, and that he always takes them to his place nearby... In fact, he told them he had one waiting there for him."

"Walker?" Brandon asked, his curiosity piqued in spite of himself.

"Apparently the blighter is enough of a regular in the West End to have invented a false identity, *and* he keeps rooms down there!" Ned ended triumphantly, until it dawned on him as to exactly what Brandon might suspect went on in those rooms, and with whom. "But of course I imagine that he only uses them to—I mean, not that anyone else—" He stopped, not daring to mention Clarissa by name.

"Yes, well, it doesn't make a difference what *anyone else* does," Brandon said pointedly. "After all, she's marrying him, isn't she?"

"Who's getting married?" Ned asked in confusion.

"Clarissa. Clarissa is marrying Waverly-Smythe. Her father told me so this morning."

"Good Lord! I didn't know!" Ned said, appalled. So this was what accounted for Brandon's foul humor. "You *can't* allow her to—"

"She's old enough to make up her own mind," Brandon snarled in warning.

"Of course she is," Ned replied, "but Waverly-Smythe is a cad of the first order! We mustn't allow her to be duped into doing something she'll regret. No decent woman can marry a man like that! I've just told you that he keeps rooms in the West End for illicit purposes."

"And so do you," Brandon commented dryly.

"But it's different with me!" Ned protested. "I do it in good fun, and I don't pretend to be anything but what I am, a skirt chaser constantly besotted by some comely woman or other. Waverly-Smythe is another sort all together. There's something perverse about him."

"There's something perverse about Clarissa's sense of loyalty, too, so you see, they're made for each other," Brandon snapped.

"Listen, grumble and fume all you like, Brandon, but you can't fool me," Ned ventured, managing to overcome his apprehension about meddling in this man's affairs once more. "You're miserable about this!"

"Leave it be, Ned," Brandon warned, menace flashing in his stormy eyes.

"No, I won't," Ned persisted. "You want her to marry Waverly-Smythe a lot less than I do."

"You're daft," Brandon drawled in condescension, hoping his attitude would put an end to the inquisition.

"Am I? Brandon, you're a law student, on your way to becoming a top-notch barrister. You should be interested in exposing the truth, not denying it!"

"It doesn't matter how I feel about it," Brandon said quietly, too exhausted to keep up pretenses any longer. "The choice is up to the lady."

"Go to her, tell her how you feel!"

"How can I? I have nothing to give her. Clarissa will conclude that I'm merely after her father's recommendation. If only she could have waited a bit for this marriage, until after Humphrey makes his decision about the internship, then maybe..."

"Brandon, if you can't go to her, talk with Manning himself. Tell him we suspect Preston has rooms in the West End, that he's carrying on with all sorts of women. What father could want his daughter to wed such a man?"

"To tell the truth, Manning isn't too keen on Waverly-Smythe. But after his daughter has declared her love, what father would take the word of a jilted lover whose sole evidence rests on hearsay gleaned from two tarts? No, Ned, I've closed my heart on the matter. Let Clarissa marry Preston. I'll survive."

"Oh, I know you'll manage, Brandon, but can't you recognize the difference between merely surviving and truly living?"

"I have the law."

"Yes, but justice won't warm your bed at night."

"No," Brandon conceded with a slow expulsion of breath, "but if I treat her with respect, she won't abandon me, either. Now if you'll excuse me, I have to prepare for tomorrow's examination. I don't want the law to follow Clarissa's example and favor Waverly-Smythe over me."

Leaving Ned, Brandon returned to his rooms to spend the evening wrestling with the justice of international law, and the injustice of his own life.

The next morning Preston glanced impatiently at his pocket watch, snapped it shut and returned it to the vest beneath his academic robes with a frown. There were still ten minutes before the final set of degree examinations would begin. He had no qualms about his performance, only the speed with which he could complete his essays, finish some work at his photography studio and return to Hertford Court to soothe his intended's skittish nerves. At this point, he wanted no female change of heart to interfere with his plans.

For the first time in years, he'd forgone the opportunity to seek prior knowledge of his examination, making no clandestine forays into the professor's files, feeling the risk of discovery outweighed the advantage he might gain. After all, the young man thought, smirking, what difference could his class standing make at this point? He'd certainly pass the examinations without difficulty, and whether he earned a respectable First or a mediocre Third, by this time next week, he'd be Clarissa Manning's husband and Dr. James Gregory Manning's newest junior partner!

Let Phillips swallow that if he can, gloated Preston as he noticed the object of his contempt enter the examination hall. Indeed, Phillips didn't look well, but that was all the better. If the fool wrote a paper anything like his last, the internship could still be Preston's. What a grand joke that would be: stealing Brandon's girlfriend, his bastard and his future all in one fell swoop! Could anything be sweeter?

Then it was too late for superfluous thought as the proctors entered the room and pronounced their sentence.

"Gentlemen, you may begin immediately."

With a cocky grin Preston opened the pages before him and began to read.

Chapter Seventeen

Four days later, Michael Humphrey rose from the conference table in the chambers shared by Dobson and Whittaker and clasped Dobson's hand in agreement.

"I tell you, sir, I haven't seen such a clear-cut decision in years, though of course that one episode of the senior preliminaries was a bit startling. Yet taken in context of Phillips' overall career—"

"Michael, you can stop selling us on the lad," rebuked Elmer Dobson with a grin. "We've already confirmed your choice for the internship. Now, do you want to notify him or should we wait for the official letter of appointment?"

"Thank you, I should like to tell him. He's due at my rooms this afternoon, and I have been working him awfully hard," admitted the demanding taskmaster, "though there's nothing better to test one's mettle than a good academic challenge."

"And we can always count on you to provide that." Whittaker chuckled, knowing the professor's tactics, and fully approving of the lawyers who survived his trial by fire. "Tell him to come round tomorrow at nine and we'll conduct the final pro forma interview."

"Yes, and see to it that he's on time. Punctuality means a lot," Dobson intoned solemnly.

"Right, I'm certain that nothing could keep him away," Michael Humphrey replied.

Brandon inserted the stubborn cuff links in his shirt sleeve and struggled to close them. What Humphrey wanted with him on a Friday afternoon after the end of term was beyond his limited imagination. He knew he'd done well on the examinations, though the results weren't posted yet and the internship in all probability wouldn't be announced till next week. The weary student had half a mind to ignore the Humph's imperious summons, but such foolhardiness wasn't in Brandon's nature. However, the answer to whatever the old weasel wanted from him this time would be a resounding no, especially if it had anything to do with the Mannings!

Since he'd refused the American's plea to speak to Clarissa about her marriage, his last week of clerking for the man had been very awkward, but he'd survived it. His final examinations were over, his university training complete, and he'd be damned if he was going to kowtow to Humphrey any longer. He might go to see his former mentor, but as of his last examination two days past, Brandon Phillips was no longer a slave to academic law, and more particularly to Michael Humphrey. He'd sweated for the right to be a free man, and earned it with every damned legal precedence he'd researched. Whatever inane request the man made of him would be summarily denied, that Brandon promised himself.

"You want me to do what? I'm sorry, sir, but I don't believe I heard you properly," the young scholar protested a half hour later.

"You heard me all right, Phillips. I said open your tie, take off those cuff links, relax and pour us a couple of drinks. You'll find the bottle behind the bust of Blackstone on your left and the glasses behind Plato." The amazement on the lad's face was truly remarkable, noted the professor with a chuckle. One of the joys of a stern reputation was watching it shattered on occasion. But maybe the lad wasn't as sharp as he'd given him credit for; certainly, he needed to be cautioned about revealing too much of himself through facial expressions—but that could wait.

"But, sir, liquor in quarters—"

"This isn't student rooms, Phillips. It is my office, and we are not talking about liquor—it is excellent cream sherry, saved for special events. Considering the work we've done together these three years, most notably this past term, we deserve nothing less, so pour healthily,'' instructed Humphrey, slapping his student soundly on the shoulder as the young man extracted the requested items from the bookshelves.

"We deserve it?'' asked Brandon in complete bewilderment. Had senility finally overtaken the razor-sharp mind of his advisor? The way he was babbling, it did seem a possible explanation.

"Of course we do. You don't suppose it was a simple matter to generate all those special projects I assigned, do you? Creating supplementary curriculum to enhance the learning experience of one as gifted as yourself, and at the same time, undo your overly independent thinking took special talent, but then, son, you were worth it. I'd say some of your work actually bordered on the brilliant.'' Taking one of the glasses Brandon had filled, Humphrey raised it in Brandon's direction. "What's more, Dobson and Whittaker agreed with my evaluation. Congratulations, Mr. Phillips, the internship is yours. You report to Lincoln's Inn tomorrow promptly at nine to take care of the final details. And see to it you're early—they're sticklers for punctuality.''

The professor's face broke into a broad grin as he read the total shock in his pupil's eyes, followed by the sudden dawning realization that this was real, his dream come true. It would have been a heady moment for any young man, reflected Humphrey, but more so for the lad who stood before him after such personal and family troubles. From out of the mire of unexpected poverty, he'd reached for the brass ring and, deservedly, gotten it.

"Sir, you're the one we should toast. I couldn't have pulled it off without your help.'' Recovering quickly, Brandon was sincere in his gratitude even as his mind weighed the significance of his new position at the Inns. Now, with his future firmly established by his efforts, he could afford to ask Clarissa to— No! Preston had already claimed her, and since he'd witnessed her happiness with his rival's love, Brandon had no cause to object.

"Bloody right, you couldn't have, especially after that damned senior paper you submitted; it almost cost the university a bloody good barrister. Yet, as peculiar a defense as it was, that examination changed your life, Brandon,'' said his mentor, not knowing how right he was.

"That it did," agreed the surprisingly calm barrister-to-be, recalling Clarissa's tear-filled eyes the night she'd confessed her authorship. He knew now she'd only taken the examination to help him, but it was too late. Tomorrow she'd wed another, and he had no right on earth to interfere after he'd tossed her aside, no matter what his feelings or his prospects might be.

Brandon hadn't attempted to sleep that night. Going to his bed would have only been a futile effort, and so he sat in his outer room, chin in hand, for the duration of the evening. But it wasn't elation that kept him awake, he thought as he studied the ruby ring he held between two strong fingers. This should have been a night filled with celebration, but instead it had become a time of mourning what could have been. He took another look at the ring and put it in his vest pocket, intending to sell it the next day. After all, why would he need it now? Dawn would herald Clarissa Manning's wedding day, and not even his acceptance into chambers shared by London's most prestigious barristers could dispel the gloom that surrounded him like a shroud.

Tonight had been a night of ghosts, as memories of the love he had known with Clarissa appeared unbidden, the specter of her smile haunting him without relief and the seductive noise of her laughter echoing in a room that had no occupant but him. Try as he might to exorcise them, the phantoms overran him until he was drained of all emotions save one—his longing for Clarissa.

It was an affliction with no cure. Even the knowledge that he had obtained the goal for which he had worked so hard these past years was no balm. The only thing that could heal him was Clarissa, and she was a remedy denied to him.

Somewhere in the background a clock chimed five in the morning.

"Four hours left till I become an apprentice barrister, and *she* becomes Mrs. Preston Waverly-Smythe," he muttered, continuing his lonely vigil as the possibility of future happiness died a little more with each tick of the clock. How ironic that he would be embarking upon his career at the exact moment she was beginning her marriage. It was as if the law were a jealous mistress bent on keeping them apart, and he could see no recourse.

Though he was patient when circumstances demanded, Brandon was essentially a man of deeds. Unable to bear inactivity any longer, he jumped from his chair and began to pace the room with furious steps, his mind engaged in turbulent speculation as he sought some overlooked solution to his dilemma.

"What *can* I bloody well do?" Brandon asked in a tone of self-derision that arose from his sense of impotence. "Plead with her as she enters the church, or perhaps abduct her? Christ's blood," he hissed between clenched teeth, "she's made up her mind. Damn her to hell, and damn me, too, for being fool enough to still care about her!"

He pounded a clenched fist into an open palm. Brandon's concentration was so intense that he didn't immediately hear the soft knocking at his door, or the half slurred inquiry that followed.

"Brandon," came Ned's excited voice, "come on, old man, answer, will you? This is important!"

Exhaling impatiently, Brandon debated the wisdom of opening his door, though finally, with a shake of his head, he turned the key, flung the door wide and encountered a slightly disheveled Ned on his doorstep.

"A little overdressed for a morning wedding, don't you think?" Brandon asked caustically as he took in the other man's evening clothes.

"One should dress for the occasion, I always say," Ned replied, a twinkle in his eye.

"You're very chipper on the worst day of my life," Brandon muttered as he moved aside.

"If you'll be quiet long enough to be pleasant, you might find that this may very well be the best day of your life," Ned said hurriedly, unable to contain his news any longer. "There's a possibility that there won't be any marriage this morning."

"What do you mean?" Brandon questioned sharply, his voice betraying the emotions that flared as a result of Ned's simple statement.

"Do you remember those two tarts I met up with a few days back? I chanced upon them again, about two or three hours ago. A couple of gins in a cheap pub made us all friends and loosened their tongues."

"What does this have to do with the wedding?" Brandon asked, ready to throttle the scamp if the boy didn't talk faster.

"Mr. Walker!" Ned replied victoriously. "He *does* have rooms off Drury Lane. My lady friends weren't sure of the exact address, but it's somewhere between Wych and Holywell."

"Is that all?" Brandon asked in obvious disappointment. It was too late to paint Preston the rake to J.G. Manning. "Even if he has a mistress, what good does that do? Society would only wink broadly, and anyway he'd be leaving her when he goes off to America with Clarissa and her father."

"Oh, there's no *one* paramour hidden away," Ned said, mystery clinging to each syllable he uttered. "This is something much worse . . . pornography."

"He collects erotica? It's not to my taste, but I doubt Manning would forbid his daughter to marry such a man."

"Good old W.S. doesn't just collect it, Brandon, he supplies it. And from what my two drinking cronies have told me, it's not the laughable stuff they're selling cheaply. It's the sort of perverse *art* that commands a high price and is sought after by private collectors. I understand, too," Ned added, his distaste evident, "that he specializes in photographing the extremely young."

"That bastard!" Brandon swore, incensed that such a snake would dare to think of making Clarissa his wife.

"You've got to tell Manning," Ned said.

"Telling him isn't enough. I need proof, and more than just the hearsay of two drunken prostitutes. Otherwise, I'll only appear the jilted ex-lover, capable of telling any heinous lie to halt the marriage. And Clarissa would certainly attribute your collaboration to the fact that you're my friend. I'm going down there now to see what I can find. If I can't get to Hertford Court before Clarissa leaves for the church, I'll meet you at St. Pancras'."

"But I'm going with you," Ned sputtered.

"No, you're not," Brandon commanded as he donned his coat and headed for the door. "You're going home to dress and then on to the church."

"But Brandon—"

"Listen, Ned, if I can't get back in time, I need you at St. Pancras to stall the wedding. Believe me, you'll be of much more service if you proceed as planned this morning."

"I may have been invited to the ceremony, but I certainly wasn't going to attend!" the young man protested loyally.

"You are now. Get going," Brandon prodded, pushing his friend out the door. "With any luck, the bride won't be going anywhere this morning."

"But how will I know what's happening?"

"If Preston appears to have been left in the lurch, meet me at Lavinia's house."

"All right," Ned grumbled. "But what about your appointment with Dobson and Whittaker this morning?"

"The hell with it!" Brandon yelled from the doorway.

With that, he was taking the stairs two and three at a time. Suddenly, hope had been resurrected, and he had become, once more, a man with a purpose. If he succeeded in preventing her marriage, Clarissa might never want *him*, but Brandon knew that at least he would have the satisfaction of saving his beloved from the likes of Preston Waverly-Smythe.

Considering its proximity to his rooms, it was amazing how infrequently he'd followed this route, thought Brandon as he hurried down Drury Lane toward Holywell Street. Though as the stench of stale urine and rotten vegetables from Clare Market filled his nostrils, he decided it wasn't so odd after all; the city fathers had been arguing about the demolition of these slums to connect the High Holborn to the Strand for over fifty years, but they were still talking, and not acting. Only those who, for economic survival or personal profit, had no choice would willingly visit Holywell Street or the narrow alleyways hidden in the seamy darkness so appropriate to the neighborhood's primary trade of the flesh.

"Hey, there, duckie, are you feeling good-natured? I can do ya fer half a guinea, easy," offered a hoarse voice from the doorway as a small woman stepped forward. "'Course if ya want to go upstairs, it's more."

"No, thank you. Actually, I'm looking for someone—"

"Now don't be funning us, lad," chided a second critic, emerging from the shadows to reveal a haggard female of indeterminate age, her hair blacker than nature ever intended. "He thinks he's too good for the likes of us, Marie, probably gets his up Knightsbridge way."

"Yeah, he don't even bow to a lady when he sees one, and me Marie Antoinette since the day I was born," cackled the first woman.

"That's not so, ma'am. I'll gladly pay you the half guinea, but all I want is some information," began Brandon.

"Ha, that's a howl! Wait till I tell the mister I been called ma'am and paid for mouthin' off when he's always after me to shut my yap," guffawed Marie. "But you keep talkin', your Lordship, you make the words sound awful pretty."

"I'm trying to find a Mr. Walker. I understand he takes pictures around here and uses locals as . . . models."

"You a friend of his?" interrupted the second woman.

"Not bloody likely," answered the young lawyer, reacting to the antagonism in the woman's voice. "He owes me twenty quid from a bet, and I want to collect before he runs off with it."

"Whadda you think, Marie? Is he one of those toffs that come round for that devil's pleasure or do we trust him?"

"Get his coppers first," advised her friend, "and then tell him. I always said Walker was no good; taking pictures of Alice was one thing, but then using Beatrice and Annie and not wantin' the likes of us . . . He's nobody's favorite around here, Governor."

"You'll find his place around the corner, third door off the street in back of the alley, number sixteen A, but I don't reckon he's there. He usually comes round at night, and don't stay."

"That's all right, thanks," said Brandon, pressing the money into the woman's waiting hand and moving on before they could accost him further. Despite the early hour, the street was busy with people coming and going, and he had no time to waste. The wedding would start in less than three hours unless he found something by then.

Slipping into the alley, he moved quickly to the third door. Despite the presence of the sun in the sky, the air was dank and shadows appeared more prevalent than light, but maybe it was his mood. As he had expected, the door to sixteen A was securely locked. Brandon followed the building as it made a sharp right turn into the alley without finding another door. There were windows back here, though, and if he were lucky, one would be unlatched. No. Damn, he'd have to make his own luck, he decided grimly as he hefted a piece of fallen slate from one of the roofs and heaved it through the glass.

Breaking and entering, vandalism, intent to steal: his lawyer's mind catalogued the crimes dispassionately as he realized no threat of punishment would stop him from getting Clarissa away from Waverly-Smythe. Not even the fact that he would forfeit his appointment to the Inns because he was out breaking the law instead of meeting Dobson and Whittaker could deter him. All that mattered now was finding the evidence that would link Preston to the pseudonymous pornographer, Walker.

Knocking the remaining glass from the frame, Brandon reached in and unlatched the window, sliding it up and looking quickly about the deserted alley before shoving the dark, heavy drapery out of the way and climbing over the sill. It was pitch black inside the room, and before he could get his bearings, he fell against a table and heard the clatter of shattering bottles.

Damn. He cursed his clumsiness. *If I haven't already wakened the dead, this will do it!* He stayed where he was, waiting for a cry to echo in the street, but nothing happened. Were noises of this sort too common in this neighborhood to attract attention? Maybe that could work to his advantage.

Peering into the dimness, Brandon was irritated at his own stupidity. Why couldn't he have brought a candle? Well, at least he had matches. Lighting one, he looked around the small room quickly: metal basins, shelves with bottles of liquid, a large table and not much else. Apparently, he'd knocked over some of the developing materials when he'd entered the dark room, but this area must be used only for the printing of the photographs.

There didn't seem to be any cabinets or files for the pictures. Where would Preston keep them? Certainly not in his college rooms—or could this Walker not be his classmate after all? The flame flickered out as Brandon spotted a door in the far wall and moved toward it. Striking another match, he noticed a small lamp on the table inside the second room and proceeded to light it.

The layout here was more typical of what he'd expected: a lounge chair piled with pillows in one corner, a high stool, a rocking chair with a child's doll, a large bed draped in black velvet against the front wall, a soiled white sheepskin rug on the floor, all apparently intended as backdrops for the two cameras, which rested on their own pedestals in the center of the room. A brocade curtain closed off the left side of the room, though Brandon doubted privacy was its purpose, not when three large mirrors reflected one's smallest movement in triplicate. Carrying the lamp, he crossed to the curtain, sending a rat scurrying from its meal of abandoned cheese and fruit on a tray at the foot of the bed. It would figure Preston was right at home here, he noted.

Behind the cloth partition stood a library table and a chest of drawers. He hoped it was the hiding place of the records he needed to incriminate the bridegroom. Damn! Was that church bell chiming seven o'clock already? He'd better hurry.

The first three drawers of the bureau yielded corsets, robes, stockings and chemises of every imaginable size and fabric, as well as some rather odd accessories: feathers, ornate scarves and shawls, lace fans and collars, elaborate hats and garters, jewelry of all descriptions, even a small gilded bird cage, but no prints or photographs. The last drawer was empty but for two locked rectangular boxes. Now what? He couldn't very well walk out of here in broad daylight carrying these, no matter how unsavory the neighborhood. Besides, they might not even contain the evidence he was after.

A quick trip to the outer room to reclaim the useful piece of slate and the prosecution was ready to explore Preston's secrets. Without compunction, Brandon found himself taking perverse pleasure in pounding his weapon against the box; if only his target were Preston's head . . . But that would come later. Suddenly, the hinge gave way and the top fell open to reveal some loose gold coins; most probably doled out to Preston's models after their arduous work. Then Brandon noticed a small notebook had been tucked against the side of the box.

Putting the pages of scribbled notes in his pocket for safekeeping, the determined hunter turned his attention to the second container.

This chest was wooden and more easily violated, despite its attendant fastenings. Within minutes, Brandon had found the scenes of hell he'd been seeking. He'd spent a lot of time at sea on his uncle's ships and was familiar with the "art" some men used for release; he'd even admired the naked portraits of a few "ladies" himself. But this—this wasn't natural; it was indecent, he reflected, thumbing queasily through the pages of nude girls and the occasional boy, alone or posed together in various carnal acts.

Ned had said Preston's models were reputed to be children, and judging from these photographs, most of them seemed too young to understand what they were doing, innocents playing at sins they didn't comprehend. Trying to ignore the rising bile in his throat, Brandon kept looking for a shot that might include Preston. Seeing a picture of a young blond girl, no more than twelve certainly, he swore at the depraved soul who'd posed her sitting on the bed looking surprised as a dog sat sniffing between her open legs. Christ, where were her parents, he fumed. They deserved to be shot, an outraged Brandon determined with a frown, wondering if the law he'd studied could ever hope to civilize people such as these.

But the next print gladdened his heart, for it was of Preston with the same child sitting naked in his lap as he suckled her breast. That was all he needed; the picture would be worth more than the proverbial thousand words. It was the price of his love's freedom. Putting the precious shot in his jacket pocket, he grabbed another handful of prints as evidence of the worm's depraved sickness and turned to the door, leaving the rest of the pictures where he'd dropped them. There wasn't much time left before the service; he'd have to go straight to St. Pancras rather than to Hertford Court.

Bam! Crack! The door smashed against the wall as a giant's foot broke the doorframe and his huge figure filled the doorway, blocking Brandon's path to the street.

"Take pictures of my sister, will ya? Let a flea-bitten mongrel nose around her, did ya, Mr. High-and-Mighty Walker? Well, I got news for ya, you mess with Freddie's baby sister and you got me to answer to, and I tell ya, you ain't much gonna like it, either.''

"I'm not Walker," protested Brandon as the behemoth lifted him off the ground by his lapels and tossed him across the room into one of the mirrors, sending shards of glass flying.

"Ya wish ya weren't, chum, but Beatrice told me where to find ya. She's not gonna be so bee-you-tee-ful for your camera anymore, neither," the man promised, yanking Brandon to his feet. "The swelling'll go down, I guess, but them teeth won't be growing back no more. Maybe we'll give her a few of yours for good measure."

Taking careful aim, Freddie launched his fist under Brandon's jaw with such force he feared at first he'd broken the man's neck, the way his head snapped back before he collapsed in a heap. Not that the scum didn't warrant it, but Freddie had other plans for him. Let the coppers earn their keep. He growled and quickly tied up the unconscious figure at his feet. Finished, he ran into the alleyway. This was one bit of information he wouldn't mind giving the police.

Chapter Eighteen

The gray murkiness of predawn light gave way all too quickly, Clarissa thought as soft, golden shafts invaded her room just after seven in the morning. The sapphire ring that Preston had given her the day after their betrothal glinted coldly in the weak light, its pale shimmer sending a shiver down Clarissa's spine.

Though it had adorned her hand since Preston had placed it there, Clarissa had found the ring an impersonal reminder of her fate, and had chosen to ignore it. Now, however, the fire imprisoned in its facets caught her eye and seemed to flare as she imagined that the jewel took on a sinister glow, branding her forever as a bride destined for the wrong groom.

With a moan of irritation, she twisted the ring around and drew the sheets over her head, turning on her side and trying to push all thoughts of the marriage from her mind in order to spend a last few moments in a peaceful cocoon that shut out the world and its demands.

A gentle tapping on her door, however, announced that this was not to be. In answer to her muffled, "Come in," there followed a soft click and the sound of dainty footsteps padding across the patterned carpet of her bedroom.

"Clarissa . . . Clarissa, dearest, it's long past time you were awake." Lavinia's low trill sounded, her forced cheerfulness made all the more patent by the heavy silence of the room.

Lord, thought the older woman as she brushed back a strand of her auburn hair and waited for some response from her niece, whatever was the matter with the girl? Though this marriage was no love match, it was true, hadn't Clarissa been the one to insist that the wedding take place? Surely she should be up and about by now. Was this obvious reticence a normal case of bridal nerves, or was it possible that for all her bravado, Clarissa really didn't want to marry Preston Waverly-Smythe? But before the concerned spinster could give voice to her curiosity, Clarissa was sitting up and preparing to begin her day.

"Good morning, Aunt Lavinia," the bride said, stretching her arms lazily. "You're up very early this morning."

"Yes, and you're not," replied Lavinia doubtfully as she peered at Clarissa's fine features, searching for pallor or some other sign that her niece was upset about the upcoming nuptials. Concerned that the girl's hesitation would be visible to her guests, Lavinia muttered, "It's highly unusual for a bride to be so casual about her big day."

"You forget the circumstances," Clarissa drawled, hoping as she rose and paced the room that her aunt was not about to start offering advice now.

"But...but you do at least *like* Preston. You've said you do. That...that *is* what you've told me, and you've surely acted as though you are fond of him when he's...when he's come to call," sputtered Lavinia, a sinking feeling of trepidation overcoming her hopes and forcing her to continue. "Yet I can't fathom why, if that's the case, you shouldn't be evincing *some* signs of happiness rather than this casual attitude."

"Aunt Lavinia," replied Clarissa, absently fingering the folds of the elaborate wedding dress that hung on a screen in the corner of her room, "don't mistake my lack of jitters for lack of enthusiasm. I'm doing what I want to do."

"Are you sure, Clarissa? Is this really a solution to your dilemma?"

"I know it is," the young woman responded, her brown eyes darkening in determination. Hadn't she asked herself that very question dozens of times since she had accepted Preston's proposal? Hadn't she spent sleepless nights wishing that it was Brandon with whom she would be spending her future and not Preston, kind as he might be?

"But my dear," Lavinia continued, horrified that in submerging herself in planning the wedding, she may have ignored Clarissa's total discontent with the match, no matter how cleverly it had been hidden, "not all women must marry. Why, I myself have received a number of proposals only to turn them down. At this very moment I am involved in a...a relationship with a man. And though he has offered me his name, I much prefer to maintain my freedom," Lavinia confessed with a blush that receded rather quickly, a pallor taking its place as she imagined James Gregory's reaction to the advice she was about to offer. "You could do likewise."

"That's all very well, Aunt Lavinia," Clarissa said, viewing her mother's sister in a new light, "but you're forgetting the baby, my child of the mist. Your situation and mine are rather different. Now that's all I want to hear about the matter. Any more will ruin my wedding day, such as it is."

"But—"

"No buts, dear Aunt," Clarissa said firmly, ushering the older woman to the door. "And remember," she added, fixing her aunt with a piercing look, "you've promised on Mother's memory to honor my confidence."

Lavinia's forlorn expression, however, was enough to soften Clarissa's heart as well as her words, so that she was prompted to add affectionately, "There's really no reason for you to worry. I know what I'm doing. Preston is a good man, and everything will turn out for the best."

With a quick nod, Lavinia hurried to her bedroom, leaving Clarissa alone to gather her courage for the coming events.

Moving to the bell cord next to her bed, Lavinia gave a tug to summon Ellen. There was no question about going downstairs until she quieted her nerves, not that she had much appetite for one of Cook's huge morning meals. Still, a lot of consolation could be found in a cup of tea. And just because she couldn't face James Gregory across the breakfast table, there was no need to deny herself whatever solace was available.

Soon a pot of steaming brew was beside her, along with a copy of the day's newspaper. Pouring the dark liquid into a floral-patterned cup, Lavinia attempted to forget her misgivings about her niece's wedding by following her usual routine. Perhaps this way, she could find a few moments of peace in what was certain to be a stress-filled day.

Listlessly, she opened the newspaper and out of habit turned immediately to the divorce column, which recorded in minute and scandalous detail the judicial proceedings of those cases heard yesterday. This was the only aspect of law that held any interest for Lavinia, and the particulars found within often-times served to confirm her wisdom in remaining unwed.

Today, however, despite Mrs. Pringle's assertion in open court that her husband, Colonel Pringle, had visited the bed-chamber of Mrs. Pringle's unwed female guest one night last November, Lavinia couldn't find any distraction from her own problems. In fact, the already distressed woman cringed in horror, certain that today's ceremony would cause her own niece's name to appear in a like column should American newspapers print such things.

"What am I going to do?" she moaned, twisting her ever-present lace hanky between fretful fingers. "If I'd been a proper guardian.... If I hadn't gone running off to my own life.... How can I stand by and allow this wedding to proceed without trying to help dear Clarissa? She's too stubborn to go to Brandon, yet my own vow of silence forbids me from telling anyone."

However, as Lavinia's eye fell once more upon the divorce column, she knew her sister would forgive her. She might have been sworn to secrecy on the love she had for Clarissa's mother, but it was that very love that compelled Miss Cooper to break her promise. She had cared too much for her sister to allow Pamela's daughter to consign herself to a life of unhappiness. With this thought firmly in mind, she reached for pen and paper.

She couldn't send a note to Brandon without arousing the servants' suspicion, but a letter to Geoffrey wouldn't be considered unusual. She'd explain the situation and implore his help. Perhaps Geoffrey's Ned could reach Brandon before it was too late. After all, what harm could it cause? If Clarissa was correct, the information would mean very little to Mr. Brandon Phillips; he'd ignore the entire situation, and the wedding would take place as planned without her niece being any the wiser. But if Brandon was the man Lavinia believed him to be, he'd put a stop to this morning's foolishness. Then Clarissa and her ex-tutor could overcome their senseless pride and put whatever had parted them firmly in the past.

The Earl of Hammerford sat sipping a cup of strong coffee and eyeing the morning suit he'd soon have to don for the infernal wedding. He hated dressing so formally early in the day, but he'd never let on to Lavinia. As far as she was concerned, he'd be dancing adoring attendance, at least as much as he could without astounding the other members of the Horticultural Society who had been invited to partake of the wedding feast.

Lord, how Lavinia and her predicaments had turned him into a patient man, he decided, thinking of her guests and the change they had wrought in his routine. In fact, this damned wedding had put him at odds with his own son, who, out of loyalty to Phillips and despite his father's insistence, had sent his regrets when the invitation had arrived. Why, the young pup had no notion at all of proper social behavior, or if he did, he refused to abide by it, the earl thought as the corners of his mouth drew downward.

A sharp rap at the door deepened Geoffrey's frown of disapproval. He'd left orders not to be disturbed.

"A note, your lordship."

"Bring it here please," he muttered, his irritation at Ned coloring his usually pleasant voice until the familiar dainty handwriting of the envelope banished his anger. When he was alone once more, Geoffrey tore open the seal like a child ripping the wrapping off a gift.

Expecting to find a little missive of love, the nobleman was astounded by the contents of his correspondence. Even when he thought Clarissa Manning was safely off Lavinia's hands, the young woman managed to create another catastrophe. The only time she hadn't been trouble was when she was being tutored by Brandon Phillips, and now Lord Geoffrey knew why. But what did Lavinia expect him to do?

He was caught in this speculation when Ned arrived, determined to make a show of acceding to his father's demands and so position himself at the church should it become necessary to stall the wedding.

"Father, I've decided you were right," the earl's offspring said in as sheepish a voice as he could produce. "I'll attend the ceremony this morning as you requested."

"Humph! That's if there's to be a wedding. Take a look at this, Edward."

Edward? thought Ned. This was serious, whatever it was. As the future earl read the letter, his raised eyebrows registered his surprise. "We've got to tell Brandon!" he exclaimed in breathless excitement, forgetting the job his friend had already assigned him.

"So it would appear," Geoffrey said, all too aware that Lavinia would find it difficult to forgive him if he did not make some sort of attempt to rectify things. "Off you go, and no dillydallying. You've got little more than an hour to give young Phillips his chance to set things aright. But just remember this, my boy," the earl shouted at his son's already retreating form, "I still expect *you* at that church at nine o'clock sharp, no matter what Phillips decides to do!"

Brandon's head pounded and his jaw ached, but why? What had happened to him? Then he remembered. Freddie—Waverly-Smythe—the wedding! Was he already too late? Why the blazes couldn't he see or move his hand to get at his pocket watch? Damn, that stupid ape must have tied him up and blindfolded him. There was no sound of anyone in the flat, but Brandon couldn't take a chance on calling out.

When I get my hands on Preston Waverly-Smythe, I'm going to kill him; that's the only possible remedy, he concluded calmly, taking inventory of the bruises he bore in Preston's stead. His head seemed to have taken the worst punishment; his arms and legs felt intact though stiff. He must be on his back on the bed, arms tied beneath him, decided the young lawyer as he felt the velvety texture of the bed covering and the support beneath him move when he shifted. If he could roll onto the floor, maybe one of the shards of broken mirror might be maneuvered to cut his bonds, as long as his attacker didn't come back to interrupt him.

Kicking his legs to propel himself forward, he inched his way across the bed till he felt nothing under his legs; only then did he permit himself to slide down the side of the covering, trying not to land with too much force.

He was in luck; within minutes of his safe arrival on the wooden floor, his searching fingers had located a sharp piece of mirror suitable for his purpose and he began the rhythmic sawing motion while his mind worked feverishly on the possibility of still being able to halt Clarissa's marriage.

"Hello? Is anybody in there?" a voice called from the street. "Brandon? Are you around here somewhere?"

Thank you, God, Brandon prayed gratefully. It was Ned! Now he didn't have to be concerned about who might hear his cries.

"Ned, in here, and hurry it up," he called as one of his bonds snapped under the pressure he exerted. "I could use a hand, old chap, and quickly. But, tell me, what time is it, and why aren't you at the church?"

"Don't worry, we can still get to St. Pancras before Clarissa," came Ned's voice. "But there's something you have to... Good God, Brandon!" exclaimed his friend, entering on the run, only to stop in astonishment at the sight of his tutor, half-trussed with pink scarves and blindfolded with a garment ordinarily intended to restrain a woman's breasts.

"Never mind the expletives, help me get loose. I found all the evidence we need to stop Preston, and was on my way to meet you, when a disgruntled relative of one of his young models showed up and mistook me for him. That's a hell of a lot better," cried a relieved Brandon as Ned removed the makeshift blindfold and the last of his bonds. "Gather up some of those prints and let's get to the church," he instructed, trying to get some feeling back into his limbs. "Freddie seems to have re-arranged Preston's filing system, but I imagine any of them will do."

"To hell with the pictures, Brandon. You don't need them now, that's why I came to find you."

"Why not? Even if the wedding were already over, we could get it annulled with these photographs. I've even got one of him with a child young enough to be—"

"I'm telling you, his scurvy pastime doesn't matter any more," Ned reiterated. "Clarissa was only getting married because she's carrying your child, and she was convinced you didn't love her, so—"

"That's why she was marrying Preston? Because she was pregnant with my child?" roared Brandon, heading toward the door. "That stupid little fool. And I thought she had half a brain!"

"Apparently she was afraid to tell you though I can't imagine why—you're such an even-tempered fellow," placated Ned hurrying to catch up to Brandon as two burly officers of the suddenly blocked the doorway to the street.

"Mr. Walker, we'd like a few words with you."

"No, no," denied Brandon, even more anxious than before to get to Clarissa's side. "That's not me, though someone else thought it was, but I'm not. If it's all the same to you, we'll be going. I have to stop a wedding so I can be married to the bride."

"Just wait a minute, chap. Step inside away from the door till we get some answers. That's better," said the taller of the two bobbies, holding his nightstick handy, while the other began to collect the randy prints from the floor. "We received a complaint about some immoral goings on here, Mr. Walker, and these photographs would seem to confirm that."

"They would if I were Mr. Walker," admitted Brandon quietly, a man of the law trying to be reasonable and cooperative though his heart demanded he take rapid action. "But at this moment, Mr. Walker, who is really Preston Waverly-Smythe, is about to wed the mother of my child unless I get there to prevent it."

"If that's the case, who are you two, making yourself at home here? A few of his older models for hire?" asked the officer holding a selection of Preston's work. "I don't see you in any of these prints."

"Look, for the third time, I'm not Walker, I'm Brandon Phillips. I came down here because I needed proof of how depraved Waverly-Smythe is so an innocent young woman wouldn't marry him."

"That's why you turned these rooms upside down and smashed the cameras?"

"No," answered Brandon wearily. Why couldn't they see the truth? "That was someone else's doing; I just broke the window in the other room to get in. Once I found the pictures I needed, I was on the point of leaving but then Freddie showed up..."

"And this is Freddie," asked the officer taking notes as he indicated Ned.

"Devil in hell, no, I'm Edward Lowell Newcomb, son of the Earl of Hammerford, ask anybody," claimed Ned. "But my friend is correct, the wedding's going to be long over unless we get out of here right now."

"Oh, we're getting out of here, all right, but you're not going to any wedding today. The Bow Street station's your next stop until we can round up this Freddie character."

"But I'm not Walker!" protested Brandon in frustration as he saw his hopes of preventing Clarissa's marriage evaporate in the face of these watchdogs of the law.

"If you're not Mr. Walker, which I still question, sir, then we have a clear charge of breaking and entering to discuss, aside from the manufacture and distribution of pornographic works," stated the unrelenting policeman.

"Look in my pocket; I have identification papers," pleaded the exasperated lawyer as manacles were attached to his wrists. Why hadn't he thought of that earlier?

"Very well, though I don't know what you expect that to prove; around here anyone can get hold of papers with any imaginable name on them. My, my, and what's this little notebook?" Brandon's heart sank; he'd forgotten that was in his pocket. "Hmm, I'm afraid, Mr. Walker, you've just given us all the evidence we need to hold you over for the magistrate: a record of payments to your models, the dates they posed and the fees you got for the prints, a nice markup I might add. And what's this special print? A favorite shot of one of your better models?"

"No! I took that picture because it shows the real Mr. Walker, I mean Waverly-Smythe, with—"

"Then you admit taking the photograph, do you? Keep your story straight, son. It don't look good if you get yourself confused," said the elder of the two. "We'll bring you down to the station, and let the detectives handle this one; it'll give them a break from the usual pickpocketing and drunken brawls."

"But he's telling the truth," supported Ned. "I came down here from the church to meet him—"

"So you fellows attend church now, eh? Looking for your next pretty little girls, maybe? Well, you can explain it all later. We were sent out to pick up a pornographer at this address and we got ourselves two—or maybe a pornographer and a thief, it's all the same to me."

"My father is Lord Geoffrey Newcomb—— 'll be Hammerford," insisted Ned vehemently. "'ll be bloody hell to pay if you don't believe ——t for us. go to St. Pancras' Church and get my father ——

Chapter Nineteen

Milling about with the rest of the wedding guests on the steps of St. Pancras, Lord Geoffrey scanned the avenue for any sign of his son and young Phillips. The Manning girl would be arriving in her carriage at any moment, along with her father and Lavinia, the signal for those in attendance to enter the church so that the wedding could begin.

Who would have thought someone as solid as Ned's former tutor could have fallen victim to a flirtatious glance, Geoffrey fumed, until he recalled Lavinia's enticing smile and forgave Brandon Phillips his indiscretion. After all, Clarissa was as beautiful in her way as his own beloved Lavinia. But there, the comparison ended; the girl had proved nothing short of troublesome, Ned's father decided.

"I've done all I can do. Lavinia can't fault me," Geoffrey mumbled into the late spring breeze as his efforts continued to yield no evidence of the errant pair. "Whatever happens, happens. I wash my hands of it. After all, why should this business involve me any longer?"

"Lord Newcomb?" came a low, discreet voice at Geoffrey's elbow.

"Yes?" the lord countered, raising an eyebrow as he fixed his stare on the nondescript gentleman who had approached him. Dressed as he was in a brown suit, this man couldn't possibly be one of the wedding guests, but rather a tradesman of sorts.

"If I could have a moment of your time," the stranger requested, motioning him to a location apart from the rest of the guests.

"I have barely a moment to spare," the nobleman answered gruffly when he spied Lavinia's carriage slowly making its way to the front of the church. "What is it you want?"

"Well, sir." The man lowered his voice and began to explain as he was joined by two similarly attired colleagues who respectfully maintained silence.

"My son is *where*?" Lord Geoffrey Lowell Newcomb, ninth earl of Hammerford, couldn't help the sudden volume of his tone. Fortunately, the murmuring good wishes that rose from the small cluster of her friends as Lavinia alighted from the carriage hid the excessive loudness of Geoffrey's question.

"At the Bow Street station, sir, if the lad is even your son. He might have stolen your boy's wallet, for all we know," said the detective. "Is Edward about five feet eight inches, black hair, brown eyes, on the slight side?"

"Yes, yes. You say he was detained in a house of ill repute modeling for a photographer of pornography?" Geoffrey whispered through clenched teeth.

"Well, he claims otherwise, sir, of course, but that is what it appears from the initial reports. We're trying to sort the matter out now before we take them in front of the magistrate."

"*Them*? Did you arrest the women involved as well?" Lord Geoffrey's nightmares were coming true; he'd hoped young Phillips had tamed Ned's wilder impulses, but it appeared not. Just when his offspring had earned a First with Honors. His academic career would be over if the university got wind of this incident. The nobleman knew he'd best get down to the station at once and settle the matter.

"Ah, actually, sir, there were no women involved, just another man," stated the detective reluctantly.

"Oh, Lord!" For Annabelle's son to be like that! The earl had trouble catching his breath. Who would have thought?

"No, sir it's not what you think. I mean, the fellow claiming to be your son says the other one is only his tutor—"

"I think I've heard enough, officer. We'd better go." Apparently those two irresponsible scoundrels, Ned and Phillips, had decided to forgo the church and spend their time in other pursuits.

"Geoffrey," Lavinia fluttered breathlessly, joining the earl on the pavement while James Gregory turned to help Clari from the carriage. "Did you get my note? Is Brandon b

"Now, now, my dear," the earl replied as the gentlemen from the police station withdrew to give him some privacy, "I sent Ned after him but to no avail. It seems my boy has gotten himself in a bit of a jam, and Phillips along with him. In fact, I must be off at once to see if I can rectify things."

"Oh, Geoffrey!" Lavinia began, horror registering in her eyes. "You can't leave! What will I do? How will I put a stop to this wedding? It's about to begin!"

"But my dear," Geoffrey said patiently as he patted her hand, "it's impossible for me to be in two places at one time. I must attend to this matter at once, or I fear we've no hope of seeing Ned or Brandon this morning."

"But the ceremony..."

"Now, now, I've the utmost confidence in you," the gray-haired gentleman soothed. "You'll think of something, and I'll be back as quickly as possible. I only regret that my rapscallion of a son has caused you any distress. When I see that boy, I'll..."

"It's quite all right, really it is." Lavinia lied as much to herself as to her love while she began mustering her strength for whatever it was she would have to do to delay the wedding.

"Then, my dear, you'd best attend to your niece," he said as he nodded toward Clarissa who, disembarking from the carriage, held the attention of the crowd. "As for me, I must be about my paternal duties, distasteful as they might be."

"Of course," Lavinia answered with a composure she did not feel. "But, Geoffrey, don't be too hard on the boy. I just know that Ned is all that you have ever thought he was."

Recalling the detective's insinuations of a few moments before, Geoffrey replied in a soft mutter. "At the moment, sweet Lavinia, I rather hope not."

Clarissa felt herself blush as she stood on the pavement in front of St. Pancras, the focus of attention for Lavinia's friends who oohed and ahhed over the elaborate bridal gown she wore.

Continuing the tradition popularized by Queen Victoria at her wedding half a century earlier, fashionable brides of the upper class still wore white gowns and adorned their heads with lace veils secured by a coronet of orange blossoms. The intervening years, however, had wrought more than a little elaboration on the simple design, as fashion had come to dictate satin brocade with flowers embroidered in silver thread.

The prevailing style also demanded the wedding dress to be heavily festooned and garlanded with leaves and orange blossoms, so that despite the approval of Lavinia's friends, Clarissa felt more like an exotic horticultural exhibit than a bride.

It was an ungracious thought, the girl berated herself as she spied her flustered aunt returning to stand beside her. The dear woman had done a magnificent job of organizing the wedding in such a short time. Lavinia's efforts were evident in every aspect of the day's celebration, and all were aimed at making this a memorable day for her niece.

Of course, all this had been done before Lavinia had learned the real reason for Clarissa's nuptials. Still, if this day turns out to be unpleasant, the young woman thought, sending a reassuring smile in her aunt's direction, it won't be through any fault of Lavinia's. I've been provided with everything a bride could wish for, except the right bridegroom, but that is my doing and no one else's.

Clarissa knew that in a few moments, her life would be unalterably changed. Though she dreaded the step she was about to take, she found that she wished to put it off no longer. It was time to end the limbo in which she found herself, the state that still caused her eyes to sweep her surroundings in futile hope, looking for someone she knew would not be there. Surely it was better to go forward and have the marriage service over and done with before she changed her mind.

Lavinia's actions, however, appeared to be in direct conflict with her niece's wishes to conclude the morning's business as quickly as possible. The older woman was dallying more than usual, keeping acquaintances engaged in chatter of no consequence so that the guests had yet to proceed into the church. At this pace, the wedding would never begin.

"Dear Aunt," Clarissa chided softly, "don't you think we might continue this conversing later? I've a bridegroom waiting for me, and by my reckoning, we're a bit late as it is."

"Of...of course, Clarissa," floundered Lavinia, desperately seeking some excuse to stall a bit more. Nervously running her hand through the faded red curls that had escaped from under her bonnet, she found sudden inspiration. "But heavens! My hair must look a sight," she pouted to her niece as the last of the wedding guests entered the house of God. "I shall simply have to redress it in the outer vestibule before I take my place inside. Surely a few more minutes can't hurt," she concluded, ignoring the mumbling she heard coming from James Gregory.

"You look fine, Aunt Lavinia. Doesn't she, Father?" Clarissa asked, waiting only a moment for his response. "Now I think," the girl continued with a smile that was not her most dazzling but was meant to reassure all concerned, "that we should begin this wedding immediately."

"But—but your dress," Lavinia blathered as they entered the anteroom of the church, "some of the floral festooning seems to be coming loose. Perhaps if we sent for a seamstress. There must be one nearby that could . . ."

"Her dress is fine!" James Gregory interjected, his patience finally shattered. "Now stop your fussing, Lavinia, and take your place inside so we can begin."

"But . . ."

"No buts, dear sister-in-law," the lawyer insisted firmly as he placed Lavinia in the care of a young man who would see the unnerved spinster to her seat. "You've done all that needs to be done. Let's get on with it, shall we?"

The woman had no choice as she was led to her place inside the house of worship, but the tears that coursed down her cheeks were not ones of joy, as her friends supposed. Oh, why couldn't she be strong or clever like Geoffrey? What *was* she going to do to halt the wedding? Her heart would *never* withstand this anxiety!

All too quickly, an organist began to play a rather obscure hymn and Clarissa, on her father's arm, made her way down the center of the church behind two little girls carrying baskets overflowing with flowers.

Though St. Pancras was not built on a grand scale, James Gregory Manning's daughter felt she had never seen an aisle as long as the one she now traveled. She had the sensation of being caught in a dream as she saw Preston waiting for her at the other end of the church.

The reality of the moment though, could no longer be ignored, and she struggled with a rising panic, afraid she would falter or turn in rapid retreat before she reached her destination. In desperation, she tore her gaze from Preston, loving as he might be, knowing she couldn't continue along this path while she saw him at its end. Instead, she attempted to concentrate on the guests who were present, hoping this would strengthen her resolution and rescue her from the utter sense of misery and apprehension that enveloped her.

Tell the truth, her heart whispered, didn't you really wish that *he* would be here to save you from going through with this?

No, she answered the troublesome specter of her former dreams. If Brandon wanted to stop this wedding, he would have tried before this morning.

Passing Humphrey and some of the dons from the college who bestowed polite smiles upon her, Clarissa recalled how she had felt last night when she had seen a letter on her father's desk, informing him that Brandon had been chosen by Dobson and Whittaker and had been commanded to present himself in their chambers this very morning to formally accept their offer. Of course that's where he was! How could she have imagined he might be here? And at that moment, Clarissa hated the law. It kept Brandon from her this morning, and after the ceremony, it would keep her from him for the rest of her life.

A few more slowing steps brought her abreast of the members of the Horticultural Society, and then finally it was only Aunt Lavinia, sitting in the front pew, who waited to see the bride pass. The dear lady tried to smile at her niece as she dabbed at her eyes with the shredded remains of a fine lace handkerchief. But the tears that flowed freely detracted from her effort. Clarissa wished she could go to her, put her arms around her, and assure her once more that everything was going to be fine, but suddenly she doubted very much that it would be.

In a daze, she heard the minister initiate the ceremony, followed by Preston's assertive voice. But just as the clergyman questioned her intent, Clarissa heard a sudden gasp, then murmurings coming from behind her.

She turned, half hoping, half expecting to see Brandon striding firmly up the aisle, but what she saw instead was the collapsed form of her aunt lying just outside the pew, its gate ajar. Without an iota of hesitation, Clarissa dropped her bridal bouquet and flew to her aunt's side, gently pushing through the ladies of the Horticultural Society clustered around their friend.

"Aunt Lavinia, what's happened?" the girl asked, her concern overshadowing all that surrounded her.

For a moment, Lavinia could manage only a feeble smile in return, apparently too weak to even conduct a characteristic wave of the lace handkerchief she clutched to her wildly heaving bosom. Then she forced herself to gasp a response. "It's my heart, my dear. I'm afraid you must get me home at once and call my physician."

"Certainly, Aunt."

"Don't worry, Lavinia, all will be fine," assured James Gregory with an awkward pat on his sister-in-law's arm.

"Yes, and while they're carrying your aunt to her carriage, let's conclude the ceremony as quickly as possible so we can join her," the bridegroom said softly in Clarissa's ear.

"Preston, really!" whispered Clarissa fiercely, "I can't do anything until I make certain Aunt Lavinia is all right. We'll take her home at once. Our marriage vows will have to wait."

"I only thought," Preston soothed, "that if anything is seriously wrong with her, your aunt would at least get to see us wed."

However, a loud moan from Lavinia followed by a shudder and the closing of her eyelids put an end to Preston's gentle argument. He was incensed that he had been stopped within a nod of becoming James Gregory Manning's son-in-law and future partner. But there was nothing he could do at the moment, he realized, as he stood watching his intended wife follow those who were carrying Lavinia down the aisle of the church, the wedding bouquet lying forgotten on the cold, stone floor.

As the horses stopped before Lavinia's house, Clarissa fought back a tear at the sight of the floral garlands adorning the front entry. The servants had been busy, on Lavinia's orders, of course, so the house would be ready to greet the newlyweds and their guests. Her aunt had gone to so much trouble for her sake, Clarissa only prayed the strain hadn't been so great it would turn the day into a greater tragedy than it already was. She'd lost Brandon and withstood the pain, but Lavinia...

Before she could voice her concern, however, the carriage door opened and her father swept Lavinia into his arms. Moving toward the house, he called over his shoulder to the man waiting on the street.

"Preston, don't just stand there like a dolt. Ring the bell and open the door," snapped the American as the groom offered his hand to Clarissa. "My daughter won't disappear on you, but right now, Lavinia is my concern. Come on, lad, move."

"Go on, Preston, I'm fine," she urged softly as she saw the veins in his neck tightening in irritation. "Father doesn't mean to be overbearing. He's just very concerned about my aunt," she confided moments later as her intended returned to assist her from the carriage.

"As are we all," Preston retorted curtly, resenting the role of lowly errand boy. Order me about like a flunky, would the great man? He'd see about that; there's a limit to what partnership will buy, Dr. Manning, but you'll learn that in time—or the world will learn the truth about your angelic daughter.

"James, calm down, and don't be so concerned," fluttered Lavinia as she was conveyed indoors. "Isn't it the bride who's supposed to be carried over the threshold, not her aging aunt? I can walk, you know."

"Not until the doctor says so," her brother-in-law said brusquely, carefully depositing his burden on the sofa in the morning room.

"There's no need to fuss so; I'm certain he'll say there's nothing seriously wrong."

"Undoubtedly," commented Preston dryly. "I mean, undoubtedly that's what we all wish."

"Yes, Aunt Lavinia, I know I do," confirmed her niece. Lavinia had been settled comfortably on the settee amid floral bouquets of lemon and orange blossoms, a delicate picture of precious femininity.

"You've done such a beautiful job of decorating the house, just as you always do everything so splendidly," she added as she viewed the white tulle swags interspersed with perfect white rosebuds. Moving to her aunt's side, Clarissa knelt and embraced her gently. "I feel so bad about your illness. I can never thank you enough for all you've done for me."

The sight of Clarissa kneeling at the old biddy's side irked Preston to the point he no longer guarded his tongue. And then there were those hags from the Horticultural Society arriving from the church even now, to fuss over Lavinia and hold her hand when they should have been shaking his, congratulating him on becoming a new bridegroom. It would have happened that way, too, if it hadn't been for old maid Cooper.

"Yes, dear Aunt Lavinia, you certainly have made our wedding day memorable," agreed Preston, his icy blue eyes catching and holding those of the older woman, as he drew Clarissa to her feet and pulled her close to him. "We can never hope to repay you. I only pray this sudden illness is quickly past so you'll soon be able to bounce our child on your knee."

Silence greeted his words, and Clarissa abruptly moved from his embrace, giving him a cold stare. He'd have to learn not to touch her so possessively, she determined. It gave her gooseflesh.

Lavinia was too nonplussed to reply, bringing her ever-present handkerchief to her mouth and coughing softly to buy a few moments to collect herself. Where in tarnation was Geoffrey, anyway? It was over an hour since he'd left her at the church. I don't know how much more of this solicitude I can bear, she thought, though at least I've held off the wedding this long.

"Lavinia, shall I have Ellen fetch you a cup of tea or a glass of water?" asked James Gregory.

"Maybe some brandy," suggested Humphrey from the door. "I've found it to have excellent restorative powers."

"Perhaps a small glass, thank you. I imagine if I just lie here quietly a while I'll be feeling better in no time. I so hate ruining your day, Clarissa, dear."

"Don't give it a second thought, Aunt. You're more important to me than any ring on my finger." Catching sight of Preston's face, she regretted speaking her heart and laughed coquettishly. "Besides, when I'm so fortunate as to be loved by an adoring rogue like Preston, I know he won't desert me."

"Not when you're the sweetness of my life," agreed her smiling fiancé, though his eyes remained frozen.

"In that case, Clarissa, would you see if Ellen is ready to serve? Then maybe you'd like to go upstairs and change out of your gown?" suggested Lavinia in a weak voice. "That way you'll be able to sit with me once the doctor's come and gone."

"Of course, Aunt," said the girl, already on her way out of the room to comply with her aunt's wishes.

"Lavinia, don't be absurd. Stop playing hostess and get some rest. No one cares about food at a time like this," admonished James Gregory. "I can't imagine what's keeping the doctor, but until he arrives, you're not seeing anyone, and Clarissa," he called to his daughter, "move your things to the room next to your aunt's. That way, you'll be nearby should she need you during the night."

"This is my house, Dr. Manning, not yours, and I hear more guests in the foyer. Let the ladies in and they'll keep me company till the doctor arrives with his little pills. You and Professor Humphrey can have a drink in the library in the meantime. Preston, there's really no need for you to stay. It's ridiculous for everyone to hover over me so," complained the attractive matron, waving her friends into the room as she shooed the men out.

"Well, James, I guess you've been told." Humphrey chuckled as he pulled a pipe from his pocket. "Let's have a smoke and let the lady have her way."

"Yes, I suppose I have no choice," admitted Lavinia's brother-in-law. "Preston, will you join us?"

"Actually, sir, I'd prefer to be useful. If you'd permit me to go upstairs, I might be able to help Clarissa move her things—"

Manning was silent for a moment, feeling this wasn't a terribly good idea, yet given other circumstances, the lad would have already been part of the family.

"All right. After all, by all rights, you're my son-in-law, I guess you can be trusted with my daughter. Go ahead."

"I'm sorry, Sergeant, but I fail to understand what this interminable delay is," complained the ninth earl of Hammerford as he made his way to the desk once again. "I have formally identified my son—"

"Yes, you have, sir, and we appreciate your cooperation."

"And you've said he's free to leave. But what about Mr. Phillips? I've spoken for him as well."

"Yes, sir, that you have, but that doesn't mean that Phillips is not also known as Mr. Walker in the Holywell neighborhood," explained the officer in charge of the Bow Street station. "The lad did possess rather incriminating evidence, you must admit."

"That's absolute rubbish," objected Ned. "Brandon achieved first place in his class at university while tutoring other students and clerking for a legal authority—"

"Then perhaps he should have known better than to break and enter another's premises," remarked the constable dryly.

"If you're so certain I'm guilty, take me before the magistrate," demanded Brandon angrily. He'd already sacrificed his career for Clarissa's sake; now it appeared he'd lose her as well unless he got to Hertford Court before the newlyweds left on their marriage trip. "With Lord Geoffrey's guarantee, I warrant he'd release me quick enough."

"Brandon, don't be hasty now. Such a charge would appear on your records once it's heard in court and it could very well interfere with your taking the silk someday," advised Geoffrey. "Look here, Sergeant, the real Mr. Walker was one of the guests of honor at the same party where your man found me. Couldn't you send someone there to apprehend him?"

"I'm afraid that's not possible, sir. That's why Detective Henley didn't ask to speak with him the first time. Without a clear complaint against the man, we have no cause to disturb him, and on his wedding day, too. Of course, once the girl in that provocative print comes forward, presuming she can identify the pornographer and give witness to his involvement, then we can proceed."

"By then he'll be halfway to Philadelphia," snorted Brandon. "What if I swear out a warrant against Waverly-Smythe? Could you act on it now?"

"Why, of course, but what charge are you making?" asked the detective, surprised no one had thought of this approach earlier.

"Theft of services. He's stolen my wife-to-be."

"That hardly seems likely, but I suppose we could investigate an alleged abduction—"

"You did say you would act on a complaint," reminded Lord Geoffrey. "And that is a valid charge. I give you my word of honor, the woman has no desire to remain with Waverly-Smythe." At least she won't once she knows Brandon loves her, added the earl to himself. "Come along, Brandon, my carriage and driver are right out front."

"But, sir, I don't think . . ." protested the bobby on guard duty as Brandon ran for the door.

"Well, go with him then, and bring back this Waverly-Smythe fellow so we can settle the matter," instructed the sergeant with a grin. That Phillips was a sharp one, all right, to formulate a scheme that had the police do his bidding. "And you, Wilson, go looking for that girl again. Her name may be Annie."

Outside the station, Brandon grabbed the reins to Lord Geoffrey's carriage from the driver waiting in attendance beside the vehicle and was in the driver's seat before the startled servant realized what had happened. As he started to protest, the carriage was already tearing pell-mell down Bow Street toward the Holborn.

"Sir, Lord Geoffrey, he's stolen your carriage and from right outside the police station, too," exclaimed the driver as the earl left the building.

"No, John, it's all right. I told him he could take it. I'm certain the police can find us transportation to where he's going. He'll just arrive a bit ahead of us, that's all."

Frowns and muttered imprecations greeted the nobleman's words, but since none of the peelers were ready to contradict him, a police vehicle was quickly brought round.

As for Brandon, he had no thought but for Clarissa. There was a clock ticking danger inside his head, and with every passing minute, he seemed to feel her growing fear. He only knew that he had to reach her before it was too late.

"There, your aunt should be comfortable enough with you settled in so nicely beside her," Preston said, patting Clarissa's hand solicitously after he had deposited the last of her books on a cherry-wood table in the room next to Lavinia's. "And, once she's tucked in her own bed, we can have the minister come around this afternoon to perform our interrupted ceremony."

"Preston! Think about what you're saying. I've *told* you that I can't marry anyone until I'm assured that Aunt Lavinia is well."

"I have thought about it, and I only want what's best for you, Clarissa," Preston continued in a soothing voice that hid the angry frustration he felt. He couldn't allow his association with J.G. Manning to just slip through his fingers because a doddering old woman had taken to her sickbed.

"I know your concern for me is sincere, but I'm afraid that I must insist we wait before we return to the altar, Preston," Clarissa said softly. Not, she admitted to herself ruefully, that she'd been looking forward to her wedding, but now as well as her own despondency she was fighting rising pangs of guilt concerning her aunt. Confiding her predicament to Lavinia had probably been more than the old dear could bear, and the idea that she might have contributed to the older woman's illness extinguished, for the moment, any possibilities of marrying Preston.

"Now, Clarissa," the dark-haired Englishman persisted more strongly than before, "I want to take care of you in times of trouble. And this, sweet girl, is one of those times. For your own good, I'll brook no argument in this."

"There is no argument," Clarissa replied, irritated by the man's sudden propensity for dominance. Didn't she have enough on her mind just now, without his exerting pressure as well? "It's a simple statement of fact. There will be no wedding until Aunt Lavinia is well."

"Then think of this," he demanded, tones of growing impatience and anger that she had never associated with him creeping into his voice, "if anything happens to the old woman, if she should die, you'd be in mourning and there'd be no respectable marriage for a year. Where would that leave you and your unborn child?"

"If that's my destiny, then so be it."

"But I won't allow that to happen! Not only would your reputation be smeared, but mine as well. You must realize that everyone would assume the child to be mine, especially since we were within moments of legally becoming man and wife!"

"I'm sorry for that, Preston," Clarissa responded, absently twisting the sapphire ring that encircled her finger, "but to be truthful, with everything that's happened today, thinking about life and death and the things that truly matter, I've begun to reconsider other things as well and . . ."

Discovering even as she spoke that she was free of the fears that had bound her to him, Clarissa began to remove the ring that had so recently held her heart in bondage. But without warning, Preston's hands came down roughly upon hers to impede her efforts.

"Now stop this. You're hysterical, overcome with emotion and you don't know what it is you're doing," he said sharply, his eyes as cold as the sapphire he had given her. "We *are* going to be married today. I'll have no more of this nonsense."

"And I'll have no more of you. Remove your hands at once," Clarissa demanded quietly but proudly. With this new insight into Preston's character, she became all too aware that Lavinia's sudden malaise, dreadful as it was, held at least one blessing.

Incensed at her cool, poised rejection, Preston couldn't contain the effect of his shattered dreams upon his emotions.

"You *will* marry me today, do you understand? In fact, you'll leave this house with me for that very purpose right now, because if you don't I'll go downstairs and tell those people that you're pregnant with Brandon Phillips' bastard."

"Lavinia already knows," Clarissa said angrily, standing firm and unflinching as he stalked closer, seeking to intimidate her with his proximity and size.

"Does she now? That's fine, but how will she enjoy hearing all her friends informed of the fact? She and her family will become society's newest scandal. What will that do to your precious aunt and her failing heart?"

Though she didn't consider capitulating to Preston's blackmail for one instant, Clarissa couldn't hide the horror that flitted across her well-drawn features at the terrible scene this monstrous man had conjured. The vulnerability in her deep brown eyes made her look so very young and helpless that Preston found her exceptionally appealing as he became aware of a familiar stirring.

That was it! He'd bind her to him in a different way, a way that depended not upon threats, but on action of the most sordid kind. His intentions lit his eyes with an ominous glisten. There was too much going on downstairs for anyone to pay attention to what he was about to do. It would be over quickly enough, and then the girl would have no recourse but to marry him. Phillips would certainly never want to touch her again after this, and what other decent man would have such an experienced woman? For Clarissa to tell anyone would merely cause an unspeakable scandal, the only possible solution for which was a wedding between them. J.G. Manning would have to accept him as his son-in-law, like it or not. Preston knew that there was no question about what he was going to do. After all, if a man wanted something, he had to seize it. And so, it was his future and not really Clarissa Manning that Preston clutched at as he overpowered the struggling girl and pulled her to him, clamping his hot, moist mouth over hers.

Anxiously snapping the reins, Brandon ignored the stares of passersby in the street outside of St. Pancras and urged the horses onward once again. He paid no heed to the loud protests from a trap he'd sent up on the footpath as he turned the carriage toward Hertford Court. As far as he was concerned when he had seen the empty church and surmised the worst, every other vehicle on the road had better watch out. With the police following him and Clarissa in danger from the husband she didn't know, let alone love, he had no time for niceties. Only when his conveyance took a corner on two wheels and threatened to overturn did he slow briefly to allow it to right itself. He was so close to Hertford Court; nothing could happen to his love now, not when he finally realized how much he loved her.

Pulling up to Lavinia's house he tossed the reins down and bounded from the driver's perch. Taking the steps at a run, he paused to rip the ornate garland from the front door. This wedding was nothing to celebrate, he fumed, and no matter how flighty Lavinia was, she should have realized that!

Brandon had just raised his fist to pound on the door when suddenly it opened to accommodate a departing physician. A doctor meant that someone was ill or had been hurt, and Brandon Phillips agonized that it might be Clarissa. Pushing past those who were gathered in the vestibule, he rushed into the house.

"Where is she?" Brandon bellowed. Chin bruised, jacket open, vest unbuttoned and shirt half undone from his race through the London streets, Brandon looked anything but a proper English gentleman as he stood poised to destroy anyone who would dare hurt Clarissa.

"Now see here, Phillips," began J.G. Manning, as he took in Brandon's agitated state, "your time for second thoughts is over. Leave my daughter alone, and have some respect for Miss Cooper. She's quite..."

"I said, where is she?" Brandon demanded again, ready to take the house apart brick by brick until he found the woman he loved.

"Why, she's upstairs, dear," Lavinia replied, recovering miraculously. Rising from her chair, she firmly shooed her friends over the threshold to the marble steps outside and shut the door in their curious, astounded faces, acting as though there was nothing unusual about this half-crazed man's demanding inquiry, or her own sudden good health.

Ignoring Manning's protests, Brandon was off, taking the stairs two and three at a time.

Outraged, Clarissa's father started after him until Lavinia laid a restraining hand on her brother-in-law's arm.

"What are you trying to do?" he yelled at the confounding and illogical woman who moved to block his path.

"Do be quiet, James," Lavinia snapped, "and don't try to interfere in something you know nothing about!" Though he found her manner almost intolerably abrasive, Lavinia's unfamiliar harshness halted Manning's pursuit.

"If you know the meaning of all this then I suggest you tell me immediately," the prestigious lawyer commanded, using his most impressive courtroom voice. But while countless witnesses and judges alike had quaked in the face of his booming imperiousness, Lavinia would have none of it.

"If you'll only be quiet, I'll explain it all," she said so calmly that James recognized perhaps it was time for him to do as she directed rather than make demands of his own.

When Brandon reached the second-floor landing, Lavinia was just beginning her tale, unaware that before she had finished the police would arrive, along with Geoffrey and Ned, to add information of their own.

Tearing along the hallway, Brandon saw empty rooms on either side. The girl was nowhere in sight.

"Clarissa!" he called anxiously, but it was silence that answered him. "Clarissa!" he roared once more in anguish. "Where are you?"

This time, he detected faint sobs coming from behind a door at the other end of the hallway. Moving as though his very existence depended upon it, he flew to the door, only to find it bolted. The muffled cries were somewhat louder now, and distinctly more frantic, so that Brandon retreated a few paces to increase the force of his impact as he threw himself against the door, shoulder first.

His initial effort produced only the groan and creak of wood being stressed. On the second attempt, however, there was a sharp snap as the door gave way and opened into the room to hang by its loosened hinges against its cracked frame.

Brandon had never known a degree of rage that could compete with what he felt when he took in the scene before him, a rabid Waverly-Smythe mauling Clarissa, whose bodice had been half torn from her dress.

Without a second's hesitation, Brandon landed on top of Waverly-Smythe, his hands closing around his rival's throat, wrenching him from the near-hysterical young woman. Yet even when that was accomplished, Brandon didn't loosen his grip as he fought the urge to kill this animal who had tried to violate Clarissa.

Blow followed blow so that the prevalent sound in the tension-filled room was the smack of clenched fists meeting resisting flesh. Though his opponent tried to throw a few punches of his own, it was useless, as Brandon vented his unbounded fury on the man he believed to be Clarissa's husband.

It wasn't until after Preston lost consciousness that Brandon realized the motionless form beneath him could no longer feel the pain he wanted to deliver. When the futility of further punishment became apparent, Brandon sat where he was, his chest heaving with exertion and spent rage.

He looked up to find a quivering Clarissa, sitting on the bed, tears covering her lovely cheeks as she stared, not knowing what to expect from him. Instantly a metamorphosis took place. The vicious emotions of a few moments before were transformed into inordinate gentleness as he moved to her side.

Clasping his beloved to him, Brandon stroked her hair and made soothing sounds of comfort, but other than that, he remained quite silent. The feel and fragrance of her filled him with such joy that he was unable to trust his voice. He didn't care if the law had marked her as Mrs. Preston Waverly-Smythe. In his heart, she belonged only to him.

Wordlessly, he swooped her up in his strong arms, stepped over Preston's still form and carried her from the scene fraught with such frightening memories for them both. With no more than a nod to the people now clustered upstairs, Brandon proceeded down the corridor to Clarissa's bedroom, leaving Manning and the police to deal with Waverly-Smythe.

Clarissa never felt safer and more content than she did as Brandon carried her through Lavinia's hallway. All the terror of a few moments before was banished as she reveled in his nearness and was lulled by the steadfast beating of his heart. Though she wondered why her family as well as Lord Geoffrey and Ned should be in the company of a band of policemen, Clarissa asked no questions. Her curiosity would be satisfied later. Right now there were more important things to be sorted out.

Distraught by the sight of his daughter's disheveled state, James Manning turned to follow in Brandon's footsteps.

"Let the young ones be," Lavinia suggested gently when her brother-in-law watched in surprise as the bedroom door swung closed behind the reunited couple.

"I only want to make certain Clarissa is all right," he protested. "And I'm afraid the evidence points to the contrary."

"James, the person she needs most now is Brandon," Lavinia said firmly. "Besides, it wouldn't do to disturb your daughter and son-in-law to be."

"But she wanted to wed Waverly-Smythe!"

"A mere formality," Lavinia said with a wave of her hand.

"What about this garbled business Lord Geoffrey has just told us, that Phillips was arrested this morning on all kinds of immoral charges? I'm not certain they've been dropped."

"Since you're such a learned barrister, or lawyer as you call it, I'm certain you'll be able to settle everything, but better do it quickly," Lavinia said, dismissing her brother-in-law's protests. "Now come along, let's see what that criminal in my bedroom has to tell the police."

Not caring what was happening down the hallway, Brandon's thoughts were centered on the woman in his arms. Though he had placed her on the floor of her room after the door had clicked shut, Brandon found he couldn't let Clarissa go. And she had no wish to leave the protective circle in which he enfolded her. So they stood, locked in embrace, each afraid after what they had endured that separation of any type might mean the other's disappearance.

"Dearest love," Brandon said at long last as his lips played gently along her ear, "I thought I'd lost you."

"No matter what, you'll never lose me, Brandon," Clarissa assured him. "Even as I walked down the aisle to meet Preston, it was you that I held in my heart."

"It's no matter. Nothing is important except that we're together at last. We'll have this wedding annulled and then we'll have one of our own."

"But Brandon, there was no ceremony this morning. Aunt Lavinia became ill, and afterward, when we had returned here, I realized the mistake I had almost made. I told Preston that I had changed my mind and then . . ."

"Hush. Let's not talk about him or the things that parted us, Clarissa," a jubilant Brandon suggested, his husky voice lovingly caressing her name. He knew all he needed to know as he removed Preston's sapphire ring from her finger and threw it in the cold ashes of the fire.

"Then what should we talk about?" she asked.

He noted the smoldering promise of passion that danced in her eyes, and felt her heart, which had finally slowed after her ordeal, begin to beat rapidly once more.

"Only this," he said as he bent to place his lips tenderly on hers, intent on demonstrating with his kiss the love he felt and the commitment he was making.

She responded warmly and joyously; when their lips parted, Clarissa had no need to discuss their future. He'd just told her everything she wanted to know.

"That was lovely," she said. Her voice was dreamy, but there was a devilish twinkle in the dark eyes that gazed into Brandon's serious face. "However, there's something *I* think we should discuss as well."

"And what's that?" he asked, a contented smile lighting his face for the first time in weeks.

"This," she declared, crushing her mouth against his to initiate a passionate spark with the sweetest abandon.

"I like the way your mind works, young woman," Brandon murmured, taking the ruby ring from his vest pocket and placing it where it belonged before he immersed himself in his response once more.

And as they warmed to the flames of their renewed passion, both Clarissa and her barrister knew that there really *was* justice in this world after all.

Epilogue

Summer of the following year was exceedingly warm in Philadelphia, and Clarissa used the letter she had just finished reading as a fan while six-month-old James Edward watched her with solemn eyes from his basket at her feet.

"You're just like your father, so serious," she told him, only to have the baby laugh in delight at her comment.

"And just as you do with his father, you can always bring a smile to our son's face," Brandon added as he entered the room, observing the tranquil domestic scene with contentment.

Scooping his child into his arms, Brandon sat next to Clarissa, glad to find a moment of peace in his busy day.

"It's official," he said to his wife, while trying to get James to laugh. "Your father's firm is establishing chambers in London. Can I leave the details of organization in your capable hands?"

"Of course," Clarissa said, happy to be included yet again in the logistics of running the family practice.

"It will mean moving to London for two or three years," Brandon reminded her.

"That's perfectly fine. Wasn't it in London that I found my greatest treasure?"

"Yes, well, it appears that I had to import mine," he replied, kissing his wife affectionately on the cheek.

"We've had a letter from Ned," Clarissa said, unfolding the paper she still had in hand.

"Whom has he fallen in love with this time?" Brandon asked with a chuckle.

"You mean whom is he marrying? He's betrothed."

"No! I never thought it would happen."

"Yes, he's to be married as soon as he completes university. From all accounts, he's quite smitten."

"Well, so am I," Brandon declared.

"Yes, I know," Clarissa said, her voice exhibiting a seductive quality as she thought of her husband's ever-increasing ardor.

"What else does he have to say?" Brandon asked, anxious to get the news from home over with and move on to other things.

"He'd like you to stand up for him if possible, and says that Aunt Lavinia is doing well and seeing more of Lord Geoffrey than ever before."

"That's no surprise. I still wonder why they haven't made a trip to the altar."

"Because some women need their freedom."

"That is one thing, my dear wife, of which I am only too aware. But there are those," he said with mock exasperation, "who manage to bring independence into their marriages."

"And along with it, passion to their husbands' beds," Clarissa replied with a sassy, self-satisfied smile.

"Hmm, yes. By the way," Brandon added, arching his eyebrow in ill-concealed suggestion, "isn't it time little James was put down for his nap?"

"He just woke up, Brandon!" Clarissa objected with a laugh.

"Ah, that's a pity," the young lawyer mourned though it was obvious as his hand moved along his spouse's shoulders that he had no intentions of giving up his plans for the afternoon.

"However, now that I look," Clarissa said, snuggling close to her husband and placing her hand on his thigh, "he does appear a bit drowsy."

"Good job, son!" Brandon exclaimed, giving the baby an exaggerated wink. "Keep this up and we'll have you a brother or sister before too long."

"You're devils, the pair of you!" observed his amused young wife.

"And you, madam, wouldn't have it any other way, admit it," Brandon demanded in his courtroom voice before his lips found Clarissa's waiting mouth.

"Guilty as charged."

"Well, then, there's nothing to do about it," Brandon murmured in a hoarse whisper between kisses, "but to pronounce a life sentence."

* * * * *

You'll flip . . . your pages won't!
Read paperbacks *hands-free* with

Book Mate • I

The perfect "mate" for all your romance paperbacks

Traveling • Vacationing • At Work • In Bed • Studying • Cooking • Eating

Perfect size for all standard paperbacks, this wonderful invention makes reading a pure pleasure! Ingenious design holds paperback books OPEN and FLAT so even wind can't ruffle pages— leaves your hands free to do other things. Reinforced, wipe-clean vinyl-covered holder flexes to let you turn pages without undoing the strap...supports paperbacks so well, they have the strength of hardcovers!

Pages turn WITHOUT opening the strap

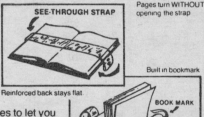

SEE-THROUGH STRAP

Reinforced back stays flat.

Built in bookmark

BOOK MARK

BACK COVER HOLDING STRIP

10" x 7¼ , opened.
Snaps closed for easy carrying, too

Available now. Send your name, address, and zip code, along with a check or money order for just $5.95 + .75¢ for delivery (for a total of $6.70) payable to Reader Service to:

Reader Service
Bookmate Offer
3010 Walden Avenue
P.O. Box 1396
Buffalo, N.Y. 14269-1396

Offer not available in Canada
*New York residents add appropriate sales tax.

BM-GR

HARLEQUIN
Romance

What do *you* want for Christmas?

Jillian in SILVER BELLS wants a safe,
conventional husband.

Holly in DECK THE HALLS wants success.

But what you wish for isn't always
what you get.
Sometimes what you get is much
much better.

Join Holly and Jillian as they discover that
Christmas is a time for
romance . . . Harlequin® romance.

Don't miss
these special Christmas Romances
coming in:

#3091 DECK THE HALLS
by Heather Allison
#3092 SILVER BELLS
by Val Daniels

DEC-1

Coming soon
to an easy chair near you.

FIRST CLASS is Harlequin's armchair travel plan for the incurably romantic. You'll visit a different dreamy destination every month from January through December without ever packing a bag. No jet lag, no expensive air fares and *no* lost luggage. Just First Class Harlequin Romance reading, featuring exotic settings from Tasmania to Thailand, from Egypt to Australia, and more.

FIRST CLASS romantic excursions guaranteed! Start your world tour in January. Look for the special **FIRST CLASS** destination on selected Harlequin Romance titles—there's a new one every month.

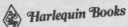 *Harlequin Books*

JT-R